"You're
What's the deal, ~~Mr. Magic Hands?~~

Cade glowered at the sound of the nickname. "You sure look like you could use some help to me. Just what are you planning to do with these?" He held up her box of nails.

Finn lifted her chin a notch. "Use them to fix my fence. They're the strongest ones I could find."

"They're also five inches long. Use these and you'll have three-inch spikes sticking out of your fence ready to skewer anyone who walks by."

"What a shame, since I have such a pleasant neighbor." Her cheeks burned. The jerk was right about the nails. Then she noticed that a few other shoppers lingered nearby, obviously listening.

"Listen," Cade said smugly. "Just one little reminder before you go off to butcher your fence. Something to remember about nails. The pointy end goes in the wood."

Laughter rippled around Finn. She wished she could jam the box right in his patronizing mouth. "I'll keep that in mind."

KIMBERLY
CATES

PICKET FENCE

HQN™

ISBN 0-373-77025-1

PICKET FENCE

This edition published by arrangement with Harlequin Books S.A.

www.HQNBooks.com

Printed in U.S.A.

In loving memory of Verna Sopher,
one of the last great ladies.

PICKET FENCE

CHAPTER ONE

IF A WICKED WITCH EVER wanted to ditch her castle to buy real estate in Illinois, any kid in Whitewater would tell you the deserted house on Jubilee Point would be the place she'd choose.

The widow's walk peering out over the Mississippi made a perfect launching pad for flying monkeys. The horse chestnut tree might not throw apples at trespassers, but half of it fell and nearly smashed Billy Callahan's big brother the night a bunch of teenagers tried to break into the house, drunk on cheap beer and Halloween dares.

Grown-ups tried to brush the whole thing off, claiming it was just a freak accident, a zap of lightning hitting the highest point near the water. Kids knew better. After all, there hadn't been a cloud in the sky the first time someone saw The Light.

Even kindergarteners knew about the creepy glow that floated past the house's tower windows on "Creature Feature" kinds of nights. Someone even painted the rusted For Sale sign with red letters: "I'd turn back if I were you." Good advice if older kids double dared you to camp out under the tree at midnight.

But the warning had no effect on the woman trying to pry the sign off the blackened chestnut tree.

In a dozen shabby rented rooms, her Irish father had filled her with tales of wicked fairies and delicious ghosts and banshees wailing in the night. Until he'd left her behind in a world of strangers who saw fairies as sweet creatures with butterfly wings who'd never steal babies from cradles.

Until he walked away making promises he never meant to keep.

No, the scariest ghost story in the world couldn't have driven the woman away from the house with its gingerbread trim and wide sweep of veranda.

When she looked at the house beyond the gap-toothed picket fence she didn't see witch-hat turrets or cat's-eye windows or trees clawing at the sky. She saw something far different.

Finnoula O'Grady saw home.

No ONE IN their right mind would have bothered removing the For Sale sign before they'd even unlocked the front door—not with movers coming to drop off a load of stuff in two hours. But Finn couldn't wait to tear the sign down, as if at any moment someone might pop out from behind the ancient wisteria vines to snatch the house away.

Absurd, to feel so uneasy, she told herself, and yet, that emotion seemed far more real than the joy that had rushed through her when the town lawyer dropped the quaint brass house key into her hand. Finn had learned a long time ago that her father's gifts could bite back, just when she least expected it.

Yet this time was different. Patrick O'Grady was dead. Finn's eyes stung—from what, she wasn't sure—grief or resentment? Her world would never be the same again. He'd made certain of that. *But what did that matter?* she reminded herself fiercely. *The house is mine.*

March Winds. The place where fairy tales lived. At least her father's brand. She'd dreamed of this place forever—on cramped twin beds in other people's houses. During visits from her father when she'd still believed everything he told her, through dark nights after she'd begun to suspect the truth: that in spite of all his promises the only home Patrick O'Grady would ever give her would be the one in his imagination.

Finn closed her eyes, her dainty sandals transforming to worn pink Keds braced on the front seat of the broken-down convertible that had been her father's pride and joy. Auburn curls whipped by the wind stung her freckled cheeks as she tried to keep her bottom on the suitcase her father had perched her atop so she could see the world whiz by.

No one had bothered much about seat belts back then. Even if they had, it would never have occurred to her father to use them. After all, he'd reassured Finn, they had the luck of the Irish.

They'd had the luck of the Irish all right. Finn grimaced. But, unlike her da, she understood sarcasm when she heard it. Any time during the past five hundred years the Irish had started rejoicing at their "luck," it was a sure bet the sky was about to fall.

But luck *had* been with them that long ago summer afternoon when her father glimpsed the old-fashioned town square draped in red, white and blue bunting and turned into the sleepy town of Whitewater on a whim.

Or had Finn's mother steered the car from heaven, guiding her little girl to the kind of town Mariel O'Grady had once dreamed of living in herself? No matter how far Finn had wandered in the twenty years since that magical Fourth of July, she could still hear the raucous cries of vendors, smell the rich scent of corn dogs and the crispy, not-quite-burned funnel cakes sprinkled with powdered sugar. She could see the bright carnival colors. Just eight years old, she'd been fiercely certain she had the most wonderful father in the world. And that he loved her. Until something about that town, those families clustered on the town green, made her doubt.

We're never going to live in a place like this, are we, Da?

She had wished the words back the minute she saw Da's face pale. *This is as fine a town as I've ever seen,* he'd said. *Why shouldn't we live right here?* He'd gathered her into his arms and she'd breathed him in, the faint bite of tobacco, the tang of mustard she'd accidentally squirted on his shirt instead of her corn dog. *That's what we'll do today! Pick the perfect house. That way I'll be able to surprise you...*

He had perched her back up on the suitcase, then wheeled the convertible out of the parking lot, leaving the carnival behind. She could still remember speeding past the cozy houses lining the street. She'd known they weren't big enough to hold Da's dreams. He headed to the edge of town.

All the finest houses are by the river, treasure, he'd insisted. *And we'll be having a fine house. Not some shack hardly big enough to make a dolls' house.*

Even though twenty years had passed, Finn's heart squeezed. She would have been happy in a shoebox as long as he was with her. But he'd swept her along on the crest of his dream that day, the way he always could. Her lonely child's heart had nearly leaped out of her chest when March Winds burst out of the trees. Towers soared skyward, windows glowing with color as if some fairy had spilled her jewel box across the glass. A white picket fence surrounded the huge gardens, roses draped over it in soft pink rainbows.

A house so perfect she had expected it to vanish like a bubble if she touched it. *Do real people live in houses like that? Truly, Da. Not just pretend?* she'd asked, wanting to believe him.

We'll *live in that house. You and me. The instant I can afford it,* Da had promised, so solemnly she had to believe him. *You'll see, Finnoula.*

Pain knifed into Finn's hand, yanking her back to the present. The house spun into sight again, not the showplace of her childhood, but rather, a shabby maiden aunt where an exquisite belle had once stood.

She glanced down at her palm. A cut just deep enough to sting oozed blood from where she'd unknowingly gripped the ragged metal edge of the sign.

You'll see, Finnoula, her father's voice echoed in her head.

Finn grimaced, sucking on the little wound. She had seen, all right. Every step he'd made along that trail of broken promises before he'd died.

She blinked back tears for the little girl who'd believed in her father so fiercely that day. For the child who slowly came to realize his promises would never come true. For the young woman who let her father catch glimpses of her contempt until his calls tapered off to silence, and she'd let that silence stand.

He hadn't even called her those last precious days before he'd died. Maybe he'd figured words were meaningless between them anymore. She'd stopped believing him years ago.

He'd asked some stranger to mail her the cardboard box he'd brought from the rooming house where he'd stayed. Such a pitiful container to hold a man's whole life, everything he owned in the world.

At least she'd thought so until she'd opened the box to see what lay inside, buried among his battered possessions a pristine envelope containing a cashier's check, her name on the top line. Her heart had thundered so hard she was afraid she'd shake all those zeros right off the check.

Shock. Disbelief. Gratitude and grief flooded through her. Until reality hit hard.

We could've had more than monthly visits and candy bars for breakfast and that sinking feeling I'd get watching him drive away. He could have come to get me whenever he wanted to.

But he hadn't loved her enough to give up his wandering, his freedom. Those were the treasures Patrick O'Grady cared most about.

Bitterness welled up inside Finn. She fought to quell it. *Don't let him spoil this day with bad memories,* she told herself.

"Giving up, huh?"

Finn swung around, the hammer flying from her fingers, the wicked steel claw thudding to the ground inches from a child's bare foot. The child didn't even flinch.

Solemn brown eyes and gypsy black curls sucked all the color from the small, heart-shaped face. An old-fashioned sundress drooped like yellow butterfly wings from the girl's narrow shoulders, the skirt's hem exposing too much of her spindly bare legs.

"I could've broken every bone in your foot!" Finn exclaimed, pressing her hand to her heart. "Didn't your mother ever teach you not to sneak up on people like that?"

Pain flared in the child's eyes, then her chin bumped up a notch. "*I* wasn't sneaking. *You* weren't paying attention."

Finn's cheeks burned. "You're right. I wasn't paying attention. I always have gotten myself in trouble daydreaming."

"Me, too." The child's lips curled in the most winsome smile Finn had ever seen.

Finn's heart warmed in spite of a twinge of nervousness. Six years of bouncing from university to university had given her lots of experience with moving vans, computers and doctoral candidates. Children were a different matter. She had wanted children in her life—lemonade stands and neighborhood picnics and Prince Charming riding in on his white horse—or tractor, as the case might be, considering all the cornfields she'd driven through to reach the town. But the Saturday morning cartoon crowd didn't exactly frequent the research libraries she'd worked in.

She summoned up a smile. "I'm Ms. O'Grady."

The formality sounded strange, but when Verna Sopher, soon-to-retire bastion of the Whitewater Public Library's children's room, had hired Finn, she had been adamant Finn use a professional-sounding name with the children.

"What's your name?" Finn asked the girl.

"Emma."

It suited her perfectly—more a character in some dreamy children's book than a modern kid jazzed up on the Internet and poisoned by too much TV.

"It's a beautiful name," Finn said.

"Yeah, well, I didn't pick it," the child said. "Bet you were feeling bad."

She felt a tug of familiarity at Emma's penetrating, dark gaze, as if they'd met somewhere before. But no. She'd only imagined eyes just like that when her father had recited a poem to her—what was it? "The Stolen Child" by Yeats. An Irishman's tale of a child coaxed to run away with "a fairy hand in hand." The refrain echoed softly in Finn's memory: "For the world's more full of weeping than you can understand…."

Finn doubted that. The child looked torn on life's hard edges, except for the fierce dreaminess that clung to her mouth like cream.

The girl pointed to Finn's hand. "Did you hurt yourself bad?"

"Nothing a little Neosporin and a Band-Aid won't cure."

"I can get the Captain to take the sign down for you," the girl offered.

"The captain?" Something about the child made Finn's imagination fill with pirates in dashing red coats and hooks where their hands were supposed to be.

"He's my grandpa."

The image she'd conjured shifted to a buzz-cut military

man in modern army green. Finn grimaced. The girl's dreaminess seemed to be catching.

"The Captain likes fighting stuff, even if it's only trees and signs," Emma said. A troubled line creased her brow. "Of course, he says only fluffies give up."

"Fluffies?"

Emma shrugged. "Babies. Scaredy cats. You know. Cowards."

"Oh." That was a word Finn knew the definition of. She just didn't like it very much. Especially when it was applied to her.

"Not that you're a fluffy for giving up this time," the girl amended. "I mean, a person would have to be crazy to want anything to do with this old house."

Finn started to bristle, but laughed instead. Plenty of people at Northwestern University, her last stop before Whitewater, would be happy to testify Finn was out of her mind.

"I live over there." The child pointed beyond a tangle of overgrown rhododendron bushes to where a log cabin hugged the farthest edge of the property. "I watch this place. Lots of funny things happen."

"I'd love to hear about them some other time when I'm not so busy. It's been great to meet you." Finn extended her hand.

Emma made a little face. "You're bleeding."

"Oh, I forgot."

"You'll forget about this soon, too," Emma reassured her. "Giving up, I mean. The Captain hates it, but he's a war hero. Not like regular people."

"You know, it's not as if I'm giving up on finding a cure for cancer," Finn teased, wanting to drive some of the solemnity from the little girl's face. "I'm just taking down a sign."

"That's a real good way to look at it. I'm sure you'll sell lots of other houses."

"Sell houses?" Finn echoed, completely confused.

"Oh, yeah. You guys call them real estate. It stinks that they stuck you with the wicked witch house first thing. But I suppose the other real estate people already tried to sell it."

Finn stared at Emma, their whole conversation shifting focus. "You think I've been trying to sell the house?"

"Who else but a real estate lady would try to take a sign down when they're wearing a dress?"

Her logic made such perfect sense Finn laughed. "Actually, I'm celebrating." She smoothed a hand over her dress, remembering how carefully she'd chosen her outfit for today, buying the perfect gown for sipping lemonade on the front porch swing.

"Celebrating what?" Emma asked.

"I'm not selling March Winds. I just bought it."

Emma's eyes grew saucer-wide. "You—you what?"

Finn fished the key from her pocket and dangled it before Emma on a key ring made from an antique spoon. "I bought it."

"That's impossible!" Emma blustered. "The house is a wreck and everyone knows it's haunted!"

"Funny, the ghost is one feature the Realtor neglected to mention," Finn observed wryly.

"She didn't tell you about all the For Sale signs disappearing? They did! Lots and lots of them! That's why they nailed that one to the tree so tight. And these real spooky lights drift past the windows late at night."

Finn stifled a laugh, not wanting to hurt the child's feelings. Emma's fear that her new neighbor could be carried off by some ghost touched Finn.

"But the scariest of all is this tree—" Emma warned, genuinely distressed. "It nearly killed Billy Callahan's brother when he tried to go inside the house last Halloween. He had to get stitches and everything."

"Fortunately the tree didn't seem to object when I went

through the house a few weeks ago." But Finn's attempt at humor only backfired, making Emma even more upset.

"*She* won't like it—you barging in on her and ruining everything!" Emma cried.

"She?"

"Addy. The ghost. She'll make you sorry you ever set foot in this house!"

"I'm Irish enough to handle a ghost or two. In fact, if I check under ghosts in the library, I'll bet I can find some old folk remedies for driving ghosts away. Like burning sage or something."

"No!" Emma cried, distraught. "You can't do that! It's *her* house! I won't let you!"

The girl unnerved Finn, as if suddenly transforming from the dreamy lost fairy of minutes before to a fiercer kind, casting in shadow a day Finn had wanted to be pure sunshine. If Emma was going to be a damper on the day, Finn would rather send her home.

"Emma," she began gently, "this is my home now. The movers are going to be here soon and I—"

"Emma!" An angry baritone roared from the direction of the cabin, something large and heavy crashing through the tangle of brush the real estate company hadn't even attempted to tame.

Finn whirled toward the sound, a man charging into view. Mahogany-colored hair in bad need of scissors fell about a face too angular to be handsome, all steely, clean lines except for a nose slightly off center, as if someone had broken it. In an act of self-defense, Finn figured, considering the way he charged toward them, his silvery blue eyes hot with fury.

Jeans worn almost white in places clung like a second skin to long, powerful legs, the butter-soft material split at one knee. His heather-blue and gray plaid flannel shirt hung open, revealing a bar of solid muscle dusted with curling dark hair.

Even more glimpses of tanned skin peeped through strangely symmetrical holes in the shirt's fabric. Triangles, lined up in absurd precision, like a chain of paper dolls. He might have been the dark, dangerous man straight out of a woman's secret fantasy if he hadn't ruined it by opening his mouth.

"Emma—what the hell did you do to my lucky shirt?" the beast demanded.

Instinctively Finn grabbed for Emma's arm, meaning to fling the child behind her, out of the path of the charging man. But the girl dug in her bare heels, facing him down.

"It's an old shirt anyway, all raggy around the cuffs."

"I like it raggy around the cuffs. It took me ten years to get it broken in this well! I was wearing this shirt the night I landed a Sopwith Camel in a cornfield—not a scratch on the plane! And the night the landing gear stuck in the Piper Cub—if I'd been wearing any other shirt, the plane would've broken apart over three different counties."

"Mr., uh, whatever your name is," Finn said, "you look like an intelligent man. Surely you don't believe a shirt—"

He pinned her with a glare. "Who the hell are you?"

"Finn. Finnoula O'Grady. I'm sure this is just a mistake."

"It's not a mistake." Emma thrust out her chin. "I cut the shirt up on purpose. I had to find some way to make quilt patches for Christmas."

"Christmas?" He bellowed. "It's April for crissakes! You can't just go cutting up other people's clothes when you feel like it!"

"You were working on that stupid old engine. I wasn't supposed to interrupt you unless there was smoke or blood."

So that was why Emma wandered around like a lost soul. She wasn't allowed to "bother" the adult who was supposed to look after her. Finn's stomach knotted with the memory of how it had felt to be shunted aside when she'd needed just a word, just a touch to drive back the fears that fed on a lonely child.

Emma's eyes burned fever-bright. "I don't care about your stupid shirt! My mom would've thrown it out ages ago."

"Your mom—" The man bit off whatever he'd started to say, his grimace telling Finn exactly how much it cost him. If anything, the fury in his eyes grew hotter. "Emma," he said, with terrifying control. "You march back over to that house this minute."

"No! You can't make me!" Emma wailed. "Don't you ever listen? She's moving into Addy's house!"

Blue eyes locked on Finn as if really seeing her for the first time. His mouth curled in a mockery of a smile. "Your husband must be a glutton for punishment."

His contempt cut deep. She'd imagined this day so differently. Neighbors welcoming her to town, maybe bringing a casserole by for dinner. But no, she gets a beast raging at a little girl who pressed hard against old wounds, awakening echoes of the childhood Finn had tried to put behind her.

"I'm not married," she said coldly. "Not that it's any of your business, Mr....?"

"McDaniel. Cade McDaniel."

"So who are you saddling with your mess, then, Finnoula? Brothers? Father? Your boyfriend? The poor sons of bitches."

Bad enough he was swearing in front of a child. He'd also made Finn sound like an irresponsible fool, accentuating just how alone in the world she really was. All the years she'd imagined having a home, she'd pictured someone to share it with—her father, a husband, children—families like the ones she'd watched so wistfully the day of the Fourth of July picnic.

She knew it was possible to build a warm, welcoming home even if there was no one else to share it with. In time, she'd imagined the rooms filled with the laughter of babies, a man who would fill her heart, fill her bed, who'd take root in this place and never dream of wandering away.

She winced, feeling vulnerable. To hide it, she shot McDaniel the "damned by the duchess" look she'd perfected in the countless schoolyards the system had dumped her in as a child. "In my experience, people who resort to swearing are either too dense or too lazy to come up with real words. You should set a better example in front of a child."

"What I say to Emma is none of your business," he said, but a dark flush rose up the muscled column of his neck.

"As for the house," Finn continued loftily. "I'm restoring it myself."

"Of course you are, darlin'." Nakedly masculine eyes raked a scathing path from her sundress to her strappy sandals as if he could see right through to where her heart was pounding. "Be sure to get Emma to help you rewire the whole place before an outlet shorts and the house goes up in flames."

"The first thing I need to fix is the fence." Finn burned with anger, hurt, frustration. She wanted things to be so different today. She glimpsed a three corner tear in her celebration dress. No matter how carefully she mended it, she could never make it like new again, just as she could never reclaim this day.

Maybe Cade and Emma McDaniel were like the Irish fairies Da had told her about, jealously guarding their domain and casting dark spells instead of flitting sweetly from buttercup to buttercup.

The child grabbed his arm, less wary of his anger than Finn felt. "You can't let her stay here!" Emma pleaded. "Tell her about the ghost! About the spooky lights in the window!"

Cade's jaw tightened. "I told you before, Emma, there are no such things as ghosts. The lights are kids trying to scare their friends. Once someone is living in the place, all that will stop."

"No it won't," Emma predicted fiercely.

Finn wasn't sure what drove him over the edge—Emma's

desperation or his contempt for what he saw as an irresponsible neighbor. Whatever the catalyst, Cade McDaniel was finished here, now.

"You will do what I say, Emma," he snarled. "Right now. March home and find some way to fix this shirt!"

"I don't know how to sew!" Her eyes blazed with emotions so fierce they seemed to eat her up inside. "Besides, you're not the boss of me! You're not my father!"

Finn reeled. So he wasn't Emma's father. Stepfather then? She wondered if Mrs. Beast knew he was swearing at her little girl?

"Mr. McDaniel," Finn ventured. "I helped a doctoral candidate in social work research blended families. Kids don't like stepparents taking charge of their world. It would be better if you let Emma's mom handle this tonight when she gets home."

"I wish to God I could, lady! And just for your information, there's nothing 'blended' about this family. That much is for damned sure."

"I hate you!" Emma cried, glaring at him.

"That's too bad. Right now I'm all you've got."

He wasn't Emma's father—her mother was God knew where. What in heaven's name was going on here? Finn wondered.

Whoever the woman was, she filled him with fury and Emma with a pain all too familiar to Finn. *How long?* A voice inside her whispered. How long before Cade McDaniel got fed up and dumped Emma with someone else?

Emma spun away from him. One small finger jabbed at Finn, reminding her even more clearly of her da's stories, bad fairies predicting doom.

"Maybe you bought Addy's house. Maybe they gave you the key. But that doesn't matter." Dark eyes narrowed on Finn. "You'll never belong here."

Finn groped for words, couldn't find them. In a flash, the child was gone, plunging through tangled rose vines and rhododendrons, disappearing like the doomsayer fairy she was, alone, so terribly alone.

Cade McDaniel just stood there, rigid as the iron rail on the widow's walk high above them.

Finn remembered so many times she'd dashed away from her father, wanting to prove to herself that he cared enough to follow. "Go after her," Finn pleaded.

"Ms....O'Grady, is it?"

Finn nodded, a lump in her throat.

"Let's get this straight. I moved out here because I wanted to be left the hell alone."

"You're not alone. You have a little girl who needs you."

He made a harsh sound in his throat. "You want a little advice about how to get along out here on Jubilee Point? You stay on your side of the fence. We'll stay on ours." He spun on his heel, stalked off—not following Emma. Rather, charging off alone.

Finn turned back to the house she'd dreamed of so long. But the sparkle had been rubbed off of the day. The windowpanes were coated with grime, the gingerbread trim drooping. She could almost hear the electrical wires crackling just as Cade McDaniel had warned—ready to set the place on fire.

And ghosted across it all she could see Emma's face, glaring as if she could see right through Finn. Hadn't the child done just that? Uncovered Finn's darkest fear?

You'll never belong here.... Emma's prediction chilled Finn's heart.

What if Emma was right?

CHAPTER TWO

CADE McDANIEL stalked under the overhang of the boat-house he'd built along the river, sun glinting on the exercise equipment he'd installed so Emma wouldn't have to hang around the gym after school while he worked out. He swore, slamming the toe of his boot into a set of weights he'd abandoned when he'd dashed off to deal with this morning's crisis. Pain shot through his foot, the clatter of iron against concrete rattling his very last nerve.

Today had been a banner Saturday at the McDaniel house, starting at seven in the morning when that unicorn notebook Emma lugged everywhere came up missing.

He'd offered to buy her one just like it the minute Ellis Drug Store opened. He would've bought her a dozen if she had just settled down. But no, she wanted the one with the wire thing that held it together all bent where she twisted it when she got nervous and the ring from his morning coffee staining the unicorn's neck. He grimaced. You'd have thought he'd smacked the damned cup down on the Mona Lisa, the way Emma had gotten on his case the day he'd made that mistake.

After turning the place upside down, they'd found the notebook behind the cushion on his side of the couch where she'd hidden it for safekeeping. He'd hoped the two of them might be able to maintain an uneasy truce the rest of the day. But no.

Miss Know-it-all, Psychobabble, Mary F-ing Poppins has to move in next door and throw Emma into a tailspin about that wreck of a house she was so crazy about. And then the woman starts pointing out everything he was doing wrong.

He scowled as green cat eyes, kissable lips and hair like autumn leaves elbowed their way into his head. That absurd dress had had all the sturdiness of a Kleenex tissue. A stray thorn could've ripped the thing right off her sweet little body. And while he was man enough to want to hang around for the show, she irritated the living hell out of him.

She had that fresh, springtime look about her that made a man want to taste, to prove all that delicious innocence couldn't be real. Creamy bare arms had seemed hardly strong enough to support the silver bangles encircling them, let alone reclaim March Winds from the rubble. Even the woman's name got under his skin. Who the hell named their kid Finnoula in rural Illinois?

But the thing that *really* ticked him off was the way she'd looked at him past the smattering of freckles on that nose of hers—all snooty and superior.

You should set a better example for a child—she'd said in that prissy schoolmarm tone. For someone who'd just been suckered into buying the county's biggest White Elephant, Finnoula O'Grady had been chock-full of advice.

But it was the woman's final plea that ate at his gut. *Go after her.*

She hadn't sounded all superior then. She'd sounded as if Emma were racing into some dark tunnel where he might never be able to find her, not running along the riverbank she'd come to know like the back of her own hand.

Go after Emma? He'd wanted to grab the woman, shake her. Why not get down to the real question? What the hell was he supposed to do with the kid when he found her?

Cade's insides twisted at the memory of Emma, her eyes

too old, feelings too easily bruised. She'd been so dreamy once, like there really were unicorns all around, and only she could see them dancing. But he didn't see that face any-more—unless he caught a glimpse of her when she didn't know he was looking. Now he knew the reason.

Emma hated him.

He'd tried to act like he didn't care how she felt about him. He had enough street smarts to know it was a mistake to let an opponent find out how bad a blow hurt you.

But this time he wasn't dogfighting a rival pilot in an Air Force training exercise. He wasn't even fighting with his fa-ther, who could take care of himself when they blew the lid off those famous McDaniel tempers.

This time he was squared off with an eighty-pound little girl who got all teary eyed for no reason—well, almost no rea-son. Cade winced at the memory of spiky lashes, dark eyes red and swollen. That damned well wasn't fighting fair.

But then, if you hated someone you fought back any way you could. Was that why she'd cut up his shirt? Some kind of kid revenge?

That Finnoula woman had claimed that the girl had made a mistake. But you couldn't accidentally dig someone's shirt out of his closet and cut triangles out of it. Sometime before you made that first snip you had to think about what you were doing. And Emma made no bones about it. Said she did it on purpose.

Cade knew what his father would have done in his place. Hand to backside—and hard. In desperation, Cade had even tried that method once—an open-handed smack on Emma's behind. But the kid looked so damned small, his hand so big. She'd peered up at him as if he were a monster. He'd sure as hell felt like one. And he'd known he'd left marks that went far deeper than the sting where his palm had connected.

No. It was far safer to hit something else.

He crossed to the punching bag he'd slung from a hook in the ceiling beam and drove his fist into the leather. The familiar impact jolted up his arm. He struck it again. Again. His eyes narrowed, feet getting lighter as he used his body weight behind each blow. He let fly a series of punishing jabs and crosses, sweat dampening his brow. The bag swung wildly on the heavy linked chain that suspended it over the ground, but the release he'd counted on since his father had first shown him how to take out his frustrations on a punching bag eluded him.

He arched his neck, kneading tense muscles with a hand still buzzing from the impact of the blows. A word in black at the top of the punching bag caught his eye.

"Magic." One of the guys from the hangar had painted it on as a joke. The nickname he'd had since high school. Cade McDaniel, the Man with the Magic Hands. Quarterbacking football games, repairing engines or romancing girls, he'd finessed them all, until people claimed there wasn't anything that McDaniel kid couldn't fix.

People still teased him about it.

Need you to work a little magic, Cade—this engine's going to blow any day. Mrs. Potter's furnace is acting up. That old sailboat of mine is leaking. They'd called him even after he'd come back to Whitewater after his stint in the Air Force.

He'd made it plain he wasn't a high school kid doing odd jobs anymore. He had his father's ailing charter business to shore up, his disaster of a family to try and sort out, and he'd wanted at least a little time to pursue his own passion—restoring the antique airplanes rich history buffs now shipped him from all over the country.

Any way you looked at it, he had too much work to do at the hangar to be replacing somebody's spark plugs. Most people had listened. A few just plain refused to hear him.

Verna Sopher, the seventy-year-old queen of the library,

was the most hardheaded of them all. She'd called two days ago. Just the thought of her made Cade smile in spite of himself.

"Kincaid, dear? Louise is making the most unladylike noises."

Louise was the name she'd given her '68 white Mustang in honor of the movie where Susan Sarandon and Geena Davis had had the good sense to drive off a cliff.

"Like what, Miss Sopher?" Nobody who'd ever crossed the library threshold as a kid would've had the guts to call her "Verna," even thirty some years later.

"It sounds like…" She paused, reflecting. "A gorilla."

He didn't even try asking how she knew what a gorilla sounded like since she'd never been outside of the Midwest.

"We could take it down to Butch at the garage," he suggested without much hope she'd let him off that easy. "He would be able to run it through his computer and see what's wrong, ma'am."

"I don't trust machines. No, God gave you those hands to fix things, young man, and you can start today by fixing my car. I haven't got time for Louise to be temperamental. I have a new librarian coming in on Monday and the children are out of school for teacher's institute."

A wave of exhaustion hit him square in the chest. A three-day weekend? He and Emma barely made it through the two-day variety. What the hell did teachers do at those institute things anyway? Besides making his life more complicated.

"The fifth grade end-of-year paper is due on Tuesday. I expect something of a rush—from the boys at least." Verna chuckled. "You can see it is imperative that Louise be in fine form. I'm depending on you, Kincaid."

He slammed his fist into the bag again. People could depend on him when it came to anything mechanical. He could run his fingers over valves and pistons and feel almost by touch what was wrong, like a doctor feeling bones to see what was broken.

He could spend all night tinkering with the intricate inner workings of an engine older than he was and never once lose patience. Because he knew in his gut he would discover a way to put it back together again, fix it, make it whole.

But Emma wasn't like that. You couldn't unscrew the head of a ten-year-old girl to find out what was wrong. It just wasn't that easy.

What had Finnoula O'Grady said when he told her he'd come to the Point to be left the hell alone? *You're not alone. You have a little girl who needs you.*

Emma needed somebody, all right. Somebody who didn't make her jump whenever he spoke to her. Somebody who could put her hair up the way the other girls did, in a bun that looked like they'd flown in an open cockpit. Somebody she trusted enough to share whatever she scribbled in that notebook with the unicorn on it.

She needed her mother, that's who. Anger burned in his gut, easier to deal with than the worry that had dogged him the past six months.

Maybe he was making a mess of things, but he didn't need a degree in child psychology to guess how tough the next few weeks would be for the kid, trying to adjust to some stranger taking over that old house.

For months now Emma had been acting like March Winds was her own private playground. She'd slipped through the hole in the fence like a mouse and disappeared into the over-grown garden for hours at a time. It might not have bothered him so much if he hadn't known the person she was hiding from was him.

He'd felt a few jabs of conscience. The property wasn't his, after all. But he hadn't had the heart to stop her. She wasn't hurting anything, and she'd seemed almost happy when she'd returned from her wanderings—her cheeks at least a little rosy, her solemn eyes ghosted with dreams. He'd never stopped to consider the effect it might have on Emma if the place sold. But then, he'd never in his wildest imagination believed anyone would be insane enough to take on that Godzilla of a restoration project.

Cade knew losing free run of the property would be hard on Emma. But in the end, it might actually be better for her. She wouldn't want to be hanging around the cabin all the time. She'd have to start doing things with other kids. Like riding her bike and buying ice cream at the Whippy Dip. Normal kid stuff. Maybe he could even get her to join a softball team.

Hitting a ball—now that was something he could teach her to do. When he picked up milk at the grocery store Friday, he'd run into Caro Bates' kid, star pitcher in the girl's softball league. The girl had been picking out stuff for a party. Brandi and her crowd of friends had gotten shy and stopped talking about party plans when they saw him. Probably heard horror stories about the monster Emma was living with.

No. He couldn't be that lucky. At least if Emma had been griping about him she'd have to be talking. Too bad he couldn't lock her in the basement with those girls. Then she'd have to talk to them. She could get past this attitude of hers.

Cade's brow creased in thought. Maybe he could do something right for a change—at least start the ball rolling. He'd helped Caro when she was stranded by the side of the road last month. Maybe he could call in a favor. Get Emma an invitation to the party. That would make the child happy, wouldn't it?

He'd still have to ground Emma when she wandered in. The kid did have to be punished for the Great Shirt Caper. But if she had the party to look forward to, maybe it would get her mind off that house next door. Maybe she'd even quit hating him so much.

Cade swiped one arm across his sweaty forehead and went in to dial the phone. Maybe he was finally figuring out how to deal with this kid thing after all.

"DROP THE NOTEBOOK on the table. You're supposed to be grounded," Cade said as Emma got up from the dinner table. For the first time he wished the kid actually watched TV. That would've made this grounding thing a heck of a lot easier. Or the phone—weren't girls supposed to love talking on the phone? Just pull the plug and he'd be done. Trouble was, Emma would barely have missed either one of them.

She glanced mutinously from him to that ratty notebook. "Why?"

"Because as long as you've got that thing with you, it wouldn't be any punishment. You spend every night scribbling in it."

"That's my private stuff. Don't you dare read it!"

Heck, you'd think she was sixteen and had something juicy in it about making out at a drive-in or something.

"I wouldn't dream of it."

She regarded him warily. "Cross your heart and hope to die?"

At least she wasn't looking quite as eager to "stick a needle in his eye" anymore.

"I told you I wouldn't look," he said. "What could possibly be so important it's got to be a big secret?" Probably ten-page diatribes about what a jerk *he* was, he thought, feeling vaguely curious. Then again, maybe not. She always looked so…happy when she was scribbling. Her eyes all soft and eager. Once he'd even heard her laughing. A rusty laugh, as if she'd almost forgotten how.

He remembered how she'd squealed with glee when they played Lion after a trip to the circus when she was four. He'd felt like an idiot, but he hadn't been able to resist letting her order him around.

For a whole afternoon he'd chased her through the house on his hands and knees, growling and tickling her tummy when he caught her. She'd used Lucky Charms to teach him silly tricks. When she'd insisted on displaying his repertoire to her grandfather, Cade had claimed he'd do anything for a purple marshmallow rainbow.

Truth was, he'd have done anything for one of Emma's smiles. But that had been six years ago, felt as strange and foreign as if it had happened to another man, a different child.

Emma regarded him warily, as if trying to figure out where his thoughts had taken him. "My unicorn book is the only thing I've got here that's mine since you let that lady take my house."

"I didn't *let* her do anything!" Cade objected. "I didn't sell the place to her!" He sucked in a steadying breath, wanting to comfort her. "I know you're upset, Emma. But it's for the best that the house finally sold. It's time you got settled here in Whitewater."

She prickled up like a porcupine. "I'm not going to be around long enough to bother. By next week I could be in New York or Santa Fe or Seattle."

The location of the last postcard her mother had sent. No return address—just a few scrawled lines basically saying "I'm alive." Cade supposed he should be grateful for that much. If anyone was going to murder Deirdre he wanted the pleasure of doing it himself.

As for Emma's objection to "settling in," Cade couldn't say much. For six months they'd both been counting the days, hoping they'd get a letter in the mail with instructions on how to return Emma to her mother.

But sometime during today's upheaval something had snapped in Cade. He'd lost his determination to resist anything that might make Emma's stay seem permanent.

"If I were going to bet on it, I'd wager you're going to be

here for a while," he said. "It's time you started making an effort. Hang out with kids in your class at school."

She thrust out her lower lip, trying to look defiant. She ended up looking small and breakable instead. "They don't like me."

"They don't even know you!" Cade brushed her words aside with a wave of his hand. "It's always tough being a new kid, especially in a town this small. But I've been thinking— maybe I can remove a few obstacles."

Emma tilted her head to one side, reminding him of a baby bird. A crease of uneasiness marked the space between her brows. "What kind of obstacles?"

"You know Brandi Bates?"

"Everybody knows her. She's the most popular girl in class." Emma wound an unruly black curl around her finger. She frowned at the ringlet, and Cade wondered if she was wishing her hair was more like the straight white-blond cascade that fell past Brandi's shoulders.

"Brandi's mom was homecoming queen when I was in school," Cade said. "Anyway, Brandi's having a birthday party tomorrow night."

"I know. She handed out the invitations in school." Emma's expression grew even more closely guarded.

"You didn't get one." Cade made it a statement, not a question.

"'Course not." Emma looked at him like he was Dumbo or something. He got a bad feeling Emma was the only girl in the class who didn't get one of those party envelopes. "Not that I care," she insisted hastily. "Addy and me need to work on quilt blocks."

Cade smiled, feeling a little surge of triumph, sure that he'd finally gotten something right. "You might have to hold off on that sewing project a little longer," he warned. "You see, Brandi's mom and I were…well, kind of friends a long time ago, so I called her up today. And guess what? She says she'd love to have you at the party."

Dark eyes widened. "You—you called Brandi's mom? Made her ask me to Brandi's party?"

He'd hoped for a reaction. No cartwheels or anything, just a smile, a thank-you. One of those quick hugs she'd handed out so freely when she was a little thing. No. He knew that was too much to hope for. But she just stared at him like she felt sick.

"How could you do that to me?" She was acting like he'd just stabbed her in the back, Brutus style.

"I'm trying to help you." Cade fought to keep his temper from flaring. "Emma, it's not good for you to be wandering around by yourself all the time."

"You do."

"I've got work to do."

"So do I," she asserted stubbornly.

"Don't you get lonely, Emma? Being by yourself all the time?"

He did. Not that he didn't love Emma. But sometimes, he thought he'd go crazy if he didn't have an adult conversation with someone.

"I'm not by myself." Emma crossed her arms over her chest. "I've got Addy."

"No, you don't." Cade flattened his palms on the table. "Addy March died a hundred and some odd years ago."

Pain streaked across Emma's face. She tossed her black curls. "That shows what you know!"

Cade's mood sank like a stone. Was the kid trying to pull his chain on purpose? Or did she really believe in ghosts? Was this a symptom of something far more serious? Damage caused by the trauma she'd been through? The possibility scared the hell out of him.

Damn you, Deirdre, he swore in his head. *What the hell am I supposed to do with her?*

"You're going to go to that party, damn it!" he roared. "And you're going to have fun!"

"I won't go! You can't make me!"

"You'll go if I have to duct tape you to one of the Bates' kitchen chairs!" Cade threatened. "This is insane! You won't talk to me! You won't talk to the kids at school."

"I have the only friend I need right next door. Addy."

"That's over," Cade snapped with the brutal mercy of someone trying to rip a bandage from a wound, knowing it would hurt, praying in the end it would cause less pain. "Ms. O'Grady isn't going to want a kid underfoot."

Fearsome anticipation lit Emma's eyes. "Wait 'til Addy gets done with her! Ms. O'Grady will be gone before school's out!"

How could he argue with that? The kid was probably right. As soon as Miss Sundress and Sunshine got a little paint thinner on those pretty hands she'd be heading back to wherever she came from.

Emma's eyes narrowed to slits. "If you make me go to that party, I'll—I'll stick sugar in your gas tank. Billy Callahan's brother told him how."

"Damn it, Emma—"

"I'll run away! I'll go find my mom!"

Cade's blood chilled at the thought that the little girl might just try it. "Don't you even think about it! If anybody could find your mother, I would have done it months ago! Dragged her back here by the hair and—"

"Duct taped her to a kitchen chair?" Emma flung back, trembling.

"Make her deal with her responsibilities," Cade ground out, clenching his jaw.

"You make me sound like cleaning the toilet. You must want to get rid of me real bad."

Guilt twisted in Cade at the thought of just how much he'd

give to be free of Emma's haunting eyes, her crushing silences, the fragility in her.

He felt as if she were one of those wildflowers his biology teacher showed him in high school—tiny pinkish white flowers that curled up their petals if anything touched it. Emma was wilting away right in front of his eyes.

Cade swallowed hard, groping for the right words, despairing that he would ever find them. He didn't want to hurt her. He knew he already had.

"Emma, I'm not very good at this, am I?"

"No. You're not." She picked up her notebook, walked into her room and quietly shut the door. Shutting him out. Shutting herself in.

Leaving him alone with one relentless, brutal question.

What the hell had Deirdre been thinking on the day she walked away?

FINN BROWSED the aisles of Farmer's Best hardware store, her shopping cart bulging with loot; plantation shutters, a kitchen garbage can and a fluffy rug to keep cold tile from waking her up during night forays into the bathroom. Providing she ever did get to sleep. Last night was no real test.

She'd unpacked until two o'clock in the morning, then dropped into bed, dead on her feet. She should've been out the minute her head hit the pillow, but the subtle noises from the walls had kept her nerves jumping.

But tonight would be different, she assured herself. She'd know what to expect. The sounds of the old house easing its bones would become familiar instead of startling her awake, setting her heart racing. Too bad the house didn't come with a knob like the one on her CD player so she could turn down the volume.

During one particularly loud series of rattles, she hadn't been able to resist the nudge from her quirky sense of humor—singing "Who you gonna call? Ghostbusters." She'd always loved the bit with the library ghost.

The awkward weight of her load shifted as she maneuvered the cart around a corner. She steadied the cardboard box protecting the shutters for her bedroom window—well, her temporary bedroom window, anyway.

The tower room up on the second floor that she'd dreamed of making her own would be far easier to spiff up without the bulk of her antique white iron bed or the gorgeous armoire she'd bought at an estate sale when on vacation last year. She'd set up camp in a room near the kitchen with a glorious bank of windows, where she could pause in her work to gaze at the river.

The room would've been perfect, if she could've blotted out the windows on the other wall, the ones that reflected the glowing lights from Cade McDaniel's log cabin. She'd promised herself her first project would be to put up window treatments so she wouldn't be reminded of the cabin and its pair of surly occupants. After all, the only reason Cade and Emma had been on her mind was because of the glow from their windows. She tried not to think how late it had been when the last light had finally flickered out.

Had Emma been crying herself to sleep over the sale of the house that had brought Finn such joy? Had Cade McDaniel had the sense to try to comfort her? More likely he'd been up late guzzling beer and watching some guy movie with cars blowing up and women running around in three-inch stilettos.

"Not your business," Finn muttered aloud to herself. Cade McDaniel had made that crystal clear when she'd tried to smooth things out yesterday. Of course, she'd failed miserably in the attempt. But why wouldn't she? She knew nothing about their situation. She only knew how she had felt when she was Emma's age. She only knew the choice her own

father had made when things got rocky—and the scars he'd
left behind.

Finn shook herself inwardly. Stewing over this wasn't
going to do anyone any good. She wasn't looking for complications in her life. And her neighbors wouldn't want anything to do with her, either. They'd just do as Cade insisted.
Stay on their side of the fence.

Fence in mind, Finn paused at a wall filled with a gazillion varieties of nails. She chose ones with heads the size of
dimes to anchor the loosened fence pickets in place. A good
start in establishing limits. One she hoped would help her
form similar boundaries in her mind.

She threaded her way toward the checkout lane at the front
of the store, trying to figure out how she was going to wedge
all of her loot into the miniscule confines of her cherry-red
Volkswagen Beetle.

She was concentrating so hard on ways to tie the hatch-
back down and still secure the shutters that she didn't see the
man staring at the meager offerings of the toy aisle. He didn't
see her, either. Broad shoulders hunched, his steely eyes fixed
on the twin rectangular boxes he held as if either the pink or
the blue Barbie had a winning lottery ticket tucked behind her
40DD breasts.

"Look out!" Finn gasped, unable to stop the collision as
the corner of her cart banged into one jean-clad leg.

Reflexively, the man wheeled toward her and dropped one
box. Grabbing the top of the cart, he yanked it to the side to
stop its momentum. Dismay rushed through Finn as she stumbled hard into the last person on earth she wanted to see.

Cade McDaniel looked even more horrified than she felt
as he grabbed her arm, helping her catch her balance. His rugged features tightened with the desperation of a fugitive
trapped between the sights of a crack SWAT team and a three-
mile drop to jagged rocks below. As to which way he'd turn,

at the moment there was no question. McDaniel was a jumper. Unfortunately the only available thing to leap into was a bin full of Mickey Mouse kick balls.

He flushed brick-red as he retrieved the fashion doll that had fallen into Finn's cart.

"You!" She gasped, Barbie's high-fashion boa looking even more outlandish silhouetted against his soft chambray shirt. She struggled to recover herself, saying, "That is, I didn't expect to see you here."

McDaniel scowled. "I need a present."

Was he getting something for Emma? He looked more like a sailor stranded on an enemy beachhead than someone seeking a peace offering.

He waved a box toward the rack of dolls. "Don't they have something like—like an Air Force Barbie? And who the hell drives a pink car, anyway?"

Finn surprised herself by laughing. "Don't knock it unless you've tried it."

"Very funny. I'm drowning here and you're auditioning for a gig on *Saturday Night Live*. How are you supposed to know which one of these dolls to buy? You're a woman. What kind of stuff did you get for your birthday?"

Finn tried not to let him see his words stung. Sometimes she had gotten wonderful presents from her father. More often, she'd gotten whatever he'd been able to grab on his way to pick her up at her latest foster home.

The year she was eleven she'd been dying for a toy horse with a mane and tail you could brush. He'd gotten her a terry cloth doll—the kind toddlers could chew on. He hadn't even noticed the bib read Baby's First Doll.

"I don't remember what I got," she lied.

"What about your sisters?" He grilled her with the determination of a cop in an interrogation room. "What did you get them?"

"I'm an only child." She admitted, suddenly quiet. McDaniel didn't notice.

"We should all be so lucky."

"I may not remember what I got for gifts, but I can tell you this much. Emma wouldn't like that doll one bit."

Cade stiffened. "How do you know? You barely met the kid."

"I saw what she was wearing, and talked to her long enough to know that feather boas and beauty parlors aren't her style. I saw a great rack of books with classics for kids a couple of rows over."

"That'd be a real thrill of a present. Just what every kid wants for their birthday. It's right up there with underwear and socks. I'll take my chances with Barbie, thanks."

Finn bristled. "With Emma's passion for history she'd probably love the book *Little Women*. It's about a family of girls in the Civil War, during March Winds' heyday." She remembered her own first foray into the world of Jo and Beth, Meg and Amy—finding between the book's cover the imaginary family she'd always wanted. A family that might just warm the lonely little girl's heart.

McDaniel recoiled as if she'd suggested giving the child a butcher knife. "The last thing Emma needs is to be stuffing her head with more of that garbage! She comes up with plenty of crazy stuff on her own. Besides, it's not even for—" He stopped dead, jaw clenched as a trio of men brushed past.

A big, mean looking one with squinty eyes sniggered. "You get lost, Magic? The power tools are this way!"

Cade looked as if they'd caught him peeking under Barbie's dress. "I'm helping her," he said, jabbing the blue box in Finn's direction.

Pig eyes laughed. "I just bet you are. The man with the magic hands."

"Cut it out, Chapman," Cade warned.

"You go on and help the little lady pick out a pretty doll, McDaniel. We're going to play with the big boy's stuff." The trio disappeared.

Finn shot Cade a look. "*You're* helping *me?* What's the deal, Mr. Magic Hands?"

He glowered at the sound of the name. "You sure look like you could use some help to me. Just what are you planning to do with these?" He held up her box of nails.

Finn's chin bumped up a notch. "Use them to fix my fence. They're the strongest ones I could find."

"They're also five inches long. Use these and you'll have three inch spikes sticking out of your fence ready to skewer anyone who walks by."

"What a shame since I have such a pleasant neighbor." Finn's cheeks burned. The jerk was right. A few other shoppers lingered nearby, obviously listening.

"Listen," Cade said smugly. "Just one little reminder before you go off to butcher your fence. Something to remember about nails. The pointy end goes in the wood."

Laughter rippled around Finn. She wished she could jam the box right in his patronizing mouth. "I'll keep that in mind."

She drifted her fingers over the doll box peeking out from under hard biceps. "You want this to be a present?" she asked so sweetly he should have known to run.

"That's what I said."

"You'll need these." She grabbed up a half-dozen rolls of the girliest wrapping paper she could find and shoved them into his arms.

His brow furrowed. "How much of this junk do I need? The boxes don't look that big."

"You'd be surprised," Finn assured him, grabbing the biggest, gaudiest sparkly purple and pink bow on the rack. She glanced around at their growing audience while surreptitiously peeling the layer of film off the bow's back.

"One thing to remember about the art of attaching bows, Mr. McDaniel." She shot him her most saccharine smile. "Sticky side goes on last."

She smacked the bow dead center on Cade McDaniel's forehead and wheeled her cart away.

CHAPTER THREE

SHE WAS LATE.

Finn scrambled up the cement steps to the arched front door of the Whitewater Public Library, her overflowing tote bag bouncing against her hip as she tried in vain to tie back the auburn waves that rioted around her face. She glimpsed her reflection in the glass door, despairing.

The roses smattering her blue cotton skirt were crumpled after tumbling from hanger to floor sometime during the night, and the blouse she'd draped over the ironing board meaning to press crisp first thing this morning hadn't seen the business end of the iron.

She stumbled and went down on one knee. Concrete scoured off a layer of skin, the sting of the scrape dismaying her much less than the feel of her panty hose tearing.

"Damn," she muttered under her breath. "Damn, damn, damn!"

People who resort to swearing are either dense or lazy. Her own words from Saturday mocked her, transposed into the whiskey-rough baritone of her next-door neighbor. She made a sour face. Cade McDaniel's silver-blue eyes and rugged features had intruded in her thoughts far too often since he'd told her to stay on her side of the fence. Not to mention the disturbing image of Emma, the doomsayer fairy with her bruised heart in her eyes. But sometimes even Finn had to make an exception to her "no swearing" rule.

She had wanted to make a good impression her first day on the job. But it was hard to look competent when you hadn't slept for two days and your alarm hadn't gone off on one of the most important mornings of your life.

The clock had been dead, along with the power in that end of the house. Heck, she would've been better off not bothering to go to bed at all, she figured, brushing a smudge off her skirt and picking up a tote that displayed a smug-looking cat in the guise of William Shakespeare.

She opened the library door, wincing at the alarm in the library staff's faces as she sailed through the adult section.

Odds were Verna Sopher was going to be taking a heck of a bite out of her.

A mix of Katherine Hepburn dignity, Maureen O'Hara flair and Queen Elizabeth I's "off with their head" decisiveness, seventy-year-old Miss Sopher had made it clear that she had no use for shenanigans in her library, whether performed by her grubby little patrons or by her staff. It was vital to set a good example.

Finn had to agree. Hadn't she told Cade McDaniel the very same thing two days ago?

Finn felt a jab of irritation as her neighbor materialized again in her mind, his arms crossed over a chest a professional athlete would envy, the undeniably sexy planes of his face looking so self-satisfied she wanted to smack him.

Sexy—yeah, sexy the way Mr. Rochester was before you knew he had a crazy wife in the attic. Sexy and dangerous as all get out. And she hadn't come to this sleepy little town looking for trouble, even if it had a mouth meant for nuclear meltdown kisses and a body that just begged a woman to make it even harder. Heck, for all she knew, Cade McDaniel had a Bertha Mason of his own.

Finn rushed headlong into the children's section. The place was already buzzing with clusters of kids—but then, Verna had said the school had the day off. Most of the present crowd looked to be somewhere between ten and twelve in age.

The head children's librarian regarded Finn over half-moon glasses, not one strand of silver hair out of place. Handing a stack of books to a pair of boys, she directed them to one of the child-size tables in the study area. Then, the older woman marched toward Finn.

"I'm so sorry!" Finn burst out, dumping her tote behind the battered oak desk.

"Ms. O'Grady, I was beginning to wonder if March Winds scared you off."

Finn stared at her. Maybe those piercingly intelligent eyes really could read a person's mind, just like all of the boys in town must have feared. "You mean the ghost?"

Blue eyes twinkled beneath winged brows as black and lovely as her hair must once have been. "Land sakes, no. I meant all the work the charming old place needs."

"Guess I'd better start with the wiring. The circuit I had the alarm clock plugged into blew sometime during the night. Normally I would've woken up anyway, but I've been having trouble sleeping."

"Is that so?"

"It's the most ridiculous thing. I keep hearing noises in the walls."

Verna pondered for a moment. "I suppose most houses have noises of their own. And older homes like March Winds would have more than their share."

"I thought I'd sleep like a baby here." One more fantasy about her house blown to smithereens. She'd always imagined sleeping there with the soundness of angels, far away from the constant buzz of traffic, the wail of sirens that kept her awake.

But in the evening, Jubilee Point was so quiet it almost pressed on her ears. She'd unpacked boxes until she'd been ready to drop. Staggered to bed, sure that this time she'd be able to sleep.

She'd barely pulled a nightgown over her head and switched off the bedroom light before it started—strange, scratching noises, little creaks and soft moans from behind her bedroom wall.

She jumped at the crash of books hitting the floor, her gaze flashing to where two swaggering boys were obviously showing off. A carrot-topped kid in a shirt that read If You Don't Win You're A LOSER made a huge display of gathering up the books, while the bruiser with fists the size of a grown man's tried to look dismayed at the disturbance they'd caused.

Miss Sopher pinned them with laser beam eyes. In an instant, the boys turned angelic. Unease nipped at Finn's already shaky confidence. She couldn't help wondering what the boys would have done if she'd tried Miss Sopher's technique. Probably break into a war dance.

Finn might not have much experience in the children's section, but even she knew the boys were not the usual patrons one would expect to find with their noses in books at eighten in the morning when they had the day off from school.

"I'm impressed," Finn offered. "When you said the kids had the day off I figured it would be a little slow here. It's gorgeous outside."

"Fifth graders. They put their final report off until the last minute. It's due on Wednesday and their teacher doesn't take any excuses."

"There doesn't seem to be many girls." In fact, none of those she could see would pass for fifth graders.

"The girls are still sleeping. There was a slumber party at Brandi Bates's house. The most coveted invitation of the year. Last May Melissa Jones tried to hide a case of chicken pox so she could go."

"Bet the other mothers were thrilled."

"It kept Dr. Flannigan's office mighty busy. Speaking of doctor's offices, I'm going to have to visit the dentist in about an hour. I had an unfortunate incident with a piece of caramel last night. I hoped we'd have more time to get you settled before I leave, but there's no help for it now."

Finn scrambled to think of the right questions to ask so that she'd feel at least semicompetent on her own. Starting to turn, her elbow collided with someone next to her, the corner of a book cover zinging her funny bone. Stifling a gasp as pain shot up her arm, Finn turned to say excuse me, but the words faltered as she glanced down into Emma McDaniel's elfin face. It seemed one fifth grade girl wasn't at the party.

The child stood so close it unnerved Finn. How had Emma crept up so quietly? Finn wondered.

She'd thought about the little girl far too often the past two days. Wondered where she'd run to, heartbroken, with no loving arms to hold her. She wondered what had happened when Emma had come face-to-face again with the angry man who was not her father.

"Emma. Have you met your new neighbor?" Miss Sopher asked.

"Yes, ma'am."

Emma peered up at Finn over a heavy stack of books, dark circles under her eyes. Even with twenty-odd other children in the room, the girl seemed entirely alone. Finn wished realizing her own dream hadn't caused this fragile little butterfly pain. She wondered if she'd ever be able to look at Emma McDaniel without feeling an uncomfortable twinge of guilt.

"Hello, Emma." Finn forced a smile.

"Emma is one of our best customers here in the children's room," Miss Sopher said briskly. "She checks out one book for every day of the week and two each for Saturday and Sunday."

Emma sneaked a resentful glare at Finn, making no bones about the fact that Finn was invading her territory here, too.

Finn's stomach sank. She felt for Emma, but the prospect of being haunted by the unhappy child at work as well as at home was disheartening. She'd come to Whitewater hoping to put her own past to rest, not to watch her childhood pain being played out by another child.

"Emma's doing this research project independently," Miss Sopher said. "It's the first time in ten years any child has been allowed to do it. The final American History report is such a big job, Mr. Jeffers has always insisted on it being a group project. But the way Emma devours books, he decided to let her do it on her own. Didn't he, Emma?"

Emma squared her narrow shoulders in spite of the heavy load in her arms. "The snooty high school library aide tried to take *Huckleberry Finn* away when I wanted to read it," Emma said, as if to let Finn know she was not a young lady to be crossed. "She said the book was too big and my brain was too small. I'd better pick out something like *Cheerleader Diaries*. But Miss Sopher told her to let me take any book I wanted. She said my mind was so hungry it'd stretch to gobble it up."

Finn's heart squeezed. She'd known someone who had "gobbled up" books once. There was so little she could picture clearly about her mother after all this time—Mariel O'Grady's features blurred by the years. Yet Finn could remember how she'd glowed when she got a new book, how she'd held it in her hands, as if it were a jewel, ran her fingertips over the title, raised it to her nose to smell the perfume of paper and leather and glue.

Finn could hear her mother reading her to sleep at whatever whistle-stop they happened to light in, Mariel O'Grady turning each character's voice into a feast for Finn's imagination. Oliver Twist and Bill Sikes, Jane Eyre and Mr.

Rochester, Ivanhoe and Lorna Doone. Sometimes Finn even found her mother crying over the volumes. Usually when Da had just convinced her to leave one behind.

But then, Patrick O'Grady liked to travel light. Finn could remember how he'd left pieces of their lives behind, too eager to get where he was going to realize how it hurt his wife and daughter to let go of their humble treasures. Books that were "too heavy," china that would only break. As long as they had each other, that was the only thing that mattered, he'd insisted. But he'd changed his mind after her mother had died. It seemed there was no burden heavier than a grieving little girl.

Finn was sure that was one thing her father and Cade McDaniel would agree on.

Miss Sopher's voice cut through the haze of memories, snapping Finn back to the crowded library and Emma's solemn, watchful eyes.

"It seems Ms. O'Grady is having trouble sleeping in her new house," Miss Sopher said.

Finn flushed, wishing Miss Sopher hadn't shared that information. The top book on Emma's pile almost toppled. Finn straightened it, scanning the title. *"Ghosts of the Blue and Gray,"* she read aloud.

"Maybe you should read this after I'm done," Emma suggested, watching Finn intently. "I've heard that reading before bed helps people sleep."

Finn figured Emma's next prescription for insomnia would be a Stephen King film fest. It was easy to see where the kid was heading—if Finn was already having trouble sleeping, Emma would love to make those long nights even worse.

She felt a bit unnerved, knowing this little girl wished her ill. She searched for a way to send the child back to a study table so she could attempt to settle in to her new job without the "bad fairy" hovering close by. *No,* not *bad fairy,* a voice in Finn whispered. *A sad fairy.*

"Did you have a question?" Finn asked, making an effort to take charge of the exchange.

"Not for you. Miss Sopher will help me." The child turned her back pointedly on Finn.

The older woman flashed Finn an inquiring glance above the rim of her glasses. But for the time being, Miss Sopher went off with the little girl.

As Finn busied herself helping the other kids, she watched surreptitiously. But in spite of the hubbub of kids whispering, giggling, even squabbling quietly among themselves, Emma seemed set apart, a princess in a glass bubble.

And Miss Sopher's subtle efforts to draw other kids into their circle failed miserably, Emma's classmates determined to steer clear of her. Finn would've liked to chalk that up to the fact that most were boys, but instinctively she doubted that was the root of the problem. The one mercy was that—for this small island of time—Emma didn't seem to care about being left out.

Aside from pausing every so often to shoot Finn dark glances, the girl looked almost happy. Her eyes sparkled with an intelligence, enthusiasm and sweet imagination that almost made Finn forget about the blue smudges marring the fragile skin beneath her lower lashes.

Emma monopolized the librarian until Miss Sopher had to hurry to leave. "I may be late myself, this morning," she said, exhuming her purse from her glass-walled office along the back wall. "But I hate to leave Emma."

"She must be excited about whatever topic she's reporting on."

"Oh, Emma finished her history paper a week ago. She's just at home here. But I can't shake the feeling that something's wrong with her this morning. She was waiting on the front steps when I got here, an hour before the library opened. And she's chattering away as if—well, if the child was one of the tin windup toys I played with as a girl, her spring would be ready to snap from being wound too tight."

Emma *did* seem wound too tight. Her books were scattered over a tabletop, her battered notebook and a pencil chewed down to a nub had tumbled to the floor. Cheeks almost feverish, she flitted to a revolving bookstand packed with paperbacks.

"She's an odd little thing," Finn said softly, something about the child pinching like a shoe that's a half size too small.

"She doesn't seem very impressed with you, either."

"I didn't say I wasn't impressed with her. There's just something…" Finn hesitated, conscience needling her.

"Different about Emma?" Miss Sopher supplied. "What a pity that is the one flaw other children can't forgive."

With two fingers Miss Sopher nipped a set of keys from the front pouch of her practical navy handbag. Her gaze pinned Finn. "You can handle things in my absence?"

"Of course." Finn attempted to reassure herself as much as she did the silver-haired woman before her. "I've handled study rooms packed with graduate students the night before their theses were due. A few kids won't be any problem at all."

"May I offer you a bit of advice, Ms. O'Grady? Never underestimate children. They're like the Mississippi River after a storm. It may seem like they're flowing along, all lazy and quiet. But take your eyes off of them, and you can be in over your head in a heartbeat."

Finn smiled wanly. "I'll keep that in mind."

She had every intention of making a seamless transition from Miss Sopher's reign of the children's room to her own. But the moment the prim coiffure was out of sight, it was open season. Noise went up a few decibels to test her tolerance level. Gestures got a little wilder to push at boundaries.

A dozen pairs of kiddie eyes fastened on Finn, and she had the sinking feeling that she'd suddenly transformed from resource to the morning's entertainment.

Emma's nerves seemed to coil tighter, too. She glanced at the clock, then started to pack a stack of books in something that looked more like an overnight case than a book bag. Intent on ignoring the other kids' antics, she looked smaller than ever, maybe even a little…scared? Finn's frustration softened into empathy.

The rest of the children seemed so much at ease, as if they'd known each other forever. While Emma might as well have been invisible.

No, not invisible. Finn saw the subtle pointing of fingers, heard the whispers. The other children had plenty to say about Emma McDaniel. Just not to her face.

Poor kid. It seemed like everyone wanted to get rid of her. Finn felt a twinge at her own anxiousness to see the girl heading out of the library.

Finn promised herself she would do better the next time Emma came to the children's room. Not let her old ghosts and nagging self-doubt get in the way.

She'd just crouched down to help a first grader find *Bedtime For Frances* when a wail pierced the clamor, surreal as the keening of her father's Banshee. Finn's hair stood on end.

Dodging the picture book crowd, their eyes pumpkin round, she ran toward the commotion. Chaos reigned where Emma had stood—a herd of the rowdiest fifth grade boys jostling for a better view, faces contorted in the nasty glee that struck terror into the hearts of shy kids all over the world.

"Emma," Finn cried.

She shoved her way into the crowd, tried to get to the little girl.

It was too late.

A screech of pain split the air.

Shoving back a pair of goggles, Cade levered himself out of the cockpit of the sweet little barnstormer he'd just taken for its first flight in sixty years, and jumped to the tarmac near the sign that identified the cluster of hangars as Flyboy's Charter and Restoration. One hand caressed the plane's belly, the engine's warmth making its skin feel almost alive. He smiled with satisfaction at a job well done. Jett Davis, the vintage beauty's owner, would be over the moon when he got this baby back.

But then, the actor who had danced his way into people's hearts in the 70s, and blazed back onto the screen in an Oscar-winning comeback took more joy in flying than anyone Cade had ever known. At least, for a very long time.

Cade shaded his eyes with the blade of one hand and peered longingly at the limitless stretch of clear blue sky. Once he'd felt the kind of kid-in-a-candy-store sensation Jett Davis did when he climbed in a cockpit. A joy, a freedom that made anything seem possible.

Back then, the people below seemed so tiny it didn't seem as if they could be weighed down with such big problems.

But he hadn't flown just for the fun of it in longer than he could remember. There was just too much to do. The restoration business he'd started was thriving. And then, there were the charter flights that still meant so much to his father.

If he'd cut them out, there would've been more time to soar away from Whitewater. But sometimes he feared work was the one thing holding his old man together. And Cade could remember all too well the kind of swath Martin McDaniel could cut when he fell apart.

Cade strode into his office, grimacing at his reflection in the glass door. His dark hair shot every which way from his flight in the barnstormer. The thick waves as unruly and unwilling to obey the laws of gravity as he was. His lean, angular face looked a little more relaxed than usual, a thin scar slashing from left to right across his square chin—a little souvenir from one of the times he'd jumped between his old man and someone who'd pissed Martin McDaniel off.

As he tossed the goggles on top of a stack of forms ordering parts from obscure places all over the world, a blinking light caught his eye. The answering machine. That was one of the things he loved best about his job—every phone call could be like opening a present—he never knew what kind of plane he might be able to get his hands on next.

But this morning, the caller would have to wait. He dialed Jett's cell phone. Grinned when the guy picked up. The voice that had made the vilest movie villains turn and run sounded groggy as hell. "'Lo?"

"Going Hollywood on me, Jett? Sound like you're still in bed."

"Never even made it that far." Jett chuckled. "The baby was up all night. I was trying to let Robin get some sleep."

The guy could have afforded an army of nannies, but he was as hands-on with his kids as he was with his airplanes. "Tell me you've got some good news for me, Magic?"

"She flies like a dream. You'll be barrel rolling to your heart's content in no time."

"Hot damn!" Jett startled a cry from the baby. "Hush, angel girl, hush. Daddy's sorry. But Uncle Magic says your plane is all ready."

Cade squirmed at the family stuff. "I asked you not to call me that."

"It just slipped out," Jett said, completely unrepentant. "I'm telling you, Cade, seeing that wife of mine bring our babies into the world is the only thing I've ever found that made me higher than flying. You should try it, buddy. Find yourself a good woman."

For some unaccountable reason Finnoula O'Grady's face flashed into his mind—her breasts soft under the thin layer of sundress, her eyes shining as she talked about turning that tumbledown house into a home. People like Jett and Finnoula would never understand why Cade wanted something different. Just a place to eat and sleep and crash when he needed to. A roof over his head with no hold on his heart.

"Thanks, I'll pass. There's only one Robin and she's married to this stuck-up movie star type who doesn't know a crescent wrench from a lug nut."

"Yeah, yeah, yeah. How's Emma?"

"Terrific. Wonderful." Except for the fact that she hates me. "She's gone."

"Deirdre came back?"

"Hell, no. Emma's at a slumber party. I've got the whole morning to myself."

"I wish you two would move out here to Montana where Robin and I could help. We could build the finest restoration company in the world. I'd bankroll the whole thing. You'd be doing me a favor, Magic."

"I'm not going anywhere."

Jett surrendered for the time being. "How is your dad?"

"Had to pick him up at the police station again last week."

"What now?"

"Witnessed a drunk hit some lady in a minivan. Chased the guy, and had him in a half nelson by the time the cops got there."

"The Captain's amazing. Might as well wear a giant *S* on his chest and a long red cape."

"It's not funny. He got a concussion and had his earring half-torn out of his ear. Hell, he's seventy years old, he should be mellowing a little by now."

"Dare you to tell him that to his face."

Cade went solemn. "He scares the hell out of me. Why does he do such crazy stuff?"

The laughter faded from Jett's voice. "Be glad he still can."

"I am. I just…wish—"

"At least he's using his powers for good instead of evil. He could be like Catwoman or Two Face." The guy *People* magazine had dubbed 'Sexiest Man Alive' was a comic book junkie to rival any twelve-year-old.

"I'll tell him you said so." The last thing Cade wanted to talk about this morning was his family. For this tiny island of time, he just wanted peace.

"Listen, I need to go. Some of us actually have to work for a living."

"Yeah, yeah, yeah. If you'd just move out here I'd show you work. You could bring the old man, too. Robin and I love him."

Everybody loved Martin McDaniel. But they didn't have to follow him around with Band-Aids and splints.

Cade hung up the phone, then shoved back the tension coiling between his shoulder blades. He wasn't going to let anything ruin his gloriously free morning. He pressed the button on the machine.

"Mr. McDaniel?" The all too familiar feminine voice jolted him. He closed his eyes, seeing Finnoula O'Grady, the triumph curving her bee stung lips as she smacked that stupid ribbon onto his head. He winced, recalling the laughter from their hardware store audience. Okay, so maybe he'd asked for it. But the woman was definitely getting under his skin.

"This is Finn O'Grady," the message continued. "Please call me as soon as you can. We have a problem with Emma here at the library." She rattled off the number. He grabbed a pencil and dialed the old-fashioned black rotary phone he'd resurrected from his parents' basement.

"Cade McDaniel here," he said when Verna's answering

machine picked up. "I got your message about some kind of problem." He chuckled. "What's the deal? Did the kid keep a book past the date you guys stamp in the cover? Don't worry, I'm good for the fine."

A deafening rattle pounded in his ear as someone obviously snatched up the receiver. "Mr. McDaniel?" Finn O'Grady demanded, breathless. "Where have you been? I called over an hour ago!"

"I was flying. That's how I make a living."

"It's not funny! I have a real problem here."

"It can't be anything too earth shattering." He said, glad for once Miss Know-it-all didn't sound so all fired sure of herself. "Emma's not even at the library."

"You don't even know where Emma is?" she demanded.

The woman made him sound like a total incompetent. "Of course I know where Emma is," he snapped.

Hadn't he dropped the girl off last night, present in hand? He'd even managed to fasten that stupid bow on to the package with Scotch tape since the sticky stuff had lost its stick after it pulled off the first layer of his skin. Not that Emma had thanked him for it. She'd acted like he was Captain Hook about to make her swim with the hand-munching crocodile.

"Emma's at the Bates' for a slumber party. I'm supposed to pick her up at noon."

"Emma's sitting right across from me. She was waiting at the library door when we opened."

Disbelief rocked Cade. "But that's impossible. Somebody would have called me."

"You were busy flying, remember? You couldn't be bothered with a phone."

His face burned. She was right. But there weren't any other messages on the machine. Caro would have known to call him at the hangar.

Anger flared. How had the kid gotten to the library?

Sneaked away from the Bates' under cover of darkness? He remembered the stubborn jut of Emma's chin, how Emma had given him her best "You're lower than pond scum" look when he'd dropped her off. He'd even gone with her up to the door. Caro had flashed her ex-cheerleader smile and promised she'd take good care of Emma. Heck, Caro had lost the kid like a cheap pair of sunglasses!

There was going to be big trouble as soon as he found out how Emma had gotten the five miles from Caro's to the library, and why no one at the Bates' house had bothered to tell him she'd gone missing.

What if Emma had decided to make good on her threat to run away and try to find her mother? The kid could be in the back seat of a serial killer's car by now!

"Mr. McDaniel." Finn's voice jolted him back from thoughts of how he was going to read people the riot act. "There's been an incident."

Incident? His old military mind-set clicked in. Incidents usually meant spy planes "accidentally" invading a hostile country's airspace. The dictator of some banana republic taken out by a strike force. Hell, the library was the one place in town Cade figured he didn't have to worry about the kid.

"Put Emma on the phone," he demanded. *"Now."*

"I'm afraid that's impossible."

"What do you mean, impossible?"

"She's not able to come to the phone."

"What the blazes is that supposed to mean? Let me talk to Miss Sopher." Verna would straighten things out. The woman always just rapped things out crystal clear.

"Miss Sopher isn't here at the moment."

She might as well have said the sun had gone AWOL. Without Verna manning the helm anything could have happened. Cade should know. He used to be the *anything* that caused the most trouble.

"Ms. O'Grady, I want to know exactly what is going on over there."

"There was a fight. Emma's in no shape to have you bellowing at her over the phone."

Cade heard some muffled noise through the receiver. If he hadn't known Finn was the Carrie Nation of the antiswearing league, he'd have sworn she muttered a curse that would make a sailor proud.

"Tip your head back," she ordered, sounding rattled. "You've started bleeding again."

"Bleeding?" Cade echoed, alarmed. "Who's bleeding?"

"Stay in that chair! Don't move! I mean it!" *Click.* The phone went dead.

Cade never knew if the handset hit the cradle. He was already running.

CHAPTER FOUR

CADE WADED THROUGH a mob of kids packing the children's room at the Whitewater Public Library, a towering Dr. Livingston overrun by hordes of pygmies.

Hot little eyes pinned him as if there were a cannibal stew pot hidden somewhere in Verna Sopher's office and they were taking bets as to who was going to be plunged neck-deep into boiling water.

Whatever drama had played out here had been a five-star event in elementary school history. And the only thing he knew for sure was that Emma had been center stage.

He winced inwardly, picturing reproachful dark eyes, arms and legs fragile as grass stems and a frame so delicate he was tempted to slip lead weights in Emma's shoes to keep a good gust of wind from sailing her across the river. Though maybe Emma's sailing away from Whitewater would be the best thing for everyone.

Palms sweating for the first time in his life, he strode up to the main desk. "Emma McDaniel—where is she?"

A frightened looking woman with the vaguely familiar face of someone he'd passed in school hallways a lifetime ago gave a wave of her hand.

"They're in Miss Sopher's office. First door on your right." He knew where Verna Sopher's office was. He'd been dragged there often enough during his "books are a waste of my time" phase.

But it wasn't Verna's voice that had taken ten years off of his life on the telephone. He rounded the corner, his eyes locking with the elfin green ones of Finnoula O'Grady. She looked like hell—pale, rumpled and overwhelmed, a stain marring her white blouse. He had a ridiculous urge to squeeze her hand, tell her everything was going to be okay. How could he know that? He didn't even know what the "everything" was.

"How bad is it?" he demanded.

He had asked Verna Sopher that question plenty of other times, when he'd jumped off the library roof and broken his arm trying out the flying machine he'd made as his fourth grade science project. When school bully Horst Chapman had knocked him out by the biography section. And six months later, when he'd sent the nasty son of a bitch to the emergency room for stitches after he'd tormented Cade's younger sister for the very last time.

But Emma was so quiet. Whatever had happened couldn't be *that* bad, could it?

"How did you get here so fast?" Finn had the nerve to ask. "Emma said the hangar is way outside town."

"I drove like a bat out of hell. You wouldn't tell me a damn thing over the phone." His gaze snagged on a wastebasket nearby. His heart clutched at the sight of a paper towel stained dark with blood. "Good God! Emma?"

"She's not hurt." Finn interjected hastily, then amended. "Not physically, anyway. But she is suffering…"

"Don't talk about me like I'm not here," a resentful voice piped up. Cade glanced around to where Finn had lined up a row of child-size chairs against the wall as if the occupants were awaiting a miniature firing squad. A petite figure with flyaway black curls and a torn pink dress perched on the edge of the chair farthest from the door. Two boys big enough to be varsity linebackers huddled as far away from her as they could get without falling on the seats of their well-worn blue jeans.

"I'm sorry, Emma," Finn began in just the right tone to calm a child's ragged nerves. But Cade's own were stretched way past the point of no return.

He wheeled toward Emma, his fists planted on his hips. "All right, young lady, you don't want us to talk like you're not here. Fine. Then how about if you tell me what the he—"

Finn hushed him under her breath, the warning like fingernails raking across a blackboard. His near-brush with swearing only ratcheted his stress up even more. "Emma, what's this all about?" he growled in a voice that made Bubba and Bulldozer shrink back into their chairs.

Emma shot the boys a hate-filled glare. "They stole something from me. I took it back."

"She's a nutcase!" one of the boys exclaimed, eyeing Emma as if she were a rabid dog. "You should'a seen her—"

"That's enough," Finn cut him off. "Name calling doesn't solve anything."

Cade scrutinized the boys' faces, noting a thin mouth designed specifically for nasty sneers. It was pure Chapman—a mirror image of his own schoolyard nemesis.

"Like I told the lady." The Chapman kid tried his damnedest to look like a choirboy. "Adam an' me found a notebook under the table. We only looked inside it to find out who it belonged to. When we couldn't find a name written on the cover, we read a page aloud to see if one of the other kids in the library would recognize it."

"Liar!" Emma flushed. "You knew that notebook was mine! My private letters to my best friend!"

Bulldozer tried to sneer past a swollen nose. "The only friend who'd like you *would* be a dead person! You can't write letters to a ghost."

Not that again, Cade thought, overwhelmed.

"Addy is real! She is my friend! She is!"

"See!" Bulldozer insisted. "That girl is plain crazy!"

Emma grabbed Cade's hand, clinging as if she were adrift on the storm-savaged river and he was her only hope of being pulled to shore. Cade's heart twisted, and he wondered just how many years it had been since she'd held his hand. She peered up at him as if, maybe, just maybe she could depend on him the way she had so long ago.

"You tell them," she pleaded. "Tell them they're wrong about Addy and me."

But how could he? Cade wondered, feeling helpless, angry. Emma *was* acting crazy. It was tearing Cade apart. Blowing any chance the girl would ever have of fitting in at school, making friends.

And no matter how hotly Emma protested to the contrary, a kid needed friends. Real, live friends who could laugh and roughhouse and share secrets. Ghosts couldn't hug you when you felt like crying.

"For God's sake, Emma, cut this nonsense out!" Cade snapped, his own cheeks burning with embarrassment for her.

Emma shrank in on herself. She bit her bottom lip, fighting to hold back tears. Cade wanted to bang Bubba's head into the wall. But not only was the kid half his size, Bubba also had a point. It *was* crazy to write letters to dead people. Cade tried another tack. "Emma, you can't be causing trouble in the library."

Emma's jaw set, mutinous. "Don't act like you're all perfect! You got in fights in the library, too! Miss Sopher told me all about it!"

What had Verna been thinking filling the kid's head with that stuff? And why did Finnoula O'Grady's questioning gaze on him suddenly make his collar feel too tight?

"You even dumped out the card catalogues once when you were so mad, and you made that stupid airplane hanging from the ceiling to say you were sorry!"

"It was an accident—the other kid knocked the file drawer off a desk when he fell." Not that it lessened the hours Verna had been forced to spend putting the file back together. Cade chafed inwardly. He wasn't sure whom he was defending himself to: Emma, Mary Poppins or the two boys who were regarding him with a whole new level of respect.

Cade suddenly felt as if Finn O'Grady had X-ray vision. He didn't want her probing feelings he'd wanted to keep balled up and out of sight where they belonged.

He groped for a shield to deflect her penetrating gaze. Settled on a method from his quarterback days—the best defense a good offense. After all, Emma had broken the rules, big time.

"Now you listen to me, young lady," Cade growled. "Lecturing me about stuff I did twenty years ago isn't going to get you out of trouble. You're not even supposed to be at the library. I left you at that party and I expected you to stay there."

The Chapman kid snickered, elbowing his friend. "Brandi spent all Saturday night whining to my sister. Brandi's mom made her ask the geek."

Cade glared so hard Billy should've had a smoking hole where his forehead had been. The kid had the good sense to shut up.

"This isn't helping the situation," Finn interrupted. "Mindy?"

She called the girl from the main desk over. "Could you keep an eye on these three, please? I need to speak to Mr. McDaniel alone."

The library aide regarded the kids as if one of them might explode at any minute. With Emma involved there were pretty good odds.

Cade stalked into the office after Finn, shutting the door behind him with a bang he hoped would rattle the Quiet Zone sign right off the wall.

"Why does she do that?" he demanded, raking his fingers back through his hair. "Run around telling people that a ghost is her best friend?" He sounded like an idiot himself, expecting Finn O'Grady to answer that. Hell, she barely knew Emma. And from what the woman had seen so far, Cade doubted she would want much to do with the kid in the future. "Emma's bound to get tormented by other kids when she talks like that. Where does she come up with this stuff?"

"I don't know why she buries herself in ghosts and letters and such." Finn flattened her hands on the desk, and Cade suddenly realized she had been trembling. "But I do know this. It's an act of God nobody got hurt today. Badly hurt."

Cade clenched his fist, shaken by the knowledge of how easy it would be to snap one of Emma's slender arms, bruise her pale skin. "You think those jerks would physically hurt her?" He'd find the boys' fathers and beat them to a pulp if those kids laid one finger on Emma.

"There are times a split lip would be more merciful than being tormented with words," Finn said.

"You've obviously never had a split lip." Cade muttered darkly. "Maybe I should find Billy Chapman's father and remind him what one feels like."

Finn looked at him as if he had just sprouted another head. "Mr. McDaniel, surely you don't mean that."

"What's he thinking, letting his boy pound on other kids like that? If Chapman doesn't have any better control over his kid than that, he deserves what he gets."

"*Emma* is the one who lashed out today."

Cade shook his head, the way he had to dispel the stars circling behind his eyes after he'd taken an upper cut to his jaw. He glanced toward the waiting room, saw the blurred outlines of the beefy boys and Emma—delicate, withdrawn little Emma. "You're kidding, right?"

"I wish I were. Both Billy and Adam could have been seriously injured."

"Maybe if Emma had been armed with a baseball bat."

"Emma hit Adam in the stomach so hard he threw up. And if her aim hadn't been a little off she would've broken Billy's nose."

Cade's eyes widened. "You mean my Emma went after those two?"

"And had them on the floor by the time I got there."

"She took both of them down at the same time?" Cade couldn't stifle a surge of pride. "Did you see the size of those bruisers?"

Finn rolled her eyes. "That's just the attitude Emma needs to hear from you right now! Why don't you just march out there and give her a high five, tell her way to go?"

"That doesn't sound like a half-bad idea," he asserted. "The Chapmans have always been bullies. And they're never happy unless they've got a whole pack of losers running with them. Before you come down too hard on Emma, you'd better find out what's been going on out of the teacher's sight."

Cade could see some of the bluster drain out of her. "As a matter of fact, I already have. I talked to some of the other kids from their class, and it's true that the two boys have been making Emma miserable. But sending them to the emergency room would hardly have solved anything."

"What would you suggest?" Cade sneered. "Sitting down with Bubba and Bulldozer to talk about *feelings?*"

Those thick, dark feminine lashes fluttered, and he knew he'd hit the nail on the head.

"Listen, Ms. O'Grady. Kids fight on every playground in America. When they do connect a punch it's almost by accident."

"Are you even listening to yourself? Bloodying Billy Chapman's nose has just given the boys another score to settle with Emma. And next time she won't have the advantage of taking them by surprise."

He tensed, not liking the sound of that, but he wasn't going to let her see she'd touched a nerve. "You're making too big a deal out of this."

"Am I? Emma told me herself that she used Special Forces moves designed to take out an enemy."

"Yeah, and I'm the Incredible Hulk." Cade gave a hoarse laugh. "She was just repeating stuff she's heard on television, trying to act tough."

"A move called a 'death shot' sounds pretty serious to me."

Cade's temples started to pound. "A death shot?"

"That's exactly what Emma called it. She showed me the technique she's been practicing, explained the damage it could do." Finn's eyes flooded with blame. "What were you thinking, teaching a ten-year-old child how to injure another student that badly?"

The muscles in Cade's stomach bunched. "I wasn't. I mean, I…" He scrambled to answer. He shouldn't have bothered. Finn was already plunging on.

"Can I suggest something without offending you?"

It was plain the only way he was going to avoid whatever she had to say would be to walk out the door. Even if he did, the woman would just follow him. "I've never known you to hold back yet with your opinions."

"You might want to think about finding someone for Emma to talk to."

"Why didn't I think of that? I'll just go down to Rent-A-Friend and check a kid out for the week."

Color darkened her cheekbones, but she refused to back down. "I was thinking more along the lines of a good child psychologist."

Cade felt like she'd kicked his legs out from under him.

Emma scared him plenty with her crazy stories. But the possibility that her maladjustment might be serious enough to need a shrink was terrifying.

"I know I've only met Emma a couple of times, but from what you've both said, there are issues with her mother."

"What did you do? Go poking at the kid to find out about her mother? No wonder Emma came unglued!"

"I'm not a complete idiot! Of course I didn't ask Emma about her mother! I've got no idea what kind of pain that little girl is feeling or why. But I do know how it feels to have a parent disappear from your life. It hurts like hell. You can't just ignore it. Emma needs—"

"What Emma *needs* is for you people to do your job. Keep those bullies off her back. Exactly where were you when this fight was going on?"

"I was…" she faltered, her eyes avoiding his. "I was helping one of the younger children. I just turned my back for a minute…. I didn't know how fast things could get out of control."

Cade glared at her, willing her to meet his gaze. "So you were nowhere in sight when those two goons were torturing Emma. What was she supposed to do? Just stand there and take it?"

Finn's eyes swept up to meet his, the green depths suddenly laid waste by uncertainty. "She could've come to get me."

Her confusion rocked Cade to the core, left him feeling strangely betrayed. "I thought you were supposed to know everything about kids. You're a kid's librarian, aren't you?"

Finn plucked at her skirt. "I worked with grad students at universities. Maybe I'm not cut out for this." She looked up at him, and he was taken aback by the stark vulnerability in her eyes. "This kid stuff is harder than I thought."

Cade didn't want to feel sorry for her. But before he could stop himself, he heard the words slip out. "I know."

His admission seemed to steady her. She reached out, laid her fingertips on his arm. It had been a helluva long time since a woman had touched him.

"Cade, I really am worried about Emma. I may be no expert when it comes to kids, but even I can see that something here is very, very wrong. While we were waiting for you I skimmed through that notebook of hers to see what the commotion is all about. Have you ever read what she's written?"

"Of course not!" He bit out defensively. "She's made me swear in blood a hundred times that I wouldn't."

"So she keeps the notebook hidden?" The woman was feeling her way along some subtle pathway he couldn't see.

"Emma knows she can trust me to give her the privacy she deserves. She leaves the thing out all over the house."

Full lips softened with knowing. "Did you ever stop to wonder why? Maybe she wants you to read it."

"That doesn't make any sense." Cade scoffed. "Why would you think that?"

"Because when I was Emma's age, I..." She stopped, looked away. "I wrote these poems—maudlin things I made everyone swear they wouldn't read. My dad. My teacher. My foster mom."

"Foster mom?" Cade looked at her more sharply, suddenly aware of how delicate the line of her jaw was, how deep the secrets in her eyes. No wonder her face had shone when he'd first seen her at that broken-down old house. He didn't want to think of Finn O'Grady as fragile, didn't want to sense any hurts in her too-tender heart. He and Emma both had enough of their own.

"I left my poems around because I wanted someone to force their way past all the defenses I'd built, show me that they cared enough to read what I'd written, no matter how often I'd told them to mind their own business."

The possibility he'd read this wrong, too, appalled him. "Well that's not what Emma's doing. She just wants to be left alone."

"Then it's working. She's so alone that she's pouring out her heart to a girl who doesn't exist. That notebook is full of letters to Addy March. The girl who lived in March Winds at the time of the Civil War. Emma sounds so lonely, so caught up in this fantasy world she's created it frightens me."

Cade shrugged. "I used to pretend I was the Wright brothers, both of them at the same time. What's the big deal?"

"There's something about Emma's entries. They're so detailed, filled with trivia from the late 1850s that my grad students would have been hard pressed to find. It's uncanny. Was her mother a history buff or something?"

"Deirdre? A history buff? I suppose if you consider Janis Joplin and Van Morrison history."

A line formed between soft, winged brows. "I just can't figure out where a child her age would've gotten so much information. And it's accurate. I even checked some resources no ten-year-old could access."

"She's a really smart kid."

"Yes, she is. She's also a very troubled one."

The girl's small, haunted face rose up in his mind, the defiance in her stormy dark eyes not quite disguising an ache that twisted Cade's heart. "Emma is going to be just fine," Cade tried to deny Finn's claim.

"You don't really believe that. Emma is hurting. Now she's striking out. I keep thinking how badly she must be suffering inside to attack Billy and Adam the way she did. Those boys are three times her size and she flew at them like a wildcat. It took all my strength to pull her off. When I did, she was sobbing her heart out. Worst of all, she wouldn't even let me hold her."

She won't let me hold her, either, he thought, helplessness gnawing in his chest. *She just huddles inside herself, so tight I can't reach her.*

"You have to do something," Finn urged. "Help her."

Cade's fists clenched, the weight of Finn O'Grady's gaze pressing into him, like a stick probing a wound. She acted as if he should know all the answers when it came to Emma's battered heart. Hell, he didn't even know the questions!

"And you're such an expert when it comes to kids?" Cade lashed out. "How many years have you been holed up in some college library reading about life in books? It's a little tougher out here in the real world, isn't it?"

He hated the stricken expression that flashed across her face. But he felt desperate to chase the expectation out of her eyes, the demand that he try harder, do better, find a way to reach the little girl with the broken heart who wouldn't let anyone hold her.

"For a woman who knows exactly how everyone else should run their lives, you've had a hell of a first day on the job, Ms. O'Grady."

He expected her to fire a verbal round from that hot Irish temper he'd seen before. He didn't expect her to sink down into Verna Sopher's chair.

For the first time he noticed how young Finn looked. In spite of her rumpled clothes and the exhaustion pinching the delicate skin around her eyes there was something fresh about her. Sweet like the roses in March Winds' garden that thrived in spite of being abandoned, refusing to die. He felt cold inside.

He retrieved the unicorn notebook and started for the door, hesitated, hand on the knob. He turned back to face her. He wasn't sure why it mattered after he'd blasted the woman out of the water minutes before. He just wanted her to know.

"I didn't teach Emma how to throw those kicks and punches. But I damn well know who did. It won't happen again."

She nodded, but she wouldn't meet his eyes. She stared down at the surface of Verna's desk, looking as rotten as he felt.

He wanted to say something. Feared he would only make things worse. "Listen," he began in a conciliatory tone. "I—"

"Don't." Eyes burning with self-blame flashed up to his. "Everything you said is true. I *did* blow it today. And Emma paid the price. Maybe I'm not cut out for this job after all."

He had wanted to take some of the certainty out of Finn. He'd wanted her to face the truths he had—that there were no right answers. That sometimes people failed, no matter how hard they tried.

But he hadn't wanted to leave her bleak. *Another slick move, Magic,* he thought grimly. *And you've got no idea how to fix it—*

He strode out of the office. The nervous little library aide had made herself a human buffer, blocking the boys on one side, while Emma perched on her little chair, the child so brittle Cade feared she might break.

"What are you gonna do to me?" Emma demanded, trying hard to look as if she didn't care.

"I don't know," he confessed. "Guess I'll figure that out after your grandfather gets back on his return flight from California and I get the chance to break his neck."

"Don't yell at the Captain. The stuff he taught me worked."

"It almost landed two kids in the hospital, from what Ms. O'Grady told me."

"The mad inside me got too big to hold. The Captain said that happens to him sometimes, too."

That was an understatement. Living around the Captain was a little like juggling lit sticks of dynamite. Even so, for an instant, Cade wished he'd been the one who'd taught her how to drop the Chapman bully like a rock.

Intense dark eyes locked on the notebook tucked under his arm, and he could almost see the relief rippling through her.

"Know what?" Emma said. "I don't care what you do to me. You can make me eat bread and water for days and days. You can lock me in the attic with the rats!"

"Oh, for God's sake, Emma, this isn't one of your story-books. We don't even have any rats."

"At least now I have my letters back." She reached out her hands with fierce satisfaction.

Cade started to hand the notebook to her, hesitated as Finn O'Grady's troubled features rising up in his mind. The last thing he wanted to do was upset Emma even more. And yet...

Cade glanced down at the battered notebook, feathering his thumb along the spiral wire that held the pages together. After a long moment, he tucked the coffee-stained unicorn back under his arm. "I'm going to keep this for a while."

"Wh—what?"

He searched Emma's face, struggling to read the emotions that flashed across it like quicksilver. "Ms. O'Grady thinks I should read the things you're writing."

Emma leaped to her feet. "You promised you'd never read it!"

Cade struggled to keep his tone firm. "I haven't decided what I'm going to do yet. But I'll be hanging on to your note-book until I figure it out."

"You can't do that!"

"Hey, geekoid, he really can't," Billy Chapman inter-rupted.

Emma glared at her enemy in surprise.

"Those are letters in that stupid notebook, aren't they?" Billy asked, even his sore nose unable to keep him from in-citing rebellion against a grown-up. "It's against the law to mess around with other people's mail. I threw an M-80 into a mailbox once and got in big trouble."

"The last thing we need is your help." Cade snapped at the kid.

But Emma seized on the idea. "I'll call the police! I will!"

"You go right ahead," Cade offered. "Then everyone down at the police station can read your letters, too."

Emma blanched in horror. "No!"

"They'd have to in order to figure out if they should put me in jail. As it stands, Ms. O'Grady is the only one who's seen your precious letters. And I'm just thinking about reading them."

"Ms. O'Grady, Ms. O'Grady," Emma wailed bitterly. "That lady is ruining my life. I'm gonna make her sorry! You just wait and see!"

Embarrassment burned up the back of Cade's neck at her threat. He'd intended to scold the kid for her outburst, made the mistake of glancing back at the irrepressible Finn O'Grady before he did. But the woman who had challenged March Winds, championed the cause of a hurt child and left poems around for a foster mother who'd never read them wasn't burning up with confidence anymore.

She sat at Verna Sopher's desk, perfectly still, her face buried in her hands.

CHAPTER FIVE

CLOUDS ROLLED IN from across the river, great, bruised billows of black and sickly green, the wind keening low in the trees. A kids' Halloween movie couldn't have created a more perfect setting for a haunting, Finn thought. But the creepy pools of shadows in the corners, the creak of wood, the moan of pipes and the soft sighing noises of the old house couldn't rattle Finn tonight. Real monsters stalked her through March Winds' shadowy rooms—self-doubt, stinging guilt and a sick dread that gave her no peace.

Finn hugged her arms tight around her middle, pressing the soft white cotton of her favorite nightgown against skin still dewy from her bath in the elegant antique slipper tub that some other eager renovator had installed years ago.

She'd done her best to wash away the grit of the day she'd begun with such grand hopes. She'd played her favorite CD of Celtic music, lathered herself generously with the precious french vanilla scented bath gel she'd bought herself last Christmas. She'd slipped into a nightgown so light and feminine it made her feel as if she were wearing fairy wings. But none of the rituals she'd developed to comfort herself had been able to banish her grinding sense of failure.

If today had been a ship, it would've been named *Titanic*— an unqualified disaster with Finn at the helm. Every time she closed her eyes, she could see them—Emma McDaniel, wild with grief and fury, battling the boys who had made her life hell. Cade McDaniel, his remarkable silver-blue eyes roiling with emotion—confusion stark across his rugged features. And Verna Sopher—when she'd returned from the dentist to find her precious children's library a shambles, Finn could've sworn that the older librarian's hair turned three shades whiter than it had been that morning.

Oh, Verna hadn't lost her temper. She had just asked questions so pointed Finn squirmed, then dealt with Billy Chapman's father with the aplomb of Sigfried and Roy handling a jillion-pound tiger. The fact that Verna had taken charge of the situation hadn't changed anything. Finn still knew that the tiger was there, and that she'd been responsible for letting it get out of control.

Why did she have to keep running into the McDaniels anyway? Whitewater wasn't a big town, but it had more than two other people in it. Why couldn't she run into an Aunt Bea clone from Mayberry or some folksy character from a Garrison Keillor story? She'd thought that coming here had been an act of fate. Were her next-door neighbors some kind of curse?

Thunder rumbled and Finn watched through the window as the stiff breeze whipped the surface of the Mississippi into foamy white peaks.

She caught a glimpse of the paint chips she'd gathered at the hardware store two days ago, the samples scattered on the wide window ledge so she could see how sunlight affected the colors.

The storm struck March Winds with a rainy fist, rattling windowpanes.

She scooped up the paint chips, half fearing the rain would get in somehow, ruin them. Like the paint chips she'd gathered in the weeks after her father had promised March Winds would be hers one day soon.

"Be thinking what color to paint your room," he'd told her

before he'd driven off that night. And she had—devoted every spare minute for months, keeping her treasures in a shoebox under her bed. She had torn pictures out of magazines, images of the perfect chair, the perfect bed, murals of knights and ladies and unicorns loving hands had painted on the walls of some other little girl's room. She'd poured her heart into the search, in spite of other children's taunts and her foster mom's worry.

That's a beautiful picture, Finn, but don't get your heart set on it.

Finn had hated the woman for that. But as months turned into years, she'd quit talking about her room, quit showing people the pictures she'd gathered. She had only dragged her dream box out from the shadows under her bed when she'd been alone. The cards yellowed, smudged from childish fingers. The pictures grew brittle, until the edges crumbled at her touch.

The day she had thrown the box away, she'd cried her heart out as desperately as Emma had at the library this morning, Finn pushing away her foster mom's arms when the woman tried to comfort her.

Finn couldn't see the lights from Cade McDaniel's cabin tonight, the storm drawing a blessed curtain between them. But the pounding rain and wailing wind couldn't stop Finn's mind from flashing again and again to images of Cade McDaniel and the little girl whose tears cut sharp as broken glass.

She wanted to go to bed, pull the covers over her head and never come out again. She wanted to call Verna Sopher and admit she'd made a mistake when she applied for the job in Whitewater. She didn't know anything about kids.

But she knew even more than Verna did when it came to Emma McDaniel.

She knew the desperate grief in Emma's heart. She just didn't know why the little girl felt it.

And Cade McDaniel with his rugged features and arresting silver-blue eyes wasn't telling any secrets. She'd been determined to dislike the man, comparing him to her father. But was he? Really?

Patrick O'Grady would never have raged or sworn to track down the parents of the kids who had tormented Finn. Well, maybe he would have blustered about it, but he'd never have really done it.

McDaniel's eyes could've melted steel when he thought Emma had been threatened. Finn hadn't doubted for a moment that he meant what he said. What kind of man seemed so angry, so bewildered, so raw? And yet, she'd glimpsed something beyond those traits in the library. Another emotion clumsy and awkward and ill-fitting, but real nonetheless.

Maybe he cared about Emma. Lord, she hoped so. The child needed it.

But Finn had no one to take care of her but herself. Strange, that notion had always made her feel strong, in control. A blessing after the chaos of her childhood. But tonight, her heart felt as if it would bruise if anyone even brushed against it.

What would it be like to have someone to talk to? Someone strong enough to ease the weight of the world from her shoulders for just a brief moment in time? To take the reins so that she could close her eyes, safe, secure for just a little while? That was why she had wanted this house, wasn't it? To build a haven for herself? But a house didn't have skin and bone and muscle. It wasn't the same as someone with shoulders broad enough, a will stubborn enough, arms strong enough to shelter her.

Someone like Cade McDaniel? The thought popped unbidden into her head.

"For heaven's sake, the man can't stand the sight of me! And I can't stand the sight of him, either!" Well, that wasn't exactly true. The man looked delicious, with his angular, tanned face, his dark, unruly hair, those long, powerful legs encased in skintight jeans. She would have liked studying the lines that fanned at the corners of those amazing eyes, the fullness of a mouth that seemed designed to melt women's knees. She might have enjoyed the heck out of it if the man hadn't had to ruin things by opening his mouth.

Stop this, Finn chided herself sharply. *You're a strong, independent woman who has finally gotten everything she wants.*

Not everything, a voice inside her whispered. Oh, she'd dated some, even imagined she was falling in love once, until a better job in a more prestigious library proved too big a temptation to resist. Love had faded into exchanging cards at Christmas. But she'd never doubted she'd done the right thing.

"I've got plenty of time to build a relationship," she muttered aloud. "There must be *some* men in this town who won't spend all their time scowling at me."

She squared her shoulders and grabbed a boxful of trash bags, then stormed up the stairs to the tower room that held her sweetest memories, her deepest pain. The room she'd chosen for her own that long ago Fourth of July day.

She attacked old boxes and papers and fallen bits of plaster, dragging bags full of refuse down the stairs until her arms ached. She tore drooping sheets of wallpaper down that had probably been there when Emma's Addy March lived in the place. It was well past midnight when she collapsed into bed, her nightgown smudged, her back aching. Yet somehow she was feeling far better than she had hours before.

Besides, there had been another benefit from working so hard, she reasoned with satisfaction. She had been so focused she hadn't heard a single noise. Not a mouse nibble or a floorboard creak or that strange hollow rhythm that must be in the ancient pipes.

She still didn't know what color she was going to paint the room, Finn thought as exhaustion overcame her. Maybe rose or peach or a glorious red. But one thing she was sure of—the tower room would be every bit as spectacular as she'd dreamed.

Everything would look brighter tomorrow, she thought, pulling the comforter up to her nose. Emma would be back in school, so she'd have no reason to see Cade McDaniel again. Verna would be at the library to run interference at least until Finn got her sea legs under her. And March Winds would heal her the way she had always known it would.

She would paint away all of her sadness, her disillusionment, obliterate those years when she'd believed she'd lost March Winds forever, just as she had somehow lost her father's heart.

TIRED...SHE WAS SO TIRED.... Finn nuzzled deeper under the covers, resisting the pull of whatever nuisance was trying to drag her from the blessed oblivion of sleep. She moaned in protest, sneaking a peek from beneath heavy eyelids. She didn't have to get up for hours. It was still dark out.

She squirmed over to the far side of the bed, away from something cold. Wet.

Wet?

She kicked one bare leg, water soaked sheets twisting and clinging to her like some kind of woman-eating vine in a Salvador Dali style nightmare.

Her eyes popped open. What in the world? Finn struggled upright. Was it the storm? Had the roof leaked? That was crazy, unless they'd had a deluge to rival the one that struck Noah and his ark. The roof was two floors up! Pipes moaned, that strange, rhythmic sound...

Oh, Lord, that had to be it! The pipes had sprung a leak! First problems with the wiring, now the plumbing! Alarmed,

Finn fought her way out of bed, reached to turn on the light, stopped. What a perfect way to electrocute herself! Cade McDaniel would just love that. She could hear that whiskey-rough voice—*Told her a woman had no business taking on that monstrosity of a house!*

Water plopped on Finn's cheeks, her arms, the top of her head, but the chill did nothing to cool her temper. The man could irritate the life out of her and he wasn't even in the room. She could handle this herself. What to do first? The water was definitely coming from someplace above her. Scrabbling for the flashlight she'd tucked beside her bed after the electricity had gone out, she flicked the light on. Shielding her eyes with her hand, she squinted up at the ceiling.

The once flat plane was bulging at the center of a dark, wet stain wider than her queen-size mattress. What the—was it moving? Finn leaped out of the way as the ceiling crashed down, hitting her bed, scattering muddy plaster everywhere. A flood of water drenched Finn as she stared at the wreckage.

The flashlight beam wavered in her unsteady hand. Just seconds before she'd been lying right where the ceiling hit. The thought made her feel more than a little sick.

Water streamed down onto her mattress from the broken end of an exposed pipe. Grabbing a crescent wrench from her tool box, Finn headed down to the basement. All she had to do to stop the flood was turn off the water main. She'd spotted it when she'd wrestled with the fuse box just yesterday morning.

She pawed through a maze of spiderwebs to reach it, feeling a small flare of triumph. She wasn't the helpless idiot Cade McDaniel thought she was. Balancing the flashlight so it glowed on the knob, she tried not to be dismayed. Crusted with rust, corroded until it looked like a misshapen shellfish instead of a knob, the water valve looked as if no one had bothered to oil the thing since indoor plumbing had been installed in the mansion.

Finn tightened the wrench around its base, grabbed the long metal handle of the tool and yanked with all her might. It didn't budge. She tried again, remembering the hardware salesman who'd convinced her to buy the expensive set, swearing the wrench would break loose anything she could find. Yeah, right. As long as Arnold Schwarzenegger was attached to the handle.

Panic bubbled up as she felt a splash of water leak through her bedroom's floorboards. If she didn't get this thing turned off before the spill reached the gorgeous hardwood in the parlor it would be a complete disaster.

She could call the water company, but by the time they got all the way out to Jubilee Point it would be too late. She bit her lower lip. There was only one thing to do. Beg for help from the one man in Whitewater she never wanted to see again.

She scooped up the hem of her nightgown and stumbled up the stairs. Bracing herself, Finn flung open the door. Flashlight in hand, she raced through the gap in the white picket fence.

CHAPTER SIX

CADE SPRAWLED ACROSS his wide bed, sheets and blanket kicked to the bottom, even the ceiling fan whirring above doing little to cool skin sheened with a fine layer of sweat. He rubbed one hand over his bare chest, hating the subtle pull of navy cotton boxers around his hips, but a man couldn't sleep naked as God intended with a ten-year-old girl in the house. Not even if he hadn't worn anything between bare skin and the sheets since he was younger than the child sleeping down the hall.

Not that he'd done much sleeping tonight. He'd been too creeped out by the letters he'd read long after Emma had gone to bed.

The kid must've exhausted herself, or she had just been doing her damnedest to confuse him again. He'd expected pretty spectacular emotional fireworks considering he'd committed the hanging offense of holding on to her precious notebook. She'd given him some eyebrow-singeing glares, but astonishingly had trotted off to bed early, inquiring after his own sleep, as well.

You must be real tired. Maybe if we both go to bed early everything will be fixed when we wake up.

What was the kid planning to do? Sneak in and suffocate him with her pillow? More likely stage a nighttime raid to take back what he'd "stolen" from her.

He'd checked on her three times and she'd been sleeping,

dark curls tossed across her pillow, her lashes fanned against baby-soft cheeks. The fourth time she had thrashed under her covers and given a long suffering moan, saying if he kept waking her up every five minutes she'd be too tired to go to school tomorrow.

That threat was grim enough to strike terror into his heart and keep him on his own side of the bedroom door. But staying there didn't give him any peace. He had just been alone with that damned coffee-stained unicorn notebook and Finn O'Grady's worried advice.

Read it…she sounds so caught up in her fantasy world it frightens me…maybe you should find someone for her to talk to…a psychologist.

He'd remembered a myth his high school English teacher had taught—something about some chick named Pandora and a box she hadn't been supposed to open. That had been a disaster, too. At the moment, he'd welcome a little plague, a simple war or two. Challenges he could meet with his hands, his strength, his brains. Instead of trying to get inside a lonely little girl's mind.

The letters did disturb him, the Emma captured in the neatly penned lines so much more alive than the child who sat across from him at the breakfast table every morning.

Cade flung one arm over his head, his knuckles whacking one of the split logs that made his headboard. He muttered an oath. So he had read the damned thing. Now what? He was used to fixing things. Figuring out what to do so problems weren't problems anymore. But how could anyone untangle what was going on inside a child's head? Or her heart?

Damn Finn O'Grady anyway, with those bright, hope-filled eyes that demanded more than he could give, and could look through a man to see secrets he was trying his damnedest to hide. Mistakes he'd made, regrets he had, uncertainty when he should have been sure…

But he wasn't sure of anything anymore, except that the woman was affecting him like a case of poison ivy. He couldn't get rid of her and she made him itchy as all hell. He'd known she was trouble from the first moment he'd seen her. Why couldn't she just do what he'd told her to and stay on her side of the fence?

He started, a fist hammering on the front door. Grinding his fingertips against his eyelids, he levered himself out of bed. It was never good news when someone pounded on the door this late. His gut clenched. Had to be the Captain. What the blazes had the old buzzard been up to now? Or was it something with the storm? Verna springing a leak in her roof, a flood threatening to burst the rivers' banks. If any of the over-sixty crowd needed a sandbagger, he'd be their man.

He staggered down the hall, banging one hip into a side table he'd made from a piece of driftwood he'd found on his favorite river island. Sliding one hand instinctively under the elastic band of his boxers, he rubbed his bruised hip as he flicked on the glaring porch light and flung open the door.

"What now?" he barked, then froze, his fingers still buried under a layer of cotton as he gaped at the bedraggled figure on his doorstep.

Finn O'Grady had breasts.

Gorgeous breasts, as a matter of fact.

Cade looked her up and down, stunned as if he'd just taken a header off a cliff. White cotton clung to curves straight out of a man's fantasy, aureoles a round, rosy mist, hardened nipples pressing like gumdrops against the water-soaked fabric. Her waist nipped in, so slender he wanted to try to span it with his hands, while ghosted against the fabric he could see a soft triangle of down as coppery as her hair.

Cade's groin tightened. It had been a hell of a long time since he'd seen the sensual secrets of a woman's naked body, and even longer since he'd touched one.

Cade shook his head, trying to clear it. Hell, he must be dreaming….

But no fantasy would be scowling like that while she was staring at the fly of his boxers.

"I'm in trouble!"

Finally something they could agree on. She *was* trouble in that getup—long slender legs that seemed to go on forever, tendrils of wet hair clinging to the delicate column of her neck, and those breasts—even thinking about them made him get hard.

"Did you hear me?" she demanded. "I need help turning off the water main. The pipes over my bed burst."

"Water…why the hell didn't you say so?" Jarred out of his sensual haze, he yanked his hand self-consciously out of his boxers. Unfortunately, that didn't do anything to hide his other uniquely male problem. "You have any idea how much damage that can do?"

Her delicate jaw tightened. "If I *didn't,* there's no power on earth that could have made me come to you for help. Are you going to make me beg?" She shifted her gaze away from his face, obviously too embarrassed to meet his eyes. Grave tactical error.

Her gaze slid down past the tanned expanse of bare chest to the unmistakable bulge in his shorts. Her eyes widened, her full lips parting in a little gasp. For a heartbeat Cade wondered if she'd make that same sound when a lover buried himself inside her.

"Beg…" Cade stammered. "Uh, no."

She wheeled around, turning her backside toward him. The change of scenery didn't cool his arousal a damn bit. Maybe he wasn't facing a pair of beautiful breasts anymore, but now he caught a tantalizing glimpse of the shadowy cleft of her bottom. Round cheeks that begged a man to cup them in his palms, urge her tighter against the part of him she'd left aching with her startled gaze.

He dashed to his bedroom, grabbed a pair of sweatpants and yanked them on, then jammed his feet into a pair of Nikes. Scooping up his terry cloth robe from the hook behind the bedroom door, he threw it across a split-log bench near Finn. "Better put this on. Don't want to show Emma the Hugh Hefner version of librarians."

Finn's brow crinkled in bewilderment. "Hugh…what?" She looked down, and blushed clean to her toes, horrified. "Oh—oh, my Lord, you can see—"

"Everything."

She grabbed his robe, clutching it to hide her breasts. Cade couldn't help thinking it was a shame. "Why didn't you say something when I got here?"

Hell, part of him was sorry he'd brought her the robe at all. But he could hardly let her freeze in a wet nightgown. He chose to avoid the question.

"Stay here. I'll get my hands on you, uh, *it* somehow. I mean the valve to shut the water off," he explained, feeling like a half-wit. So much for being Mr. Focused-in-an-emergency.

"Stay here? I'm going with you!" she asserted stubbornly.

"One of us is staying with Emma," Cade snapped, the tension of the day and night finally getting the better of him. "I'm not leaving her alone in the house. Now, do you want me to shut off the main or don't you?"

"Emma. Oh, Lord, I didn't think of that. Look in the south corner of the basement. You'll see the wrench I tried to use right beside it."

Cade tried to distract himself by imagining the kind of tools she would have. The damn things were probably pink. Grabbing his own toolbox from under the sink, he started for the door.

"Wait." Finn grabbed his arm, skin to skin. It jolted him clean to his toes. "Take this." She thrust her flashlight into his hands. Her face turned pleading, so vulnerable it made him want to gather her in his arms. "That house is…is all I have in the world. My first home since…my mother died."

"I know."

He ran toward the latest disaster—but couldn't stop wondering if the more dangerous one was waiting back at his house, emotions stripped bare in her eyes, her wet cotton nightgown clinging to a body he knew he'd be thinking about for a very long time.

FINN PACED the hunter green and navy blue braided rug before the cabin's huge fieldstone fireplace, feeling so agitated she wanted to start flinging things off the mantel—the intricate model of the *U.S.S. Constitution,* a wooden rendition of a paddle wheeler called *Quinlan.* Antique books on every kind of transportation there ever was, from Celtic chariots to elegant carriages to airplanes and cars stretching back before the Model T.

For a man so all-fired passionate about learning how to get himself from one place to another he was taking his time walking five minutes across the garden to put her out of her misery.

What in God's name was taking him so long?

He'd been gone for two hours. It seemed like forever. The only sign he was even alive over there was the occasional glimpse of light through the overgrown bushes and twisted, newly leafed trees. She'd marked the time, trying to figure out what room he was in each time a yellow glow flicked on somewhere in the vicinity of her house.

She'd even heard a car drive up a while ago—not that she'd been able to see who the visitor was. It appeared that, surprisingly warm, welcoming and relentlessly masculine as the cabin was, McDaniel had designed it so that he could feel as if he was the only person in the world.

Broad sweeps of windows gazed out across the river; the waters, fed during the storm, rushing swiftly along under the watery glow of the moon waning in the rain-washed sky. Windows toward the cabin's back and on the road side of the house were tucked strategically as if he'd planned to curtain them from the world outside with clumps of trees and shrubs.

Maybe Cade McDaniel wanted to block out the rest of the world, but Finn wasn't wired the same way. Not knowing what was going on was driving her insane. She'd considered waking Emma up, bundling the kid in some clothes and dragging her across the garden to March Winds. Surely the girl could finish the night sleeping on the parlor sofa. Then Finn could see for herself what was happening to the house she loved.

Deciding that was the only answer, she'd gone on a mission to find Emma's room, opening door after door, glimpsing a cluttered office, a master bath with a Jacuzzi tub big enough to swim laps in. She'd found a guest bedroom stuffed with out-of-date fitness equipment, and last of all, a bedroom rustic and masculine as all the others, yet containing little touches, to betray the fact that a ten-year-old girl lived there.

Emma's toys and books looked out of place beneath a deer antler chandelier, her clothes delicate and pale where they lay strewn across the bold red, green, black and yellow strips of the wool Hudson's Bay Blanket that served as a bedspread.

Books teetered in a stack beside the bed, looking as out of place as the child who slept, balled up under the covers as if she were trying to make herself small enough to disappear. The only thing that looked feminine was a picture frame, decorated with glittery rhinestones.

When Finn crept in, held it to the faint light filtering through the window, she'd been able to make out a woman with dark hair and a defiant face, holding a much younger Emma in her arms, as if daring anyone to try and take her away.

Finn's stomach wrenched, and she'd set the picture down with a sick sense of déjà vu, remembering rooms she'd temporarily camped in as a kid, rooms that held no piece of who she was. And where, once she left, nothing of her would remain, as if she'd never been there at all.

She'd slipped out, closed the door, surrendering the idea of waking the child. She didn't want to have to look into Emma's haunted eyes and somehow see her own.

Helpless. Finn had never felt so helpless—not since she was a little girl. She'd sworn she'd never feel this way again. Promised herself she'd handle crises with aplomb. Be strong, independent, never have to depend on anyone again. She'd told friends and colleagues her mantra a million times. Repeated it to herself over and over as she taught herself to change the oil in her own car, install a new shower head, replace leaky faucets. But not once had she shared the secret she'd wrapped in those words like a code.

Never *have to,* ah, therein lay her secret. *Have to* was far different from *wanting to, choosing to,* finding someone you loved enough, trusted enough, knew well enough that you could dare to try—to let them shift some of the burden off of your shoulders. Work together to slay whatever dragons came their way. She'd dreamed of her own knight errant a hundred times.

But she wasn't any closer to finding that kindred spirit than she had been at twelve. And tonight fate, with its usual nasty sense of humor, had left her no choice but to depend on a man she'd been butting heads with from the first moment she'd laid eyes on him.

And whoa, honey, had she laid eyes on the man tonight. Finn hugged herself tight, the folds of his robe enveloping her with his scent, the uncomfortable intimacy of the terry cloth abrading her skin with the knowledge that McDaniel had shrugged this very garment over his naked shoulders, the cloth drying the dampness from his skin after countless showers. She wondered if Emma's mother had worn it, as well, the woman in the picture sweeping out of the gorgeous bathroom wearing his robe, stripping it off at the side of the bed before flinging herself naked into McDaniel's arms.

Why the heck did the vision bother Finn so much? Maybe because Emma's mother had that bold look men found so seductive, that recklessness, the daring that made one think of stiletto heels and red dresses slit at the thigh. While Finn was as homespun as the white picket fence she'd always dreamed of.

Maybe, a voice inside her whispered. But when Cade McDaniel stared through her wet nightgown, he'd almost made her hair catch on fire. Finn pressed one hand above her breast, tingling. His reaction had been pure male—the image of that athlete's body taut and sleek and well muscled, the only thing keeping his most intimate secrets from her that band of navy cotton boxer. She swallowed hard, remembering how his fingers had been buried under the elastic band, his thumb hooked on the outside of the boxers. All it would have taken was one brief downward shove and she would've been able to see more than just the shape and length of his arousal.

An impressive one at that, she knew, judging by her own limited experience.

The kitchen door swung open. Finn jumped guiltily as if McDaniel could read her mind. Her cheeks burned, but she rushed to meet him, everything driven from her mind except worry about her house.

"Is the place all right? You've been gone forever!" She

slammed to a halt, staring at his face. Not a wisp of male arrogance clung to his sensual lips, his eyes didn't hold the sense of triumph she'd expected—or irritation for being dragged from his bed.

The knees of his sweats were darker where he'd knelt in water, but they'd started to dry. His tennis shoes were soaked. But it was his eyes that made Finn freeze in her tracks, her stomach knotting, her hands fisting in the pockets of the robe.

"What is it?" she asked, a catch in her voice. "Tell me."

"The house will be fine. I even saw your Shop-Vac in the basement and used it to clean things up before there was any more damage."

"But that's—that's good. Why don't you look pleased with yourself? You should be gloating right now. Or at least having to try hard not to."

"I went upstairs to check where the leak was. What I found was…damned disturbing. Someone has been in your house."

"What? That's impossible. The pipes are old. They just burst."

"Someone took a hacksaw and cut them on purpose."

Finn reeled, clutching the edge of his knotty pine table. "You—you mean, while I was at work someone broke into my house?"

"The pipes would've started leaking as soon as the saw bit through them. The leak would've started dripping through inside an hour."

"But I was home all night! I would've heard—"

"Not with the storm making such a racket."

"Oh my God. There was a stranger in my house while I was—was lying there, asleep."

Cade dragged out a chair and gently guided her to sit in it. "I'm afraid so. I had Skip Wilkins out—he's a cop, a friend of mine from high school. I'm supposed to bring you in to talk to him in the morning."

"Why would anybody do such a thing?"

"I sure can't figure it out. You'll have to check your stuff, see if anything was taken. But it didn't look like a burglary."

"Oh, God. I have to—to go home—see…"

"You can't go back there tonight. They dusted for prints— hell, it's a mess. Crime scenes usually are."

"My house is a crime scene?" Finn pressed her hand to her mouth, feeling like she was going to throw up.

"Listen, you're going to sleep here tonight. I convinced Skip you were too tired to know your own name, let alone be able to answer questions coherently."

"What if someone breaks in again?"

"The cops will be watching the place. You take a hot shower, get a few hours sleep, then you can face all this in the morning. Come on—"

She was stunned by how gently he helped her out of the chair. He led her to the bathroom, even turned on the taps. Water steamed up the mirror over the double sink. She leaned against the side that looked empty, no toothpaste holder or toothbrush or soap to show it belonged to anyone.

Cade grabbed a towel out of the linen closet—a surprisingly thick, rich, burgundy bath sheet, big enough to wrap around his six foot three body.

"Finn?"

She started at the sound of his voice. "What?"

"I'll lay one of my shirts out on the bed."

"That'll be fine. Thanks."

"I don't want to scare you, but we figure it has to be something personal. They didn't seem to take anything, just wanted to destroy…" He stopped, and Finn wondered if he could see the stark horror on her face.

"Don't worry," he said. "There has to be an answer somewhere. Some kind of a trail we can follow, if the storm didn't wash it all away. There were metal shavings all over the floor.

They'd cling to shoes. And footprints—we'll have to find some wherever they broke in. Don't worry. We'll find them."

"I'm...scared."

"I know you are. I'll have a drink waiting for you when you get out. I sure as hell could use something."

He turned on the jets, the Jacuzzi erupting in whirls of steam, then he slipped from the room, leaving Finn alone. She stared at the foaming water, watching it rise.

But even after she sank into the tub, felt the heat seep into her stiff limbs, she couldn't keep from wondering who had stolen into her precious house. She shuddered, wondering where they had been, how long they had watched her before they were sure she was asleep.

How had they broken in? Had they crept past her bedroom door? Paused to watch her sleep? Had they smiled, knowing what they were about to do? Guessing how much more deeply this would hurt her than stealing a VCR or stereo or TV?

They hadn't just stolen things that could be broken or replaced or forgotten about. They'd struck at the house itself, her dream, and damaged it as deeply as the lightning bolt had damaged the horse chestnut tree in the yard, left her feeling burned black like that tree, broken and torn.

Finn shivered in spite of the hot water washing over her. Who could hate her that much? And why...?

Why had the person attacked her? What had they wanted? And more terrifying still, what might they be willing to do next?

FINN PADDED on bare feet to the kitchen, Cade McDaniel's soft flannel shirt skimming the middle of her thighs. Her hair, towel dried, tumbled about her face, her fingers smoothing the butterscotch and blue plaid shirttails down as far as they would go.

He stared at her a long minute, his gaze flicking, almost involuntarily down her bare legs.

"I dropped part of your robe in the tub," she said self-consciously. "I laid it out to dry."

"No problem." He'd shed his damp sweatpants and showered himself, obviously more quickly than she had, in the smaller bathroom that was Emma's. Dark green running shorts molded to his narrow hips, leaving most of his legs bare. His skin gleamed, his hair drying, light from the chandelier constructed of artfully arranged twigs picking out gold highlights amid the dark strands.

Her girlfriends at Northwestern would've called him sex-on-a-stick. But all Finn could think of was how solid he looked, with those broad shoulders and hunter-gatherer eyes, a certain primitive power about him that would make an intruder think twice before breaking into his home.

But Finn—with her Pollyanna innocence and her tiny frame—any burglar who'd staked out the place would figure she'd be a pushover.

Finn curled her fingers in against her palms to hide their trembling. All she'd ever wanted was a home of her own— March Winds, the place of her dreams. Now all she could do was wonder how she was ever going to get the courage to go back there or spend the night at her house alone.

Cade rose and crossed to the cupboards, reached up to the highest shelf and took down a bottle of Glenmorangie. Brushing a thin layer of dust from it with a dishtowel, he set the liquor down on the table. She didn't know much about liquor, but even she knew this particular bottle was expensive stuff.

Before she'd seen the cabin, it might have surprised her that Cade McDaniel wouldn't just grab the first brand on the shelf. But the man's home had been crafted by someone who cared about how he lived, the rooms put together with an attention to detail and comfort that hinted at someone far deeper than McDaniel's quick temper and bad attitude would suggest.

Had he decorated the place himself? Or had Emma's mother been the one who'd blended the rich comfort of a 1900s Adirondack camp, the time-mellowed gear of outdoorsmen of old and a rugged pioneer style of beauty that whispered of the first explorers who'd wended their way along the river?

Cade thumped two heavy glass tumblers on the knotty pine table and scooped the bottle of Glenmorangie up in one strong, tanned hand.

"I don't drink whiskey," Finn said, eyeing the bottle dubiously.

"You do tonight." He poured two fingers worth of Glenmorangie into each glass. He shoved one toward Finn, his mouth crooking in an encouraging smile. "Come on, Ms. O'Grady. I hate to drink alone. It's the least you can do after getting me out of bed at two in the morning."

She forced the corners of her own mouth upward. It quavered. Taking the glass gingerly between her fingers, she wrinkled her nose and took a drink.

Her eyes stung as the liquor burned down her throat, and she had to fight back a cough. But a warmth she'd needed badly spread through her veins, steadying her at least a little.

Cade downed a mouthful, as well. "Feel better?" he asked, setting the tumbler back on the table.

"Some," Finn admitted.

"Good. Because we're going to have to talk about some things you're damned well not going to like. I wish there were another way to get to the bottom of this. But there's not."

He braced himself, elbows on the table, silvery eyes fixed intently on her face, Finn could tell he'd been preparing what he was going to say the whole time she was in the tub.

"There's no good way to say this, so I'm just going to

spit it out," he said. "You need to start thinking—is there someone who would want to hurt you? An ex-husband? A boyfriend?"

"No!"

"Normally, I'd say it was nobody's business. Hell, I'm a private man myself. But there must be some reason you moved to a town where you obviously don't know a blasted soul. There's nothing wrong with trying to get a fresh start. But if some jerk of a guy is the reason you left Chicago, then I'd say he followed you."

"I moved here because I wanted a home." Her eyes teared up, stinging. "A home! Is that so much to ask?"

He reached across the table, covered her hand in his. His long, calloused fingers engulfed hers, so strong, so tender, completely unexpected. "Of course that's not too much to ask. But sometimes...hell, sometimes whether something is fair or right or not doesn't seem to matter much."

His voice turned rough with the last few words, a distant pain darkening his eyes. For an instant Finn wondered if he was thinking of her at all.

He looked at his fingers, curled so naturally over hers. Slowly, he drew his hand away. Finn drew her hand close to her body, chafed it with her own fingers, trying to recapture the warmth she'd felt for just that brief moment. She couldn't do it herself. She let her hands fall to her lap.

"I don't have a boyfriend or a husband, ex or otherwise. Ever since you got back from the house, I've been driving myself crazy trying to think of someone who might have broken into my house. But there's no one in my life who would do that kind of damage. You'd have to—to *care*, wouldn't you?" she asked, peering up at Cade as if he had the answers to her question. "You'd have to care fiercely to risk sneaking into the house while I was there. To try to hurt me like that?"

"I suppose."

"My father was my only family. And he's dead. I had friends at the different universities I worked at, but I never stayed in one place long enough to really get close to anyone. Just made the kinds of friends you go out to lunch with, talk to at work. As for boyfriends—nothing serious. There's not a person in my life who should care enough about me to do such a thing." Finn's throat swelled shut, the words sounding so sad, pathetic even to her own ears.

Cade looked down at his tumbler, almost as if he were trying to give her privacy to tuck away her hurt without somebody watching. He swirled the amber liquid around the glass. But in spite of the fact he wasn't watching her with those keen eyes, she knew his mind was still probing, trying to find the answers.

"Any chance someone you've met along the way could've fixated on you? Somebody who might not like the idea of you moving four hours away from the city? A guy at the grocery store you went to back in Chicago? Or somebody where you used to work?"

"That's crazy!" But what could be crazier than someone sneaking into her home, creeping to the second floor and sawing through the water pipes while she was lying asleep in the house and could wake up at any second?

Oh, sweet heaven, Finn thought. What if she *had* awakened and gone to see what the noise was? If she'd discovered the intruder, God knows what could have happened to her. Her blood ran cold.

Worse yet, what about the other noises she'd heard over the past few nights? What if this hadn't been the first time this person had broken into March Winds? What if the intruder had been in her house before? She shuddered. "Mr….Mr. McDaniel—"

"After tonight, you'd better call me Cade. I *have* seen you in a wet nightgown." Finn knew he was trying to distract her, strangely enough, trying to make her feel safe. The whole transparent nightgown incident didn't seem nearly as terrible when compared to what had come after.

"Cade." Finn used his given name on its own for the first time. It sounded strong, no-nonsense, with a hit-me-with-your-best-shot kind of muscle behind it. Like he was.

She swallowed hard. "This may not be the first time someone's been there."

His eyes sharpened. "Why do you say that?"

"Since the night I moved in I've heard noises."

"What kind of noises?"

"I thought they were just old house sounds. You know. The pipes groaning, the doors creaking, the floorboards settling. The kinds of sounds that would make a kid say the place was haunted. That's why I looked the way I did at work today. All rumpled and flyaway. I hadn't slept for two days."

Cade's mouth set, grim. "It's a damn good thing you slept through whatever happened there tonight. People who break into houses don't like to be surprised."

Finn's hand shook as she took another sip of whisky.

"I'm sorry. I don't mean to scare you. But whoever sawed through those pipes meant business. Have you noticed someone following you around?" Cade pressed. "Turning up places unexpectedly?"

"No!" The thought terrified her. "There were a few grad students who were a little odd—not bad kids or frightening in any way, just different enough that the other kids hung back from them. I tried to make them laugh."

"What about since you've come to Whitewater?"

"The only people I know here are Verna and you and Emma. And I've been trying to stay as far away from the two of you as I can get. Not that it's done me any good."

"You're telling me." A smile ghosted across his face for a

heartbeat, then vanishing. "You're a beautiful woman," he pressed her. His eyes warmed, intense, and the flannel shirt suddenly felt thin as morning mist. Finn squirmed inwardly, remembering how those eyes had heated when they'd seen her shape through the wet cotton of her nightgown. "You've got the kind of body that could turn men's heads. It's possible some guy—"

"No!" Finn's chair scraped against the slate floor as she stood up, spun away from him, pacing toward the kitchen door. "Open your eyes! I'm not the kind of woman who makes men act crazy! I'm a librarian with freckles and red hair that goes every which way and…oh my God, why is this happening to me?"

She wanted to hide her face from him, wanted to catch some glimpse of her house to reassure herself it was still there. Finn cried out, her toe stubbing hard against something on the floor beside the door. She glanced down, froze.

"Cade," she breathed, her voice trembling. "I know. I know who did it."

"Who?" He bolted out of his own chair, stalked over to her, his face hard with anger, anticipation. If he'd been ready to blacken Billy Chapman's father's eye at the library that morning, he now looked ready to beat some invisible foe to a pulp. To guard her, Finn knew. Her chest squeezed.

Cade grabbed her arms, forced her to turn toward him. She stared at his bare chest, the curve of his collarbone, the stubborn square of his jaw. It hurt too much. She couldn't look him in the eye.

He hooked his finger under her chin, forced her head up, until she was pinned by those mist-blue eyes. "Who did it? Finn, tell me."

What could she do? What could she say? The truth. Hard. Heart-wrenching. "Emma."

"That's impossible." Cade glared down at her, furious, disbelieving. "I was here all night. And trust me, I didn't sleep a wink after reading that damned notebook you were so dead set on my seeing. Besides, where the hell would she get a saw? And cutting the pipes? How would a little girl know to do that?"

"I don't know. You'll have to ask her."

"I'll admit, Emma's got problems, but there's absolutely no way she would do that kind of damage. I'd stake my life on it."

Finn pointed downward, hating that she had to do it, knowing it would hurt him. His gaze followed her gesture to the mat by the door. His fingers clenched on her arm until it ached.

Child-size tennis shoes stood in a puddle on the mat beside the door. Flecks of metal gleamed on rain-soaked pink canvas and clung to frog-green shoelaces.

"No." The denial tore, ragged edged, from Cade's throat. "Not Emma."

CHAPTER SEVEN

CADE STOOD, silent for what seemed like forever, trying to take it in. Emma. *His* Emma had caused the disaster he'd been trying to shovel out of for the past two hours. Emma had broken into Finn O'Grady's home, sent water gushing over the second floor. Only pure luck kept the sodden one hundred and fifty-year old plaster ceiling from crashing down on a sleeping woman's head.

Had Emma realized what she was doing? Horror dug deep in Cade's chest. No. Emma couldn't have known what would happen. A grown-up couldn't have predicted just where the plaster would give. She'd meant to cause damage, take some kind of kid revenge for what happened at the library today. That's all.

Maybe, Cade thought with sick certainty, but if Finn hadn't awakened, Emma's intentions wouldn't have mattered a damn. Finn would be in the emergency room right now, injured God knew how badly and it would have been Emma's fault.

Cade staggered to the sink, braced his hands on the granite edge, cold sweat dampening the back of his neck.

No, not Emma's fault. My fault.

He was the one who hadn't paid attention to the signs, who hadn't wanted to admit just how bad things had gotten. Hell, Finn had only known Emma since Saturday, and she'd seen trouble coming.

"My God. I…I can't believe…" A groan tore from Cade's throat. "How the hell can this be happening?"

"I know it's a shock. I'm sorry."

"*You're* sorry? You tried to tell me she was lashing out. That someone was going to get hurt. I yelled at you and told you to mind your own business. But you didn't know her before…before her mother left her. Emma was—"

"Shh." Finn held a finger to her lips, bobbed her head toward the hallway beyond the kitchen. Cade detected the creak of a heavy split-log door on its hinges, the quiet click of the door latch catching.

Emma. She'd been listening to the whole damned thing. Cade should have guessed. He'd been raised in a family of fuse-lighters. And not one of them would set off an explosion like this and go to sleep without seeing the fireworks go off.

Cade stalked toward the back bedroom and shoved open the door, banging it hard against the side of Emma's dresser. But the huddled form in the bed only gave a muffled snore to add to the illusion she was sleeping.

Cade flicked on the light and grabbed the edge of Emma's wool blanket, hauling her covers clear to the floor, but she still didn't move. For a heartbeat he wanted to shift into denial. Emma looked so fragile against the absurdly masculine sheets, with their army of block printed bears marching between bold red-and-green stripes. But her pale ankles were speckled with dried mud above the crescent that marked the place where her tennis shoes reached.

Cade grabbed her around the waist and flipped her over. Emma cried out in protest, rubbing at her eyes.

"Stop it…sleeping…" Emma moaned.

"Don't even try it," he growled, hauling her into his arms. She came awake in an instant, kicking and struggling, fighting against him physically the way she'd been fighting against him with her heart since the day she'd arrived on his doorstep.

"I didn't do it!" she wailed. "I didn't do it!"

He didn't say a word, just banded his arms around her until she surrendered to his superior strength. She went rigid, but he could hear her breath, quick, light, afraid. Like a kitten he'd once found caught in some careless woodsman's trap.

He marched to the kitchen and sat her butt square on the edge of the counter, one arm on either side of her, the cupboards behind her so there could be no escape.

He stared into that small, heart-shaped face, her skin ashen except for two hot spots of color high on her cheeks, her eyes blazing as defiantly as her mother's ever had. *Oh, God,* he thought, terrified for her. *Don't be like Deirdre… You can't be like Deirdre….*

"What the hell were you thinking?" Cade bellowed. Emma clunked the back of her head against the knotty pine cupboard door as she instinctively tried to back away. But there was nowhere to go.

"Cade, maybe we should all just calm down here. Sit down and talk about this like reasonable people." Finn pulled out a chair, as if willing him to put Emma in it. Gullible woman. Did she really think the kid would sit there, chastened and obedient while he verbally whaled on her? Emma would squirm down from that chair and be off like a shot before he could say three words if he gave her half a chance.

"Back off," Cade warned Finn. "I'm going to do this my way."

He felt a surge of kinship with Emma as she squared her delicate shoulders and glared at him, giving as good as she got.

"I didn't do it!" She insisted again.

"Didn't do what?" Cade demanded. She caught her lower lip between her teeth and shot daggers at Finn. Cade stormed over to the mat, grabbed Emma's tennis shoes and plopped them, soaking wet, right in the lap of her nightgown. "Explain this, little girl."

Emma glanced down at the shoes, mud and water spreading a dirty stain across Hello Kitty. Emma's face crumpled with fury. "I don't care! I'm *glad* I did it. I'm glad! Addy doesn't want anyone but me at her house and neither do I!" Her feverish gaze shifted to Finn. "Why don't you just go away? Leave us alone! Me an' Addy aren't hurting anybody!"

"Aren't hurting anybody?" Cade raged. "The ceiling fell in, for Christ's sake!"

Emma gaped at him, appalled.

"Right on Ms. O'Grady's bed." Cade hoped like hell to drive the gravity of the situation home.

"I hurt Addy's house?" Emma asked in a small voice.

Cade swore, feeling helpless. She still didn't get it. Didn't care about real people, live people, or regret what she'd done to one. "The hell with the house! Do you know what could have happened to Ms. O'Grady if she'd been hit by that plaster when it fell? It's damned heavy, Emma, like...kind of like rocks. How'd you like that to fall on *your* head?"

"She made you take my letters!" Emma's chin quavered. "I just wanted her to go away!"

"Well, Ms. O'Grady's not going anywhere and you're in deep trouble. What you did is against the law, Emma! I had the cops over there. Right now they're looking for a criminal who broke into that house and did thousands of dollars worth of damage."

Emma's eyes widened, fearful. "Are they gonna put me in jail?"

Cade's stomach plunged, not knowing what to say. The child wouldn't go to jail, but there would be serious consequences. Finn's house had been vandalized. Plenty of people would press charges. And there was no question about keeping Emma's adventure from the cops. Skip would damn well expect an explanation before he ended his investigation.

Finn swept over, her hand curving over Cade's bare arm, the swell of her breast brushing against him, nothing but a thin layer of his shirt between his skin and hers. Even dire as things were, his nerve endings sizzled with awareness of the sweet woman smell of her, the yielding softness he knew would fill a man's palm.

"You're not going to jail, Emma," she said, so calmly, they both turned to stare at her. "What you did was very wrong. And there will be consequences. But you're not going to jail."

Emma shuddered, her eyes glistening with tears. "I didn't—didn't mean to—to hurt anybody. I just…Addy's house is the only place I'm happy in the whole wide world and I can't go there if *she's* in it." Emma pointed at Finn, her voice cracking.

"Emma, you had no business—" Cade began.

"Why didn't you go away?" Emma sobbed. "Why didn't you just go away? I want my mom! I want my mom!"

The plaintive cry sliced, razor-sharp down Cade's back. He wanted to scoop Emma up, hold her tight, crush the sadness out of her. He wanted her sweet and laughing again, her eyes shining. He wanted to be flying, a thousand miles away from here, in the vast blue sky where no one could ever find him.

"Emma, you can come to Addy's house. In fact, I'll expect you there every day, front and center, the minute I get home from work."

Cade jerked around, gaping at Finn. "Have you lost your mind? She's never to set foot on your property again, or I swear I'll—Emma, I'll crack your butt so hard they'll hear it clear across the river in Iowa."

"Cade, please. Wait just a minute. Listen."

Cade started to swear, stopped. *If you'd listened last time she asked you to, maybe none of this would have happened.*

"Emma caused a lot of damage tonight. I think it's only fair that she be the one to help me clean the mess up."

Why hadn't he thought of that? "I'll do it," Cade insisted, feeling a flicker of hope. "I'll fix the pipes and the plaster-work. You won't even know there was any damage when I'm done with it." She wouldn't even have to call the insurance that way. Maybe Emma wouldn't be in quite as much trouble.

"I'd welcome any help I can get with that part of the restoration. But cleaning up that mucky plaster, that will be Emma's job."

"You can't make me," Emma protested, but she sounded uncertain.

"The hell she can't! You listen to me, young lady. We're going to do whatever we have to to make this right."

"This is between Emma and I," Finn interrupted, taking the shoes off of Emma's lap and tossing them into the kitchen sink. "Here's the deal I'm offering you. You do the fair thing and clean up the mess you made. I'll do what I think is fair and share March Winds with you."

"Sh-share? You can't share a house," Emma said in confusion.

"From what you've said, you're already sharing it with Addy. And, to tell you the truth, I always intended to share the place with my da."

"Da? Is that your dog or something?"

"It's an Irish way of saying Daddy."

"So where is he? Your daddy…I mean, your da?"

"He died a few months ago."

"Oh." Emma fidgeted with a tail of wet ribbon on her nightgown. "If he's dead he can't live in Addy's house anyway. Why can't you just find another one?"

"For God's sake, Emma!" Cade protested, but Finn didn't look the least offended.

"I'm afraid another house just wouldn't do. March Winds is as special to me as it is to you. See, we never had a home when I was a little girl, at least not after my mother died. Da left me at other people's houses all the time."

"My mom left me, too."

Finn's gaze softened. "I bet that makes you sad."

Emma darted a glance at Cade, then lowered her gaze and nodded. Cade wished to hell he hadn't had to see the expression on her face. Knew he wouldn't forget it for a really long time.

"On one of my da's visits, we found March Winds and he promised it would be my home someday."

Cade watched the emotions chase across Finn O'Grady's animated face, feelings too close to the surface, too easily read, too vulnerable. He winced inwardly, remembering how harsh he'd been the first day he'd met her, his acid comments about a lone woman buying a house that was in such rough shape. How someone else would have to clean up her mess— her husband, her father.

But there was no husband. And her father—he had left her in foster homes, where she didn't belong anymore than Emma belonged here.

"So your da kept his promise?" Emma asked.

"Not exactly." Pain darkened Finn's expressive green eyes, and Cade wondered what had put it there. Or who? This father she'd been talking about? Some other man? He felt the urge to find whoever it was and plant his knuckles square on the bastard's chin.

Emma peered up at Finn, with the wariness of a fawn taking its first step out of the cover of woods. "My mom just left. She didn't even promise to come back."

No, she'd just vanished. No forwarding address. No phone number. She'd just fallen off the face of the earth and left Cade and Emma to the torture of not knowing where she'd gone, if she was coming back. Could there be anything more cruel?

"She's coming back, Emma," Cade insisted, sounding far more certain than he felt. "I know her."

But did he? He'd never have believed Deirdre would abandon her little girl and walk away.

Finn seemed impervious to his torment. She continued as if she and Emma were the only two people in the world. "My da promised I'd have a home when I was eight years old."

"That's a long time to wait. You're real old now."

Finn forced a smile. "Thanks a lot, kid!"

"So did he buy the house for you and give it to you before he died, you know, like a present?" Emma asked.

Finn's features tightened, her spirit so bruised Cade could feel the pulse of pain. "No. It wasn't like that at all. He left me money. So much money he must have had it forever. Enough so that he could've bought the house at any time. When I was your age it would have meant the world to me."

Cade didn't want to see the raw spots in Finn O'Grady's heart. He and Emma had far too many of their own.

"Then why didn't he buy March Winds way back then?" Emma asked. "He promised."

"I suppose that having a real home was my dream, not his. He loved wandering around the country more than he loved me." Finn hesitated, her soft brow wrinkling in thought. "No, that's not exactly true. He loved me. He did. But his freedom was everything to him. And it's hard to have adventures with a little girl hanging on your arm."

"Tell me about it," Emma agreed. "We get in the way. Lots."

Finn chuckled, a rueful, feminine sound that grabbed Cade, square in the chest. "Everyone gets in the way sometimes. And we think it's always bad when we do. But it isn't. Living alone, you kind of miss tripping over someone else's shoes in the hallway, and the clutter of extra plates to wash and the sense that someone is near to you and cares."

"Yeah. Living alone stinks." Emma agreed, so heartfelt Cade winced.

"Hey, I live here, too," he said.

Emma gave him a long-suffering glance full of understanding far too old for such a little girl. "Just 'cause other people are around doesn't mean you're not alone."

Point taken. Cade remembered back twenty-some years to his own parents' house, full of people and chaos and lives being lived. How many times had he stood in the middle of it all and felt as isolated as if he were the only person in the world?

Emma was right. There might be two people living in this cabin. But there was no denying the truth. Both he and Emma were alone.

"Anyway," Finn broke through his thoughts, "that big old house is so empty sometimes it makes me feel sad. Missing him. Missing the time we were supposed to spend there. And besides, it *does* get kind of creepy at night, just like you told me. I keep hearing these noises in the walls. I thought for a while it might be mice. But to make sounds that loud, they'd have to be wearing army boots. Then I thought maybe it was a ghost."

"It was me," Emma admitted, sheepishly. "You sure don't scare so easy."

"You've been breaking into the house all this time?" Cade exclaimed. "How long, Emma? How long have you been doing it?"

Emma shrugged. "Since a week after I got here. There's a little square door right near the ground. It was loose. I squeezed into it."

"A door?" Finn prodded.

"Like a trap door. The kind in mystery stories. I brought

a flashlight and there was a tunnel, like, that went to—"
Emma pressed her fingers to her lips, as if trying to hold the
words inside.

"Spill it, Emmaline Kate," Cade commanded. "Every detail."

Emma turned pleading eyes to Finn. "It's my secret. I'm
the only one who wanted it. Nobody else would even have
found it if it weren't for me."

"Found what?"

"Addy's book."

Cade groaned. "You didn't just break in to the place? You
took something? Emma, that's *stealing.*"

Emma caught her bottom lip between her teeth, trying
hard not to cry. "Please don't take it away from me. Addy's
the only friend I've got. If I don't have her book I—I'll just
wither right up and die."

"Nobody's going to be doing any dying around here,"
Cade warned, driving his fingers back through his still-damp
hair. "And that's the end of it."

But how could you keep a little girl like Emma from wilting away right before your eyes? Not her body, maybe, but
her spirit. That spark that made her the Emma he used to
know. You couldn't make her flourish again, grow strong inside by force. Maybe a woman would know what to do
with her—someone like Finn with her nurturing heart and
tender, healing voice. But Cade didn't know any way to attack a problem besides wrestling the damned thing to the
ground.

"Can you show Addy's book to me?" Finn asked so gently that it made him feel even more like a bear, blundering
around, smashing things whether he meant to or not. Breakable things like Emma's feelings.

Emma slid down off of the counter, and padded reluctantly
back to the bedroom he'd given her. Cade heard her mattress

squeak, being shoved aside. Hiding contraband under the mattress—the oldest childhood trick in the book.

Emma returned moments later, a red leather volume clutched to her breast. Gilt roses decorated the cover. Tooled in gold were the words Addy March, Her Book. The damned thing was probably worth a fortune, Cade thought in dismay. And the kid had it squished under a mattress!

"Addy's father gave this to her right before he went away to war," Emma explained. "Told her to write in it every day, then when he got back he could read it and know everything she was dreaming about and doing while he was gone. He said that way they wouldn't miss each other so much. I can't write to my mom. I don't know where she is."

Or even if she's alive. Cade tried to crush the fear that rose, unbidden. The state Deirdre had been in when she left—anything could've happened. And she wouldn't trust him. Wouldn't tell him...

But why would she? Cade thought. He'd failed her, just as he was failing her little girl.

Finn held out her hand to Emma, asking without words for the child to give her the book.

Cade couldn't stand the agony of indecision on the little girl's face, the abject misery. "It belongs to Ms. O'Grady," he said, more sternly than he intended. "Give it to her."

Emma's eyes welled up with tears, but she didn't even try pleading with him. For some reason Cade couldn't begin to understand, that hurt.

Ever so slowly, Emma held the volume out to Finn. Finn took it, cradling it tenderly as Cade sensed she would have cradled Emma, if the little girl would have let her. She opened the book with something like reverence, her slender fingers delicate on the aged paper. Even from where he stood, Cade could see a careful, child's script inked across the pages in old-fashioned letters, all points and swirls.

PATCHED CLOTHING

Solution: 5 letters

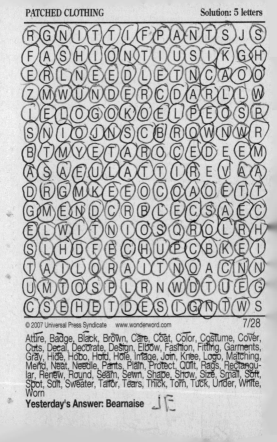

```
R G N I T T I F P A N T S J S
F A S H I O N T I U S I K G H
E R L N E E D L E T N C A O R
Z M W U N D E R C D A R L L W
I E L O G O K O E L P E O S R
S N I O J N S C B R O W N W R
B T M Y E T A R O C E D E E M
A S A E U L A T T I R E V A R
D R G M K E E O C O A O E T T
G M E N D C R B L E C S A E C
E L W I T N I O S Q R O L R H
S L H D F E C H U P C B K E I
T A I L O R A I T N O A C N N
U M T O S P L R N W D T U E G
C S E H E T D E S I G N T W S
```

© 2007 Universal Press Syndicate   www.wonderword.com

7/28

Attire, Badge, Black, Brown, Care, Coat, Color, Costume, Cover, Cuts, Decal, Decorate, Design, Elbow, Fashion, Fitting, Garments, Gray, Hide, Hobo, Hold, Hole, Image, Join, Knee, Logo, Matching, Mend, Neat, Needle, Pants, Plain, Protect, Quilt, Rags, Rectangular, Renew, Round, Seam, Sewn, Shape, Show, Size, Small, Soft, Spot, Suit, Sweater, Tailor, Tears, Thick, Torn, Tuck, Under, White, Worn

Yesterday's Answer: Bearnaise

S THE BOURNE ULTIMATUM	.. (PG13) .. Advance Tix on Sale Now
S RUSH HOUR 3	(PG13) .. Advance Tix on Sale Now
THE SIMPSON'S MOVIE	(PG13) .. (12:00 / 2:10 / 4:20) / 7:20 / 9:40
NO RESERVATIONS	(PG) .... (Digital) (12:05 / 4:15) / 7:15 / 10:15
HAIRSPRAY	(PG) .... (Digital) (12:45 / 4:10) / 7:30 / 10:10
CHUCK & LARRY	(PG13) .. (Digital) (12:20 / 4:00) / 7:25 / 10:20
HARRY POTTER 5	(PG13) .. (Digital) (12:15 / 3:45) / 6:55 / 9:55
LICENSE TO WED	(PG13) .. (12:10 / 2:25 / 4:35) / 7:10
TRANSFORMERS	(PG13) .. (Digital) (12:25 / 3:55) / 7:05 / 10:00
SICKO	(PG13) .. 9:50
RATATOUILLE	(G) ..... (12:30 / 3:50) / 7:00 / 9:45
LIVE FREE OR DIE HARD ...	(PG13) .. (12:35 / 4:30) / 7:35 / 10:05
KNOCKED UP	(R) ..... (12:40 / 4:05) / 7:40 / 10:25

NA 16   (330) 723-4416

THE BOURNE ULTIMATUM ...	(PG13) .. Advance Tix on Sale Now
RUSH HOUR 3	(PG13) .. Advance Tix on Sale Now
THE SIMPSON'S MOVIE	(PG13) .. (Digital) (11:30 / 12:00 / 2:10 / 2:30)
THE SIMPSON'S MOVIE	(PG13) .. (Digital) (4:20 / 4:40) / 7:10 / 7:40
THE SIMPSON'S MOVIE	(PG13) .. (Digital) 9:30 / 9:50
NO RESERVATIONS	(PG) .... (Digital) (12:15 / 2:40 / 5:05)
NO RESERVATIONS	(PG) .... (Digital) 7:30 / 9:55
I KNOW WHO KILLED ME	(R) ..... (Digital) (12:20 / 5:00) / 7:45 / 10:20
WHO'S YOUR CADDY?	(PG13) .. (Digital) (11:45 / 2:30 / 4:45)
WHO'S YOUR CADDY?	(PG13) .. (Digital) 7:05 / 10:00
HAIRSPRAY	(PG) .... (Digital) (11:40 / 12:10 / 2:50 / 4:25)
HAIRSPRAY	(PG) .... (Digital) 7:00 / 7:20 / 9:35 / 9:55
HARRY POTTER 5	(PG13) .. (Digital) (3:30)
HARRY POTTER 5	(PG13) .. (Digital) (11:35 / 12:05 / 12:25 / 2:35)
HARRY POTTER 5	(PG13) .. (Digital) (4:00) / 6:45 / 7:15 / 7:50 / 10:15
CHUCK & LARRY	(PG13) .. (Digital) (11:40 / 2:20 / 4:50)
CHUCK & LARRY	(PG13) .. (Digital) 7:25 / 10:05
LICENSE TO WED	(PG13) .. (Digital) (12:05 / 2:15 / 4:35)
LICENSE TO WED	(PG13) .. (Digital) 7:35 / 10:05
TRANSFORMERS	(PG13) .. (Digital) (11:55 / 3:55) / 6:55 / 10:10
ATATOUILLE	(G) ..... (Digital) (11:50 / 4:10) / 6:50 / 9:40
VE FREE OR DIE HARD	(PG13) .. (Digital) (11:35 / 4:05) / 7:15 / 10:15
IRATES OF THE CARIBBEAN .	(PG13) .. (Digital) (12:30 / 4:15) / 7:55
ICKO	(PG13) .. (Digi...

TS 41

"This was written during the Civil War," Finn marveled, scanning page after page. "Every detail of Addy's life. This is where you got all those obscure facts you wrote in your notebook, isn't it, Emma?"

"I read what Addy wrote, just one day at a time to make it last longer. Then I write back. I try to do what she's doing— like make cherry jam and—"

"That's why you crammed all my glasses with that glop you made out of maraschino cherries and red Jell-O," Cade said, rubbing his aching head with his fingertips. "You were trying to do what it said in this book?"

"That's why I cut up your lucky shirt, too. Addy was making a quilt block pillow for her mom for Christmas. I thought if I made one for my mom, too, maybe she'd come to get it. My mom loves presents."

"Oh, Emma." Cade's chest felt like it was going to split open. He could picture Deirdre at Christmas, waking long before dawn, sparkling brighter than the lights on the Christmas tree as she shook any package with her name on it. Where had that Deirdre gone?

"I used your lucky shirt on purpose," Emma confessed. "I thought some of the lucky would rub off and make her come get me for sure."

Finn feathered her fingers over Emma's cheek. The child backed away. Finn dropped her hand back to the book and Cade saw understanding fill her eyes. "Where did you find this, sweetheart?" she asked.

"In the secret room where they hid the bad soldiers that sneaked away from prison."

Excitement brightened Finn's face for the first time since she'd arrived, soaking wet, on his doorstep. Eagerness spread a flush, dainty as roses, across her cheeks. "The Marches were hiding rebel soldiers?" she marveled, as enthusiastic about the damned book as Emma was.

Emma nodded, her small face brightening, too. "Addy's mom was from Virginia and had lots of boys in love with her before Addy's father swept her off her feet and took her to Illinois. When those boys escaped, they came to her house for help. But the people in town were suspicious, and they even dunked Addy's mom in the river to try to get her to tell them where those soldiers were. But she never said a peep. Addy's book is full of stuff like that."

"We can look it up in the library, see if we can find more information. I knew we were close to Rock Island. The prisoners must've escaped from there. Emma, will you show me—"

Hell, she was looking at the kid as if Emma had given her a pot of gold instead of causing disaster in her house! Cade's gut clenched. Deirdre had had that gift—the ability to make people believe in her—even her craziest schemes. And what had it brought her or anyone else who loved her? Nothing but pain and disillusionment. Reality crashing down on their heads as mercilessly as Finn O'Grady's ceiling.

"No," Cade asserted sternly, determined that *this* time he was going to take control of the situation before it careened into a brick wall somewhere. "Emma's not going to show you anything. She's not going to your house. She's going to stay the hell away from March Winds and that's the end of it."

Finn stared at him, disbelieving. It cut him to realize the woman was sure she could reason him out of his decision. "But Cade—"

His hands clenched into fists. "You can't reward her for bad behavior. I won't have it."

"What in the world is the matter with you?" Finn's eyes snapped irritation. "Can't you see? We're finally getting someplace."

"There is no 'we.' Emma is my responsibility. Maybe if somebody had held her mother accountable she wouldn't have dumped Emma—son of a bitch!"

Cade could've kicked himself at the stricken look on the child's face. What the hell was he thinking, saying a thing like that in front of her? No help for it now. That was the problem with words most McDaniels had never understood. Once you said them you could never take them back.

"Emma, go to bed," he said briskly. "There's school tomorrow."

"I don't want to! She said I could share Addy's house!" Emma edged toward Finn as if the woman could protect her from his decision somehow. The child's delicate frame close to Finn's, close, but not touching. Sensing that "mother earth" would comfort her, defend her in ways Emma thought more important than wrestling bears and keeping wolves from the door. Even bloodying Billy Chapman's father's nose.

"This discussion is over."

Cade hated himself as Emma flinched away from him.

"Please," she whispered, so desperate, so broken. "I promise I'll be good."

Complete surrender. Cade wished he didn't know just how much it had cost her. Wished he could do anything, say anything except crush the spark of hope in Emma's dark eyes.

"It's over, Emma. Done. This is how it has to be. Now, get to bed."

"Wait!" Finn exclaimed softly, sadly. "Emma, don't forget this." She handed the red leather book to Emma.

The kid looked at her as if her hated enemy had turned into a blasted angel. "I can—keep Addy's book?" Emma held it as if it were the Holy Grail. One diamond bright treasure snatched out of the rubble.

Cade swept it out of her grasp, surprising both Emma and Finn. "Absolutely not. You stole this. It's going back to the person it belongs to."

"I'm giving it to her," Finn objected. "Cade, she didn't mean to—"

"Nobody ever 'means to.' But that doesn't cause any less damage. Emma's got to be taught a lesson. And I'm the rotten bastard who has to teach it to her."

Cade shoved the book at Finn. Finn took it, only because he hadn't left her any other choice. Cade started to put his hand on Emma's shoulder, meaning to nudge her toward the door.

Emma jumped away as if he'd burned her. "Don't touch me!" she cried.

"Oh, sweetheart—" Finn mourned.

The tenderness broke Emma as his temper never could. Tears welled over her lashes, but she didn't stay to let anyone see them fall. With one last, hopeless glance at the book, she fled from the room.

Cade tensed as he heard the bedroom door slam, the creak of Emma flinging herself, headlong on the bed, muffling her sobbing into the pillow as if her heart would break.

Cade stood in silence, Finn deathly still long moments that seemed to spin on forever. What the hell was there left to say? Cade wondered bitterly.

Plenty.

He tried to back away from it, get out of it. It wasn't necessary. He was a private man. It wasn't her business. But they'd made it her business tonight. Both he and Emma.

He looked at the woman standing beside his kitchen table, his flannel shirt worn and washed not nearly as soft as her heart.

"How—how could you do that to her?" she whispered, her own voice breaking around the edges.

Cade sagged down into a chair, burying his head in his hands, trying to find the words. "Sit down," he ordered her.

He could sense her stiffening, drawing away from him, horrified, no doubt at what a hard son of a bitch he was. Hell, he didn't blame her. But he had to tell her. She had to know.... There was no help for it now.

He lifted his face, looked into those eyes that saw far too much, reached far too deeply.

"Please." His plea reminded him all too painfully of Emma's moments before. He counted on the fact that Finn had a far softer heart than he did.

She peered into his face, a long, quiet, searching. He didn't want to wonder what she saw. Or if it would drive her away.

He breathed a sigh of relief as she moved to her own chair, sat across from him, still cradling Emma's precious book as if it were the broken-hearted child.

He glanced longingly at the Glenmorangie, still perched on the table. But this kind of trouble was nothing whiskey could help.

He braced himself, met her gaze unflinchingly, a soldier again, facing enemy fire. Knotting his fingers together and resting them on the table, he looked her, square in the face.

"It's time I told you about Emma's mother."

CHAPTER EIGHT

EMMA'S MOTHER?

Cade's resolve swirled in Finn's mind. She should be rejoicing at his willingness to answer some of the questions, solve some of the mysteries that had formed the little girl Finn was coming to care about, whether it was wise or not.

And yet now, all of a sudden, she wanted to cover her ears, wanted to run back to her own house with its broken water pipes and damp floors and the fingerprint dusting stuff the police had left all over the scene of the crime.

Yet there hadn't been a crime at all, except the one that had been wreaked upon a ten-year-old child's sensitive heart.

Finn folded her hands together and laid them on the table before her, trying to calm herself. The night seemed like some kind of bad dream. But this was real.

She, Finnoula Eileen O'Grady—the woman who hadn't set foot outside her door after eleven at night since she was in college—was alone in a stranger's house at four in the morning. Sitting, naked except for his flannel shirt, across the table from a man changeable as a thunderstorm, hot-tempered as a lightning strike. A fiercely proud fighter who held his vulnerabilities tight against his chest, concealing them, she sensed, even from himself.

But Finn had caught a glimpse beyond this intensely private man's battered armor of sarcasm and fiery temper. Past the strength of body and will that defied anyone to doubt him, believe he couldn't meet whatever challenge came along with his own wits and steely determination.

Yet in the past hour Finn had seen so much more—the desperation that plagued him, the self-loathing beneath his belligerence, the fight in him, so infuriating, so strangely moving, as he battled to do the right thing—refusing to surrender the struggle even after he failed.

Yet the prospect of Cade McDaniel letting her past his guard alarmed Finn. His emotions too hot to handle, promising to burn.

"Maybe this isn't such a good idea," Finn said, fidgeting with a button on Cade's flannel shirt. "You don't owe me any explanation about Emma's mom."

"After all that happened tonight, yeah. I think I do." Cade stared down at his knuckles, and for the first time, Finn noticed a U-shaped cut, the blood dried on what was obviously a wound fresh tonight.

"You hurt yourself," she said, wanting to delay, give him time to think over this decision he'd made to tell her things she wasn't sure she wanted to know.

"The corrosion took a bite out of my knuckle. I suppose I was asking for it. I expected to go in and just whisk that valve around with my bare hand. But you were right about the damned thing being stuck. Hell, it was almost as stubborn as Emma's mother." He flexed his fingers, staring at the cut as if he could see another wound, far deeper.

"You must have loved her very much," Finn observed, uncertain why it bothered her to say so.

"I did." He ran his thumb over the cut, the rippling muscles of his naked chest rising and falling on a sigh. Light glistened on the morning stubble shadowing his jaw, making him seem even more untamed, more dangerous than ever. "From the time we were kids, she followed me around. Hell, I couldn't turn around without stepping on her. But then she grew up, and everything was different."

Finn's imagination filled with images of a young Cade McDaniel. He would have been a beautiful boy—the planes of his face not yet roughened by the harsher side of life, his nose not yet broken. And his eyes—she tried to picture those silvery depths in a boy's face, filled with a boundless thirst for adventure, no shadows to haunt him, no regrets.

She imagined the beautiful woman in Emma's picture trailing around after him, hero worship setting her wild, defiant eyes aglow. What would it be like? To have loved someone that long and to lose them? Was that the source of the pain Cade tried so hard to keep hidden behind his remarkable eyes?

Finn hated the desolation etched deep in Cade's face, couldn't resist the instinct to help him. If he were determined to talk about the woman, then she would open the door. "I saw her picture in Emma's room. She's lovely, Cade."

Cade's gaze flicked to Finn's, guilt darkening his ruggedly handsome features. "If you only knew how many times I wanted to take that frame off of the nightstand and bury it someplace so I wouldn't have to see her."

Another facet in this increasingly complicated man. She'd have wagered anything—even her precious March Winds— that Cade McDaniel was not the kind of man who would tolerate things that chafed at his emotions. And the ragged edge to his voice, warm as whiskey, exposed just how raw seeing the photograph made him.

"I'm glad you didn't take it from Emma." She was. She hadn't really been sure what he was capable of once she'd watched him snatch the book from Emma's hands.

His gaze captured hers, held it a long moment, a quiet supplication that made Finn's heart skip a beat. "Even I'm not that big a bastard, Finn."

"I didn't say that you were," she stammered, flushing.

"But you were thinking it."

How could she deny it? He was right.

"We do seem to keep butting heads, don't we?"

"Yeah, but who would've thought a little thing like you would have such a hard one? I've crashed into linebackers that have more give in them than you do, lady." Lips unabashedly sensual curved in a rueful smile. Empathy and undeniable attraction welled up in Finn, and she reminded herself fiercely that it was Emma she was trying to help here. Cade was a grown man. He might be hurting, bruised, but he could take care of himself. While the child, whose sobs had quieted in abject exhaustion, was so fragile, so helpless.

"It must be hard for you, going into Emma's room every day, seeing the childhood sweetheart you lost."

"My sweetheart?" Cade's head jerked up. He shook his head as if trying to clear it. "You thought Deirdre and I were—" He gave a bitter laugh. "Deirdre's not my lover. She's my sister."

Finn reeled at the revelation, scrambling to make sense of it. She'd been so sure he was Emma's stepfather, or her mother's boyfriend, something with a dashing, romantic flair. Cade McDaniel had that wild, almost primal power thrumming just below the surface, one that made a woman think of RAF pilots fighting for the skies above World War II England, or a smoke jumper skydiving in the middle of a raging forest fire. Even the scar across his chin whispered warning.

It was hard to believe the man *had* a sister. But then, he'd hardly sprung, full-grown, out of a cockpit, his jeans already skintight, his nose slightly off center, his body hard sculpted with the muscle and sinew shadow and light in the rustic kitchen made look like a work of art.

"Emma is your sister's child?" Finn marveled. She wasn't sure why she felt a flood of relief. But maybe her reaction wasn't so strange. She wouldn't wish anybody a broken heart.

"But how—why did you end up with her?"

"Guess that's what I've been trying to figure out. Life around Deirdre has always been rocky. But this disaster with Emma, this is the worst it's ever gotten."

Finn quavered inside, her memory filling with images of Emma—the deep hurt in the child's face, the damage so easy to sense behind those dark eyes. Someone had caused that damage.

"Did your sister hurt Emma?" Finn asked in a small voice, remembering with horrifying clarity a doctoral dissertation she'd helped a social work student research. She'd gathered the books, the articles, tucked them behind the library desk while the student went to retrieve the ID they'd left at home. The library had been so quiet. Finn had just flipped open one of the books to see… She'd still been crying over the pages when the student came back.

"Yeah. She hurt Emma."

Breath hissed between Finn's clenched teeth. "Oh, Cade!"

His quick mind registered what she was thinking in a heartbeat. "Oh, she didn't hurt Emma physically. Not with her fists or even her hot temper. Sometimes I think the kid would have preferred that to what happened…"

Cade turned the bottle of Glenmorangie with his long fingers, sending flashes of light bouncing off of the glass. "And every day since, I've been thinking about what I'm going to say to her when she comes back."

He sank back in his chair. "It still seems so crazy. Just another night at the hangar. I'd been searching the Internet for vintage parts. It's not like I can go to the hardware store and pick up a propeller for an old barnstormer, if you know what I mean. I got home late. This car I'd never seen was parked in front. A bashed-up piece of junk, filled with God knew what. Cardboard boxes and suitcases. I thought someone must've broken in."

"So I suppose you did the wise thing, stayed in your truck and dialed the police on your cell phone." Finn smiled.

"I went into combat mode. Even pilots learn how to fight without their airplanes."

Finn imagined Cade, stealthy as a panther, every muscle in his body tensed and ready to attack. He'd be in his element, then. Not bewildered and bashing into more subtle, fragile things like people's feelings.

"The lights were off. I didn't turn them on. I just eased my way through the front door, ready to grab whoever it was by the throat. Nearly broke my neck on a pile of stuff just to one side of the door. Hell, I felt so damned violated, someone in my home. The way you must have felt tonight."

Finn nodded, remembering that stomach-churning horror she'd felt knowing stranger's hands had touched her things, breached the haven where she felt safe, left her wondering if she'd ever really feel safe again.

"Moonlight was filtering in," Cade continued. "You know, from all those windows toward the river. I could make out a shape curled up on the couch. Funny, but I didn't stop to think how strange that was. I mean, what self-respecting burglar stops to take a nap?"

She smiled at the image. "The only thing I can think of worse than discovering your house has been burglarized would be finding the burglar still there."

"Skip would tell you that's when things get dangerous. But I was glad the bastard was still there. Couldn't wait to get my hands on 'em.

"I crept up and grabbed whoever it was, ready to land the cleanest left hook of my life. But it was no man on that couch. Not even some brainless teenager. When I dragged the intruder up to face me it was like lifting a damned puppy dog, someone so light, so small."

"Emma?"

Cade nodded. "She started screaming. I heard someone scramble to turn on the light. The lights blazed on and for a moment I couldn't see. This woman shrieked behind me, hammering me with her fists. 'Put her down! You're scaring her!'" His features twisted in anguish, regret.

He arched his head back, his corded throat exposed, vulnerable in a way Finn sensed this warrior rarely let himself be. He closed his eyes, and Finn could feel him slipping away, carried on currents of memory to a place he didn't want to be.

His voice dropped low, gravelly with pain. "That's when my world turned upside down."

"WHAT THE HELL?" Cade wrestled the kicking, scratching little fireball he held to a standstill, trying not to crush her in his arms as he wheeled to face the woman screaming in his damned ear.

Dark hair, stormy blue eyes, a face far too thin and drawn.

"Deirdre!" He felt like the bundle in his arms had landed a kick to his solar plexus.

"Damn it, Cade, I told you to let her go!"

Her... Cade looked down into the face of the person trapped in his arms. Black curls, a heart-shaped face that reminded him of the cameos his mother used to wear on lace blouses. The child's cheeks were bright red from her struggles, her eyes wide and terrified, but still full of fight.

"Son of a bitch!" Cade exclaimed, sick at the fear he'd put in the kid's eyes. But this wasn't just any kid. This had to be... "Emma." He choked the name out loud. "Oh, God, Emma, I'm sorry. I didn't know it was you."

The kid still regarded him as if she expected him to gobble her up like the Big Bad Wolf.

"I'm your uncle. Uncle Cade. Remember?"

The kid didn't look convinced. She wriggled, trying to escape his grasp. He wanted to hold on, but he made himself shift her to the ground.

She darted behind her mother to peer at him. Cade struggled to grasp the changes five years had made in this child he cared about. She'd grown taller, thinner, so fragile, she could have broken in half when he grabbed her that way. Her dress was clean, but awkwardly mended, a strange, old-fashioned kind of thing Deirdre never would've been caught dead in, even as a child. A white gauze bandage wrapped Emma's left hand.

"Emma, did I hurt you?" Cade asked, sounding gruff even to his own ears.

"Yeah. You squeezed my ribs like the corset Laura wouldn't wear at night in *Little Town on the Prairie,* even though Ma said she should."

Totally confused, Cade glanced from the child to his sister.

"Don't even try to figure it out. She's always talking about books."

"Deirdre, what are you doing here?" Cade asked.

"I got a gig in Chicago. I was just passing through and I thought Emma ought to see the old homestead."

Cade's gut instinct flared. "The old homestead would be the Captain's place on Linden Lane."

He remembered Deirdre at the clapboard house, a bundle of energy, irrepressible. Trying to do everything he did, only better. She'd been so full of joy, laughing and bright, hell on wheels, but man, giving life a helluva ride. They'd been a family then. Maybe the Captain and their mother didn't make much sense as a couple, when he sat down and thought about it, but they'd been a family. Until the night he'd blown everything out of the water.

"The Captain and I aren't speaking at the moment, in case you've forgotten."

Hell no, he hadn't forgotten—the ugliness, the anger between them when he'd left the Air Force to come home after his mother's death.

"It's been five years. He's not going to be here forever."

"What was it Mama used to say? Heaven wouldn't have him and the devil's scared he'd take over. You might as well give up on us, big brother. I have. Want to know how I got in?" Deirdre paced to the window, frenetic, edgy. "You'd better get new locks. These are absurdly easy to get past."

"You broke the lock?"

"Hardly anything so crude. One of my boyfriends taught me how to pick the little suckers. It was an emergency. Emma had to go to the bathroom."

"I did not," Emma protested.

Deirdre tossed her hair. "If you're planning to argue with everything I say, you'd be better off heading to bed. In fact, that's a stellar idea. Give your uncle a hug and march into that bedroom and go to sleep."

"Don't want to."

"Do it, Emma. Now! Your uncle is letting you stay. It's the least you can do. I told you to hug him—"

"I don't want a hug." Cade meant to add *unless she wants to.* But something in the little girl's face stole the words from his mouth.

She was peering up at her mother, looking so scared. "I'll hug him if you come with me to bed, mama. It feels too—too big here."

The hardness fell away from Deirdre's face for just a moment. She feathered her hand through Emma's curls with a quiet desperation that spooked the hell out of Cade. "This is the way it's supposed to be for little girls. Lots of room and a yard to play in. Did you see the size of that bed? See how much room you can take up before I come in there."

Emma clutched her mother so tight Cade thought her arms might break. Then the little girl slipped back to the bedroom and shut the door.

Cade tensed, hands on hips. "Damn it, Dee, what the hell is going on? Something's not right here."

She laughed, that bitter laugh he hated. "In *our* family? When were they ever?"

"We loved each other."

"They loved you. I loved you. Not bad if you're the golden boy. When you're the child from hell it's a little different."

"Nobody felt that way!"

"You missed the best parts, off keeping the skies safe over America."

"Dee, are you all right? And what was that bandage on Emma's hand?"

"Oh, that." Deirdre chewed at the inside of her bottom lip, a dead stress giveaway from the time she was a kid herself. "Grease spattered her arm when she was sleeping by a grill in the place where I was playing."

"What kind of place?"

"They hardly book acts like mine in the local library."

"Emma was sleeping in a *bar?*"

"Only when I can't find a baby-sitter. I find her some out of the way place to set up camp, make sure she has plenty of books and she gets along all right."

"Are you crazy taking her places like that? Any psycho could take a look at her and—" The possibilities were endless.

"I do the best I can, Cade." Pain cracked her voice. "I know that's never good enough. And of course, *you'd* do it better."

"Well, I sure as hell wouldn't take a kid into a goddamn bar!"

"Talent scouts from a big name record label were coming to hear me. It was my big chance."

"I've heard that before." The thought of Emma in the dark, smoky confines of a bar made him mad as hell. No wonder the kid looked so pale and thin. She'd have to be up half the night. "So, what happened? Did they sign you to a five-year deal?"

"I spent the performance in the emergency room getting Emma patched up. While I was there, I got to thinking."

Deirdre thinking? The notion made him twitchy as the devil.

"I can't take this anymore." Deirdre's voice broke. "I can't take care of Emma the way she needs me to. And my music— I'm never going to make it like this."

"You've got to make a choice, Deirdre. What are you? A musician or a mother? It's time to pick one or the other."

"You're right," she said in a small voice. "There is only one thing I can do. But it's hard, Cade. It's so hard."

He knew what it meant to walk away from dreams. He'd traded test-pilot adventures for the lone hangar on the White-water airstrip. Most times he figured he'd done the right thing. He wished he had their mother's way of smoothing troubled waters with one of her loving smiles. He wondered if Deirdre was right and those smiles had fallen on him more often than they had on her.

"So you've made mistakes, Dee. Who hasn't?" He grabbed Deirdre's hands, holding them tight. "There's still time to make things right. I'll be here for you and for Emma. No matter what."

The devil-may-care mask slipped, leaving Deirdre strangely more familiar, more heartbreaking than moments before.

"I'm counting on it," she said.

CHAPTER NINE

FINN WATCHED EMOTIONS play across Cade's face by the light of the twig chandelier, her throat aching. A lock of dark hair tumbled across his brow, a silky contrast to the rigid planes and angles of his stubborn jaw. But whatever blow had caused the scar that etched a thin line through the stubble shadowing his chin shrank to nothing beside the wound he was probing now.

"Next morning, I woke up to Emma screaming, sobbing," he said, "clutching a note. Deirdre had made her choice, all right. She'd left Emma's stuff in that pile by the door then driven away without even saying goodbye."

Finn imagined Cade, frantic with worry for his sister, furious at her betrayal, deserted and left with a hysterical little girl. "It must have been awful."

"Emma was terrified of me. Who could blame her? I went a little crazy myself when I realized what Deirdre had done. I mean, what the hell did I know about kids? Especially a little girl like her? Maybe I was her family, but I didn't even know her. I might as well have been a total stranger."

Finn hurt for him. This man, so fiercely self-reliant he looked as if he could move mountains with his bare hands. Finn couldn't bear to see him so alone.

Not pausing to question, she surrendered to instinct, reaching across the table, squeezing his hand.

For a long moment, Cade stared in surprise at the place

where their hands joined, as if he were trying to unravel some mystery hidden where the hard tanned length of his fingers lay covered by the softer weight of her own.

Warmth seeped through her palm, Cade McDaniel all bone and sinew and work-roughened skin. Yet beneath her touch she sensed artistry, as well, deft, clever hands that had worked on this cabin, fashioned the delicate ship models, done their best to care for an abandoned little girl.

Cade slid his thumb along the inside of her wrist, as if seeking softness in counterpoint to the hard truths he revealed. Finn shivered to awareness, feeling cracks spread through the armor Cade fought so hard to keep in place.

"I kept telling myself Deirdre would be back," Cade said. "She'd get to Chicago and realize what she'd done. She'd finish this latest gig and come get Emma. I counted on it. Emma did, too."

He raised his eyes to Finn's. "It's been six months. Deirdre's dropped a couple postcards in the mail to Emma, telling her she loves her. She's sorry. This is all for the best. No return address. No way to trace her. Just a different city, a different state somewhere down the road. Until now—" His throat worked convulsively, as if some secret part of him didn't want to say the words out loud, afraid they would make his worst fear real. "Now I don't know if she's ever coming back."

Finn squeezed his hand so tight her own fingers burned. "She won't stay away forever. Even my father couldn't do that."

Cade pulled his hand away from her, shedding comfort, restless again, wild. "And if she comes back, then what?" he demanded harshly. "Do I hand Emma over to a woman who deserted her? Who'd just keep dragging her from place to place? Hell, it had been five years since Deirdre saw me. She didn't know me anymore. I could have been a drunk, a mean son of a bitch who wouldn't give a damn about the kid. I could've been the kind of bastard who'd say the hell with the responsibility and stick her in some foster home."

Finn flinched, her own pain swift, sudden. Cade cursed under his breath, touching her cheek in regret. "God, Finn, I'm sorry. I didn't mean—"

Finn evaded his touch. Hugging his flannel shirt tight against her breasts, she paced to the bank of windows staring out on the storm-washed river. "I'm a grown woman. I shouldn't let it sting this much. My father did say the hell with responsibility. You might have done the same."

Cade crossed to stand beside her. He turned her to face him, hands abrading the soft fabric on her arms, his breath feathering her cheek. Awareness sizzled between them as his gaze held her, a plea to understand.

"It's just—when I think about what might have happened to Emma, it scares the hell out of me. Who knows how much I might have changed in the time Deirdre was gone? She didn't even bother to find out. She just dumped her daughter in my lap and ran. What was she thinking, leaving that little girl with someone like me?"

How many nights had he spent lying awake these past months, searching desperately for an answer?

"Deirdre trusted you," she said.

"More proof that my sister is out of her mind," Cade observed bitterly. "Just look at what a bang-up job I'm doing when it comes to the kid."

"You're here," Finn insisted. "That means something."

"Yeah. I'm here. Deirdre's not. And all this time, I've been trying to make sense of it. How could she just leave the way she did? Why would she do such a terrible thing? That's when I realized the truth." A flash of pain streaked across his handsome face. "It's my fault she got so out of hand."

"Don't you think that's going a little too far?" Finn cautioned. "You're her brother, Cade. But you're not responsible for her decisions."

"Aren't I? Whenever she'd get in trouble, I'd jump in and fix things—fight her battles, take the blame, do whatever I had to do to make sure she wasn't punished. Truth to tell, I thought the kid was a riot—it was all a big joke, the crazy things she'd do."

"Your reaction isn't hard to understand. She was your sister. You loved her."

His features softened with yearning. Finn could almost see him probing beyond the veil of hurt.

"She was so damned fearless back then," Cade remembered softly. "I was too much of a wild kid myself to realize the damage I was causing. I taught my sister that she didn't have to take the consequences for anything she'd done. Someone else would take the blow for her."

Envy stung Finn. What would it have been like to have a brother who loved her so much that he'd step between her and an angry father or mother? Protect her, without thinking about the cost to himself? Deirdre McDaniel had had that all her life, and she'd betrayed that trust, taken advantage of that love, just as she'd trampled selfishly across her daughter's heart on her quest for the fame and fortune she'd probably never find.

Wistful, Finn murmured, "Deirdre was very lucky to have you."

"She was lucky all right." Cade stalked across the kitchen, brushing Finn's words aside. "So damned lucky she's made a mess out of her life, and Emma's."

"It was your parents' place to discipline her, Cade," Finn warned. "Not yours. You were a boy yourself."

"Yeah. A stupid, selfish—" He swore, striking one fist hard against the black granite counter. "You don't understand, don't know what I—"

He stopped, features stark with pain. "It's my fault Deirdre got out of hand. I can't fix that now, but I'm not going to make the same mistakes with Emma. That's the end of it."

Finality hardened the curve of his mouth—a hanging judge passing sentence on himself. "You head on in to sleep," he ordered curtly. "Take my bed. I'll sleep on the couch."

She felt a dangerous urge to touch him again, take her fingertips and smooth away the worry lines marking his face. She wondered what he would look like if the tension coiling through him were ever banished, if he were free, in his element, soaring through the sky without the weight of the world on his shoulders. Emma's world. His sister's.

She wanted to offer him comfort the only way he might not refuse. "My legs aren't nearly as long as yours are. Let me take the couch. You've had an even tougher night than I have."

He pinched the bridge of his nose between his thumb and forefinger, his lashes drifting closed. For the first time Finn noticed dark circles smudged beneath them. "Just do what I tell you for once, will you?" He pleaded far more than commanded. "I want you in my bed."

Finn stilled. Cade stiffened as if realizing what he'd said, intentions that might have been far different. A shiver ran down Finn's spine at the memory of quicksilver eyes peeling away the fine layer of cotton nightgown, a molten gaze that should have heated the dampness right off her bare skin.

His voice dropped low, gravelly. "Take my bed, Finn. Please."

Cade McDaniel's gruff brand of chivalry.

"Okay," she agreed, more touched than any polite, polished offer could have made her.

He shot her a look of surprise mingled with gratitude. "If Emma and I are gone before you wake up, don't sweat it. I'll have coffee on."

"I don't want you to go to any trouble."

"You should've thought about that before you woke me up." He crooked her a smile that made her knees feel wobbly, her chest feel tight. "I'll be at your house in the morning to start cleanup duty, as soon as I drop Emma off at school."

"It will have to wait until evening," Finn protested. "I have to work."

"Not tomorrow, Ms. O'Grady," Cade said. "Don't worry. Verna owes me. I'll call her in the morning and let her know what happened. She's used to disaster where we McDaniels are concerned."

Finn fretted her bottom lip, sheepish. "I did a pretty good job of wreaking havoc in the library myself today. If I don't show up for work tomorrow she's going to be sorry she ever hired me."

Cade gave her a long, measuring look. "I doubt that. You give a damn about the kids who come in that library door. Verna cares about them more than anything at all. That's why she waited so long to retire. She didn't know there were people like you left in the world. Maybe I didn't, either." He rolled shoulders broad and glistening in the lamp's soft glow, gave her a rueful smile. "It's been a helluva night, Ms. O'Grady."

"Why is it that I think you've had worse ones?" The words slipped out before Finn could stop them. A muscle twitched in Cade's jaw.

He crossed to the table, took the tumbler to the sink. Kept his back to her, unapproachable as ever, every line of his powerful body blatantly signaling their conversation was over.

But as Finn peered at the rippling muscles of his back, the rigid line of his spine, she sensed some jagged secret still lodged like a thorn in his soul.

She wanted to cover his wounds of the spirit. Wanted to

give him peace. But every instinct in her heart rebelled at letting him close the door between them just yet.

Mustering her courage, Finn went to him. She flattened one hand against his back, her fingers spread, her palm tingling, his body living satin beneath her touch.

"There's something you're not telling me, Cade," she said. "What is it?"

He growled something, low in his throat. For an instant, Finn heeded the warning, started to back away. No matter what he'd revealed to her, Cade McDaniel was still as unpredictable as the storm that had slashed across the river hours before. He might be hurting, but wasn't a wounded animal the most dangerous kind?

But something in the set of his shoulders, the droop of his dark head wouldn't let her turn away. Scarcely believing her own foolhardiness, she slid her arms around him, laid her cheek against his back. Cade's muscles turned rock-hard, stilled, like a beast poised to take its prey. Finn felt wide, wide-open to him, her breasts flattened against his hard, athlete's body, her breath soft against the heat of his skin.

"Tell me," she begged.

He wheeled around like lightning, catching her by surprise. Her body so close to the front of his that the hardened points of her nipples skimmed the naked plane of his chest. He caught her face between callused hands, desperation and something more flaring in his quicksilver eyes.

"I told you too much already," he ground out, driving his fingers back through her hair, his gaze searching her face as if she held answers to questions he'd been asking forever.

"Maybe Emma's right. That house is bewitched, and you've cast some kind of spell on me. I don't talk about things like this, damn it. Not to anyone. Not ever. But you—"

Hot eyes raked her, raw with need that went far beyond a

touch, worlds away from simple comfort. "You make me want…make me *feel*…." He all but spat the word.

A firestorm of emotions, a wilderness of confusion lanced through her as he glared at her with the wariness of a lone wolf fiercely determined he'd never take a mate, yet craving nonetheless…craving a closeness he would never allow himself to have.

Finn's head swam, her knees trembled. Shuddering with needs of her own, she arched her back, bringing her breasts in firmer contact with Cade's naked chest. Offering him her softness in a world far too stony and unyielding.

Fire blazed in his hard, masculine features. Finn's eyes widened as she felt another part of him rising in response. He battled for control, not of the physical, but of something more ephemeral, more terrifying.

She saw a clash of wills in his silvery gaze, saw him grasp for the thing he understood best.

Passion. Recklessness.

Hot, masterful, his mouth crashed down on hers, hungry for something too dangerous to name. Diving deep into a force of nature he could understand.

Finn moaned, her fingers curling against the rough mat of hair spanning his chest. He crushed her closer, and her arms slid around his lean waist, flattening her body full-length against his.

His tongue swept a fierce line across the seam of her lips. She opened them on a gasp, and he plunged inside. Big hands gathered up the flannel shirt, exploring her back, her waist, her hips, ranging up and down, until one palm skimmed beneath the cloth to curve on bare bottom, pulling her hard and tight against pure male arousal.

Finn cried out in surprise, Cade releasing her as if his hand had caught fire. They sprang apart, regarding each other with wary, passion-hazed eyes.

Finn pressed her hand to her throbbing lips, wondering if she'd ever be able to breathe normally again. Cade's chest heaved, his face sharp with animal hunger. Finn wondered if his heart was thundering as wildly as hers was.

"Cade, I—" Finn stammered. Stricken with shyness, she dipped her head to avoid his probing gaze. Down the crisp mat of dark hair, past the ridged muscles of his stomach, along the ribbon of dark hair that disappeared beneath the waistband of his running shorts.

Finn caught her bottom lip between her teeth as her gaze collided with soft cotton molded over his erection, the cloth leaving nothing to the imagination. She'd felt that rigid length against her femininity, felt stunned that she could have awakened such a potent desire in a man like the one standing breathless before her.

She expected him to make some effort to hide his reaction. Knew modesty dictated she should have turned away herself. Instead, she raised her eyes to his face again, feeling open to him in a way that left her more vulnerable than she had ever been with a man before.

Finn shoved away her own doubts, dared to reach out to him, cupping his face in her hands. Stubble prickled her soft palms. "Cade, I—"

"No." He manacled her wrists with his fingers, dragged her hands away from his face. "I don't know what I was thinking—kissing you like that. Telling you…" He winced, as if hearing every word he'd said replayed in his head, regretting every one of them.

"Is it such a terrible thing? Wanting to be close to someone? Wanting to be touched when you're hurting?"

"Touched? Lady, I was all over you like some crazed teenager with his first lay. But don't get any ideas with those damned dreamy eyes of yours. My reaction meant about the same thing as a revved up kid's would, Finn. You need to understand that. Sex is a place a man can dump emotions he doesn't want to feel—distract himself from—"

"*That* was just a *distraction?*" Finn knew he was battling to throw up his defenses, but that didn't keep his words from hurting.

"Exactly," Cade said firmly. "Now, you've heard enough sad family stories for one night. I wouldn't have told you this one except that I couldn't stand the thought of you believing I took that book away from Emma for no reason except stubbornness and male pride."

Finn peered past the bluster, the wall he threw up before the world. "Why does it matter what I think?" she asked softly.

He blinked hard, stared at her, his mask slipping again for just a moment, his features vulnerable, bewildered. "I don't know," he said. "But it does. Finn, I…didn't want to hurt her."

"I know," she said. But he had.

Just like he'll hurt you if you give him a chance, her heart warned.

"There are times we just have to tough things out when we screw up. This is one of those times for Emma." Cade insisted, more to himself than her, as if to steel himself to meet Emma's desolate gaze in the morning.

Finn wanted to argue, take Emma's part, but the time wasn't right. Perhaps later when the chaos of tonight had a chance to fade in Cade's memory. Caution nudged her, maybe something darker, a survival instinct Finn hadn't even realized she possessed.

"Maybe it isn't such a good idea, you coming to my house in the morning. I could hire someone to do the ceiling. Send you the bill."

"No."

Finn jumped at the stony tone of his voice. "I fix what damage my family causes. *I do.* Understand?"

Finn blushed, fidgeted, wondering how she'd stand it. Cade filling up March Winds with his big body, every move, every word reminding her of the few reckless moments she'd spent under his hands, under his lips. "Really, I think I'd rather…"

Silver blue eyes pierced hers. "If you're worried about that kiss, forget about it. It won't happen again."

Even if she lived a hundred years she'd never forget the searing heat of Cade McDaniel's mouth on hers.

Finn shivered, stung by the knowledge of how easily he would forget it. But for tonight, there was nothing left to do. Nothing but sweep the tatters of her own shaken pride around her and leave Cade alone.

Alone to gather up the broken memories of his sister, his sense of guilt, confusion over the kiss he and Finn had shared. Time to sort things out again, and bury them deep, the way he wanted to bury the photograph in Emma's room, yet couldn't.

Finn huddled deeper into Cade's flannel shirt, remembering with a guilty twinge how warm he'd been, how solid in her arms. "Good night, Cade," Finn said softly. "I wish…"

She wished Emma's mother hadn't abandoned her, wished she'd known what a decent man Cade was, before she'd labeled him a beast, wished he would kiss her again that way and mean it.

"I do, too," Cade said. "But that doesn't change a damned thing."

Finn turned, padded barefoot out of the kitchen, down the corridor to Cade's master bedroom.

Mellow, honey-colored logs scalloped their way from ceiling to floor, a thick, wool rug spilling bold graphic colors beside the bed. On the dresser, an antique ivory comb stood sentry beside a bottle of aftershave and a handful of screws and coins filled a pottery bowl.

But the neatness of the rest of the room clashed with the king-size bed near the wide-open windows. Sheets tangled in disarray, covers kicked to the end of the bed, pillows bunched up and shoved every which way.

No question that even before Finn had arrived on his doorstep, Cade had been having a bad night.

What would it have been like if they'd been reckless enough to follow where their kiss had tried to lead them? If he'd scooped her up and carried her to this bed, kicking the door shut behind him. Pulling his shirt from her shoulders and laying her naked on this bed?

What if he'd stripped away his shorts, and she'd felt the power of his need for her between her thighs, skin to skin, nothing at all separating them.

But that would be mere illusion. Worlds of difference stood between them. To him, their physical joining would be nothing but sex—stark, raw, cold with a strange anonymity. She'd be a willing female body to lose his pain in for just a little while.

For her…his touch would reach far deeper.

Oh, God, what was she thinking? Touching him, kissing him, letting him slip into her heart? And what would it be like tomorrow? Cade in her home? In her life?

But not in her bed, Finn resolved firmly.

No, a wicked voice whispered in her head. *He may not be in your bed, but you're spending tonight in his.*

Finn crossed to the vast expanse of mattress, lay down on it gingerly. She eased the sheets over her body, the scent of Cade swirling around her, masculine, outdoorsy, with an exotic tang of adventure, an unexpected intimacy that unnerved her.

She flicked off the light, darkness blanketing her. She felt wrapped up in the man who still sat in the other room, enveloped in him as surely as she'd felt in those brief heady moments she'd spent in Cade's strong arms.

How had it happened? she wondered. How had she ended up sharing a kiss so hot her bones melted? She wasn't a woman who kissed strange men, no matter how sexy they might be. In the few relationships she'd had she'd been cautious to a fault, not that any of the men she'd been involved with could hold a candle to Cade's physical magnetism.

But it wasn't Cade McDaniel's movie star body that had moved her, or his face with its dangerous good looks and delectably masculine mouth. It was his courage, his honesty as he'd spoken to her in the confines of the night-shadowed kitchen.

He'd stripped himself barer than she'd been in her wet cotton nightgown, exposed his emotions, his past regrets. He'd made so sure she knew everything he'd done wrong, every detour, every fall.

And in all that time, he didn't realize there was only thing that mattered. Something he didn't have to tell her at all.

He might be flawed, might have made mistakes with Emma and his sister, Finn thought, smoothing her fingertips across his rumpled bed. But there was one thing Cade McDaniel hadn't done.

He hadn't walked away.

ST. MARY OF THE HILLS cemetery nestled like a green jewel amidst the bustle of Chicago, the rolling hills of the Irish Catholic cemetery serene, peaceful in ways Finn's father never had been. It seemed impossible that he lay here now. Or that some inexplicable force unleashed by the night she'd spent with Cade and Emma McDaniel had driven her to return to this silent, lonely spot.

She hadn't visited the site since the day of his funeral. And after his final betrayal hadn't expected to visit again very soon. But here she stood, remembering the day she'd laid him to rest. The sun had been shining, her father, even in death, having a flair for the ironic. The service attended only by one or two strangers, sweet-faced older women. Finn saw them through the haze of disbelief and the bitterness that had colored her life for so long whenever she thought of how her father had failed her.

Your father was a remarkable man, one woman had told her with tears in her age-worn eyes. *I swear, but there is no one on earth like Patrick O'Grady.*

I hope not. Finn had stifled the words. *For the sake of their daughters.*

And yet, she hadn't been able to deny her grief for all the roads he'd never taken, the love he hadn't wanted, the home he'd run away from. She'd been so determined to put the past behind her, dub her father a loveable failure, an irresponsible dreamer who would have done better by her if he could.

She'd tried so very hard until she'd gotten the package that had changed her life. Finn hugged herself, remembering the day the battered cardboard box had arrived at her apartment, the address marked in her father's spidery hand, the hospital return address stamped in a corner.

Ever so slowly, Finn had opened the lid. Fingered the familiar things inside it—her father's tin whistle, the one his ancestor had brought from Ireland. His shamrock good luck charm. A threadbare tweed jacket her mother had surprised him with years ago. But amid the detritus of his whole life lay an envelope, far too crisp and new to have been lost among her father's motley belongings very long. Finn had pulled the envelope from the box, split the seal with her fingernail, then drew out the cashier's check inside.

She brushed a wisp of hair from her cheek, the breeze wafting through St. Mary's like a mother's hand trying to dry away tears.

Finn fought back the fresh wave of pain, and focused on the scar on the well-tended turf—grass growing over the grave site, but not completely healed. One more whisper, reminding her of her father.

But he was dead now. At peace, please God. Resting here, beside Finn's mother.

Not that anyone browsing through this cemetery would have known Mariel O'Grady ever existed if they'd walked past this place eight months ago. There hadn't been a marker in sight except a number on a metal stake—plot number 4682—until Finn had ordered this small rectangle of granite after her father's funeral.

Her father had always meant to buy a grand gravestone. He'd told Finn so, on the rare days their brief visits together had included a trip to St. Mary's. He'd always insisted his Mariel would have the best, with one of the quotes from the books she loved carved into glistening white marble. Nothing but the best was good enough for Da's wife. So that's what Finn's mother had ended up with. Nothing at all.

An ache clenched tight around Finn's heart and suddenly she was a child again, standing beside her mother's grave, hair pulled back into braids so tight her eyes felt stretched, last year's patent leather shoes pinching. Her father, weeping bitterly as she held tight to his hand. *How could she do this, Finn? How could she leave me?*

Mom had left Finn, too. But she didn't say it.

You've still got me, Da, Finn had told him. *I promise I'll never go away.*

But Da was the one who'd gone away. Not like her mom had, snatched away against her will. Da had made the choice to leave Finn behind. Again and again and again.

And now? He'd done it one last time. Turned her world upside down, left her with a thousand burning questions that he could never answer.

"Why, Da?" she murmured aloud. "Why give me the home I always wanted now, after you're dead? Money you must have been saving up for years? Why didn't you at least tell me what you were doing?"

So I'd know you were trying to keep your promise after all?
So part of me wouldn't despise you?

"Why didn't you tell me before it was too late for us to heal?" Finn knelt down, pulled a weed crowding the pristine new stone. Surely everything would have been different then. Finn wouldn't have spent her whole life trying to find a place to belong. Wandering like her father did.

No, Finn thought fiercely. She was nothing like her father had been. Maybe she'd moved around more than most people in the years since she'd gotten out of college. But that was only because she had no roots to hold her. Now she had the house she'd always dreamed of. It changed everything.

But it didn't answer the mystery she'd spent a lifetime trying to unravel…and now her father never could.

"Did you ever really love me, Da?" she asked. She reached into her jacket pocket, hand closing on soft, worn fabric. She drew out a ragged terry cloth toy.

Baby's First Doll, faded letters read.

She laid it on the grave.

CHAPTER TEN

CADE PULLED HIS TRUCK to a stop and put it in park in front of his childhood home, his shoulders so tense that by the laws of physics his muscles should have snapped. The sleepless night had left him feeling as if someone had given him two black eyes, but he'd rather have done twelve rounds in the ring with the Incredible Hulk than face the prospect of the day ahead of him.

He'd dropped Emma off at school, feeling like a monster for not letting the kid stay home. She'd looked so drawn and stoic, like he was sending her to be burned at the stake.

As for fire hazards—he'd run into one of his own this morning in the form of Finn O'Grady. Offering her his bed had seemed a decent enough gesture last night. He just hadn't thought far ahead enough to realize he couldn't take Emma to school come morning until he was fully dressed—and every stitch he owned was tucked away in the bedroom with the new town librarian.

He'd knocked softly on the door, hating to wake her, trying his best to give her the heads-up he was coming into the room. But Finn hadn't made a peep, didn't so much as twitch an eyelash as he slipped through the door.

Soundless, on bare feet, he'd crossed to his chest of drawers, trying not to look at her as she lay oblivious on his big bed. The way he figured, between him and Emma, they'd taken enough advantage of Finn already. But as he retraced his steps toward the door, jeans, shirt, boxers and hiking boots in hand, he'd caught a glimpse of delicate bare ankle against the dark backdrop of sheets.

He'd made a stab at being a gentleman, but he was no saint. His eyes traced a path along her body, to the rise of hip, swell of breast, curve of shoulder.

Finn lay curled like a kitten, fast asleep, her face half-hidden, her hair tumbled about her face in rich, silky waves. She'd kicked part of the covers off, one leg bared beyond the sheet from hip to toe. Slim white arms hugged a second pillow tight against her. Cade caught himself wondering if she'd sleep the same way with a lover, fling her leg over him, nuzzle her face against his neck, hold him in her arms so he couldn't slip away.

Cade pushed the memory away and leaned his forehead against the steering wheel. Thoughts about Finn wouldn't help him scale the next mountain he had to cross this morning: filling his father in on the change of work schedule and informing the old man that Emma was grounded, their adventures off-limits at least for a little while.

No question how the Captain would react. Martin McDaniel didn't suffer frustration gladly. But for once he'd just have to deal with it. Cade was handling things his way this time. He didn't want to stir up his father's legendary temper and he sure didn't want to dig up old failures. But the Captain had had his chance years ago with Deirdre. And he'd blown it clear out of the water.

Cade turned off the engine and stashed the keys in his bomber jacket. Bleary eyed, he looked at his childhood home.

The scene of the crime, Deirdre would call it, Cade thought with hard humor, certain his sister could list every sin committed against her. All the knock-down-drag-outs, the explosions and the mutinies. Every mistake their parents made that had twisted Deirdre's life and turned Cade into the man he was.

He wondered if Dee remembered there had been laughter in the small house, too? Wild roughhousing when the Captain wasn't too tired or stressed or angry. Cookies and milk and tender kisses in the days before their mother faded away into silence, Emmaline McDaniel not able to dive and race and fly and joke and do the heart-pounding, pulse-racing things that made the rest of her family feel alive.

Cade wondered what his sister would think if she saw the house on Linden now. It hadn't changed since the day they'd moved into it. Precise, well cared for, its windows flanked by crisp black shutters.

The Captain's white Jeep parked in the driveway, tires with traction like a tank, fog lights marched across the top. A genuine preserved rattlesnake head dangled from the rearview mirror, fangs drawn.

The eccentric vehicle fit Cade's father to a *T*. Cade opened the pickup's door and climbed out, trudging up the sidewalk to the front door. He hesitated a moment, then tried the door handle.

Unlocked again. Cade scowled. He and the Captain had fought about the state of that door a dozen times. Whitewater might be a small town, but that didn't mean some lowlife wasn't going to show up on the doorstep and try the lock.

The Captain just smacked his lips in satisfaction and said an intruder in the place would make his day. He couldn't stand the boredom of so much peace and tranquility.

Cade rapped on the doorjamb, then walked inside. "Captain? It's me. Cade."

A still formidable man of seventy strode into the blue painted living room, his silver hair gleaming, his lived-in face ferociously alert, his morning can of Coke in his hand. "I was hoping you'd be somebody interesting," the Captain grumbled. "One of the ladies in the next house or some solicitor I could throw off my property by the seat of his pants."

"Sorry to disappoint you."

"I figured I'd see you at work this morning. I'm coming in late. It was past eleven by the time I logged in at the airport last night."

Eleven…three hours before Emma had sneaked into March Winds. When Cade might have had time to stop her if he'd watched her more closely, listened more sharply. But hell, he had to sleep sometime. Cade crossed to the recliner, but he was too restless to sit down.

"Head in to work whenever you want," he said, pretending to look at an old football trophy on the shelf. Most Valuable Player, all conference. Back when he'd had magic hands. He couldn't imagine why the Captain kept it. "I just wanted to tell you that I won't be there."

"You won't be at the hangar?" His father stared as if Cade had just claimed he'd decided to go without his head for a few days.

"The world's not going to end if I take some time off," he hedged. "Jett's new toy is all ready. I don't have to start my next project right away."

"You don't *have* to!" Martin exclaimed in disbelief. "You usually can't wait to get your hands on a new piece of machinery. What's wrong? You sick, boy?"

"Do I look sick?"

"No. You look like you're up to something. I see that look on your face. You're keeping something from me. It won't work, you know. I'll take Emma to the Whippy Dip and bribe the secret out of her by feeding her as many triple berry sundaes as she can eat."

"That would be just great," Cade grumbled, knowing the Captain would make good on the threat. "Feed the kid enough ice cream and you could make her sick to her stomach, too."

"What do you mean 'too'? What am I getting blamed for this time?"

Cade jammed his hands in the pockets of his leather jacket and turned to face his father. "We've had a real exciting few days while you were gone."

"That's something different." The Captain frowned. "If things are going to get exciting I'm usually in the middle of them."

Cade rolled his eyes. That was his father, all right. A master of understatement.

"So, you going to tell me what I missed or keep me in the dark?" The Captain was almost wistful, for God's sake. No wonder. He loved confrontation, thrived on upheaval. Cade could hold his own in any fight, but he would've surrendered his wings to be as far away from Whitewater as possible these past few days.

He peered into his father's expectant face wondering where to begin. "March Winds sold."

"You've got to be kidding," the Captain said, astounded. "What kind of a nutcase would buy that old place?"

"The new librarian."

"And people think librarians are smart." The Captain took a swig of soda and made a face as if it had gone flat. "I always said nothing good would come of being locked up indoors with a bunch of books all day. I wish Emma would get outside more—do something constructive like—"

"Learn how to fight?" Cade supplied acidly. "She took out two kids at the library Monday. You'd have been so proud."

"She did?" Keen blue eyes widened with such enthusiasm Cade wanted to shake his father until the old man's false teeth rattled out of his head. The Captain positively sparkled. "That's my girl!"

Cade crushed the memory of his own first reaction when he'd heard of Emma's clash with this generation's Callahan bully. Cade had swelled with pride, elated Emma had gotten back some of her own. But the disaster with Finn's pipes put the whole thing in a different light.

It was a slippery slope from knocking Billy Callahan's lights out to the damage she'd done to Finn's house. Damned if Cade would let the girl's wily renegade grandfather encourage her to break even more rules.

"If Emma had been in school, she would have been expelled!" Cade snapped. "This is no joke, Dad. I've got enough trouble handling the kid without you egging her on!"

The Captain smacked his Coke down on a table. "I taught you to fight, didn't I? And you were damned glad I did, as I remember it. Some older kid pushed your hand into dog—"

"This isn't about me, damn it!" Cade roared, trying hard not to remember just how good it had felt when his small fist had knocked the wind out of the jerk who'd tormented him. "Times have changed."

"Not as much as you think." The Captain crossed his arms over his favorite T-shirt, blocking the letters that read Drive It Like You Stole It—one of the gag gifts the cops had given him on his seventieth birthday.

"That kid never bothered you again, did he?" the Captain demanded. "And I bet those rotten little bastards who've been tormenting Emma won't be bothering her again, either. It's a question of survival."

"It's a question of learning to get along in this town!" Cade argued. "Emma is going to be living here, who knows how long. And she's going to have to find a way to fit in with the other kids somehow."

"Deirdre will be back." The Captain had been saying that for the past five years. But then, Special Forces soldiers were trained never to give up. Cade had always figured Martin McDaniel had been saving up plenty to say to his daughter when he finally collared her. Deirdre must know it, too. One more reason to stay the hell out of Dodge. But arguing the point with his father was a quick road to nowhere. Better stick to the facts.

"Here's the deal," Cade said. "For the next month Emma's grounded. She goes to school, comes home. That's it. You want to see her? Fine. Come to the cabin, where I can watch you two like a hawk."

"You don't trust Emma with her own grandfather?" the Captain demanded, thunderous.

"Call me crazy, but no. If I could get away with it, I'd ground you, too, since you taught the kid the stuff that got this trouble started. Last time I left her with you, you showed her how to throw death shots."

The Captain snorted in disgust. "It's not like she could really hurt anybody. There's nothing to Emma! Besides, I told her to be careful." Blue eyes narrowed. "You're acting pretty strange for a kid who spent half his life in the principal's office for scrapping. This isn't about a fight. There's something else on your mind."

Cade's jaw clenched. He didn't want to tell his father about last night's disaster. But there was no point in even attempting to keep it quiet. Martin McDaniel would find out anyway, even if there were parts of what happened Cade wanted to hide, things too emotionally raw for the Captain to know.

Cade planted his hands on his hips, met his father's gaze head on. "You want the whole story? Fine. I'm going to be over at March Winds the next few weeks, helping the new owner to fix it."

"You are, are you?" Laserlike eyes pierced Cade. He could feel his father trying to peel back layers of defenses, find whatever lay underneath. "Verna Sopher said the new girl's a pretty young thing. Maybe I'll stop by and ask her for a date." His father flashed a devil's grin.

Problem was, he might just do it. That was the last thing

Cade needed—the Captain sniffing around Finn and discovering what had happened last night in the cabin's kitchen. He'd be incorrigible if he figured out Cade had already kissed her.

"She's not your type," Cade said, with a dismissive shrug. "The woman's a librarian, for God's sake."

"Verna Sopher was quite a spicy little number in her day. If I hadn't already asked your mother to marry me, I might just have swept Verna right off her feet."

"With a judo throw or a right cross?"

"Very funny." The Captain puffed out his chest, offended. "I'd sooner cut off my hand than strike a woman!"

Cade didn't want to be taken in by his father's charm. He tried to hide a smile behind a grimace. "Bet one or two women took a swing at you."

"Yeah, but it was worth it." The Captain cracked a thousand-watt grin. They laughed together, and for just a moment if felt good enough to drive back the shadows. But his father wasn't about to let go.

Lines deepened between the Captain's shaggy brows. "Now, why don't you tell me the reason you looked so bad when you came in here? Like a whole panzer division rolled over your head? Come on, boy. Spit it out."

Cade's chest tightened at the very real concern beneath the bravado in his father's eyes, eyes still so young in an old man's face. There'd been a time Cade had believed there wasn't a problem in the world his mighty father couldn't tame. Both of them knew better now.

"The reason I'm helping the librarian has nothing to do with the way she fills out her jeans." *Or her wet nightgown.* "Emma broke into March Winds last night."

"She broke into someone's house?" The Captain scowled.

"It gets a whole lot worse. Once she got in there she sneaked up to the second floor and flooded the place."

"That doesn't make any sense!" the Captain objected. "She's ten years old, for God's sake! Why would she do something like that?"

"Emma wants the woman out of the house. I may not like the fact that Emma busted Billy Callahan in the nose, but I realize how good it must have felt to her to fight back. That's what she was doing at March Winds. Fighting back the best she could, devil take the rules. I just can't figure out what put it in her head—cutting those pipes. If she saw it on some television show, or—"

"She didn't just leave the bathtub running or something like that?" the Captain asked, more subdued than Cade had seen him in five years. "She actually cut the water pipes?"

"Took my hacksaw to them. It's the damnedest thing. I would have bet my life the kid didn't even know water came in pipes, let alone could figure out how to find the main on the second floor and cut it."

"Why that conniving little monster!" The Captain swore, low under his breath. "That's why she showed all the tender interest in my old covert operations lately! Fire or water, that's how I told her I used to flush enemies out of hiding."

"*You* told her how to do it?"

"I didn't think she intended to use the things I told her! There aren't many nests of enemy officers in Whitewater. At least, not that I knew about."

Cade wished he could blow up at the old man, vent his anger, frustration, downright fear for Emma. But there's no way the Captain could have guessed Emma was devious enough, desperate enough to be making plans to cause such mayhem on her own.

"The house is a mess. You should see it."

"I'm the one who told Emma what to do. Maybe you should go to the hangar and I should fix the house."

"It's plaster work. Detailed as all get out in that old house.

You'd lose your mind in no time and start breaking windows or something."

The Captain shrugged, resigned. "Sounds like I've caused the little lady enough trouble. Maybe you'd better take care of things for her."

"I'm sure as hell going to try. And as for Emma—I'm going to try to do right by the kid. What I think is best for her. But sometimes I worry—" Cade heaved a weary sigh. Where to even begin listing his fears where Emma was concerned. The child was so fragile on one hand, so dangerously resourceful on the other. At least now he knew where she'd gotten the idea to form her plan of attack. He and the Captain were going to have to be careful what they said around the girl.

Cade's one hope was that actually seeing the damage done would slow Emma down a little next time, make her think about the consequences before she jumped in over her head.

A nice hope, Cade thought with a tug of despair, but none of the Captain's disasters over a lifetime had made him more cautious. And it seemed that delicate, feminine little Emma was more a chip off her grandfather's block than Cade would have believed possible.

Suddenly the old man surprised him, clapping him on the arm, scattering insights that were starting to depress the hell out of Cade.

"Don't you worry about our little Emma," the old man said. "She is my granddaughter, after all."

"That's what worries me," Cade muttered. The Captain's granddaughter. Deirdre's daughter. No wonder he couldn't sleep at night.

The phone rang. The Captain strode into the kitchen to answer it, his voice so young, vigorous and full of humor he sounded barely twenty while Cade felt a hundred years old.

There were times he figured his father was taking some

kind of twisted revenge for Cade's wild teenage years. Martin McDaniel trying to give his son as many gray hairs as possible. The cops had even given him a surprise party for his seventieth birthday after the old man had caught a hit-and-run driver, single-handedly wrestling the drunk guy to the ground. The man had ripped the Captain's piratelike gold hoop out of his ear, but the cops had gotten the collar and the Captain had gotten the kind of adrenaline rush he thought far too short in supply during the "golden years" of his life.

It was amazing. No one could deny it.

No one who heard about the old man's escapades could get over the Captain's courage or grit or downright fearlessness. Yeah, Cade thought, remembering the lines under his father's eyes, the thinning of arms that used to bulge with muscles. It was just terrific. Unless the man in question happened to be your father and you lived in fear he was going to break his neck one of these days.

Pride and exasperation warred in Cade, accompanied by a hard kick of dread somewhere in the gut. The Captain was the only family he'd had for years while Deirdre and Emma were out of his life. His father was so strong, invincible. But age was a relentless enemy, creeping up even on the Captain. It was damn tough watching a superhero start to stumble over skyscrapers he'd once leaped with ease.

But Martin McDaniel would even give the Grim Reaper a run for his money. The old man had a head hard as concrete and the heart of a lion. A hero in every sense of the word, if only it wasn't for the bitter side, the ugly edge that had slipped out now and then, and made a hell of a nasty splash during the dark days when Cade returned home after his mother's death.

It had been damned hard to shove his father's beast back into the bottle of Jack Daniel's. And by the time Cade managed to get the job done, it was too late. Deirdre was already pregnant, unmarried, defiant, as if she lived to fly in her proud father's face.

Mom would have known what to do. How to calm them both down. Cade didn't have a clue how they'd manage without her.

An ache twisted somewhere in his chest. He wondered if Deirdre even remembered the picnics, sailing on the river, playing touch football. The Captain starting the charter business so Cade would have something to come back to when his time in the Air Force was done.

Not that Cade had figured on ever returning home. He'd been thirsty for new places, new challenges, imagined his life with boundaries farther reaching than the skies he loved to fly.

While their mom—she'd been wired so much different. God, how she'd loved quieter things, poking around in antique shops, learning about history. She'd been the one who'd sparked Cade's interest in the earth-shattering days when aviation was brand-new. Still a miracle, inspiring awe.

She'd let him rattle on about the *Kitty Hawk* and Lindbergh's *Spirit of St. Louis*. Never got bored as he told her the latest theory about what had happened to Amelia Earhart when she'd disappeared.

He winced at the memory of the sunporch, her special haven from the upheaval of everyday life with a trio of wild McDaniels. She'd kept two little chairs nestled close to a delicate piecrust table, even though the second was rarely used. Every afternoon, she'd taken refuge there, sipping tea from bone china cups so thin they felt like eggshells. There were times Cade had joined her because he felt sorry for her, sitting there, alone.

He'd been so afraid he'd break one of his mom's delicately painted treasures with his awkward boy hands. Not that she would have said a cross word, just tucked the shards quietly away, like she did when she got trampled over by her bois-terous family.

He stopped, aware his father had returned to the room, the Captain watching him as if trying to read his mind. Cade won-dered if the Captain ever thought of his wife, or still blamed Cade for the accident when everything went wrong. But they didn't talk about it—no, not about things that really mattered, that cut you deep and left you bleeding.

"That was Doris, the dispatcher down at the police station. She's going to drop a cherry pie off as soon as she's done with her shift."

Doris was still trying to repay the Captain for the night he'd stepped between her young cop husband and a gang of street toughs on their way to the big city looking for trouble.

Cade's heart hurt with a mixture of love, respect and fear that one day even the Captain's formidable luck would run out.

"If Emma wasn't grounded, we could take the pie and two forks down to the river and eat 'til the damned thing was gone. But I suppose there's no way I'm going to get you to change your mind about this whole grounding thing."

"Not a chance."

"Well, then. Might as well lay it on the line. Just how long are you planning to keep my grandbaby in the brig?"

Cade met his father's gaze. "As long as it takes."

"Takes to what?" the Captain demanded. "Break her spirit? You've got to admit, Cade, it was damned resourceful of her to come up with a plan like she did. If she ever got in real trouble without some grown-up around to help her, you'd be glad she was smart enough to get out of it."

"She didn't get *out* of trouble, she got *in* to it," Cade re-minded him. "She's grounded and grounded she stays, long enough to keep her from doing something crazy like this again."

The Captain's face fell, and he rubbed his bristly morning chin. "That might take a really long time. That girl's got a mighty hard head on those itty-bitty shoulders."

"Tell me about it," Cade groaned.

"You know, maybe we should talk this over before you get so set on the sentence you passed. I mean, doesn't she deserve a trial by her peers or something?"

"You want me to argue the case in front of Ms. Norton's fifth grade? Come on Dad."

"I was thinking I could help you figure things out."

The idea of his seventy-year-old hellion of a father being Emma's peer almost made Cade laugh, but the Captain would see that as a break in Cade's battle line and that was all the encouragement the old man needed.

"Maybe you could lighten her sentence," the Captain wheedled. "Have a heart, son. I'm sure Emma's real sorry."

"Have you forgotten the kind of trouble that kid caused?"

"No. I just…sue me. I like to spend time with my grand-daughter. I went five years without her, you know." Shadows fell in the Captain's eyes. Cade knew just how badly Emma's absence had hurt him.

But not badly enough to find Deirdre, tell her he was sorry for the wedge his anger had driven between them. Still, Cade thought, what could the Captain really have done? Apologize for being himself?

"As long as you come to the cabin you can see her whenever you want." Cade resisted the pull of sympathy the Captain had already figured out was his very best weapon.

"I can see her under house arrest. How much fun can we have with you standing guard over us?"

"Hopefully not as much 'fun' as you two have been hav-ing lately," Cade said. "I could use a little peace."

But peace was going to be in very short supply in the next month, Cade figured, as mutiny settled into the Captain's craggy face.

No question. This was going to be a very long siege.

CHAPTER ELEVEN

"WHAT YOU NEED, flyboy, is a good old-fashioned roll in the hay."

Cade blinked hard, gaping at Finn perched on the top of a ladder, her slim legs spattered with plaster, her breasts straining against a white T-shirt so old and thin he could see through it when the afternoon sun blazed into the huge arched window beyond.

"What the hell?" Cade choked out.

Finn started, turned toward him, the breeze from the wide-open windows and doors feathering auburn curls about her throat, her face so creamy smooth and her body so hard-on sexy he ground his teeth.

"Did you say something?" he demanded sharply.

"No." She looked so damned surprised he had to believe her. Her eyes glowed like she'd been a million miles away, dreaming of some woman thing like wallpaper or curtains or black satin sheets—

Black satin sheets? Cade amended in irritation. No, that was more of a man kind of thing. One more facet of the X-rated fantasies that had been tormenting him since the night two weeks ago when he'd made one of the biggest mistakes of his life: Being driven by some desperate instinct to kiss Finn O'Grady and thinking he could relegate it to the back of his mind.

The back of his mind—that satin sheet place where his

subconscious was muttering comments like the one a moment ago and his body was being tortured with instant replays that kept his nerves on edge, remembering just how sweet and hot and soft she'd felt crushed against him. The way her lips had opened beneath his with a generosity that stunned him. How her gasp of response had tasted when he'd thrust his tongue into her mouth, a shot far more intoxicating than the whiskey they'd used to steady their nerves after he'd returned from her vandalized house.

He did his damnedest to quell the image of the new town librarian draped across his bed, her skin glowing, her full lips parting, moist and berry-red, fresh as summer. But it only made the ache in his groin worse.

"Cade?"

He snapped back to the present, unnerved as if she'd been able to see what he was thinking, from her red hair tumbled across his pillow to the black satin he'd imagined beneath her. The midnight color setting her creamy skin aglow with the luxurious perfection of a pool of velvet cradling a handful of pearls. No wonder she was looking at him as if he'd lost his mind.

"Do you need something?" she prodded.

His mouth went dry.

Oh, he needed something all right, he thought, angling the all-too-honest front of his jeans away from the woman. But he wasn't about to tell her what that "something" was.

What was it Jett's wife had said on his last visit to the family ranch in Montana?

"It's a scientific fact that men think about sex every six seconds. It's just not natural, Cade. A gorgeous man like you living like a monk. I know you keep insisting you don't want any complications in your life, but if you'd just give 'so-and-so' a chance."

Theresa, Kathy, Susan, Stephanie, Jan, fill in the blank

with whoever had caught Robin Davis's eager matchmaking eyes lately. Since she and Jett were so head-over-heels happy, she thought everyone else should give marriage a whirl. Like it was all white veils and great sex and Christmas dinners by candlelight. Of course, Cade doubted the Davises used the same criteria the McDaniels had to judge whether a holiday had been successful or not.

Success meant that no one had told anyone else at the family table to go screw themselves.

No, Cade had been enough of a lunatic to actually spend one Christmas Eve at the Davises. To Robin and Jett, holiday meant playing footsie under the table, stealing kisses under the mistletoe, touching each other every time they got a chance as they put their kid's new bike together while a fire roared in the fireplace.

They hadn't left Cade a whole lot of doubt as to what they'd be up to as soon as the bike was safely tucked under the tree. Robin might as well have tied one of those bright red ribbons around her waist.

Even Jett had looked like he felt sorry for Cade when Cade couldn't take the domestic bliss another minute and fled up to the guest room.

"I know what you need, Cade," Robin had insisted with a sigh. "Call it women's intuition. Too bad you don't listen."

Cade grimaced. It was bad enough listening to Jett's wife rattle on about his "needs" when she was sitting five feet away from him. But hearing her misguided but well-meaning advice echoing in his head when she was nowhere in sight was a pain in the neck he just didn't need.

Especially with Finn O'Grady driving him slowly out of his mind.

Only two weeks had passed since the night he'd kissed her so hard her hair should've caught fire but it seemed like forever. Imprisoned in this room, surprised by her sweet laughter, trapped with her pleasure in the most insignificant things.

Things he'd never even notice on his own, like raspberry jam on warm bread or a wren lugging a twig twice as long as it was to build a nest in the gap by the nearest downspout.

Sure, Finn had her moments when she was overwhelmed. But she tried so hard to make the old house beautiful in her eyes, make the best out of soggy plaster and hairline cracks and pipes he'd worked for days to replace. That kind of resilience wasn't natural, damn it. But then his new next-door neighbor was all about porch swings and picket fences.

She might as well be building prison walls as far as he was concerned. But the glow always fled her eyes when she thought of Emma. The corners of her mouth would tip down, her lashes dip low. She'd cast Cade a look so dark with regret he had to turn away. It would have been easier if he hadn't known how much she cared about the kid. If he hadn't told her so damn much, spilling out secrets like some kind of idiot. Sometimes she even gave him these long, sad looks as if…

As if she wanted to touch him again.

Not with that burning, clean passion, all physical, elemental, but with tenderness, as if she wanted to take away *his* pain.

Cade stiffened, feeling hunted, trapped. What the hell had possessed him, letting her past his guard like that? He didn't want her help and he sure as hell didn't want anyone to feel goddamn sorry for him. He could handle whatever curves life threw him. He'd had plenty of practice.

His only purpose in opening his mouth at all had been to help her understand why Emma was acting out. The kid was a mess, but maybe, just maybe doing the best she could.

And Finn *had* gotten the picture. He'd seen it in her all too sensitive face, the sadness in eyes deep green as forests he'd flown over, her mouth soft with knowing just how it felt to be a kid left behind.

Yeah. He'd given Finn every reason in the world to hurt for Emma. And hell, he could understand the urge to try to fix things for the girl. For God's sake, he'd felt the same thing. Problem was, Finn's idea of what the kid needed was the exact opposite of his.

Cade glowered at her, wondering when she'd start her next campaign. He'd known five star generals who could take lessons from her on strategy.

"Am I doing it wrong?" Finn demanded, challenging him with her gaze. Her paintbrush poised above her head, a drop of sweat trickling down her throat, disappearing into the shadowy hollow of cleavage exposed by the shirt's V-neck.

Cade focused on it, preferring to feel aggravation. Whatever happened to the good old-fashioned kind of shirts Verna wore, Cade wondered. Ones that actually covered women up to their chins? There had to be one in that maze of boxes piled all over the hall beyond the door, the ones with lacy bras and delicate nightgowns peeking out of their cardboard tops.

Finn brushed dust self-consciously off of the seat of her cutoffs with her unoccupied hand. The shorts fit her like a coat of paint on a Ferarri, a three-corner tear just below the pocket on the left cheek of her bottom. Her panties? Lipstick-red.

"It was wonderful of Verna to give me night shifts this week so I can help with the repairs," Finn said. "I know she did it as a favor to you."

"She's all heart," Cade growled, knowing what Finn said was true. The way he saw it, he'd be a lot better off if the women in his life quit trying to do him favors.

It hadn't been quite so bad the first few days he'd worked at March Winds. She'd been skittish and shy, blushing every time he got near her. She'd worked harder than most men and she sure didn't handle a hammer like a girl.

She'd said little about Emma. But he'd known that was too good to last.

By the time the "quiet" and "shy" had worn off Finn O'Grady, he'd wanted to ring his niece's neck for getting him into this mess.

But the ache in his groin wasn't Emma's fault. The kid hadn't made him kiss Finn. He'd done it himself—a distraction, he'd claimed.

Well, he'd distracted himself, all right. Until now, he was so busy trying not to think about getting that woman in bed, she was on his mind most of the day.

Better than the alternative, he thought, with a twinge of guilt.

He sure as hell couldn't stand to think about the little girl who dragged herself around the house, a dejected Tinkerbell fading away in *Peter Pan* when not a soul was clapping.

Speaking of Emma... Cade glanced at his watch, let fly a low curse. "Damn, I should've left to get Emma forty-five minutes ago," he said, dumping tools in a bucket and giving it an aggravated glare.

"Go ahead."

"Leave my tools dirty?" The woman might as well have told him to put sugar in his gas tank.

"I'll clean them," she offered. "No problem."

Her offer offended the blazes out of him for some reason he couldn't put his finger on. "I don't leave messes for other people to clean up," Cade said, grabbing a rag and cleaning off his hands as best he could.

"Terrific. Go get Emma and bring her back here. The tools will be waiting for you and I made some fresh lemonade. It will taste good after a long day in school."

Finn's lashes fluttered, so innocent he wanted to dump the nearby bucket of water over her head.

"Don't even try to sneak that one around me," he said, tossing the rag and groping at his belt for his cell phone. "I said Emma wasn't to set foot on March Winds' grounds and I meant it."

Finn heaved a sigh that should've shaken the rafters. "Cade, it's been two weeks. Hasn't she been punished enough?"

"You think this is *my* idea of fun?" Cade asked. "Keeping Emma penned up in the cabin with nothing to do but pout and scowl at me and needle me with every weapon of irritation in her ten-year-old arsenal?"

Cade scrolled through the cell's phone book to find John Glenn Elementary, thanking God he'd had the foresight to include entering the number—one more fragment of the meticulous preflight plan he'd made since his niece was dumped on his doorstep.

"Maybe if Emma makes you miserable enough you'll see reason," Finn suggested, about as helpful in the crisis as a pickup with velvet lining its bed.

He gave a harsh laugh. "I always thought grounding kids was such a good method of punishment. How come no one ever tells you that the stupid grown-up who imposed the sentence gets the worst end of the deal?"

The school number popped up and he hit the call button with a ferocity that should've shoved it halfway through the phone.

"Maybe the reason it's making you so uncomfortable is because you realize what you're doing is wrong—in your subconscious, I mean. It takes a big person to admit when they're wrong."

He held the receiver to his ear. "I'm not that big a person, obviously. And I'm not wrong. Damn it, why doesn't someone at that school pick up the damn phone?" He glared at his watch again.

"John Glenn Elementary, Mrs. Sedgewick speaking," a breathless voice came over the line.

"Cade McDaniel here. Would you tell Emma to sit tight? I'm on my way."

"Emma's not here, Mr. McDaniel," the school secretary said with a distinct chill.

"She's not…there?" Panic squeezed Cade's gut, a dozen possibilities as to where his niece could have gone racing through his mind. Not one of the options good.

Finn froze on her perch on the ladder, her face going white as the plaster. Cade could see her assessment of the situation was even more grim that his was. "Emma's gone?" she asked, pressing one hand to her chest. "Cade, what—"

He waved his hand to hush her. "What the—what did you people do with the kid?" he snarled into the phone.

"It seems as if *we* should be asking *you* that question. School was out almost an hour ago."

Cade glanced at his watch. "Forty-nine minutes. I screwed up. But that's no reason for you to lose Emma!"

"Emma tried to call you. You really should have some way she can get a hold of you in an emergency. You wouldn't believe the kinds of trouble children can get into when you're not watching."

Oh, he'd had a healthy respect for the chaos theory of children ever since Emma had come back into his life.

"Perhaps you should see about a cell phone," the secretary suggested smugly.

"I'm talking to you on my cell right now!"

"But I could have sworn…" the secretary fumbled, nonplussed. "I sat right here and watched Emma try to call you. She hung up and said you were always forgetting about her."

"I've never forgotten that kid in my life! I just lost track of time—" Cade's hand clenched, and he paced to the window, furious with himself. "Damn it, where the hell is my niece?"

"She called Captain McDaniel to come get her."

Cade leaned one shoulder against the wall, a tremor of relief working through him. Emma hadn't run away, taken off with some crazed idea of finding Deirdre. The Captain had her safe. The old man might have his shortcomings but as Martin McDaniel was fond of saying, nothing would hurt his grandbaby while he was around, even if the whole Russian army decided to invade Whitewater.

"What a remarkable man, the captain is!" the secretary crooned. "My, the adventures he's had! Emma told me all about them while she was waiting. Tell me, what is it like to have a father like that?"

"Like living in a wooden barrel with a box of lit fireworks," Cade said. "How long ago did they leave?"

"Twenty minutes ago," the secretary said, sounding confused by the fireworks reference. "Maybe more. I was just telling the first grade teacher what a fine old gentleman—"

Cade cut her off with a brusque goodbye and pressed End Call. That "fine old gentleman" was the craftiest SOB Cade had ever met. He wouldn't take Emma back to the old homestead and wait for Cade to call. No, the Captain would mount a full frontal assault to find out what the devil was going on.

He'd be out to the cabin at a speed that would set Skip Wilkin's radar gun screaming. Hell, it was a miracle he hadn't charged in to March Winds already, those streetwise eyes assessing the situation in a heartbeat.

The situation? A voice in Cade's head argued. What situation? That Cade was helping a neighbor? Meeting his responsibilities when it came to damage Emma had done to the woman's home?

No. There was something far more personal Cade didn't want the Captain to know. That Cade was more turned on by the new librarian than he'd been the time he'd stumbled on the whole cheerleading squad skinny-dipping in Fire Lake. And all his father would need was one good look to get the lay of the land.

Damn. Cade had to get out of here. Now.

Cade clipped the cell back on his belt. "I've got to head home," he said, trying to maneuver his broad shoulders past the ladder half-blocking the door. But in his haste, he cracked into one of the ladder's legs. Finn cried out, fought for balance as the ladder bucked, shooting her off the top rung. Cade grabbed for her. She smacked into him, knocking them backward over a roll of wire. He twisted his body, trying to break her fall.

Pain jolted his right elbow. Breath whooshed out of his lungs, the back of his head banging hard against the floor, the drop cloth protecting the wood doing little to cushion the blow.

They fell in a heap, Finn's paintbrush flying. Out of the corner of his eye, he caught a blur of wooden slats, the ladder tumbling toward them.

Cade rolled Finn underneath him, cupping his big body around her smaller, more fragile one in an effort to shield her as the ladder glanced off of his shoulder. One wooden edge grazed his temple before the ladder fell with a crash to one side.

For a moment, Cade's head swam. The reason? He wasn't certain. The crack on the head or the far more dangerous blow of Finn's curves and hollows melded so intimately against him as the weight of his body pressed down on hers.

Breasts crushed against his chest, her legs tangled up with his, the subtle hill of her femininity cradling the part of him that had been causing so much trouble moments before.

She fit him like a damned glove, Cade thought, trying to clear his head. He imagined being gloved tight inside her.

"You hurt?" he ground out, levering himself up just a few inches, one hand braced on the floor.

"I don't think so. Are you all right?"

His head started to throb, and his shoulder ached where

he'd broken their fall. But that wasn't the reason he was having a hard time remembering how to breathe.

She smelled so damned good he wanted to eat her up. She felt lush and deliciously soft underneath him. And her lips were so close he could feel her quick bursts of breath on his mouth.

His heart hammered, and he ran his hand down her bare arms, as if to prove to himself nothing was broken or swelling. "You scared the hell out of me! All these tools and such scattered around—you could've hurt yourself, bad."

"You took the brunt of the fall." She smiled, a sweet, shaky smile that made Cade wonder if his legs would ever hold him up again. "My hero."

Cade growled under his breath, not liking the pictures the woman painted in his head, the possibilities. Wondering what it would be like to be a hero to someone like Finn, to commit to being the man always there to break her fall.

No, he didn't have it in him to be a hero for anyone. But man, oh, man, what he wouldn't give to kiss a few of the lady's bruises away.

Her fingertips brushed his hair back from his forehead, tracing a sore place where something hit on the way down.

"You're bleeding," she said, drawing his head down. "Let me see."

He resisted for a heartbeat, then let her pull him closer, taking his chin between her soft fingers, and angling his face so she could see the scrape.

The tender concern in her eyes drove him over the edge. The rest of the world forgotten, he did what he'd been wanting to do for days. His mouth opened hungrily over hers, the hard line of his body taut, imprinting itself on the yielding femininity of hers.

Finn gasped, her arms closing convulsively around him, breasts arching even tighter against his chest. Cade groaned, shifting his jean-clad legs against her long, slender bare ones, instinct parting and nudging and moving ever so subtly in the kiss until he sank into the place he wanted to be.

Her thighs warmed the outside of his, his hardening shaft pressed against the fly of her shorts, nothing but two layers of frustrating as hell denim and a pair of lipstick-red panties preventing the skin-to-skin contact he was burning for.

What the hell was he doing? Some far-off voice of reason demanded.

He didn't care. Adrenaline pumped through his veins, thick and hot, in a way he hadn't felt in years. He couldn't resist the wildness in it, the primal response of body to body.

Through a haze of desire, he heard a hollow, wooden noise, something else falling around them, no doubt. Falling away like his hold on reason. Voices intruded, and he didn't want to hear them—

"Hey, boy, where the hell are—"

The voice doused Cade's passion like a bucket of ice-cold water. He struggled to find his bearings, tear his mouth away from Finn's. But the woman had threaded her fingers back through his hair, holding his mouth to hers.

"Whoa, there!"

Even Finn heard the low whistle. She released her hold on Cade. They tried to scramble apart, guilty as two sixteen-year-olds caught by their folks steaming up the windows in the family station wagon.

Cade rolled off her, and stared at his worst nightmare—the Captain, his ice-blue eyes blazing keen, Emma, holding the old man's hand. The Captain had smacked his hand over the kid's eyes.

"So *that's* the lay of the land." The Captain gave them both a long, streetwise stare. "When the school called, I figured there must've been some disaster, an accident, a plane crash.

My son's got a pilot's sense of time—never been late in his life unless there was hellacious weather involved. Looks like you've been stirring up storms in here, all right, young lady. Just not the kind the weather channel would be reporting on. But then, the weather channel is meant for family viewing."

Emma was scrabbling at the Captain's hands, trying to pry his fingers apart.

As soon as Cade had untangled himself from Finn, Martin McDaniel surrendered his efforts to blindfold his granddaughter. He bowed gallantly to Finn, offering her his hand.

"She fell off the ladder," Cade growled, clambering to his feet.

"Cade caught me," Finn stammered breathlessly, her cheeks fire engine-red.

"I can see he did."

Cade wanted to elbow the old man aside and haul Finn up himself, but she'd already put her hand in the Captain's. Martin McDaniel pulled her gently to her feet. Cade's irritation sharpened when the old man didn't let go of her hand.

"So you're the young woman I've been hearing so much about," the Captain said, eyes twinkling. "Funny, you don't look like a wicked witch."

He cast a teasing glance Emma's way. The child glared at Finn, confusion in her dark eyes, as if trying to decide how to react after Finn had risen to her defense two weeks before. Decisions, decisions, Cade thought as he watched the kid try to figure out whether or not she still wanted to turn Finn into stone.

Finn laughed, trying to hide how flustered she was. "No crystal ball, no flying monkeys, not even a smidgen of green makeup."

"No, your face is more red, I'd say." Martin McDaniel arched one bushy eyebrow.

Finn pulled her hand out of his grasp. She flushed so dark her freckles disappeared.

"This is my father, the Captain," Cade snapped.

"Martin. Call me Martin."

Cade did a double take. The only person who'd ever called the Captain by his first name was the old man's sainted mother. Cade had figured that even in the heat of passion his own mom had called him by his rank. Not a picture he wanted in his head at the moment. Hell—not ever!

"I'm Finn." She peered at the Captain, completely oblivious to the sharp intelligence in his eyes, a baby bunny under the all-seeing gaze of a hawk.

"Finn. Verna has told me all about you. And of course, Emma's given her opinion, as well. And Cade—well, it's obvious what my son thinks about you."

"I think she's a woman whose ceiling fell in and she needs some help," Cade said firmly.

"When I got here, you were looking like the ceiling fell, all right. Smack on your head. Haven't seen you that dazed since you kids were waterskiing in the river and Caroline Bates lost the top half of her bikini. Though I always figured she did it on purpose to get your attention."

"Damn it, Dad—cut it out!" Cade jerked his head toward Emma who was looking at him, big eyed and all ears.

The Captain didn't even blink. He just laid one finger along his stubborn chin. "You're a mystery, all right, Miss Finn. Been hearing opinions about you as changeable as the sky during spring—tornado weather, storms and the sweetest weather you can imagine. I suppose I'll have to figure out which one of these folks is right about you. But then, I should be up to the task. One of the things they look for in the Rangers is a quick judge of character. Got to size up the enemy—or friend in a heartbeat."

"*He's* the one who taught me how to kick Billy Callahan's behind," Emma said, proudly, an attempt to drive a wedge between her grandfather and the woman she might still decide was her enemy.

Martin grimaced. "Never underestimate a McDaniel. Emma may be a little thing, but she's got fighting blood in her. My son, too. It's the loving part of life that comes hard to us."

Cade could almost have sworn a shadow crossed his father's face. But then, the Captain rarely showed any emotion save charm or outrage. He didn't believe in regret.

"Can I offer you some lemonade and the best sugar cookies this side of Chicago?" Finn offered, a gentle understanding in her voice as if she could read things in the Captain's face Cade couldn't see, hear things in his voice Cade couldn't understand. The openness in the woman's gaze was way too easy to read.

Cade remembered how Finn had touched him, the night in his kitchen and moments before on her bedroom floor, as if the loving parts of life came natural to her as breathing, and she wanted to give him some kind of CPR of the spirit. But one thing he knew for sure, he didn't want that part of him revived—the vulnerability, the need, the peril of depending on someone for an emotion as ephemeral as what? Love?

Cade's blood ran cold at the danger in it.

"How about it, Emma?" Finn coaxed. "We can have a little snack on the porch and talk. See if your grandpa here can figure out whether or not I'm after your ruby slippers."

Emma regarded her warily, a little spark of hope brightening her face. "You mean, have it here? At Addy's house?"

"No way," Cade cut in. "You and the Captain and I are marching home, right now. You need to get going on your homework. Tell Ms. O'Grady goodbye."

Emma looked at Finn, so quiet, resigned. "Bye." Finn hustled to the kitchen, grabbed the pitcher out of the refrigerator and a tin of cookies from the counter. "Take these with you."

"That's not necessary," Cade said.

"I know it isn't. I want to. Emma, I made the lemonade the old-fashioned way. With real lemons." Finn held out the glass pitcher to the child. Emma's gaze fastened on the bright yellow peels floating in the liquid. "Just like Addy would have made it."

Emma drew closer, took the pitcher carefully in her hands as she peered into the sweet mixture. "I never tasted it with real lemons," she said. "Just powdered stuff in envelopes."

"I can teach you how to make it."

Emma looked up at her from beneath curly lashes and caught her lip between her teeth as if trying to fight something inside her—hope.

Finn glanced from Emma to Cade, and amended her offer. "Maybe."

"Or maybe not," Cade said. "Back to the cabin. Now. Both of you." He steered his father and niece toward the door, didn't know what to do when Finn thrust the tin of cookies hard into his midsection. His hands closed around the container reflexively. The tin, hard and cold where she had been so incredibly soft. He drew himself inward, trying not to remember.

"I'll be seeing you later, Miss Finn," the Captain said, regarding them as if he could read their blasted minds. "Keep this son of mine on task. You never know what's going to happen when his mind starts wandering. People lose all track of time. They fall right off of ladders, and next thing you know…you end up in a heap on the floor. Anything could happen."

Cade ground his teeth, remembering the "anything" that had been hardening, thickening where it pressed against the crux of Finn's thighs, how he'd felt the heat of her legs through his jeans.

"Home." Cade groaned, steering his father and Emma toward the wide-open back door.

"Cade," Finn called after him. "Your tools."

"Let 'em rust!" he said, herding his family away from this house, this woman, the spell March Winds and its resident dreamer were casting.

On the Captain.

On Emma.

On him.

He didn't intend to glance over his shoulder. Couldn't stop himself. Finn stood in the doorway, her hair red as sunset, her mouth tender, generous as her body, warm as her heart.

The kind of woman who could make another man forget. That picket fences could be far more dangerous than flying, a free fall into the disaster he'd watched in the clapboard house for so many years.

He was a McDaniel, after all.

He was better off on his own.

CHAPTER TWELVE

FINN WANDERED through rooms of the home she'd wanted forever, her slipper-clad feet guided by moonlight, her instinct for the corridors and pathways of home already honed with the unbearable sweetness of fingertips tracing a lover's face in the dark.

She longed to wrap herself up in the comfort of that familiarity, to close eyes itchy with exhaustion and rest muscles aching from the hard physical work she'd used to fill every moment she hadn't spent at the library during the past two weeks. But tonight a new yearning refused to let her rest, leaving her unsatisfied with plaster ceilings and wood floors, warm rugs and gleaming fireplace mantels and furniture lovingly placed by windows she peered through alone.

She hungered for touch, a man's breath, hot and alive against her throat, a mouth eager and seeking on hers.

Cade.

Her whole body burned as if he had made love to her, right there on the drop cloth covered floor, penetrated her with a force far more powerful than his hard, athlete's body.

He'd drowned her in his need, his confusion, the battles raging inside him spilling between them in a wordless flood.

Finn pushed open the porch door and slipped out onto the veranda, the quiet of the night closing around her. She hadn't wanted to care about Cade, she thought, trailing her hand along the porch rail as she followed it the length of the house.

From the moment she'd met him she'd known he was trouble. One of those deliciously sexy, difficult men she'd once joked with friends should be relegated to a "ten minutes in a closet" kind of affair.

She hadn't bargained on his sense of humor, or imagined how his skill with his hands would affect her as she watched him, not just slap plaster into place as expediently as possible, but rather coax out a subtle piece of March Winds' soul.

In the time she'd spent with him, something had changed, shifted, ensnaring them both in a magnetic tug as primitive as gravity and as inescapable. Passions simmering for days finally boiled over, leaving Finn wondering whether she was relieved or disappointed that Emma and Cade's father had interrupted them.

Because if they hadn't…

Finn tingled all over. Would she have thrown caution to the winds? Would she have let him…

Let him?

No, nothing so passive, she admitted to herself, her cheeks burning. She'd wanted him as fiercely as he'd wanted her. Her hands had been hungry for the feel of him, the muscles cording his back, the silkiness of his dark hair under her fingers, his mouth, wet and wide devouring her as if he were starving for the taste of her.

Maybe in her secret heart every woman dreamed of a man desiring her that way. But those fairy tales always ended in a happily ever after, the hero riding home on his white steed with his lady fair in his arms. Irish legends, like Irish fairies, were a stormier breed apart, with shadows and tempests and tragedies to haunt the soul.

Somehow Cade seemed far more like the Celtic warriors her father had spun than the earnestly sweet Prince Charmings that peopled her foster mother's bedtime stories.

Finn caught her lip between her teeth, searching the moonlit garden for a flicker of light, any sign that Cade and his cabin were real.

What was he thinking right now, alone in his split log bed? Was Cade as deeply shaken as she was at how completely they'd poured themselves into each other for those moments they'd lain together on the floor? Defenses crumbling, raw emotion melding more than lips, twining more tightly than legs and arms ever could? Breaching places more intimate than mere layers of cloth could separate?

She blinked hard as something fluttered in her line of sight, a distant smear of white crossing from Cade's land onto the grounds of March Winds. Rubbing her eyes with her knuckles, she tried to sweep away the blur floating steadily down the riverbank. A fairy light, a fallen star trying to find its way back into the sky.

But when she opened her eyes again, the white smudge moved closer than ever, drifting toward the silvery ribbon of river just visible beyond her garden.

The back of her neck prickled, Emma's whispers of Addy's restless child spirit echoing through Finn's memory.

Tentative, silent, she moved toward the pale, drifting form on the horizon, unable to resist its pull. Was there a lonely spirit wandering?

Her pulses fluttered. What if it was Cade, as restless as she was? But with his tall frame he'd tower far higher than the small white shape moving inexorably toward the river.

The shape seemed to walk, phantomlike onto the water, beyond the ragged, dark border of shore. Finn shivered, tempted to flee back into the house.

But some unseen force held her. She hesitated, the breeze dusting her curls against her cheeks, her heart hammering loudly in her ears. Poised, between reality and the mystic world Emma believed in, Patrick O'Grady's realm of fairies and ghosts and dreams that could never be real.

Wood splintering shattered the silence, a splash banishing the mists filling Finn's imagination. A child's scream of terror, horrifyingly real, iced Finn's veins.

Emma!

Finn bolted toward the river, branches tearing at her arms and legs, her slippers flying from her feet, unheeded. The riverbank disappeared behind the hulking shape of a shrub, Finn losing sight for a moment of the precious white shape of the child.

Oh, God, she prayed, don't let her be in the river! No more splashing, no sound of flailing—had she bumped her head? Slid into the water, unconscious? Helpless?

Finn could barely swim herself.

"Cade!" Finn shouted. "Cade, help!"

But the cabin was too far away, the walls too thick. He'd never hear her. Never get to them in time.

She burst past the wall of vegetation, moonlight pouring down on the old dock, its rotted wooden planks a dangerous pathway into the river. A wail split the silence, desperate, heart wrenchingly scared, but blessedly very much alive.

Finn neared the dock, saw the child hanging on, her arms wrapped around a dock post, her body buried to the waist beneath the break in the wood planks she'd fallen through.

"Hang on, sweetheart!" Finn called.

"Can't…" Emma sobbed. "Can't hold on."

"Yes you can! I'm coming, baby!"

Finn's imagination flashed horrifying images, Emma disappearing through the breach in the splintered wood. The child caught in the river's merciless current, being dragged like a fragile leaf under the dark water and whisked away downstream where Finn could never find her.

Finn stumbled on the edge of the dock, skidding on her knees, her breath freezing as she heard the wood start to give underneath her.

Emma shrieked in terror, sliding down a little farther and for an instant Finn feared she'd startled the little girl into releasing her grip on the post.

"Hold on! I'm here, Emma. Just a few seconds longer!" Finn urged, pleading, praying, promising God anything if He'd just let her get the child to safety.

Finn flattened herself on the splintery surface spread eagle, trying to distribute her weight across the boards, not knowing how many were rotted, how much weight they would hold. Knowing the surface beneath her could give at any moment.

But she had no choice. Emma was scared, tired, disoriented. The little girl couldn't hold on forever.

Finn edged toward her. "Grab my hand, honey. Reach for it. You can do it."

"No! The—the river will get me, just like Addy's mom!"

Finn's heart twisted. Even here, her very life in danger, Emma was still linked to the house, the people who'd lived here a century and a half before. Finn eased closer, could see the child's arms shaking with fatigue.

"I won't let the river get you. I promise, sweetheart. Grab onto me."

"C-can't."

The wood groaned under Finn.

Shoving ever so carefully with her toes, Finn moved closer, closer to Emma. The child's face, stark in the moonlight, her dark eyes huge in her small white face, her fingers in a death grip upon the weathered wood.

Would Finn have to pry them away? Her stomach lurched. If Emma fought her, the chances of the dock holding beneath the extra weight were slim.

Finn managed to curve one hand over the child's icy fingers. She didn't try to loosen Emma's grasp, just covered her hand, making sure the little girl knew by touch that she wasn't alone. "Emma?"

Emma peered up into Finn's face, her lips blue with cold, her chin wobbling. "I w-want my mom."

"I know, baby. But I'll take care of you. Just grab my hand and I'll pull you onto the dock."

"It'll break!" Emma sobbed.

"I'll hold on to you, no matter what," Finn promised fiercely. But if the worst happened could she get them both to shore? Fight the spring-swollen current with a flailing, terrified child in tow?

Finn had to distract Emma, give her the courage to reach for Finn's hand. A reason to take that chance.

Addy… Even terrified as she was, Emma had spoken of Addy….

She forced her voice into soft, soothing tones. "I've got hot chocolate up at Addy's house in green bunny mugs. And a quilt to get you warm. Addy…Addy misses you, Emma. And so do I. You have to come and see her."

"C-come to Addy's house?" the child echoed, plaintively.

"As soon as I get you back to shore."

"B-but *he* told me I couldn't."

"Your uncle Cade will be so glad you're safe he'll change his mind. I promise, Emma. Reach for me, sweetheart. I won't let go."

Emma sucked in a shuddery breath, then in a heartbeat released her grip on the post and grabbed for Finn's hand. Emma's nails dug deep into Finn's skin, the child clinging for dear life. Finn grappled for a hold on her, locking fingers tight around Emma's wrists. She pulled, tried to drag Emma up, out, but the wood beneath her groaned, the child whimpering. "It's sticking me in the tummy."

"You need to help me, sweetie. You can do this. You're strong."

"No I'm not."

"Remember what you did to Billy Callahan! Use your

legs. Just imagine you're climbing the tree where I saw you that first day. We'll pop you right out of there together and then we'll go to Addy's house and get warm. On the count of three, now. One. Two. *Three.*"

Emma's eyes flashed with determination, suddenly, painfully reminding Finn of Cade.

Finn hauled back, Emma scrabbling for a foothold. Slowly, Emma slid toward her, chest on the dock, hips, thin damp legs in a twist of nightgown. "I've got you, Emma. I've got you," Finn soothed. Finn eased herself backward, the dock creaking as she hauled Emma with her toward the river-bank.

"Finn!" Cade's rough, alarmed voice echoed through the darkness. "Emma? Where are you?"

"The dock!" Finn cried. "Cade, hurry!"

Relief swirled through her as she heard the sound of foot-steps running toward them. Suddenly a horrific crack of wood splintering drowned out Cade's shout. With strength born of desperation, Finn yanked Emma into her arms, and hurled herself backward.

Hard, masculine hands clenched on Finn's shoulders, and she all but flew the last few yards off of the unstable dock.

She thudded hard against Cade's chest, Emma, Finn and Cade tumbling to the ground in a heap. Safe. Thank God, safe.

Cade clutched both of them in a grip so tight it drove the air from Finn's lungs. But Emma struggled, kicked.

"Let go!" she wailed. "Let go!"

Cade loosened his grip on them, and Finn fell back to the ground on one elbow. "God, Emma! Are you hurt?" he asked.

"You're okay, aren't you, sweetheart?" Finn asked.

Emma rubbed her stomach with one hand. "The wood scratched me."

"That's all?" Cade demanded, so sharply the little girl jumped. "You're sure?"

Emma sniffled, bobbed her head.

"What the hell are you doing out here? It's the middle of the night!"

Emma scrubbed at her eyes with her fingertips. "Don't… know. I was in my bed. Sleeping. Thought it was a…dream. But it was real." Her voice quivered.

Finn caught hold of Emma's hand. "She must've been sleepwalking. Some kids do that when they're under a lot of stress."

"But the door was locked!" Cade exclaimed, disbelieving.

"She must have unlocked it."

"Son of a bitch!"

Finn could feel Cade's big body shudder, knew the horrible scenes playing through his mind, Emma wandering, innocent, asleep, toward the treacherous water.

"Thank God you saw her!" Cade choked out, trying to gather the child close. But Emma went wild in his arms.

"Don't you touch me!" Emma shrieked at Cade, scrambling to Finn like a little monkey, clinging to her with heartbreaking desperation. "I'm going to Addy's house! She promised!"

"What the hell?" Cade stared, as hurt and confused as his niece was.

"Hush, Emma." Finn hugged the child, stroked her dark, tangled hair. "You gave your Uncle Cade quite a scare."

"*He's* the one who scares people!" Emma said. "He made my mom run away!"

"Oh, honey," Finn soothed, "he didn't make your mother leave."

"Yes he did!" Emma cried brokenly. "It's all his fault!"

"What the—?" Cade shook his head, bewildered. "Emma—what are you talking about?"

Emma's small body trembled. "My mom got so scared of you she won't come back, 'cause you yelled at her! Just like you yell at me about Addy!"

"Your mom and I argued." Finn could see Cade struggle to keep his voice level. "But I never scared Deirdre in her life."

"You didn't want her to like her music! You told her she had to pick! I heard you!"

Cade's face went ashen in the moonlight. "Oh, my God, Emma."

"She didn't pick me! Why didn't she pick me?" Emma sobbed, burying her face in Finn's neck.

Cade reached toward Emma, froze as the child instinctively flinched away from him. His fingers curled into a fist, fell to his side, so strong, so suddenly utterly helpless.

"Hold on to me!" Emma begged Finn. "You promised you wouldn't let go!"

"Cade, she's just disoriented, upset," Finn said, her heart breaking for both of them. "Once we settle her down we can explain."

"Explain what?" Cade asked hoarsely. "I did tell Deirdre she had to choose. I just never thought she'd… Emma's right. It is my fault. Just like this is my fault." He waved toward the treacherous, dark river. "My God, she could have drowned!" His voice caught. "Take her…to March Winds. Take her."

Finn wrapped her arms around Emma, balancing the child on her hip, the girl small for her age, but awkward to carry. Arms straining, Finn trudged toward the house, with its bunny mugs and its ghosts that whispered to lonely little girls. Cade McDaniel followed behind her, the weight of little Emma's world bowing down his broad shoulders.

CADE PROWLED the confines of March Winds' parlor, the fire Finn had insisted he build crackling in the white marble fireplace. Warm and dry, Emma huddled secure among the plump cushions lining Finn's white wicker rocking chair. The child clutched a mug with both hands, a quilt tucked around her, the room filled with the sweet, rich smell Cade remembered from childhood.

His mother had made hot chocolate every Christmas morning—let him and Deirdre spray whipped cream out of a can, decorate the top of their cups any way they wanted. With mountains of the fluffy white stuff, red and green sprinkles, sugar stars or broken bits of candy cane.

Strange he should remember Christmases past right now, with spring bursting all around him and Emma barely escaping drowning in the river. Then again, maybe not so strange to recall those all too brief pools of peace in his parents' rocky marriage. Security he'd craved, but known even as a boy was unstable as the black ice that lured unwary skaters onto the river.

But with Finn, there were no undercurrents waiting to sweep peace away. She soothed the craziness of the hour before so naturally. Moving about in that feminine way that still mystified him, as if she knew secrets of the universe no man ever could—how to weave peace, coax out secret hurts lodged like thorns under a child's skin, or a under a man's.

He watched Emma sip her cocoa, a whipped cream mustache clinging to her upper lip, feeling as if he had to do something, say something. But every time Emma caught him looking at her, she dug herself deeper into the chair, as if trying to wedge herself into it so tight he could never haul her back to the cabin.

She should be turning to me, a voice inside Cade cried out.

Hell, Finn wasn't Emma's family. But Cade had no more idea how to soothe his emotionally battered niece than scale mountains on the moon.

"Feel better?" Finn asked—Cade wasn't sure who.

Emma shuddered. "It never happened like that before."

"Before?" Cade echoed, feeling sick to his stomach. "You've gone sleepwalking before?"

Emma eyed him warily. "Dunno. I just wake up outside sometimes. When I have bad dreams about my mom."

"It must be scary waking up outside, in the dark all alone," Finn sympathized.

"Yeah. Until I go see Addy."

Cade ground his teeth, trying not to bite the kid's head off. "You mean you come over here? All by yourself? In the middle of the night?" While he lay there, sleeping, completely oblivious.

Emma nodded.

Cade shuddered inwardly. No wonder Emma had been able to find her way over to March Winds the night she'd pulled her stunt with the water pipes. The kid had gone to the house before with no grown-up within hearing range, no one to help her if she'd gotten in trouble.

She was too young to realize that her midnight wanderings in an old house like this were an accident waiting to happen. If Finn hadn't moved into March Winds, hadn't gotten to know and care about Emma, God only knew what might have happened. It had only been a matter of time until something terrible had occurred. The kid was a ticking time bomb.

"You're lucky you didn't break your neck in here in the dark!" Cade said, fighting back the image of Emma hurt, alone.

"It wasn't dark. After the first time I hid some candles inside the coal door. Just in case."

Could things get any damned worse? "You were wandering around this house with lit candles? You could've set yourself on fire!" Not to mention the house. Cade shuddered, thinking of those long, flowing nightgowns Emma preferred. Old-fashioned looking things with puffy sleeves and hems down to her toes. One careless move could've meant disaster.

Emma's lower lip thrust out. "Addy used candles sometimes and she wasn't any older than me. Well, mostly Addy used oil lamps, but you wouldn't let me borrow any of yours."

Cade remembered Emma eyeing lanterns hanging in the rafters from his camping days, how she'd suggested they use them instead of electricity, "like a real cabin." So that's what she'd been up to. Hell, she was as crafty as the Captain.

"I stuck a flashlight over there, too. Got to see to light the candles. You know."

"Then why bother with the candles at all?" Cade demanded. "The flashlight makes more sense."

"But it wasn't the same. I was real careful with the matches and stuff," Emma defended, turning to Finn. "The candlelight made the whole house look so pretty and soft. I'd go from room to room and look at the carvings on the fireplaces and the paintings on the ceilings, and think that's what it must've looked like when Addy was alive."

Finn crossed over to her, stroked her curls. "So, all those stories about ghost lights drifting around March Winds at night were true. *You* were the ghost."

Emma peered up at Finn, so earnestly Cade felt like his chest was going to crack. "I didn't mean to hurt anything. Nobody else wanted March Winds. And nobody wanted me."

"Emma—" Cade protested hoarsely.

"It's true." Tears welled up in Emma's eyes. Her throat worked as she tried to hold them back. Another McDaniel trait—Cade thought. Rage if you want to, yell and scream and hit back. But show grief? Heartache? Sorrow? No, never let 'em see you cry.

"My mom doesn't want me and you don't, either."

Finn gathered Emma up in her arms, sank down in the rocking chair, holding the little girl so naturally Cade could hardly bear to look at them.

"Sometimes it feels that way, doesn't it?" she murmured

into Emma's curls. "I know. When I was little my da left me, too. I didn't know why."

"I do," Emma quavered, looking straight into Finn O'Grady's earth-mother eyes. "My mom didn't want me 'cause I'm bad. I did bad things while mom was playing her music sometimes, just so she'd have to come talk to me. I didn't even care if she yelled. I did bad things here, too. An' now Uncle Cade hates me."

Finn's eyes met his, the woman silent for once, knowing…this was between him and Emma, alone.

"Emma, I don't hate you." Cade fought to keep his voice from cracking.

Emma shook her head, so sad, so certain. "It's not your fault. Nobody wants me to be their little girl."

Cade stared into Emma's woebegone face, groping for the right words, knowing whatever he said next would stay with this sensitive lost soul forever. But she'd know if he were lying, stretching the truth, trying to make her feel better. If that happened, she'd never be able to trust him again.

He neared the rocking chair, knelt down so he was face-to-face with his niece. "I want you."

"Why should you?" Emma's bottom lip trembled. "You don't even like me very much."

Is that what she believed? "You're wrong. I love you. I just…haven't had very much practice."

He heard Finn catch her breath, felt the intensity of her big heart reaching out to him until he could *feel* her, like a gentle hand on his shoulder. He hadn't felt gentleness in such a long, long time.

Emma sucked in her left cheek and cuddled deeper in Finn's protective arms. The child's brow crinkled as if trying to peel back layers, see into his soul. Cade wanted to look away, so she wouldn't see how damned scared he was, how uncertain. That no matter how much he loved this child or how determined he was to do right by her he'd fail in the end.

"Emma, I know you're scared right now. I'm scared, too. But if you'll give me the chance, I promise I'll do whatever it takes. You can be my little girl forever."

He sensed Finn tensing, as if something he said had worried her. Was she afraid he didn't mean what he'd said? He damn well wasn't a man to go back on his word like Finn's old man had so many years ago. But this was about Emma. Cade focused on the little girl.

"You've been waiting and waiting for my mom to come back." Emma's gaze faltered. "I have, too."

"Not anymore." Cade searched for some way to make her understand, reached back into childhood for the right words. "I want you, Emma. For keeps."

The words hung between them, long moments that seemed to stretch into eternity. Cade wanted to swoop in on her, grab her up out of Finn's arms, make Emma see he'd never made a more solemn promise in his life.

But the first step had to be hers. A leap of faith from this child he'd hurt so badly. He held out his arms, hoping, praying, counting on the courage he'd seen reflected in his little niece's face.

Come on, baby girl. Cade pleaded with his eyes. *Take a chance.*

Emma straightened, Finn's grasp on the child loosening ever so carefully. Emma glanced up at Finn, and Cade saw Finn smile encouragement. Slowly Emma climbed down and faced him, closed the space between them. She held out her hand as if to seal their pact with an earnest handshake. Cade didn't take it.

With a groan, he gathered Emma in his arms and held on tight.

An hour later he watched her as she lay sleeping on Finn's bed, so small, so fragile, snuggling into the covers and into Cade's life.

"I meant what I said," he murmured, aware of Finn standing beside him. "About doing whatever it takes. But I don't know what the hell I'm doing. How to make her happy. I want her to be happy, Finn."

"I know."

"Help me."

"I'll be right here for both of you."

But wasn't that dangerous, too? Leaning on someone? Depending on them? Someone whose soft eyes reminded a man just how hard-edged his life had become? Finn slipped her hand into his. He let his fingers curl over hers. What the hell was he getting himself into?

It didn't matter. He was already in way over his head.

CHAPTER THIRTEEN

THE CHILDREN'S ROOM looked like an earthquake had struck, crayons and scraps of colored paper littering the craft table, empty cartons of milk and three kinds of cookie crumbs scattered across the blanket where the preschool crowd had just finished snacks. A parade of tissue paper monster faces peeped out from under the giant construction paper bed Finn had created on a bulletin board to highlight her first selection for story hour—an adorable lap book revealing the truth every child knew—that there were monsters under the bed. But the story's goal had been accomplished. The monsters appeared to be a distinctly friendlier variety than those described by the kids at the opening of story hour.

She waved to her pint-size audience as their parents herded them home, the kids' favorite pajamas rumpled, their dolls or teddy bears or stuffed dogs bumping along behind them as they dragged them across the floor.

If teacher's institute day had been a disaster, bedtime story hour had turned out to be a delightful surprise. The best time of her week, Finn thought, tired but satisfied. Nothing like a flock of sturdy three- and four-year-olds to build up your confidence, adoring you from the moment you opened your mouth to read.

It would have been perfect if the giant bed hadn't reminded her of a certain log cabin and monsters she'd glimpsed in the silvery blue depths of Cade's eyes. He'd changed the night Emma fell in the river. The wall he'd built around himself was crumbling. He was feeling things he'd been resisting, imagining the rest of his life in ways he'd never intended to, weaving Emma into the fabric of his own forever.

Finn replayed that night when they'd come so close to losing Emma over and over in her mind, remembering the stark vulnerability in his face as he'd told Emma he wanted her for keeps….

Sometimes, now, Finn caught him looking at her with new intensity and glimpsed emotions she couldn't exactly put her finger on. He was grateful for her help with his niece, Finn kept telling herself. Desperate and determined as he was to help Emma, he'd been forced to depend on Finn in a way she sensed was foreign to this proud, independent, emotionally wounded man. But what would it be like for Finn to hear him say the words he'd said to Emma to her?

She'd always wanted to hear them from her father. But that wasn't the image that kept her up at night now. What would it mean to Finn as a woman? To hear Cade McDaniel claim that he wanted her—not just for sex. Lord knew there was no denying the chemistry between them. But for more than that…for keeps.

Finn caught her bottom lip between her teeth, an uncomfortable heat simmering beneath her skin as she imagined a life filled with Cade McDaniel's soul-blistering kisses. She had no business thinking such inappropriate thoughts here with a giant stuffed Winnie the Pooh peering down at her. Not to mention the little blond boy busily trying to feed his construction paper monster to a shark hand puppet in the corner—no mother in sight.

He seemed occupied at the moment, so she grabbed the garbage can and headed over to start cleanup duty when she heard someone come up behind her. Figuring someone must have misplaced their blankie, she turned with a smile, "Can I help…you?"

Cade stood like a giant amid the child-size chairs and tables, a smile crooking the left corner of his mouth. He smelled so good and looked even better in his leather bomber jacket and vivid green shirt. "Hi."

"Is Emma all right?"

"She's fine—well, I think she's fine. She's with the Captain. First unsupervised visit since she got out on parole."

Finn chuckled. "A night to yourself and you come to the library?"

He shrugged, looking a little sheepish. "Guess I was just passing by and saw your car…."

Her lingering pint-size patron pushed between them, waving his tissue paper creation at Cade. "I know why you comed. It was on the sign Miss Gravy put on the door. Come to story hour if you got a monster under your bed."

"Absolutely," Cade said so earnestly Finn couldn't help but be charmed.

"Miss Gravy is real good about beds an' things."

"Thanks for the tip." Cade raised one brow in teasing speculation. Finn couldn't decide whether to laugh or crown him.

"Fictional beds," she said. But not fictional monsters, the thought stole in. Real monsters were in Cade's eyes, the kind of sad that comes from families with secrets.

"Did you ever see a bed bigger 'an that one?" The boy thrust a grubby finger at the construction paper creation on the wall. "Bet it's the biggest bed in the whole world."

"I've seen a bigger…" Finn started to answer automatically. "I mean I'm sure it's not the biggest…uh, Tommy, shouldn't your mom be here to pick you up?"

Most of the preschool parents stayed and shared the experience with their toddlers. This little towhead had been dropped off at the door by a whirlwind in chartreuse Capri pants and a midriff baring top.

"She gots to pick up my sister."

"Then maybe you can help me find Mr. McDaniel a book—" Finn shot him a warning glare.

"About beds." Tommy insisted.

"Trust me, I can handle my bed just fine, partner. I won't need an instruction manual when it comes time to…check under the covers."

Finn whacked him as Tommy bolted off to the bins filled with picture books.

Even with the child out of earshot, Cade leaned so close his warm breath feathered the sensitive skin of her neck. "The kid doesn't have a clue what we were talking about," he whispered.

"But his mother will when he heads home and recounts the whole conversation," Finn whispered back. "You want to get me fired?"

"Definitely not. I can speak for the whole McDaniel clan when I say that." His eyes warmed.

"Then why are you here?" she asked, still astonished to see him, curious, secretly pleased.

"The truth? Call me crazy. I… Hell, I spent the first few weeks after you moved in trying to avoid you. Now…guess I'm like the kids in the library. You're definitely growing on me…and not just because of the monster you left under my bed."

Finn laughed, a tingle of awareness delighting her at the sensual undercurrent in his words, and in the simmering heat in his eyes. "I'm quite sure I didn't leave anything under your bed," she insisted.

"Could've fooled me. After that night when you stayed, my pillow smelled like you. All flowery and fresh…like rain. The damned thing hasn't been the same since. Ms. O'Grady, do you believe in fantasy?"

She deliberately misunderstood him. "It's a children's librarian's job to encourage make-believe."

"That's a load off my mind, because I've got this bit of make-believe I'm hoping you just might encourage. When I was in high school I had a helluva creative imagination. I'd think about taking a girl back into the stacks—you know, those real dark corners where nobody ever goes and—"

"You wouldn't dare!" She ground the heel of her foot into his instep, but it was too late. His eyes glittered, telling her in no uncertain terms that he knew she was as turned on as he was, just thinking of his hands on her in the shadows.

"Oh, I was too scared of Verna to try it back then."

"I should hope so!"

Cade's gaze skimmed down her body. "Now, I'm still scared of Verna, but I figure you might just be worth taking a chance."

Taking a chance? What was he trying to tell her? Something more than teasing? Making her tingle in ways a librarian definitely should not be tingling while in charge of the children's room? She barely heard the rear entry door swing open.

"Well, well, well," purred the curvaceous blonde who'd dropped Tommy off an hour before, sashaying into the room. "Cade McDaniel in the library. If I hadn't seen it with my own eyes I never would have believed it."

The secret teasing vanished from Cade's eyes. He gave the newcomer a stiff nod. "Caro."

The hair at the back of Finn's neck prickled with dislike. Why? Because Tommy's mother was stunning? Or because of the way she looked at Cade? As if she knew every plane and hollow of his sexy-as-all-get-out body. Caro walked over to him and kissed his cheek.

"How's Tom?" Cade asked.

"Oh, Tommy's fine." She waved a vague hand toward the toddler in the corner.

"I meant your husband."

Caro shrugged an elegant shoulder. "He got promoted. Has to travel all the time. You should stop by, Magic. We could talk over old times. I'm head of the reunion committee and we would love to get some pictures to put on the invitations—past and present, you know. Who would be more fitting for those shots than the two of us? The football hero and the homecoming queen."

"I'm way past that stage of my life. Thank God," Cade said. "Have you met my new neighbor? Finn O'Grady."

The woman stared as if Finn had just appeared out of thin air. Caro extended a perfectly manicured hand, rings flashing. "We haven't officially met yet. I'm Caro Bates. Tommy and Brandi's mother. For a woman who just moved to Whitewater you've made quite a splash, Ms. O'Grady. People are still talking about that unfortunate incident with the fifth graders in the library a few weeks ago. It must have been so difficult for you."

Matched against Caro's creamy, perfect complexion, Finn felt like her freckles must be glowing like Rudolph's nose. "I'm just glad no one was badly hurt," she said.

"I still feel terrible about what happened with Emma. I suppose I should have watched her more carefully, considering…" She lay a proprietary hand on Cade's arm and fluttered her lashes. "Now, don't get all defensive, Cade. You know as well as I do what a handful Emma's mother was."

Cade's eyes narrowed. His temper sparked, dangerous. "You weren't exactly an angel yourself as I remember, so why don't we leave my sister out of this."

"You see how he is about that sister of his," Caro sighed, turning back to Finn. "Say one word about her and he turns into a regular pit bull. Maybe I should have thought twice about…well, doing a favor for an old friend. But I've never been able to deny Kincaid anything he asked for."

"Kincaid?" Finn's gaze flicked to Cade's. He glowered.

"It's his mother's family name," Caro supplied. "He hates it. When we were going steady I used to call him by it whenever I got mad. He does have a temper, you know. All the McDaniels do. When he called about Emma going missing, well…I'd never heard him that angry before."

Realization dawned on Finn. "You're the woman who was supposed to be taking care of Emma at the slumber party and lost her."

Caro gave one of those silvery laughs Finn had thought only existed in books. "It's something of a bad habit, I'm afraid," Caro said. "From the time we were in high school, I always seemed to lose things around Cade. Remember the time I lost my bikini top when we were skiing in the river? Not all I lost that day, was it Cade?"

"What day was that?" Cade asked, feigning boredom. "I spent my life on that river in high school. Don't remember anything in particular."

Caro thrust out her lower lip in a pretty pout. "No wonder I came to hate the place. Cade built this sailboat, but he'd only sail alone. Said there wasn't a woman on earth he'd take out on the river. He liked the quiet. Can you imagine? Why, if I hadn't lost my temper over the time he spent on that boat I might be Mrs. Kincaid McDaniel right now."

Finn felt a hot jab of something disturbingly like jealousy. In high school when Caro had been pushing her pom-poms, Finn had been working two jobs, determined to save enough to put herself through college. Dating had been what other girls did. Girls with real parents who bought them pretty dresses.

Caro smiled her toothpaste ad smile. "Finn…it *is* Finn, isn't it? Strange little name. I consider it my civic duty to fill you in on a piece of common knowledge since you're new in town. Don't break your heart by being drawn in by Kincaid's charm. He's one gun-shy man. Not that I can blame him, after the way his parents...well, you wouldn't know anything about that since you just moved here. And Cade wouldn't even share the most dreadful parts with people he loves."

"Caro, thanks for reminding me," Cade said. "I'd almost forgotten."

Finn felt the jealousy twist deeper, wondering what he was thinking of—Caro missing that bikini top, the glory of being a teenager, just discovering the mysteries of your own body or "the dreadful parts" of his family's past. Cade looked as if he could read Finn's mind.

"You know, I haven't taken that boat out in over a year," he said. "What do you say, Finn? Feel like getting to know the river?"

Finn felt as if he'd doused her with cold water. Oh, Lord! He was flashing that knock-'em-dead smile not at the perfect Caro Bates, but at *her*, neon freckles and all. "I've never been around water much," Finn stammered. "I don't swim very well and..." She glimpsed Caro's not-so-smug face. Suddenly drowning seemed a better choice than wimping out. Finn forced a smile. "I'd love to go."

Caro tossed her hair. Her mouth pinched with disgruntled lines. "Don't say I didn't warn you. Cade McDaniel isn't the marrying kind."

"Deirdre would agree with you on that one," Cade said. "Considering the women I dated."

Caro grabbed Tommy and swept out, the empty library silent, unnerving. Finn rubbed her palms on her skirt, feeling unsettled. "What a horrible woman." The truth slipped out. But Cade hadn't thought she was horrible, at least for a while. Caro Bates had all but said he'd taken her virginity. But then, he was a grown man, and not cut out to be some kind of monk. Not that his sex life was really any business of hers—past or present.

"So you, uh, played on the river as a kid?" Finn couldn't help asking.

"When things got rough at home I'd turn into some kind of modern day Tom Sawyer."

He was trusting her. She sensed just how hard it was for this intensely private man.

"It's so quiet out on the water, Finn. You know? So peaceful. Caro never did know when to shut her mouth."

Finn tucked a strand of hair behind her ear, the auburn hues suddenly seeming garish compared to Caro's locks of fairytale gold. "She's very pretty."

"If you like plastic. Everything about the woman is fake. Fake nails, fake eyelashes—and trust me, in high school she wouldn't have filled out her blouse half so generously without fist-size wads of cotton batting."

"But you almost married her?"

"Hell, no!" He looked so appalled Finn had to believe him. "It's damned embarrassing. But I guess you should never count on a sixteen-year-old guy with a hard-on being very discerning." He shook his head in disgust. "It didn't mean a damned thing."

He looked like it mattered to him—a lot—that she knew that. But then, hadn't he said Finn was a distraction when he'd kissed her the first time?

"I've never even gotten close to marrying anyone," Cade said. "I swore I'd never end up like my parents." A lifetime's worth of dread haunted his eyes.

"I know what you mean," Finn confessed. "Sometimes I'm scared of that myself. That I'll be like Da and never belong anywhere no matter how desperately I want to. That somehow, I won't be good enough to…I don't know, fit, I guess."

"That's ridiculous," Cade bit out, defensive as he'd been of Deirdre moments before. Finn's heart skipped a beat. "Any town would be lucky to have you. And now you've got the house. I've been thinking I'd like to keep helping you with the restoration since you've done so much to help Emma. And me."

Cade cocked his head, regarding her, suddenly solemn, reminding her of Emma's gaze, probing beneath layers of denial to where the pain lived, the doubts. "Finn, what's wrong? You look…sad all of a sudden. Tired. As if you're scared to…I don't know what."

She hadn't admitted her fears aloud to anyone. But somehow she knew Cade McDaniel would understand if she just had the courage to trust him with this, the most fragile part of herself. "Don't you see, Cade? This is it. The place where the rubber meets the road. Where I'll find out the truth about myself. Whether I'm strong enough to really put down roots. To *stay*."

"Of course you'll stay," Cade began, looking a little unnerved. Finn touched his arm, hushing him with the plea in her eyes.

"When your own parent rejects you, you figure there must be something ugly inside you," she continued. "Something wrong. You're dead sure that when the rest of the world figures out what it is they'll reject you, as well. Or maybe you're just so afraid of people seeing that—that fatal flaw that you run the instant you see doubts in their eyes when they look at you."

"If anyone is flawed it was your father. Not you. He was a fool not to treasure you the way you deserved," he said so gently it astonished her. "Hey, look at it this way. You're the first person I ever asked to go sailing with me. That has to count for something."

Her smile wobbled, nervousness and pleasure warring in the pit of her stomach. "I suppose so."

"Unfortunately, there's one small hitch in the plan. The boat leaked like a sieve the last time I took it out and I haven't had time to repair it."

"But you—you made it sound like…?"

"Something about the way Caro was treating you really ticked me off."

"Maybe you are crazy."

"Not really. If I close my eyes, I can see us together, the sails full, skimming through the waves. I can see you lifting your face into the wind, the way you do when you walk through the garden, or stand on the riverbank just as the sunset's turning the sky pink."

Finn flushed, remembering the times she'd done just what he described, wondering if Cade suspected she'd been thinking of him when she stood out there on the river bank. "How…how did you know…?"

"Like I said, you're growing on me, Finn O'Grady. I catch myself watching you. Listening for your laugh. When you're not around it's too quiet. Not the kind of quiet I used to crave. It's more…I don't know, peaceful, somehow, to have you around, hear your voice, watch your eyes shine. I've never felt that way around anyone before."

"I'm glad." Finn smiled into his eyes. "Listen, Cade, if we can't go sailing, what would you think of…of going on a treasure hunt?"

"Not many pirates on the Mississippi, I'm afraid."

"Not that kind of treasure. I'm going into the attic this Saturday, to see what's up there. The whole place is packed with things no one has bothered to move for a hundred years. I know Emma would be over the moon at the chance to paw through the trunks and boxes and such. I'd love it if you'd come, too."

"Thanks, Finn. For thinking of her. Knowing her. Trying so damned hard to find ways to make her smile. We'd almost forgotten how."

She wondered if he realized that he'd included himself in the last. She wanted him to smile. Wanted to make him laugh out loud. Wanted him to trust her enough to share the secrets that haunted his eyes. It was amazing. He'd lived in one town all his life, just like Finn had longed to. But his life hadn't been storybook perfect, either. At least, not *yet*. Hope fluttered to life inside her. Maybe children's librarians encouraged make-believe, but Cade made her long for something *real*.

"Finn…"

She loved the sound of her name on his lips, the way he looked at her now, mystified, wary, but warm. He cupped her face with his palm, his touch so warm, his eyes whispering secrets she knew he wasn't ready to admit even to himself.

Something was changing between them, greening like the shoots in her garden. Coming alive in a way that awed her, frightened her. Something as miraculous and fragile as the first blossoms in spring.

Something that might just be…love?

CHAPTER FOURTEEN

SUNSHINE SLANTED through the attic windows, setting dust motes sparkling like powdered gold. Emma glowed with the zeal of a treasure hunter who'd just discovered the mother lode as she ordered Cade to unearth yet another Civil War–era trunk from beneath the spiderweb strewn rafters.

He wrestled it out, amazed that he was spending Saturday afternoon cooped up in Finn's attic, and even more astonished that he was enjoying it. He'd shut off the tape in his head reminding him of the hundred and one things he needed to do. Did his best to focus on one little girl and whatever would put twinkles of pleasure into her eyes. But concentrating on Emma was no small feat with Finn whisking around the attic, bursting with an enthusiasm that made Cade ache, feel as if he could never get enough of watching her. Wanting her.

The booty from their two-hour excavation stood in a mound near the attic door, things Finn intended to use decorating the house beneath them—an old-fashioned rug beater, a copper teakettle thick with patina, an old linen apron dripping with a yard of handmade lace. And a squat wooden biscuit bowl, worn smooth inside from generations of making a family's bread.

Emma gave the woman no peace until Finn had promised to show her how bread rose and let her punch the dough, just like Addy did in that old journal. Cade smiled inwardly. Finn had broken his resolve about the journal over a plate of pasta when the three of them had gone to the elementary school's annual spaghetti supper. Not his usual way of romancing a woman, but Finn hadn't seemed to mind the mayhem one bit. And Emma had gained points among the other kids, being seen with the ever-more-cool new librarian.

Yes, the red leather journal was Emma's greatest treasure now, displayed with loving care on the nightstand beside her mother's picture. The kid was more obsessed with life in the 1860s than ever, but then, Cade was beginning to understand her temptation to travel back in time, at least in her imagination. Life in present day Whitewater hadn't been any great shakes for the girl.

But that was going to change, even if he had to dig through every spiderwebby trunk in three counties. He went down on one knee and attempted to tug it open, but the lid held firm.

"This one is locked," Cade announced, trying to pry the metal tongue out of the groove that latched the trunk closed. "We'll either have to find the key or get a professional to open this, otherwise we could damage the lock mechanism."

"Rats," Finn grumbled. "I've just got a feeling about this one. Bet it's something wonderful." She was so damned adorable his temperature jumped a notch.

"People only lock up treasures," Emma insisted, eyeing the trunk with a measured determination that tempted Cade to laugh. "If Jesse James was here, he'd stick dynamite in the lock and then hide and push down the plunger thing to blow it up just like on those Road Runner cartoons you like, Uncle Cade."

Finn raised one slender brow, smiling at Cade with her eyes.

"Yeah," Cade said, ridiculously pleased that he'd turned the kid on to his own favorite childhood cartoon during the past week. "Just one problem. There's never much left of Wile E. Coyote when they're done."

Emma considered for a moment, then shot him the most full-throttle grin he'd ever seen on her face. A damned miracle. Cade's chest hurt at his niece's courage. She'd taken giant steps, trusting him in ways he wasn't sure he would have had the guts to if the situation were reversed. And Finn had been a big part of that transition for both McDaniels.

It hadn't been easy making those changes, that much was damned sure. In spite of all his resolutions and Emma's best efforts, things between the two of them had been plenty uncomfortable during those first few nights after Emma's near-plunge in the river. Finding something they could do together and both enjoy proved one heck of a challenge until during an early morning race to find a fugitive tennis shoe he'd run across the scraps from his lucky shirt stuffed under her bed.

By the time Emma got home from school, he'd dug out the shoebox full of thread and stuff he kept on the top shelf of his closet. And after homework was done, he'd helped her patch together the pillow she wanted to make while they'd watched old cartoons together.

He still chuckled every time he remembered how awed she'd been as he demonstrated the sewing skills he'd learned stitching together canvas sails for his model ships and making repairs on his uniforms in the Air Force.

Finn thumped the heel of her hand against the trunk lid. "I guess we'll just have to be patient," Finn sighed, as disappointed as Emma was.

"No we won't! I almost forgot!" Emma enthused, her face suddenly brightening. "Give me a paper clip." Emma pointed to a stack of photographs someone had clipped together under the title "Old Settler's Reunion."

Cade exchanged a surreptitious smile with Finn as he handed the clip over, watched Emma straighten it ever so carefully—the artist about to work a masterpiece. Emma stuck the tip of her tongue out and caught it between her teeth, her dark eyes narrowing as she inserted the tip of metal wire into the tiny keyhole.

Of course, it was ridiculous—no way the kid was going to get the trunk open, but she looked so damned cute, a miniature outlaw in a pink polka-dotted dress and tousled black curls. Breaking into a treasure chest was something he might have tried twenty-five years ago.

"Maybe my mom didn't teach me to sew or make lemonade 'cept with powdery stuff," Emma said. "But she showed me how to do…this."

Click!

The mechanism sprung open, reminding Cade sharply of Deirdre's smugness the night she'd broken into the cabin, telling him his locks needed work. What had she said? That one of her boyfriends had taught her how to pick locks for fun?

What kind of man picked locks for fun? He tried to imagine the people Emma had been around, the lessons she could have learned in the kinds of dives Deirdre worked in, searching for that impossible dream. Anger heated his belly. Yeah, Emma didn't know how to make real lemonade, but the kid could probably tell you exactly how to put together a killer whiskey sour.

"Emma, you're a genius!" Finn raved, sweeping Emma into a hug. She danced the child around in a celebratory circle.

But it was Cade Emma turned to, glowing with hope, searching for approval. "Look, Uncle Cade! I opened the treasure!"

"That's great." He tried to hide his unease. Emma never could be fooled. He hated seeing the uncertainty in her eyes. But there was no point admitting to his reservations about this particular talent of Emma's and how she'd come by it. It wasn't as if his irresponsible sister was ever going to get the chance to teach the kid such dangerous things again.

Better to distract Emma with the trunk's contents. He hoped it was something cool for the kid—some Civil War bayonets or swords or something.

"Let's pop the top off this baby and see what's inside," he said. Emma fell for it, hard. He pinched together two metal tabs and the metal tongue popped free. Cade stepped back. "Go on, kiddo, you do the honors."

Finn slipped her hand in his and squeezed hard as Emma flung back the hammered tin lid. Emma gasped, Cade feared in disappointment. He'd wanted to discover something wonderful for both Emma and Finn, the need to please them marrow-deep in a way he hadn't felt since Deirdre was a bright-eyed little girl. But the trunk's content didn't look like much of a treasure to him. A bunch of old clothes, a crumbly wreath of some kind of dried flowers. There weren't even many interesting colors of cloth Emma could use for quilt blocks. Just oceans of foamy white lace, a thick, bumpy homemade-looking kind.

"There's bound to be something awesome in the attic somewhere," Cade reassured both of them. "We just have to keep on looking."

"Nothing could be more awesome than this!" Emma said. Delicately, as if she were picking sugar roses that might crumble at a touch, the little girl lifted the fragile flower crown out of the trunk, the wreath trailing a length of veil delicate as mist.

"Do you have any idea what this is, Uncle Cade?" Emma breathed. "This is Miranda's wedding dress!"

"Who?"

"Addy's sister," Emma supplied, turning to face him, glimpsing Finn's hand in his before Finn pulled away.

"I read about the wedding in Addy's journal," Finn offered, putting her hand almost guiltily behind her. "Miranda's betrothed was a cavalry officer from Virginia. He slipped through enemy lines and married her—"

"In that old gazebo by the river," Emma took over eagerly, "just like Miranda always wanted. It was nighttime and there were paper lanterns strung in the trees and they all pretended for just one night that there wasn't any war and they didn't have to choose sides. Addy said it was the happiest day in her whole life."

Just thinking about weddings had always made him twitchy as hell. But this time it was different. Still scary as hell, but scary in the same way he'd been just before he'd made his first HALO jump from a plane in boot camp. Yeah, Finnoula O'Grady gave him the same adrenaline junkie rush of a high-altitude, low-opening parachute jump. But there was no way he was ready to admit it to anyone but himself.

"Hmm." Cade grimaced. "I always knew love makes people do crazy things, but crossing enemy lines seems just plain stupid. Couldn't they have eloped on the other side of the border where the groom wasn't as likely to get a bullet in the back or a quick trip to prison as a wedding present?"

"Addy's mom wouldn't travel all that way. Lots of people in town were mad 'cause Addy's mom was from the South. Maybe she was scared they would burn up the house. Or maybe her mom was too sick. Addy got all worried 'cause her mom got real skinny and didn't sleep anymore and her eyes got real big in her face."

A faraway expression shadowed Emma's features, Cade's edgy awareness of Finn and weddings and love blessedly doused by anger at the knowledge Emma was worrying about Deirdre—the mother who hadn't even bothered to drop her a lousy postcard in almost two months.

"Grown-ups can take care of themselves," Cade said brusquely.

"Sometimes they don't do a very good job," Emma observed. "Kids have to help." She rummaged in the trunk, coming up with a dress so delicate an angel might have worn it.

"Finn, it really is Miranda's wedding dress! I know it is! See the thistles embroidered on the sleeves?"

"Thistles?" Cade echoed, determined to put the brakes on his all too vivid imagination. "I pulled plenty of those out of gardens when I took care of lawns as a kid—nasty, thorny, miserable weeds. You mean this Civil War chick put them on her wedding dress on purpose? Go figure. Maybe she had a more realistic view of marriage than most."

He wanted to remind himself exactly what he thought of the whole marriage bit. Expected at least some token protest at his cynicism from the woman who challenged everything he'd been so damned sure of. But Finn might as well not have heard him. Her face softened, a sweet flush sweeping her cheekbones as she brushed tender fingers over the embroidery. "Miranda's fiancé was born in Scotland. She wanted a touch of his home about the wedding, too."

"That's just like a woman." Cade grumbled, trying not to let that dreamy look of hers get into his head. He already spent half the night thinking about getting her in his bed. Adding forever to that was just plain crazy, wasn't it? "The man was already risking his life so she could have her wedding where she wanted it," he complained. "It's not as if the poor guy would give a damn about a bunch of eentsy-weentsy flowers stitched on sleeves."

"As a matter of fact, Angus loved it," Finn said, her lips more kissable than he'd ever seen them. "Miranda snipped one of the flowers off of the sleeve so he could take it with him when he went back to war. He kept it in a pocket over his heart."

"You know, I never got that whole knight thing. Getting tokens from their ladies fair, all those ribbons and such. Why didn't the ladies give their heroes something useful—like a really sharp pocketknife?"

Finn laughed and looked at him in a way that made him

wonder what she'd do if he slipped loose the bandana she'd used to keep the spiderwebs out of her hair.

"With the war and all, it would have been a big deal for Miranda to sew a new dress, especially one so fine," Finn said, dreams dancing in her eyes. "Addy tells in her journal how Miranda stitched on those sleeves all through the winter."

She closed her eyes, running her fingertips over the sleeves, searching them by touch. Cade wanted her fingers on him. Imagined them learning him by touch, searching…for what? A way into his heart? But there wasn't any, was there? At least he hadn't thought so until Finn had swept into his life.

"I can't imagine the hours it took to embroider this, and then just to—yes! Here it is!" Her eyes fluttered open, her face glowing the way it did when he'd just kissed her. She took Emma's fingers, traced the outline of a square. "Can you feel where she patched the hole cutting Angus's scrap made?"

Emma glowed, nodding until her curls bounced. "Uncle Cade, feel it!" Emma grabbed his hand, shoved it down atop Finn's, only the layer of fabric between their palms. Sensation rippled through him, so intense it terrified him, touching Finn O'Grady through a wedding gown a hundred and fifty years old.

The cloth was so thin he could almost see his fingers through it. Women back in that time had bundled themselves up from chin to toes, everything about their bodies wrapped in mystery. What would it have been like for a man back then, to see pink shadows of his lover's arm, the shape of it, the smoothness? A soldier, gone away so long, far from the soft, beautiful things in life? Not missing just any woman, but the *one* woman he loved?

Cade doubted there would have been any rolling around on the floor with a proper Victorian lady, the way he and Finn had, the desperate touching, the hot kisses, yet…had passion really changed that much? Or had it always been that way when a man wanted to lose himself in a woman so badly his whole body burned with the need? Not *a* woman. *His* woman. A feeling of possession Cade had made damned certain he'd never known.

He kept his face averted from Emma's gaze and Finn's, trying to hide the emotions rocking through him. Taking his time tracing the tiny stitches where a woman had mended the fabric, where she'd willingly cut into something she'd loved so a man could carry a piece of her with him. It was crazy, cutting a hole in something like a sleeve. No easier to mend so it didn't show than the holes Emma had cut in his favorite flannel shirt.

But this woman had cut her wedding dress on purpose. Hell, she could've snipped off a bit of the hem, or a strip of fabric from the inside-out part of the dress, someplace where it wouldn't have shown. But she'd cut the best part—the part she'd worked longest on, hardest on, dreamed over during countless firelit nights. It was just the sort of crazy, loving thing Finn O'Grady would do if she loved a man. *If she loved him,* a whisper tantalized Cade.

"I wish we could make a wedding," Emma said longingly.

"What?" Cade started as if the kid had slipped ice down his shirt. He hooked a finger in his collar, tugging at it. The top button was still unfastened. Why did it suddenly feel like he was choking.

"You mean *go* to a wedding, don't you, sweetheart?" Finn amended, looking almost as flustered as he was.

"No. You could be the bride and Uncle Cade could be the groom and I could wear a dress with a blue sash and be Addy."

Cade stiffened. He should've seen this coming. The kid wanted a mother and who'd make a better one than Finn? He wanted to protect the kid from disappointment. And yet, if he was honest, hadn't he just been thinking of Finn in that blasted white dress? He swallowed hard. The hell with being honest. "Emma, marriage is a real serious business. And Finn and I—well, we're…just friends…"

Yeah, buddy? A voice mocked him inside his head. *When's the last time a friend gave you kisses so hot your hair should've caught on fire?*

Finn must've been thinking the same thing. Her cheeks grew redder than a stop light.

"Uh, *special* friends," he amended, feeling like an idiot.

"Weddings are lots of fun," Finn intervened. "But they're kind of like Christmas. You just have to wait until one comes up. People have to fall in love and—and— You can't make that happen even if you want to." She faltered, glancing at Cade, hastily tearing her gaze away. His heart thudded hard against his ribs. *Even if you want to?*

Emma made a face. "I know that. I'm not stupid. I didn't say I wanted to *have* a wedding. I said I wanted to *make* one."

Cade and Finn traded bewildered looks. "I'm not getting this," Cade said. "You want to explain the difference?"

"You know. Make a pretend wedding, like you were Miranda and Angus and I was Addy. It would be so pretty with the lanterns in the tree and we could bake a cake and dress up in all the old clothes and it would just be the most amazing, wonderful thing that ever happened in my whole life!"

Cold sweat prickled the back of Cade's neck. "You're ten. Believe me, something better than a make-believe wedding is bound to come along."

"Maybe. But you don't know for sure," Emma wheedled, looking too wise for her own good. "What if I'm right? What if this is the best thing that will ever happen to me? And what if I miss it?"

Damn the conniving little Captain clone! She was getting to be as dangerous as her grandfather when he wanted something!

"You won't miss it," Finn tried to mediate. "Maybe a wedding is a little extreme, but you and I could dress up and have a bridal tea. A pretend bridal tea," she clarified. "Think of the fun we could have."

"I am thinking about the fun I could have. *Making a wedding.*" Emma flashed him the Big Eyes. Hell, the Air Force should have a weapon that convincing. "Please, Uncle Cade. All you'd have to do is stand there most of the time. Men don't do anything at weddings anyway. The girls do all the fun stuff."

Cade knew just how Wile E. Coyote felt when he was hanging on to the edge of a cliff by his fingernails. He was slipping and Emma hadn't even brought out the big guns yet. Meet Finn O'Grady in a wedding dress, pretend or not? That would be just plain crazy. Wouldn't it? "If men don't do anything at weddings why do you need me at all?" he asked. "Can't you just pretend a groom and be done with it?"

She sidled over to him, slipping her small hand in his. She was a true McDaniel. Show no mercy. Cade peered down at her, his throat suddenly tight.

"You promised you'd do whatever it takes to make me your little girl. Sometimes dads have to play silly stuff with their kids. It's a rule."

The corners of Cade's mouth twitched in spite of himself. "Yeah? And exactly where did you find this rule?"

"Ask any kid. They'll tell you." Emma's bravado faded, and she suddenly looked uncertain. "But maybe you shouldn't have to do silly stuff. You didn't get to be my dad on purpose."

"I'm not your dad. I'm your uncle." *Yeah, an uncle who missed five years of her life. What's the big deal about playing some game of make-believe if the kid wants to? If it will make Emma happy?*

Oh, it could be a big deal all right—pretending to marry Finn O'Grady. There was something about the woman that scrambled a man up inside, made him question decisions he'd made years ago to charge on through life, unencumbered, free of chains, responsibility, a family, children.

"The dress probably won't even fit." Finn tried to come to his rescue. "People in the 1860s were much smaller than we are. Emma and I read it in one of the books we found on Civil War life, didn't we, sweetheart?"

"Yeah. They got malnutrition," Emma supplied. "It's not like they could pick up fresh fruit and vegetables at the grocery store." She paused, and Cade could almost hear the gears in that little brain of hers steaming.

"How about if I make you a deal, Uncle Cade?" she asked sweetly.

"A deal?"

"If the dress fits Finn, you play wedding. If it doesn't, I won't bug you about it anymore. Cross my heart." She drew a giant *X* on her chest.

Cade glanced at Finn, weighing his chances. From what Madam Librarian had said, the chances of the dress fitting were slim. *I hope to hell you're as good at this research stuff as you are at kissing,* he thought.

"Okay. It's a deal." Why the heck was Emma grinning like that cat in the *Alice in Wonderland* movie she'd watched about three zillion times? The eternal optimism of youth? She'd be crushed when she lost this inning, but he'd find some way to make it up to her.

Cade extended his hand to shake on it, but Emma shook her head. "Cross your heart," she insisted. Cade rolled his eyes, drawing an *X* on his shirtfront.

"Repeat after me," Emma said officiously. "I, Uncle Cade, swear to do what Emma wants if this really teensy old wedding dress fits Finn, no matter what."

Cade repeated, solemn faced.

"You look mighty sure of yourself, young lady," Finn said.

"Yeah, well, the Captain taught me poker and I figure I've got better than average odds the dress'll fit. Addy says her sister's the tallest girl in all of Whitewater."

"Hey, wait a minute!" Cade exclaimed, something like panic flaring in his chest as he glared at his niece. "That's not fair!"

"Don't worry, Cade. Tall is one thing. But I'm sure I'm too…well, curvy, to fit the bodice."

Cade couldn't keep his gaze from flicking down to Finn's breasts. Curvy, hell. He knew just how lushly those soft globes filled his hands. Maybe she was right. Finn looked as if she was remembering his fingers measuring the sweet curves. Cade tried to steel himself against the inevitable stirring of arousal.

Hell, think of something, anything to distract himself… multiplication tables, backwards. The periodic table from the chemistry lab in high school….

Finn slipped behind an old folding screen, Emma bounding after to help with buttons and laces or whatever a dress like that used for fasteners. He turned his back to the screen, the rustling sounds of Finn undressing doing little to get his mind out of the bedroom.

He'd be lying if he said he hadn't imagined those sounds plenty of times before, but in his fantasy he'd been the one helping Finn peel away layers of clothing, not his niece.

Long minutes later, he heard a whoop of triumph, Emma dancing out to him, her face aglow.

"I win!" She howled. She batted thick lashes so innocently Cade couldn't help laughing. "Who would'a thought?"

"You," Cade said, remembering what this kid's bloodlines were. He should've known better. But no. Here he stood, fleeced by a pint-size pirate with the best poker face he'd ever seen. No way around it now. He was going to be face-to-face with Finn in an antique wedding gown. At least he'd get part of the bridegroom thing right. He'd spent plenty of time concentrating on what he'd do to her luscious body the first night he made love to her. Not that he'd figured it would be a wedding night. Even a pretend one.

"The Captain says you should always know the odds before you place a bet," Emma interrupted his wayward imagination.

Great, Cade thought. She could pick locks and win at gambling. Those were terrific life skills for a ten-year-old girl. But she could also smile up at him like he'd hung the moon.

"Never say I don't admit when I'm beat," he said, ruffling her curls. "Remind me never to play cards with you."

"We can make the wedding when I start summer vacation! It'll be like a big celebration. Getting out of school."

The last shades of Cade's fantasies about Finn melted away as he detected a wistful note in Emma's voice. He knew Emma couldn't wait to get away from the daily reminder that she didn't fit in. He wished there was something he could do about it. He'd felt a flicker of hope at the spaghetti supper, Finn drawing the kids around Emma with that charm even the toughest bullies found hard to resist. But Emma was going to have to build on that herself, get up the nerve to try.... Whoa, flyboy, put the brakes on, he told himself. Do what Finn told you to and let Emma handle it her own way, in her own time. Last time he'd tried to push the poor kid into Whitewater's Elementary School social scene had been a complete disaster. But maybe if he just gave her a nudge, put the controls in Emma's hands.

"Maybe you could invite one of the girls from school," he suggested. Was he out of his mind? He'd already agreed to make a complete fool out of himself in front of Finn for the kid. Not to mention skating on thin ice with his own unruly emotions where the woman was concerned. And now he was suggesting an even bigger audience to blab the tale of this pretend wedding all over Whitewater? The guys at the hangar would never let him hear the end of it.

"Invite kids from school to my party? They wouldn't come."

"There's got to be some other girl who'd like to make a wedding. I mean, if you think it's so cool."

"I think that's a great idea, Cade," Finn called from behind the screen. "Jenny Johnson checks out thick books packed with history just like you do, Emma. I'll bet she'd jump at the chance to dress up in antique clothes like the ones in *Little Women* if you asked her."

"Umm." Emma scrunched her lips together, and Cade could feel her tightening up inside. Afraid—afraid that he'd force her hand, turn the pressure up to high and ruin everything. Rejection was an ugly thing to risk, even for a grownup. And Emma had suffered the harshest rejection of all—from her own mother.

"This inviting a friend thing is just a suggestion," Cade said. "It's your call, Emma. Only do it if you want to."

"Okay." Emma searched his face as if trying to decide if he really meant it. Whatever she saw there helped her relax, at least a little.

Back in jeans and a T-shirt, Finn emerged from behind the screen, the bandanna abandoned, her cheeks pink, her eyes soft, shy in a way he'd never seen them.

Cade felt a rush of sensation under his rib cage, reached for humor, wanting to make both Finn and Emma smile. "I'm amazed you've got the nerve to show your face out here, lady, after helping the kid sucker me into this wedding deal. I thought you were supposed to be some top-of-the-line research librarian. So much for the accuracy of all those books you read on Civil War life."

"Research usually focuses on the norm," Finn said, chagrinned. "There will always be exceptions."

"And you're one of them," Cade said truthfully. "In more ways than I can count."

She'd shattered all his expectations, his preconceptions. Shaken up his world and left him bewildered. He'd spent a lifetime in a family with secrets. Always wondering what lurked behind masks. He'd never known anyone as real as Finn, her heart wide-open, her eyes so honest a man couldn't stop himself from trusting her.

But he'd trusted before—blindly, adoringly—only to discover that everything he'd ever believed in was a lie. A lie that had come to light because of him. *I didn't know! I didn't mean to*—

The age-old protest rose up inside him. But he was old enough now to know the excuses didn't matter. The consequences were the same.

"Cade?" Finn called him back from the waves of guilt rising inside him, tightening the muscles in his shoulders, creasing his face.

Her face swam into focus, and he felt a fierce need to gather her into his arms, wash himself clean in her sweet, healing embrace. Love, so freely given. How did she do it? He wondered. After her father had deserted her? When she'd been bounced from foster home to foster home, never having a place to call her own? Why wasn't she bitter? Suspicious? Why hadn't she built protective walls around the vulnerable places in her heart?

Why hadn't she given up?

The question staggered him, a sucker punch from out of nowhere, setting his gut burning. Is that what he'd done, all those years after his world had fallen apart? Given up?

Cade McDaniel a quitter? No, he'd just chosen to take control of his own life. Put your happiness in someone else's hands? A man might as well jump out of a plane with a parachute bought at the Goodwill store.

But why should Finn trust anyone after what her father had done to her? Maybe it was a question of simple courage. Who would've thought that this slip of a librarian could teach a breakneck flyboy what it meant to be brave?

"Cade?" Finn said again, a worried edge to her voice.

"Don't worry, Finn," Emma piped up. "I bet I know why he got all quiet. He's feeling left out. I mean, it looks like you and me are getting to do all the fun stuff with the wedding and all."

Cade's face burned. "I'm not quiet. I was just thinking."

"I'm thinking, too." Emma dove back into the trunk. "The next thing we've got to do is find something for you to wear, Uncle Cade."

"No. No way!" Cade objected. He'd agreed to play wedding. Surely that was sacrifice enough. Unfortunately sometimes God had a really nasty sense of humor.

"Don't worry, something awesome just has to be in here." Emma practically tipped headfirst into the trunk like a magician's assistant about to disappear. "If Miranda saved her wedding dress, she must've saved Angus's clothes, too."

"I wouldn't count on finding the uniform," Finn warned. "Remember, the Confederates lost. Whatever Angus wore must've gotten pretty ratty."

"Yeah," Cade agreed, relieved at the idea. "Trust me, kid. I know how men think. He would've tossed his uniform at the end of the war."

"Like you tossed that raggy flannel shirt I cut up?"

Cade winced. Point well taken. He still hadn't been able to throw the shirt away. He'd shoved the damned thing in the back of his closet.

Emma dug into the trunk again, coming up with a mass of gray wool. Cade's heart sank as she shook out a coat in Confederate gray. Hell, his neck was starting to itch just looking at the thing. But there was something intriguing about seeing something this close up that had survived a hundred and forty-odd years and a war that had torn the country apart.

Divided it, just like his family had been.

But finding the thing interesting and wanting to truss himself up in it and go out in public were two completely different things.

Emma's triumph faded as she held the coat up toward Cade. "Oh, no!" she wailed. "Why'd you have to be so—so big? This thing will never fit!"

She was right. Thank God.

But the kid's credo was Never Surrender. "I've got an idea! Maybe if we cut the coat right up the back and sew a piece of cloth in we can make it stretch."

Finn snatched the jacket out of Emma's hands as if she was afraid the kid might whip a pair of scissors out of her pocket and start hacking away. "This is an historical artifact," she said in a stern librarian voice that was downright adorable, not to mention more than a little sexy. "We are not cutting up an original Civil War uniform, young lady. Not even for the wedding of the century!"

Emma's face fell.

"I'll just wear a suit," Cade said, grateful for his narrow escape. "I would have looked like an idiot in that kind of getup anyway."

"You would've looked dashing!" Emma mourned.

"Dashing? Where the…where did you come up with a word like that? You're a kid, for God's sake!"

"I collect chewy words I read in books. But the other kids look at me real strange when I try to use them."

"You just keep right on using them, sweetheart," Finn said, giving her hand a squeeze.

Emma gave him the once-over. "You know you really are handsome, Uncle Cade. For an old guy."

"Thanks a lot. I think."

Emma turned her gaze to her partner in crime. "Don't you think he's handsome, Finn?"

For a heartbeat, Finn faltered, her lashes dipping to hide those too honest eyes. Eyes he'd seen heat up when he'd kissed her. She liked his face, his body just fine. No question. But what would she feel if he let her see past them, to the inside where the ugly parts hid?

Did she sense his self-doubts? She gave him a playful shove. "Move over, Mel Gibson. It really is too bad the uniform doesn't fit. Emma's right, you know. You're perfect for the role of a Civil War soldier, stealing through enemy lines."

Cade's imagination flared with fantasies of another kind. Maybe dressing up in costume wasn't his thing. But undressing Finn when she was in costume—that was a game he'd enjoy. Jett had embarrassed the hell out of his wife at dinner one time when he'd told Cade about the anniversary present he'd given her one year, raiding the costume department to surprise her.

She always said she fantasized about being ravished by a sexy pirate, Jett had teased unmercifully. *So I turned up with my cutlass drawn ready to board her.*

Cade imagined carrying Finn to bed, his hands fumbling with the strings of one of those corset things, trying to free her breasts so he could taste them. An uncomfortable tightness spread across the front of Cade's jeans, and this time even multiplication tables couldn't cool him down. Appalled, he fought to keep from embarrassing himself in front of Emma. He grabbed Finn's bandanna, holding it oh-so-casually in front of the fly of his jeans.

"I'll look perfect dressed in a suit," he insisted, trying to think of something, anything, except Finn all trussed up and eager beneath him. "I leave the acting to Jett."

"Jett?"

"Uncle Cade makes planes for movies and stuff. He's friends with Jett Davis."

Finn gaped at him. "The Jett Davis I saw with an Oscar in his hand just last year?"

Cade shrugged. He made it a habit not to talk about his relationship with Jett. People would either try to pry out secrets from the poor guy's private life or they'd think Cade was trying to play big man himself. But now that Emma had brought the subject up, there wasn't much he could do to dodge it.

"Jett keeps his Oscar in the bathroom," Cade said, trying to make light of the whole thing. "That way anyone who goes in there can pick it up and practice their acceptance speech in front of the mirror."

Finn laughed. Cade wondered what she'd make of Jett and his family—if she'd see past the fame and wealth to the truly decent people beyond.

The Jett who never took anything too seriously. Except his family. Cade had never known a guy so crazy in love with his wife and his little boy. And now Jett had a baby daughter. Cade remembered painting her name on Jett's plane. *My Alyssa.*

Envy stung, surprising Cade. He'd rarely felt jealous of his friend before—not of his success, his wealth, not even of his world-class collection of vintage airplanes. He'd just felt lucky to be able to help restore them, and to have Jett's blessing to fly them whenever he got the urge.

But there was no way to borrow Jett's home life, his children's squeals of delight when Daddy came through the door, his wife's adoration, the soul-deep love and trust in her eyes.

Cade never imagined he could even want to see those emotions in a woman's face. Until Finn…

But what if Jett's wrong about this happily ever after stuff? What if I've been right all along?

The thought killed the last of his hard-on like a splash of ice water.

Hell, am I capable of opening myself up that way even if I wanted to? Cade wondered. *Leaving myself open for the kind of heartache I saw in my mother's eyes?*

And yet, hadn't his mother been the one who had crossed enemy lines?

"All this wedding stuff is making me hungry," Emma said, closing the trunk with a thump.

"You don't want to keep looking around here anymore?" Finn asked.

"Maybe later. But not today. I already climaxed."

Cade's head jerked toward the kid, he heard Finn's soft gasp. "You what?" he said.

"You know. Climaxed. Don't you know what that means?"

He knew, all right. Maybe he hadn't followed his little fantasy to the end a few minutes ago, but he had no delusions he would've finished it off in his head later that night, once he got Emma to sleep and lay alone in his bed.

"The climax is the best part," Emma explained, as patiently as if he was the school dunce. "Like in a story. It would just get boring and ruin things if it kept going too long. Today's like that, too. We already found the treasure."

Embarrassment faded, Emma's childish wisdom sinking in.

We already found the treasure.

Her words echoed through him.

Maybe, Cade thought, just maybe Emma was right. Question was—what was he going to do about it?

"Hey, kid, how about starting to carry some of the stuff we found down the stairs?" he suggested.

"Will you feed me when I get to the bottom?"

"You bet."

Emma scooped up an armful, and headed down, her curly

dark head disappearing in the stairwell. Finn started to follow suit, bending down for the wooden batter bowl.

"Wait." The request sounded urgent even to his own ears.

She tilted her head to one side, giving him that look that unnerved him, as if she were listening, really listening, instead of doing what most people did—trying to think of what they had to say next.

"What is it?" she asked. "Are you worried about what Emma just said? Don't. She has no idea…about what the word might mean to you and me." Finn flushed. "I mean, to any grown-up."

"I figured that out. She did have me thinking there for a minute, though."

"I'll bet." Wicked twinkles lit up green eyes.

"Listen, I was wondering. Maybe you'd like to go out to dinner next Saturday."

She grinned. "You know I love eating dinner with you and Emma." It had gotten to be a habit lately, sharing dinner, sharing laughter, sharing plans for this Godzilla of a house.

"I want to take you someplace where the food doesn't come in a Happy Meal bag." Cade felt his face heat.

Finn brushed a wisp of hair off of her cheek with the back of her hand. "Oh, Cade! Emma would love that! I can't wait to tell her!"

"She's not invited. Not this time." He shoved his hands in his jean pockets, feeling as awkward as a teenager. "I'm asking you for a date."

"A date?" Finn echoed.

"I mean…an official date. You and me." He'd been damned careful not to call the time they'd spent together lately dates. Not that it had changed that butterflies-in-the-stomach kind of anticipation he'd felt every time he knew he was going to see her.

He waited as she nibbled at her lower lip. It was never good news when it took a woman this long to answer.

"I'd like that," she finally said. "But I don't know if it's such a good idea. Emma's just getting settled and it might confuse her. Make her hope…well, you know. Maybe we should take our time. Think about it."

"I have been thinking about it. About us." Us. The word felt right on his tongue. She peered up at him, and he could see images of their roll in the drop cloths reflected in Finn's eyes.

"About us, Finn. Together. Not just sex."

"Oh." She swallowed hard. And he would've bet his pilot's license she'd been thinking about him plenty, too.

"This is the part where you say yes, you'll go out with me."

Her lashes fluttered. He weighed his chances of kissing her into saying yes. But before he could move she gave him a nervous smile.

"All right. Yes."

Cade grinned, figuring he could try the kiss later. "I'll pick you up at six."

"Great."

She started to turn away, try to hide her sudden discomfort. He wasn't ready to let her go just yet. He caught her arm, loving the feel of her under his palm.

"Hey, Finn?"

"Yeah."

Cade couldn't resist running his thumb along the tender skin of her inner arm. Her breath tripped, her eyes dark with desire locking with his.

"You've got great legs. I wouldn't mind if you wore something that shows them off on Saturday."

"I suppose I can dig something out of all those boxes stacked in the hall."

"I'll make you glad you did."

Hell with waiting to kiss her. He could hear Emma downstairs, plundering Finn's cookie jar. He was hungry for something sweet himself, and Saturday was still a long way off.

He curved a finger under Finn's chin, saw her eyes widen, her lips tremble. He brushed a kiss across her lips, exploring them with a soft, slow heat.

Sensation speared through him. She tasted like summer. Like sunshine. Like hope. And he could feel her, lighting him up inside where the darkness stayed.

Stop. You have to stop.

His instincts flared, his head clearing just enough to get a grip on things—the sounds of Emma a floor below, the delicious feminine hills and valleys of Finn's body, ready, so damned ready to melt into his.

She moaned as he drew away, ever so carefully, as if he feared she might break.

But she wasn't the one in trouble here. Much more of a taste of her and he knew exactly what would shatter.

His own self-control.

"Saturday." He promised. He wasn't sure which one of them. No doubt this was going to be the longest week of his life. But he didn't know if that was a good thing or a bad thing.

He'd have time.

Time to second-guess. To think. To drive himself crazy wondering if he was just plain losing his mind.

Or if he was losing something far more dangerous to Finnoula O'Grady.

His heart.

CHAPTER FIFTEEN

FINN JUMPED as the grandfather clock in the hall chimed five-forty-five, fifteen minutes until Cade would arrive. Eyeing her reflection in the full-length mirror for the tenth time in an hour, she tried to smooth an imaginary wrinkle out of the green satin sheath she'd bought on a dare at an upscale Chicago boutique. She'd been shopping with a cluster of library aides when centerfold gorgeous Belinda Tucker had waylaid her. "Every woman needs a dress that makes her feel irresistible," the younger woman had claimed. Finn figured she was right.

Not that Finn had ever actually worn the dress. But she hadn't been able to bear taking it back, either. Looking at herself now, she could see why. The gown fit her in a way that made her cheeks heat, the silky fabric clinging to her breasts, the neckline dipping low. The rich green hue warmed her fair skin to alabaster and made her eyes shine like a dew-kissed Irish glen. While beneath a hem far more daring than she'd ever worn before, her legs seemed to go on forever in their fine silk stockings.

It was true, she'd nearly shipped the dress off to the Goodwill when she'd packed her apartment to move to Whitewater. But in the end, she hadn't been able to do it, the dress a slightly guilty secret tucked away with what had once seemed only hopelessly romantic dreams.

Yet, now that Cade McDaniel had charged into her life…

At the thought of Cade's bold stare, Finn's hand fluttered up to the hint of cleavage exposed by the dress's neckline.

"Is this going too far?" Finn asked the woman staring back at her, a worried cast to her mascara-clad eyes. Finn glanced at her bed, strewn with other outfits, tried and discarded. Full skirts and soft, creamy blouses. Dresses so summery and flowing that they would've been perfect for a garden tea.

No question she would have felt far more comfortable in one of them. Something easier to keep in place, to hide from the frank appraisal of Cade McDaniel's potently male gaze. But in all Finn's wardrobe, only this dress did what Cade had asked, showing off the legs he'd called great.

A shiver of pleasure rippled through Finn. She'd never thought her legs were anything special until Cade had complimented them in that rich, sexy tone. But now that she noticed, they were kind of nice. Long and softly curved, with fine-boned ankles and small feet.

Just thinking about him looking at her in this dress, his eyes hot, their lids heavy, started her body tingling beneath the sheer cups of her prettiest bra. A feathery sensation that kept right on traveling down her midriff, past her navel, to dip beneath the wicked red ribbon that darted in and out around the top of the garter belt and panties that had never seen the outside of her drawer. She still blushed when she remembered the day she'd received them, a not-really-funny gag gift from the same library aide who'd browbeaten her into buying the green dress.

It had been her birthday when Belinda presented her with a mysterious cotton candy–pink and white striped box in the staff break room. Delighted and surprised at the gift, Finn had opened it in the midst of the lunchtime crowd.

"Every woman needs a pair of fuck me panties," Belinda had insisted, laughing as Finn shoved the lingerie back into the tissue before anyone else could see them. "Even if you just keep them in your drawer."

Finn stammered. "I'm sure a lovely young girl like you gets plenty of use out of something like this. But since I haven't even gone out on a date in over a year…"

Belinda had regarded her with a critical eye. "You're not exactly ancient, you know. Bet you could look pretty hot if you made a little effort. Wear something so a man could see that you actually *have* a nice body. You've got to be prepared. Never can tell when Mr. Sexy Man might come along and turn your burner on high. And even if that doesn't happen, they'll make you feel gorgeous all on their own."

Belinda had been right about that much, Finn had reasoned as she'd eased the wisp of black lace over her hips. Even if Cade didn't see them, they'd make Finn feel prettier, more confident, wouldn't they? And if they did get…well, carried away…

She moistened her lips at the picture flickering across her imagination, Cade's blue eyes narrowing as he hooked his thumbs beneath the ribbon waistband, sliding the panties down the curve of her bottom, baring what lay beneath the fragile barrier.

Not that she planned to seduce him or anything. She just wanted to feel feminine down to her very toes. Elegant, for once, instead of cute, sexy instead of wholesome.

Yet she couldn't deny that when she and Cade were alone together, they tended to lose control.

Finn pressed a hand to her tripping heart. "What if this dress is too much? What if Cade shows up in jeans and a nice shirt? What if I look ridiculous?"

But there wasn't time to change even if she wanted to. She could hear someone driving up to the house. Not the customary rumble of Cade's truck, a richer sound, deeper.

Moments later, a knock sounded at the door, its distinctive rhythm as familiar now as Cade's voice. Her hand flitted to her hair one last time, tucking a stray curl back into the tousled chignon she'd managed to scoop her hair into.

She sucked in a deep breath as she crossed to the door, then flung it open. "Hi!" she said, forcing a confident smile. But it died on her lips as Cade turned toward her, a bouquet of spring flowers in his hand, delphiniums and daisies and fragrant white stock.

"Whoa," he drawled, low, his eyes roving over her so intimately Finn felt as if he'd skimmed her with those strong, tanned hands. "You trying to drive me crazy in that dress? You're gonna make it mighty hard to keep my mind on getting us to the restaurant on time."

Finn flushed with pleasure, smoothing the front of the sheath with hands suddenly unsteady. "I was afraid this would be too dressy. I guess not."

Cade seemed like a stranger—nothing at all like the man she'd come to know, his well-worn jeans, comfortable boots, shirts unbuttoned beneath the hollow in his muscular throat as if he couldn't bear to be closed in, even by something as soft as a flannel collar.

Tricked out in his navy blue suit he looked perfect all right, just like he'd told Emma when the three of them had been rummaging in March Winds' attic. Although perfect was a pretty bland adjective, when it came to Cade McDaniel at the moment. Mouthwateringly sexy. Primal. Ruthlessly masculine in a way that made everything woman in Finn melt.

"You look wonderful," Finn stammered. "I never expected—"

"That I actually owned something better than—what did Emma call it? My ratty lucky shirt?"

"If you wanted to make an impression, it worked. You look…so different."

That was the understatement of the year. The suit might have been made to order by one of Jett Davis's tailors, it fitted Cade's muscular body so exactly. The jacket skimmed without a ripple across his broad shoulders, the knife-blade creases in his pants making his long, powerful legs sexier than ever.

A cotton shirt so white it all but blinded Finn gleamed, crisp against his tanned throat, a silk tie the shade of lapis lazuli setting his eyes burning blue as the heart of a flame.

"Want to put these in water?" he asked, thrusting the bouquet toward her, a little sheepish. "I saw them in the florist window on the way to drop Emma off at the Captain's. I thought they looked like you. All fresh and sunny. Maybe some of those deep red roses would have been better after all." His eyes went smoky beneath thick lashes and she knew he'd left sunshine and lemonade behind and was imagining sultry summer nights and skin too hot to even bear the touch of sheets.

"No!" Finn insisted, weak-kneed. "These are beautiful. Exactly the kind of flowers I love." She placed them in a cream-colored ironstone pitcher filled with water. Trying to get her thundering heart back under control, she retrieved her beaded bag from the couch.

Cade offered her his arm, leading her out to yet another surprise in the driveway.

Finn felt as if she'd just stepped back into an old Cary Grant movie as Cade opened the door to some kind of vintage Porsche. She'd never seen a more beautiful car, top down, its white hood flaring, rich, deep accents of chrome gleaming as if it was only minutes from the showroom instead of God knew how many years old.

"Where's your truck?" she asked, struck completely off balance.

"At home." He shrugged, and her mouth went dry as the

silky ends of his freshly cut dark hair brushed the white of his collar. "I only take this out on special occasions."

Finn's pulses fluttered as she jack-knifed herself into the car, remembering why she never bought clothes with hems above the knee. The clinging green sheath rode up her thighs, all but showing the tops of her stockings as she maneuvered herself into seats that seemed to sit mere inches above the road.

Cade whistled, low, didn't even bother to pretend he wasn't looking at the wisp of black lace slip that crept out beneath the hem of her dress.

After getting her settled, he strode around to the driver's seat and slipped into the car, as if he were a foot sliding into a well-worn boot. It fit him—the rosewood steering wheel under the curve of his strong hands, the leather of seats that seemed to glove his big body to perfection.

Sexy. Dangerous. Unique with a kind of Humphrey Bogart flair. He surprised her, and yet, seeing him in the vintage car, in his elegantly tailored clothes—it all somehow made sense. A side of Cade Finn had never expected.

He started the engine, whisking them onto the road. Finn wondered where he was taking them as the Porsche ate up the miles. The whole town would be talking about this date of theirs come Monday. Anyone this dressed up in Whitewater's simpler restaurants would be sure to draw plenty of gossip.

"You okay?" he asked, glancing over at her across the small space that separated them. "It's not like you to be this quiet."

That's because every time I look at you I can't think of anything to say that doesn't sound like complete drivel, Finn thought.

"Sorry," she said. "I guess it just feels strange. You know. To be going somewhere together without Emma."

"Mind if we agree not to talk about Emma tonight?"

"I suppose not." Terrific. They hadn't even gotten to the restaurant and he was putting the one subject that might have distracted her offbounds.

"I want to use this time to get to know you better," Cade said. "And maybe you'd better get to know me before…" He stopped, his intense gaze flicking to her face for an instant from the road rushing below them. Something in the blue depths haunted Finn.

"Before what?" she asked softly.

Cade turned back to the road, but not before she'd seen the uncertainty, the vulnerability in his strong, rugged features. "Before this thing between us goes much further."

He sounded like he was a werewolf by night or something, hiding some terrible flaw. He'd always seemed so desperate to keep his freedom. Why was it he suddenly seemed as if he were trying to give her a chance to run?

"We've been spending most of our free time together for almost a month now. I know everything I need to know about you," she said, laying her hand on his sleeve, the muscles of his arm rock-hard, tense beneath her touch.

"Honey, if I told you the half of it—"

"You can tell me anything you want. It won't matter. I think people show exactly who they are by what they do. Actions, not words. I've had my eye on you a lot these past weeks, Cade McDaniel."

"What about your hands?"

She warmed to see the harsh lines of his profile soften, his mouth crook into that smile that made her feel all shaky inside. He slid his hand off the wheel, cupping her knee with one work-hardened palm, giving her a suggestive squeeze that made her hot all over. They'd done their best to keep their hands to themselves with Emma around. But it hadn't been easy.

"We do seem to have a problem when the two of us are together," Finn said, cupping her hand over his, delighting in the heat of his palm through her stocking. "Have you noticed?"

"If I notice you much more we're never going to make our reservation in St. Louis."

"St. Louis?" Finn repeated, astonished. "It'll take three hours just to get there!"

"We're not driving." He wheeled the Porsche into what looked like a small airport. "We're flying." He gestured to an airplane that looked small enough to be one of her foster brother's plastic models on the nearby runway. And she'd thought the idea of going out on Cade's sailboat had made her nervous.

Finn's heart pounded as he pulled the car to a smooth stop inside a hangar marked Flyboy's Charter and Restoration.

"This is my shop," Cade said, ejecting himself from the sport's car seat as smoothly as James Bond. He rounded the car with catlike grace to open her door.

Far too soon Finn stood staring up at a plane that looked older than dirt.

"You expect me to get in *that?*" Finn gulped with a flutter of panic.

"You afraid of flying?" Cade frowned, as if the thought hadn't even occurred to him.

"I don't know. I've never been in an airplane before. Guess I always thought that when I did finally take the plunge it would be in something a little bit…er, bigger. And, um, newer. This one looks like it could've been parked next to Wilbur and Orville Wright's plane. You know. The What's-It's-Name?"

"The *Kitty Hawk.* This plane was built during the Second World War." Pride lit his face. "A Grumman Avenger. Patrolled for submarines, dropped a few bombs. One of the sweetest little birds ever to ride air."

"So how did you get this…Avenger? It looks like it should be in a museum, not on a runway."

"My flight instructor, Vic Madsen, was a vet who'd flown one of these during the war. Restoring this plane, piece by authentic piece was his life's passion. Mine, too, from the first time I caught a glimpse of it. I was fifteen and so air-crazy Vic took a liking to me." Cade smiled. "Good thing, or he probably would have had to kill me. I gave the man no peace until he'd explained every inch of this machine to me, let me polish it, work on the engine. It felt…I don't know…almost holy, working on this plane. Thinking of the men who died flying her."

"You bought it from Vic then?"

He laughed. "No way in hell I could ever have afforded a plane like this. It's worth a fortune. Vic didn't have any kids of his own, so when he died he left her to me. Said I was the only one he could trust to treat her like the jewel she was. When I fly her, it's like I can feel Vic right there with me. Vic and all the other pilots who kept the oceans safe."

Finn touched the fuselage reverently. "I love old things. It's as if they carry the imprint of the people who loved them. And if you press your hand against them, you can almost feel a heartbeat."

Understanding swept between them, so deep Finn's heart ached.

Cade smiled. "That's it. Exactly how it feels. Every time I climb in this plane." He turned to her, touchingly earnest. "I know she looks old, and small, but she's perfectly safe, Finn. I swear it. If there was any danger there's no way I'd put you on her."

It was true. He cared for her. It was etched in every line in his handsome face. Finn wanted so much more. Afraid he might read her dreams in her eyes, she tried to tease him. "I'm sure the plane's safe and you can fly it just fine. The hard part is going to be getting me into it while I'm wearing this."

She flattened suddenly damp palms against the green silk sheath that clung to her hips and skimmed along her thighs.

"I know you wanted me to wear something that showed my legs," she said, cheeks burning. "But when I try to clamber up into that cockpit, you might be able to see even more than I intended."

Cade shot her a pirate's smile. "Wish I could say that's exactly what I planned. But it's gonna be a completely unexpected fringe benefit. Of course, I could promise to be a gentleman and keep my eyes trained someplace else. But you, above anyone, know I'm no gentleman."

"No. I know your secret. You *are* a gentleman. You just don't like anyone else to know it. Well," she said sucking in a deep breath. "I guess we might as well get this over with."

Cade climbed up onto the wing of the plane, his expensive suit doing nothing to hinder his innate animal grace. Hunkering down, he held out his arms.

"We're never going to get to St. Louis. You're going to be in the nearest emergency room with your back in traction," Finn grumbled.

"I'm tougher than I look. Try me."

Try him? A wicked voice whispered in her ear. *Oh, wouldn't you just love to?*

Feeling vulnerable in a way she never had, Finn stepped into Cade's reach. His hands spanned her rib cage, and before she could stop to think, she was weightless, being pulled upward until her strappy black sandals came to rest on the wing of the plane.

She was close enough to feel the warmth of Cade's body scarcely an inch from her own. Knew she'd barely have to lean forward at all to feel him, solid, hard, from her breasts to her thighs.

Her sandal heel started to slip. Cade clasped her to him, holding her tight.

"I—I didn't mean to—I mean, I slipped!"

"I'm glad you did," Cade murmured, sliding his lips to the sensitive hollow just below her ear.

Finn's nerve endings sizzled to life, the hot, moist feel of his breath tantalizing her, his mouth stealing a kiss.

"You always smell so damned good," he growled hoarsely. "Fresh. Clean. Like lemonade on a hot summer day."

"I was going for something a little more exotic to match the dress," Finn said.

"Did you say erotic?" he teased. "Trust me, sugar. You're the sexiest woman I've ever held in my arms."

"Which just goes to show you spend way too much time with your head stuck in old engines."

"Never saw much worth comin' out from under for, until you wouldn't stay on your own damned side of that fence. Now, get in the plane, woman, or the whole town'll be talking about the new children's librarian and the renegade flyboy. Your reputation will be shot."

"Promise?" The word trembled, soft, vulnerable. "I've been a good girl way too long."

"You can't help being good. You're just made that way. I keep hoping some of it will rub off. Maybe you'll save me after all."

She wanted to ask what he meant. But he'd changed the mood again, quicksilver fast, scooping her up in his arms with a laugh and sliding her into the cockpit. He buckled her in, as if she were precious, as if he wanted to make damned sure he didn't lose her.

She watched him, silent, as he maneuvered himself into the pilot's seat, fastened down the airplane's hatch and went through his preflight checks. Then they were taxiing away from the hangar, taking their turn on the airstrip, its blue lights twinkling.

"Ready?" Cade asked, shooting her a grin that made her

breathless. "I used to think that flying was better than sex. Now…" His gaze heated, his mouth parting as if he wanted to taste her. "Now I wonder…maybe I was a little hasty in that judgment. Guess we'll find out. Sometime."

"Sometime," Finn said as he thrust the plane throttle forward. Her stomach rioted with butterflies as the plane lifted into the air, Cade guiding it with strong, sure hands. Hands he wanted on her body as much as she wanted him. She flew.

She'd never felt so free.

Ten minutes passed, soaring through skies blue as Cade's eyes. Suddenly he shot her a smile. "I want to show you something important. Hold on."

He spun the plane, wings circling around and around like blades on a propeller as he looped up and over like a roller coaster at the same time. Finn shrieked, laughed, fingers digging into the sides of her seat to keep slipping off the edge of the world.

Cade righted the plane, smoothed it into a straight, gliding line.

"Wh-what was that?" Finn stammered, still holding tight to her seat.

"A barrel roll. Did you like it?"

"I…yeah. It was scary. Wonderful. Never felt so— so…alive. But why is it so important?"

"I just wanted you to know." His voice dropped low. "That's how I feel every time I kiss you."

CADE HELD HER HAND, walking down St. Louis's well-lit streets toward the restaurant district, a breeze, soft and cool, wafting in from the river. "This is where Lindbergh was from, you know," he said. "He named the plane he flew on the first trans-Atlantic flight *Spirit of St. Louis*. Can you imagine what it must have been like? Doing the impossible? Being the first man ever to make it across that ocean? We do it every day, now. Like it's nothing. But back then, he could have died. It took a hell of a lot of courage."

"It sounds like something you would do, if you ever got the chance. But not in one of these new, state-of-the-art planes. No. In something like we flew down here in. Something old. The size of a large cat."

He laughed. "That would be the challenge. I can't help it. I've always liked old things better."

"Just not old houses, huh? You didn't have such a high opinion of my common sense when I bought March Winds. Explain the difference between my house and your—well, your car, your plane, your…everything else."

"You have a point." He chuckled. "Guess I always messed around with planes, cars, machines that could take me away from Whitewater. A house has to stay put."

"That log cabin of yours isn't exactly on wheels."

"No. But it doesn't look like it belongs here. That made me feel better, for some reason."

"And that reason would be?"

"I thought I didn't belong here, either. Now, I'm not so sure."

Finn peered up at him, his profile rugged against the streetlight's glow. "Why the change?"

He shrugged, staring meditatively out across the water. "If I'd done what Jett wanted, moved my business to Montana, Deirdre would never have been able to find me. Hell, we hadn't had contact for almost five years. If I'd moved away, I wouldn't have been here for Emma. And…I would never have found you."

Love welled up in Finn. Love and hope. Seeing the light in Cade's eyes made her believe in destiny even more fiercely than she had when she was a little girl. "Maybe I would've ended up in Montana," she said. "It's not like I was born and raised in Whitewater or anything."

"Maybe not. But you belong to March Winds more than that house could ever belong to you. All the years I've worked on old things, I thought I was the one in control. That I chose what to do and what not to. Lately, I've come to realize something strange. We think we find our own treasures. It's not true. Somehow they find us."

She smiled at him, all lit up from inside, slipped her arm around his waist. She fit him exactly, felt warm, womanly, soft. Understanding things he wasn't quite ready to say.

"So when did you discover this fascination of yours for machines any sane person would've taken to a dump?"

"The Porsche I picked you up in was the first. It was built the year I was born. My parents gave it to me when I was fifteen. Talk about a heap of junk! I think Mom hoped restoring it would keep me out of the cockpit for a while. My flying scared her. Guess no matter how old you are, your parents think somebody should hold your hand when you cross the street. You know how it is."

"Uh-uh." Finn tried to think of something to say, pass off as an agreement. But Cade wasn't fooled.

"No, you don't know. Do you, Finn?" He skimmed his fingertips across her cheek, his chest burning with empathy.

"Whenever my da showed up for a visit, he wanted me to be his baby. Hold his hand. Need him. I suppose that's natural."

"No." Cade snapped. "There's nothing natural about a parent expecting their child to hold their hand. It's supposed to be the other way around."

Outrage fired up in him. The thought of Finn abandoned, alone…like Emma, but without even a hard-case uncle to catch her when she fell.

"What were you supposed to do the rest of the time, when he wasn't there?" Cade demanded. "Damn it, it isn't fair. A kid shouldn't have to put up with that garbage from the parent who is supposed to take care of them."

"Kids will put up with most anything when it comes to a parent's love. Take whatever they can get. Scraps, if they're the only thing left to them."

"Emma's not going to have to live like that anymore. Deirdre doesn't want her? Fine. Emma's mine now."

Finn stopped, turned to face him. "Just because Deirdre doesn't want Emma with her right now doesn't mean she'll never want her daughter again."

Cade swore under his breath.

"More importantly," Finn continued. "Emma will always want her mother, even after the hurt Deirdre's caused her."

"That's crazy!" Cade argued. "Emma won't—"

"Trust me, Cade. This is one thing I do know about. And I can tell you this, too. Hard as it might be, if Emma has any chance to heal this thing between herself and her mother, you have to let her do it. Do you want her carrying this rejection? This emptiness? This pain for the rest of her life?"

"She will anyway. Deirdre dumped Emma on my doorstep. I'm just picking the kid up."

"It's one of the things I admire most about you," Finn said softly. "Emma's lucky to have someone who loves her as much as you do."

"Damn." Cade swore softly. "I'm doing it, aren't I?"

"What?"

"Talking about Emma. We agreed not to."

Finn smiled. "I don't mind. I love her, too."

"You do, don't you? I wish…"

"What?"

"Nothing. She just—she deserves to be loved, you know?"

Finn stopped, looked up at him, her face so tender, so warm. "So do you, Cade."

His heart tripped. For a heartbeat he forgot where he was. Forgot everything except the need to crush her against him, kiss her until he couldn't breathe.

"I'm not an easy man, Finn. To live with. To…" He couldn't say *love*. But damn it, he wanted to. He hedged, taking a safer turn. "To be in a relationship with. I'm set in my ways. And I've got a hell of a temper. I don't know if I can change, even if I wanted to."

"You don't scare me, Cade."

"*You* scare *me,* woman. Plenty."

"Just think of me like…like flying across the ocean. It may be scary when you lose sight of land, but once you find your way back where you belong…"

Where he belonged? When was the last time he felt that, really? When he was sixteen? Before that? Had he ever?

Her eyes gleamed, soft…he knew damned well what it meant. Love…that she loved him…

But he couldn't let her say it, couldn't admit what he was feeling himself until she knew the truth. Wasn't that what tonight was really all about?

She needed to understand what made him who he was. What secrets he'd kept. Lies he'd told. What he'd done and failed to do.

Secrets…

He'd spent a lifetime keeping them.

He'd never been tempted to break the silence until he'd glimpsed a chance for redemption in his Irish angel's eyes.

CHAPTER SIXTEEN

SULTRY, SOULFUL jazz filled Ella Fitzgerald's, the St. Louis club with music rich as chocolate cream. Finn sank into the booth Cade had reserved for them in an out-of-the-way corner of the dark paneled room, her eyes drifting shut as a regal black woman in red velvet sang Cole Porter's haunting plea for "Someone to Watch Over Me." The heartrending strains sank into Finn's very skin, a treat even sweeter than the chocolate-covered strawberries she'd nibbled for dessert at the five-star restaurant she and Cade had left an hour ago.

She smiled at the man sitting across from her, seeming so confident, so strong, yet beneath it all, so anxious to please her. A dozen times, she'd caught him watching her, an uncharacteristic vulnerability behind his flashing white smile, uncertainty in that blue gaze that had once seemed unyielding as granite.

When she thought of how much planning had gone into the evening, it touched her to the heart.

"You've surprised me again," Finn said, letting her pleasure dance in her eyes. "This place is wonderful. How did you ever find it?"

"I was raised on Ella Fitzgerald. So when I heard this place existed I had to come take a look. My mom was crazy about jazz. Used to play it all the time at home and sing— she had the most beautiful voice. Soft, like you could bruise it without even trying, kind of lost, so you kept thinking about it a long time after she'd gone quiet."

"It must have been wonderful to hear her."

"One of my favorite things when I was growing up. I was a such a restless kid. But when she'd start singing, I'd stop. Listen. But it hurt, you know? Even as a kid, I knew the sad in those songs was real. Inside her."

"I wonder if she realized you knew her secret," Finn said.

Pain flashed across Cade's handsome features.

"I'm sorry. It's none of my business. It's just—strange, how your parents' pain can haunt you, color everything in your life in a way you never imagined. You can spend your whole life trying to find your way out from under the shadow."

"Sometimes, you never can." Cade's face darkened. He swirled his tonic water and lime in a circle. No alcohol to-night, he'd told her. Not when he was flying. But she'd never seen him look like he needed a drink more. "There are things that stay with you forever. You start thinking, wonder-ing…what if I could go back, change it. What if I hadn't…" His voice trailed off. "Funny, even as a kid you think you could have stopped it. Changed it. Fixed it."

"When you grow up you should know better," Finn agreed. "But you still feel as if you're the one who failed somehow. Whenever I think of the money my father had squirreled away, I wonder why he didn't come and get me all those years ago. Why he never wanted to make a home with me. I was his daughter. I tried to believe so hard that he loved me. He loved his freedom more."

"You don't know that. Things happen. Strange things you never plan on. They twist you around, leave you hanging without a net. Sometimes you come crashing down and take people you love with you. Even if you don't mean to."

He brooded, staring into his glass. "Maybe it was like that

for your father. I never met him. Don't know anything about him. But I do know how it is to get caught in a tailspin that tears out of your control. When Deirdre got hurt, how the hell could I know—"

He hesitated, and Finn sensed that maybe this moment was what tonight was all about. His edginess. His vulnerability. The darkness in his beautiful eyes. "What happened?" she asked.

"I was sixteen. Obsessed with getting my pilot's license. It was all I could think about. I lived at the flight school, working to pay for my lessons. I'd leave before anyone else was awake, and I'd come home after they were asleep. I was running on empty, but I didn't give a damn. I was too obsessed to see how it was affecting my sister. Deirdre sneaked out and hitchhiked to the hangar one night. Later Mom told me Dee had said that she missed me."

He swallowed hard. "But hell—why would I have noticed? I was a big tough guy, with more important things on my mind than the little sister who adored me. She stole in and climbed up on the wing of the plane I'd been scrubbing down. Started dancing around out of my reach."

"That was a pretty spectacular way to get your attention. And make you furious in the meantime."

"I wish I could say I was afraid she'd get hurt. Truth is I was scared she'd get me in trouble and I might lose my job. No job, no flying lessons. You know what my temper is like. It was even worse back then. I made a grab for her. I just…just wanted her to get down off the damned plane. She fell. Crashed down on the open toolbox Vic had left there a little while before."

"Oh, Cade. It must have been awful."

"She hit the ground so hard—cracked her head, her ribs. It was the most horrific sound I've ever heard. I'll never forget what she looked like, sprawled there like a broken doll, bleeding. I—I couldn't wake her up, Finn. She just…just lay there."

"It was an accident. I understand that you felt badly you hadn't been paying so much attention to her, but that's just a part of growing up. There's not a big brother in the world who hasn't wanted to ditch his kid sister at one time or another."

"But Deirdre needed me. I was her anchor. The thing that kept her feet on solid ground. She always said I was the Golden Boy. She was right. I tried for years to deny it, because it hurt too much to face the truth. Both my parents loved me more than they loved my sister."

The guilt haunting his eyes broke her heart. "Was that your fault?"

"I don't know. It must have been on some level. I felt so guilty about it, I tried to make up for it by loving Deirdre myself. Let her tag along everywhere with me. Watched out for her when the Captain lost his temper or Mom gave her the Big Chill. But I could never understand why, you know? What was wrong. Then Deirdre fell. I thought she was dying. We rushed her to the hospital and I thought—I thought this is it. This is the *worst* thing that can ever happen to me."

Cade sucked in a shuddery breath. "I was wrong."

Finn bridged the space between them, covering his hand, her fingers doing little to cover the long, strong expanse of his own. "You got through it, Cade. You survived."

"My family didn't. I think my mom started dying the day we took Deirdre home from the hospital. I'll never forget her face. She never really looked me in the eye again."

"Because of an accident?" Finn heated with outrage for the boy Cade had been. "That was hardly fair!"

"Not the accident. What came after. Because I knew…" Cade turned his hand beneath Finn's, held on, tight. "Christ," he ground out. "I've never talked to anybody about this. Ever.

So why—why do I have to do it tonight? With you? I wanted this to be…special. A night you'd always remember."

"It is. What could be more special than you sharing with me pieces of yourself you've never shared with anyone else? I know you well enough to realize just how rare this is, how hard this is for you. But I want to know everything about you, Cade. All the things, dark and bright, that made you into the man you are."

"It's ugly, Finn. So damned ugly."

She scooped up his hand, turned it to find a freshly healed scar across one knuckle, a place where something had cut, deep. She kissed the pale line, willing him to feel the tenderness crushing her heart. "We all have ugly places inside us. The miracle is being able to trust someone enough to let them see it and have faith that they won't turn away."

"Aren't you afraid of that? That turning away? Sometimes I think if you did, it would tear me up inside."

"I'm not afraid. Not with you. My father was a man forever running when things got hard. You're a man who stays."

"I ran like hell once. Into the Air Force. I just couldn't stand it anymore—watching my family fall apart. Knowing the secrets. Certain that without my screwup the poison would never have spilled out."

"That wouldn't mean the poison wasn't there, whatever it was. Something would have opened the wound. That's what happens. The pressure builds—however long it takes—days, weeks, years. And then it bursts. That's what has to happen before wounds can heal."

"This one never healed. Now it never can. It's too late."

"I won't believe that." She lay her hand along his cheek, felt the subtle prickle of beard spanning his closely shaven jaw. "Tell me. What is it? Hurting your heart so?"

Cade caught her fingers with his hand, held her still as he turned to bury his lips in her palm. His eyes closed, face tightening beneath her fingertips as if he were expecting a blow.

"Swear you won't ever tell anyone," he said, lifting his face, probing her very soul with his gaze. "No matter what happens between us. There's been enough pain."

There had been. Finn could see it, twisting in his chest, darkening his eyes, hard and merciless where it clung about his sensual mouth. "I swear."

A hoarse laugh tore from Cade's throat. "You know what's the most amazing thing of all? I believe you. Sometimes I wonder if I've believed in anything…anyone since that day in the hospital. Especially myself."

Cade's lashes drifted down, his voice low, ragged. "Seemed like we'd been in that damned waiting room forever. All night, anyway. The Captain had gone home to let out Deirdre's dog. He figured that if she woke up and found out we'd neglected the mutt she'd explode."

Cade paused. Finn let the quiet stretch between them until he was ready to go on.

"Strange, isn't it?" he said. "She was so crazy about that mangy stray. Let it sleep on her bed, treated it like a baby. She called him Spot. Made the Captain a little nuts—like he was always trying to figure it out. Sometimes I think he believed Dee did it just to irritate him. My father always called 'em as he saw 'em. The dog was coal-black, not one speck of white."

"Sometimes people see things other people don't," Finn said. "My father always saw rainbows and fairies, even when things were as bleak as they could get."

"You've never even met Dee. Funny, you should know. Sometimes late at night when she couldn't sleep she'd sneak into my room to talk. Talk about anything except what was really hurting her. Dee told me she'd named the dog what she did because he was her one soft spot. I knew what she meant. A safe place she could let all her defenses down."

"She obviously could do the same with you. She was lucky. If I'd had a big brother I could talk to I'd have been in heaven."

"I didn't listen. At least, not all of the time. I just let her ramble on until she went to sleep. She'd take up most of the bed, sprawling out until I was balanced on the very edge of the mattress. I always swore when I had my own place, I'd own a bed so big no one could ever shove me off."

"So that's the story of the King Kong–size mattress."

"Once I got it I slept alone. Not that I was a monk. I wasn't." Blue eyes pierced hers, relentlessly honest.

Finn swallowed hard, not wanting to think about Cade in the arms of another woman. It was absurd to think he'd been celibate since his fling with Caro Bates. He was the most physical man she'd ever met, oozing testosterone, so hot he'd probably had his pick of women. But that didn't make it hurt any less.

"We're both grown-ups, Cade. That's understood."

"Is it? I never understood. Not really. It just never felt right, bringing a woman to the cabin." He seemed to grope for words, an explanation. "It was my place, you know? Felt like an intrusion."

"Your soft spot?"

His mouth crooked in a weary smile. "Maybe so. I never thought of it that way."

"Truth is, we all need one. That's what I've been looking for my whole life."

"That's what I figured Deirdre had been doing. Looking for someone to love besides that old dog. And me." He sighed, let his eyes drift shut for a long moment. "When Emma was born, I thought Deirdre would be the best mother in the world. She had so much love dammed up inside her, just waiting for her to give it away. How the hell did it go so wrong?"

"I don't know. Maybe if you tell me what happened the night she was hurt I'll be able to understand."

"Right. The accident. I guess I got offtrack. Hell, no wonder. I'd rather talk about anything else. But that won't change it, will it, Finn? Or help you know who I am. And I want you to. All of it. So you can decide…"

He was really afraid she'd think less of him once she knew whatever this secret was, Finn thought. He even feared she might leave him. "I'm listening," she prodded gently.

"I'd offered to go take care of the dog," Cade said, "but I was still so shaken up, the Captain wasn't about to let me drive. He's a hard son of a bitch, my father. Had to be to survive in combat. But he was so damned *kind* to me that night. Didn't yell about the accident, blame me for what happened. Just…took care of me in a way he hadn't since I was a little boy. He said he'd seen other guys through things like this in the war. Promised he'd see me through it, too."

Finn imagined the gruff Martin McDaniel in the midst of traumatized young soldiers who blamed themselves for disaster, wracked themselves with survivor guilt. *Why did he get hit with a shell…torn by shrapnel…why did he lose his leg or his hand or die on that bloody ground instead of me?*

"I laid down on the couch. Guess I fell asleep. I can remember, I couldn't get warm."

"Hospitals are always cold." Finn remembered feeling small, her fingers icy as she huddled in a hospital waiting room while her mother died. The nurse had been so gentle with her, but she'd heard enough to know—if her mother had gone to the doctor sooner, she wouldn't have died. She'd always tried so hard to save money. And there hadn't been any insurance. She'd been sick before Da left on his trip, selling whatever it was he'd been selling at the time. Insisted it was just something she ate. By the time he'd gotten home a week later, her appendix had ruptured. A raging infection had set in. She was dying. Finn remembered her mother, tossing and turning in the small hospital bed, telling Da over and over that she was sorry.

Cade kneaded his forehead with the tips of his fingers, as if trying to rub out the memory, the pain. It didn't help. Finn could see it, raking him with sharp claws beyond his eyes.

"The doctor came in and started talking to my mom. They didn't know I was listening. But I couldn't help it. I wish I hadn't, Finn. Wish I'd been anywhere but trapped in that damned green room where I heard…."

He clutched Finn's hand, tight, and her heart ached at his trust. He let her lead him back to places he didn't want to go.

COLD. THE PLACE was so cold. He couldn't get warm. Cade huddled on the couch, his long legs cramped, his stomach still sick as images flashed through him every time he closed his eyes. Deirdre, blood trickling across the concrete from the gash on her forehead, her body curled up as if someone had kicked her in the ribs.

Still, lying there so still, like a doll he'd broken.

Was she cold, wherever they'd taken her? He should find her, make sure she had blankets. He was her big brother, for chrissakes. He was supposed to take care of her.

But he'd been yelling at her, mad as hell in those few, precious moments before the unthinkable happened, before she fell.

Since then? Mom kept insisting Dee would be fine as the hospital ran their eight gazillion tests on the unconscious girl. But the Captain—he'd taken one look at his daughter and gone stone-cold. Cade knew the truth in that instant. His father, who'd seen far too many broken bodies and far too much death, wasn't sure she was going to make it.

The old man had gone into his under-fire mode, taking care of business, not letting anyone see how scared he was. Cade wished he hadn't known, knew he wouldn't even have guessed the truth if he hadn't caught that glimpse of his father's face before the Captain could shutter his real feelings away.

Deirdre was going to die, the words thundered through Cade's veins. Even if she made it, she might never be right again. She'd taken a bad blow to the head, and landed on a stray toolbox on the way down, shattering ribs. Whatever happened to his sister, one thing was certain. It was all Cade's fault. Cade crushed his eyes shut, feeling the hot shame of tears. He'd never wanted anything more than he wanted his mom to hold him. But how could he ever ask her to do that now?

"Mrs. McDaniel?" The doctor in green scrubs walked into the room, empty except for Cade and his mom. The man sounded edgy as Cade felt. "We've got the test results back. Is your husband here?"

Cade wanted to leap from the couch, grab the guy by the throat, making him spit it out—whatever the news was. But his stomach heaved, and he curled up, deeper inside himself, praying with every fiber of his being. *Let her be all right God please let her be all right God please let her be all right…*

"Captain McDaniel had to step out for a moment," his mother said in that bruised voice Cade hated. "Please, whatever it is, I have to know—"

"As we discussed, it's likely your daughter will need a kidney transplant. There's considerable damage. It may straighten itself out, but I think you should know what you're looking at. If we need a donor—"

"That won't be a problem. Her father has already said he'd give Deirdre whatever she needs."

"Yes, Captain McDaniel did say that. Unfortunately, it's not that simple."

"Wh-what do you mean?"

The doctor hesitated, and Cade sensed the tension dialing up a notch. "Maybe we should step into the hall. It's quiet out there right now. Your son…he's had a rough night. There's no need for him to hear." The doctor's voice trailed off.

Cade's whole body quaked. Why was the doctor taking her in the hall? To give her terrible news?

"Of course," his mother said, her voice shaking.

Cade heard footsteps on tile as the two grown-ups stole out into the hallway. In a heartbeat he scrambled up from where he'd lain, moving silently to the door. He had to know—whatever it was, he had to know.

"Mrs. McDaniel," the doctor began. "We've done preliminary checks. You're not eligible to be a donor—a history of kidney stones and infection has left scarring."

"Then Deirdre's father will give her a kidney."

"I know he was ready to. In fact, I think if he had his way, the minute I told you there was trouble, he wouldn't even have bothered waiting for anesthesia. He'd have hopped up on the gurney and taken his own kidney out to give to that little girl in there."

"Yes. My—my husband would," his mother's voice cracked. "He was a war hero, you know. There's no one braver."

"I'm sure that's true. But there's just one problem. Captain McDaniel is not Deirdre's father."

Not Dee's father? Outrage boiled up in Cade. He waited for his mother to blaze up with indignation, tell the doctor he was an idiot. Even gentle as his mom was, she had to know this guy was implying the unthinkable.

But she stammered, faltered. "Not—not her father? Are you sure there's no mistake?"

"There's no mistake. I had them run the test three times. The result was the same. It's biologically impossible that Captain McDaniel is her father."

Cade reeled, clutched the back of a chair to try to catch his balance in this crazed, shattering world.

He waited for his mom to argue, explain—tell the doctor anything. That Deirdre was adopted. Was that the big secret?

Maybe that was why she never felt like she fit in—but why hadn't anyone told him? Or at least told the doctors the minute they knew she might need a kidney? If she was adopted there was almost no chance any of the McDaniels would be a match. No one would know that better than the Captain. Cade's head throbbed. It didn't make any sense.

"Does my husband have to know?" his mother asked. "Captain McDaniel…he thinks Deirdre is his. I never told him it was possible she is another man's child."

Cade's stomach heaved. He couldn't suck air into his burning lungs.

"I don't know how we can keep the truth from your husband if Deirdre's kidneys get past crisis stage and he's ineligible as a donor. He's the type of man who will demand to know why we can't use him."

"Yes. He is," Cade's mother said faintly. "But maybe—maybe Deirdre will get better without the transplant. You did say it was possible."

"Possible. Not likely."

"Then I'll have to pray for a miracle, won't I, doctor? No one in my family can ever know…."

They'd talked a few moments more, but Cade didn't hear them. He sank down into the chair beside the door, buried his face in his hands. He was still there when his mother walked back in.

He heard her breath catch, a horrible, broken sound rising in her throat. "Cade!" she cried his name. "You didn't hear that! Tell me you didn't hear."

He raised his face—contorted in anguish, streaked with a boy's shameful tears.

"Mom…how could you?"

She broke to pieces right before him. He could see it in her eyes.

"Oh, God, baby!" She hadn't called him that since he was

in grade school. He'd hated it even then. Now, it made him feel shattered inside, small, weak. He wanted her to tell him it was all a rotten dream, wake him up in his own bed, Deirdre sleeping down the hall with that shaggy dog of hers. Everything could go back to the way it was before.

"Mom, tell me…tell me it isn't true."

Tears welled up in her eyes. "I wish it wasn't. But…oh, Cade. You're so young. How can you ever understand?"

She tried to hug him. He pulled away, scared he might start crying like the baby she'd called him.

"You're a smart boy. You know that your father and I haven't always been happy. We're too different. We always were. I thought—he was so handsome, your father. So sure he was right. And I was the wife he wanted. He was determined to make it work. By sheer force of will."

"You're not telling me anything. I know…" About the Big Sad inside her. About the tension that always sparked between his parents, ready to erupt into flame. He'd always felt a little like he was walking blindfolded through a minefield, waiting for the next explosion. The house would be so quiet for a while and calm, anyone on the outside would've sworn they were the perfect family. But from the time he could remember, Cade had known it was only a matter of time before disaster struck.

But this? This was beyond anything he could imagine.

"Mom, how could this happen?"

She was supposed to be the good one, the gentle parent Cade had done his best to shield from his father's rough edges, the perfect angel who always did the right thing. Who made hot chocolate at Christmas when the Captain's temper flared, put bandages on scrapes on Cade's knees and on his heart. She wasn't supposed to be the one who hurt him, betrayed his father.

She sank down in the chair beside him, sucked in a shuddery breath. "You were two years old when it happened. Such a little boy. Crazy about airplanes even then. I think both your father and I had hoped once we had a child that things between us would get better. But—much as we both loved you, it couldn't change the fact that we didn't love each other—at least not the way we should have."

"Mom, I don't want to know—" Any of this, Cade thought wildly. Wishing he could tear it out of his head, plug up his ears, turn back the ugly plastic clock on the waiting room wall.

"But you do know. You listened at the door, Cade. It's only right, now you hear the whole truth."

"I was scared Deirdre was dying! Just wanted to hear…if she was going to be all right. I didn't want to hear this! I'm your kid, for God's sake! I shouldn't—shouldn't have to know…"

That you cheated on my father, lied to my sister, betrayed me…

"You say I was two—what'd you do with me when this crap was going on? Park me in the next room with my toy trains or something?"

His mother's cheeks burned, hot spots of color on ashen cheeks. "Of course not! Do you really think I'd take my child with me when I was having an affair?"

"I didn't think you'd have an affair *at all*. Now I know the truth, how am I supposed to know how low you'd go?"

She flinched back as if he'd slapped her. Cade wanted to grab her hand, tell her he was sorry. God, he didn't want to hurt her. But his whole inside felt chewed raw. "I suppose I deserve that. You stayed with our next-door neighbor. Another Army wife. We helped each other out when the men were on assignment."

Cade clenched his jaw, rigidly silent.

"Your father was somewhere in South America, on one of

those covert missions he loved so much. I was lonely. There was a man selling instruments to the school band. He played saxophone so beautifully it made you want to cry. He was only going to be in town a few weeks. It seemed so harmless at first, just flirting with him, feeling young again, pretty. I didn't mean to love him."

"You can't love some other guy!" Cade cried. "You're married to my dad!"

"That doesn't mean you can't love someone. Only that you can't be with him." Sorrow, loss cut deep in her voice. It terrified Cade to realize she still missed this jerk. Was that why she'd sung all those sad songs? Why it made his heart hurt sometimes to hear her?

"So why didn't you just leave?" he demanded, putting his worst fears into words. "Dump Dad and I and run off with this—this musician asshole? At least that would have been honest."

"There was never any question of leaving. We both knew that from the start. I had you and your father and he…he had a wife and children, too. We didn't mean to hurt anyone. But we couldn't help the way we felt. Those three weeks were our only chance to be together. We took it."

Cade strangled a sob.

"I don't expect you to understand. Maybe you will someday, when you're a man. When you love someone of your own. I never meant for it to happen."

"Then why didn't you stop it! You had this guy's baby and you didn't even care!"

"There were times I wondered, once Deirdre was on the way. Times I was afraid she might be his. But I convinced myself I was wrong. Your father came back home to the states two weeks after my saxophone player left. There was no way to be sure. It was easier to try to forget. Even though part of me always hoped…"

"Hoped what? That Deirdre was his kid? That's sick! You lied to me and Dad! And Dee? What about her? She's never thought you and Dad loved her. Always knew something was wrong! If she finds out it'll destroy her!"

"Then we can't let her find out, Cade." His mother clutched at his hands, desperate. "Deirdre can't ever know. Or your father."

"But the doctor said he'd have to tell—"

"Only if Deirdre needs a kidney. She's a strong girl. She'll fight her way out of this. She has to."

"So dad doesn't know what you did?" Cade accused. "That's just great."

"What could it do but hurt him, Cade?" Tears slid down his mother's face, a face Cade had loved so much, thought so beautiful. His mother—who'd been his angel, who'd always keep him safe. "You don't want to hurt the Captain like that, do you?"

"I didn't sleep with some—some stranger. You're the one who did this!"

"Yes. I did. And if Deirdre hadn't gone to the hangar after you and gotten hurt, no one would ever have known."

Guilt jolted through Cade as if she'd hit him with a hot wire. "You're saying this is my fault? It's because of me?"

"No! That's not what I meant!" his mother cried, dismayed. "I just—things happen we don't intend, Cade. Accidents… Sometimes all we can do is try to keep people from getting hurt. You're a good boy, Cade. Almost a man, really. You've taken care of Deirdre her whole life. And me…"

She looked down at her hand, twisting the Captain's plain gold band circling her fourth finger. "You've taken care of me, too, when your father's lost his temper and we're fighting. You think your father and I don't notice what you're doing— getting in trouble to distract us, anything to draw fire onto yourself so we'd stop hurting each other with words we can't ever take back."

Cade flushed, his secret laid bare. "Why do you fight all the time? Why can't you…just love each other, like you're supposed to?"

Her hands fluttered, helpless, hopeless, as if trying to catch some answer he could grasp. She surrendered, letting her hands fall into the lap of her blue-flowered skirt. She stared down, pale, all torn up inside.

"Why did Deirdre fall off of that airplane?" she asked. "It just happens, Cade. It just happens. But what happens next is up to you. Swear you'll never tell."

He'd sworn. To keep the truth from his father. To keep it from Deirdre. He just hadn't realized how much silence could feel like lying.

He'd prayed night and day that Deirdre would heal on her own, that his father would never find out. It would kill the Captain to know his wife had cheated on him. The Captain was so damned proud. And Deirdre—

He couldn't even think what the truth would do to her.

He'd promised he'd never ask God for another thing, if He'd just let Cade's family go back to the way it was before that horrible night.

He'd been too young to know the truth.

Even after Deirdre healed, the secret kept safe. Even after the Captain carried her in from the car in his arms and laid her on the couch and his mother bustled around, trying to act like everything was okay.

Even then, Cade's world could never be the same again.

FINN WATCHED as Cade pulled himself out of the raging waters of memory, knew that this proud, strong, honorable man had plunged himself into his worst nightmare for her. To be honest with her. So she could see the wounds still seared in his spirit.

All she could see was a sensitive boy trapped between two unhappy parents he loved.

"I think that night in the hospital was the last time my mother really looked me in the eye," Cade confessed quietly. "It ate at her, my knowing what she'd done. Changed everything. The Captain could tell something was wrong—spent the next years as if he were being stalked by some danger he could feel but could never get his hands on. He was used to fighting, going head-to-head with anything that threatened his family. The not knowing—it triggered the soldier in him. And Deirdre—it was as if that knock on her head had jarred loose any survival instinct she'd ever had when it came to the Captain. She got wilder than ever, hell-bent on defying everything my parents stood for. She said life was too short to give a damn what other people thought."

"I can see why a sixteen-year-old would blame himself for what happened. Kids think everything is their fault. But you're a man now. You know better. In one way, your mother was right. Accidents happen. You have to know she didn't really blame you. What happened between your parents when you were two years old wasn't your fault."

"But what happened after the accident *was*. I ran, Finn. Got the hell out of there the minute I was old enough to enlist. Swore I was never coming back. I'd join the Air Force and fly myself away from the pain, the secrets, the lies." His face contorted in anguish still so fresh it broke Finn's heart. "I tried to forget. Forget I had a family. I had my own life to live."

"There's nothing wrong in wanting to live your own life, Cade," she said, gently. "Every person has that right."

He angled his face, the glow from the candle on the jazz club table searing his features with red light. "Did I? Did I have the right to walk away when I knew it was only a matter of time before it all boiled over? Deirdre was my little sister. I was supposed to take care of her. Maybe if I had she wouldn't have abandoned Emma the way I abandoned her.

And my mom—she'd made a bad choice, but she was still my mom. She needed to know I loved her, no matter what she'd done."

"She knew you better than anyone, Cade. You're the most loving man I've ever known. She had to know that, too."

"Then why did it eat her up from the inside out? The guilt? The shame? Why didn't she tell me she was so sick? She wrote that it was nothing—one little snip and the doctors said it was no problem. That's what she told me. She pretended everything was going to be all right when the whole time she knew…she was dying, Finn. Breast cancer. It was stage four by the time she even bothered to go to the doctor. Why did she wait so damned long? I think…I think she wanted to die."

Stark anguish burned in his vivid blue eyes. Finn's heart broke. God in heaven, that was the horror that haunted Cade. Somewhere inside him he really believed that he'd killed his mother.

"You can't know that, Cade. Lots of people try to ignore symptoms when they're sick. My mom did, and it cost her her life. You'd think if people sensed they were sick they'd run straight to a doctor, but it's not always that way. Sometimes they know something is really wrong and are too scared to face it. If the doctor doesn't give them the diagnosis, it can't be real. No matter what the case, you're not responsible for her death."

"I could have made her go to the doctor. I would have seen something was wrong."

"There were other people around your mother who could have done the same thing. Your father. Your sister. Your mother's friends. You're not responsible for saving the world. You're not even responsible for saving your parents."

"I suppose it's a good thing you think that, because I sure as hell didn't. The Captain started drinking. Things got so ugly between him and Dee, it still makes me sick when I think… By the time I got discharged, Mom was a week away from the end. She said she was sorry for letting things get so out of hand. Asked me to take care of them. She said I was the only one who'd ever been able to handle the Captain and Dee. If I'd been there…"

Cade's voice cracked. Tears burned Finn's eyes. Hadn't he suffered enough? How could his mother have done that to him? Laid that burden on his shoulders? The woman had to know Cade would carry those words with him for the rest of his life.

But the woman had been dying. She must have been afraid—afraid for her husband, her daughter. Blaming herself for what had gone wrong. Just like her son had blamed himself for so many years. She might as well have put him in charge of a ship that was already sinking.

I wouldn't have done that! Finn told herself fiercely. *I wouldn't have done that to my child.*

She could see him so clearly, Cade at twenty-one, so young, so vulnerable beneath his hell-raising facade, dressed in the Air Force uniform he loved. On the brink of having the life he'd dreamed of, before his broken family had snatched him back to Whitewater, back to the memories, back to the disillusionment he'd tried to leave behind.

Who would have guessed that this man who'd spent most of his life in one place, surrounded by parents and a sister, the white picket fence life Finn had thought perfect—who would ever have guessed that he could be every bit as alone as she was?

Maybe even more so.

Loneliness in a crowded room had to hurt even worse than the solitary life Finn had known. To be exposed, raw, while in the midst of people who should have seen how you were hurting, felt how you were struggling, known that you were drowning. People so self-absorbed, they didn't have a clue.

What would that do to a person, when not even the people who were supposed to love you would hold out their hand to pull you from the river? The way Cade had reached out to Emma.

Finn fought back tears, understanding the wildness in him, the fear of being cornered, trapped, responsible for anybody's happiness but his own. God, the panic must have almost killed him when he woke up and realized Deirdre had abandoned Emma. That the shattered little girl was his responsibility to care for, love, protect.

She could hear what he was feeling, knew it as clearly as if he were able to say it aloud.

I don't know how to love. I got it wrong last time. Everything wrong.

Finn peered into his haggard face, wanted to kiss him, cradle him, comfort him as he should have been comforted as a boy.

Love doesn't have to hurt, she wanted to tell him. *Give me a chance to show you. I love you. For who you are. Not for what I need you to be.*

She loved him.

Finn staggered under the weight of the truest thing she'd ever felt.

But she couldn't tell him now, now when her declaration of love would be forever bound up in his memories of pain. She wanted so badly for this heart-weary man to feel joy.

"So," Cade said, a shudder of something like relief rippling through his broad shoulders. "That's it. The whole, miserable story."

"And you've been taking care of your family ever since," she said.

"I didn't do such a great job with Deirdre. It's hard to watch out for somebody who's always taking off in a temper, disappearing. But I figured if I stayed here in Whitewater, she'd be able to find me if she needed me. And the Captain—the ornery old son of a bitch. I'm proud of the way he pulled himself together, got off the bottle. I love him, Finn. It's just…sometimes he's so…I don't know, larger than life, I feel like I don't have room to breathe."

"And now you have Emma to take care of. More responsibility you didn't ask for."

"Who would've thought that would be a good thing? Change the way I see everything. The world. My life. She's my second chance, Finn—to get this family thing right." Silver-blue eyes narrowed, so intense Finn expected the tabletop to catch fire. "Emma's not growing up in the kind of chaos I did. I'll do whatever it takes. Even if it means taking my sister to court."

Dread feathered along Finn's spine, something in the steely resolve in Cade's features making her fear for him. "Do you really think taking legal action is a good idea? I know how angry you must be and how hurt. But Deirdre is Emma's mother. Nothing will ever change that."

"And nothing will ever change the chaos around my sister. I'm going to protect Emma from that, damn it."

Finn ached. If only it was that easy—to hold back life's craziness, to control the madness of hurt and pain and costly mistakes just because you wanted to. If only you could make life perfect….

But no one had the power to hold back life's pain. Not even Cade with his battered heart and his steely, calloused hands.

What would happen to Emma if he pursued some ugly scene in court? How would Cade feel when he saw how torn Emma would be, when he learned the inevitable—that the child still wanted, needed her mother?

It was only a matter of time until the pain and chaos he was trying to hold back broke free and crashed into them all. And when it did—Cade would believe that he'd failed.

The thought of him devastated, full of self-blame raked at Finn's heart. *I'll be there for him,* Finn vowed fiercely. *I'll find a way to help him understand....*

That's what she'd do. She'd love him through whatever happened.

For the first time in his life, Cade McDaniel wouldn't face the world alone.

CHAPTER SEVENTEEN

THE PORSCHE was built for speed, but Cade slowed it to a crawl as he eased the machine along the winding river road to Jubilee Point. Finn's soft, drowsy face nestled close beside him, her gaze turned up toward the stars sprinkling the sky. He didn't want this night to end. Didn't want to leave Finn on her doorstep, give her time to think too much about what a mess she was getting herself into.

He'd warned her he wasn't an easy man to live with. Let her see the ugliness, touch the places in him that were afraid to trust. He'd taken her by the hand and led her through all his failures, his doubts, his decision to remain alone.

She'd listened, so loving, a healing, soft rain on a fire-seared forest, whispering of a chance at new life. But then, Finn believed in miracles, taking shattered little girls and broken-down old houses and making them better than new. And him?

Was it possible she could see beyond the rubble of his past, to the man he was meant to be? Might *still* be if he took the most terrifying risk of his life and admitted he loved her?

Loved her? That was the easy part. Finn was a woman born for loving. But building a life with her…making a home… that was something far more dangerous.

What did he know about happily ever afters? The story-book ending Finn O'Grady deserved? White picket fences and arms full of babies, children he could screw up as badly as his parents had him and Deirdre?

Cold sweat prickled the back of his neck.

Time. He'd give Finn time to think about what he'd said before he asked her to risk—what? Forever? The rest of her life? With a man who had crashed and burned so badly before?

What if she *did* think about it and changed her mind? Panic fluttered through him. There were a hell of a lot of men who would leap at the chance to love a woman like Finn. Men far better equipped to keep her dreams safe. Dreams every bit as big and beautiful as her heart.

But the mere thought of another man touching her, making her laugh knotted Cade up inside so tight he couldn't breathe.

Her head tipped toward him, as if she wanted to lay those rich red curls against his shoulder, would have cuddled close if the stick shift hadn't been in the way. And for the first time that night he wished he'd brought his truck so that, right now, he'd be able to feel the sweet weight of her pressed against his body.

"It's amazing to think we flew way up there, through all those stars," Finn said with a sigh. "Imagine hundreds of years ago, men on ships, sailing—they never would have dreamed it was possible to travel that way."

"They traveled by starlight, too. See the one right up there? The bright one?" Cade took one hand from the wheel to point. "That's the North Star. It never moves. Even as a kid it fascinated me. Knowing that before all the machines, the navigation systems, even before people had compasses, that one little light in the darkness was leading lost men home."

She caught his hand, pressed it against her cheek, gently rubbing her satiny skin against his knuckles. She kissed them, and Cade's throat squeezed, tight.

"You're not lost anymore. And me...I'm finally home." She sounded so certain. He wondered what that felt like—to know in your heart, trust the way Finn did. He wondered if he could ever have that kind of faith.

He pulled the Porsche to a stop beneath the shelter of a porte cochere overrun with wisteria vines that made him itch to get out his hedge trimmers. He'd have to move fast, he thought. If Finn saw the things in bloom she'd never let him trim them back. She loved life, eager, bursting, determined to flower.

Funny, he'd spent his whole life trying to cut back tangles, tear away vines, tame chaos. He'd never stopped to see the beauty in all that wild, enthusiastic clambering toward the sun. But maybe Finn was right. When the wisteria draped itself in purple blooms, it would be all the more beautiful, allowed to grow its way through all the barriers that tried to hold it back.

Sliding the stick shift smoothly into Neutral, Cade turned off the engine. He searched out her hand in the darkness, held it. How could something so soft, so feminine, be so strong? Stronger than any man had the nerve to be.

"So what happens now?" he asked, wishing he could see her face. As if in answer to prayer, the moon drifted, a bar of soft, silvery light finding its way through a break in the vines to illuminate Finn's face.

Cade's breath caught, she was so damned beautiful. Her eyes shining, her throat white in the moonlight, her lips full and tender and begging to be kissed. Her fingers tightened on his, as if she'd never let go. "Come to bed, Cade. I want you."

Had he been waiting forever to hear her say that? He should have jumped at the chance, hell, he'd all but taken her right on the floor the day she'd tumbled off the ladder. If they hadn't been interrupted would he have had any problem burying himself inside her? Easing the terrible ache she stirred in his shaft? It wasn't like a guy's erection had many scruples once it was hard and ready. And he'd been both, what seemed forever, in the days since Finn had charged into his life.

"You're sure?" He could hardly believe it was his own voice, questioning her, giving her a chance to back away. What was he? Out of his mind? "Finn…hell, I've been half crazy, wanting to make love to you so damned bad. But now—it's different, now. Now that you know about everything…it's not just—"

"Just what?"

"Just sex," he admitted hoarsely. "Hell, who am I trying to kid? It was never just about sex. That scared the hell out of me, but it couldn't stop the wanting, the needing… Night after night I'd lie in my bed, imagining what it would be like to bury myself inside you. To have you want not just my body, the way I could make you feel. Not just the thrill. To have you want *me*."

She laid her hand lightly along his jaw, looking straight into his eyes, the way only she could. "It took me hours to get ready tonight. I almost didn't have the nerve to wear this dress. And when you see what's underneath it…" She gave a shaky laugh, he could almost feel hot color riot onto her cheeks.

"You make me feel like I'm on fire, like my skin is too hot to hold me and everything inside me is melting. Into you, Cade. Until there's no room for anything else. And nothing could ever come between us."

Cade hardened, ached, burned. He climbed out of the car, stalked around it, opening the door. Finn swung her long legs toward him, the moonlight giving him a glimpse of pale skin above the top of her stocking, and something so hot it all but drove him to his knees.

"A garter belt?" he rasped.

"One of the girls at the University gave it to me. Called it…well, never mind. She said I might—might actually need it someday. I didn't believe her. Couldn't imagine anyone making me feel this way." She rose to her feet, a little unsteady, a little uncertain. "I guess I was hoping tonight…"

"Son of a bitch!" Cade swore, sweeping one arm beneath her knees, the other under her shoulder, as he whisked her off her feet. She shrieked in surprise, clung as he clamped her hard against him, striding up the stairs to the door.

He never knew how the hell she opened the damned thing, crazy as he was to get Finn to her bedroom. But at last they reached the tower room on the second floor. When had she fixed it up? Had she worked on it when he was at the hangar? It shone, freshly painted, a soft, buttery yellow, as if she could never get enough sunshine and light. White gauzy curtains draped back from the four poster bed she'd set in the center of the room, where she could see the river from the gleaming bank of windows. A miniature step stool tucked close to the sky-blue comforter, so she could climb up to the high ledge of the mattress.

The whole room smelled of Finn, that fresh, woman smell, not too sweet, but feminine in a way that made a man want to sink into it, exotic, otherworldly, welcoming, like slipping between cool sheets on a hot summer night.

He kissed her, devoured her body through its layer of green satin, knowing black lace waited beneath, feeling the side of her breast crushed against his chest, the sleek line of her leg draped over his arm, the eagerness of her mouth under his.

Shaken by the fierce passion she fired in him, he drifted her toes down to the thick, hooked rug with its whimsical sprinkling of white woven stars. She whimpered in protest as he loosened his hold on her.

"Wait," he said. "Just a minute." He stepped away from her for a heartbeat. Worry creased her brow, drove back the haze of desire that veiled her lovely face.

"What is it?" She trembled. "What's wrong?"

"I want to remember," Cade growled fiercely, his gaze raking her from the crown of her head to her sandal clad toes. "What you looked like tonight before…when everything's perfect. Everything's possible. Even a woman like you wanting me."

Her eyes glowed, like she was all lit up inside. His heart hurt as she gave him an angel's smile. "Not just wanting you, Cade. Loving you." She confessed it so easily, quietly, the words roaring through him like flood tide. "I love you."

Cade groaned, fierce triumph raging through him. He drove his fingers back through her hair, knocking loose the pins that had held the tumbled mass off her slender neck. The curls tumbled loose over his hands, spun silk against the rough places, the hard places life had worn into his body, his heart.

She loved him. He should have wanted to run like hell. He always had before. When a woman had wanted more of him than he feared he could ever give. But Finn's confession unleashed something primal in him, beyond his power to control.

And he knew why knights had stolen women they wanted, scooped them onto horses and carried them away, to secret castles where they could make their chosen lady love them. But Finn was the one who'd carried him away. Out of bleakness and shadow, into her fairy garden.

He kissed Finn as if he could draw her very essence deep inside him, to light his way as she led him out. Out into a world he'd thought beyond his reach. A world he wasn't even sure existed. One he'd only glimpsed in the starry lights in Finn's green eyes.

He fumbled for the zipper that ran the delicate length of her spine, slid it down the deliciously feminine path to where her bottom swelled beneath the satin, begging for his hands.

He palmed the soft hills, pulling her tight against the erection, full to bursting beneath the fly of his pants. He'd never felt so hard. So damned ready.

Her dress fell open, slipping down the length of one arm, and he glimpsed her bare shoulder, a river of creamy soft skin framed by the low cut slip that ended at the small of her back. He nipped at the pale column of her throat, sucked ever so gently at the sensitive point he'd raked gently with his teeth, silky hot skin beneath which her pulses were racing.

He drank in the tremor of pleasure radiating through her, heard her gasp, her own eager hands running over his back, her breasts against his chest, nipples hard as pearls, ready for the sweep of his tongue.

She loves me, he told himself with savage triumph, the need to claim her driving to the very marrow of his bones. *She loves me.*

He stripped the dress down her body, then caught the thin ribbon straps of black slip and eased them off until the garments fell to a sweet, crumpled pool on the floor. Finn stood before him, her chin tipped up with a heart-wrenching hint of vulnerability, waiting to see his response in his eyes, discover what it did to him, seeing her all but naked for the very first time.

The black bra she'd confessed to choosing so carefully cupped full breasts, her aureole just visible through the delicate lace veil. Panties and garter belt straight out of a man's most sensual fantasy encircled her hips. The dark tops of her stockings accented the fragile white skin of her thighs.

She'd dressed for him tonight. To turn him on. Fire him up. The thought penetrated through the desire hazing his mind, touched a still tender place in his chest. How could he even begin to tell her what she did to him.

"You're so damned beautiful," he murmured.

She looked him straight in the eye, the way only Finn

could. He drowned in the wide, green meadow depths. "I wanted to be. For you. Tonight."

Her courage amazed him, her willingness to leave herself so vulnerable…to him. "You think I need black lace and red ribbon?" he rumbled, low in his throat. "Garter belts and hems up to your thighs? I have to admit, you look like my hottest dream, sexy as hell, but it's not lace that turns me on whenever you're in reach. Hell," he laughed raggedly. "Even when you're on the other side of that damned picket fence. I just *think* about you and I get hard as steel."

Delight flooded her face, her cheeks flushing beneath their sprinkling of freckles. And Cade swore, in time, he'd kiss every one of them.

He covered her mouth with his, tongue tracing every curve and dip and corner of her lips. His hands ran wild, feeling her all over, the lush, generosity of her body, her spirit making him weak in the knees. "It's not the lace…the damned silk dress that makes me crazy. It's *you*," he murmured hotly against her throat. "Your skin, so damned soft. The way you smell like lemonade on a scorching summer day, the way your breath catches when you laugh. And those eyes—the way you look at me, as if there were no other man on earth."

She clung to him, kissed him, driving him wild. "There isn't anyone like you. I've been looking for you for such a long time."

"Ahh, Finn," he groaned, skimming the cups of her bra down until her nipples popped free, candy-pink, sheer temptation. He leaned her back over his arm, all sleek, supple woman, soft and sweet-smelling, her breasts arching toward him. He bent down took the hard little nub between his lips, suckled her, taking his sweet time, tormenting her with the pull of mouth, the sweep of his tongue until she was moaning, trembling.

"Please, Cade." Her fingers curled in his shirt, as she

pleaded, breathless. "I want to see you. Taste you. Your bare skin. That first night when I came to your house in the rain…you were just in your boxers. I thought…I'd never known a man could be so beautiful."

"I was a first-rate bastard," he said. "I'm sorry."

"You spent most of the night helping me, in spite of all the growling. That's what really matters, you know. Jumping into the breach even if you don't want to, doing whatever you can."

"You wanna know what made me so mad?" He pulled away, long enough to rip his necktie loose, hurl it toward the slipper chair Finn had tucked in a corner. "That wet nightgown of yours. You were all pink and soft and curvy underneath it. I could see everything. Your nipples, hard from the chill, your navel, that dark little triangle between your legs. You made me hungrier than I'd ever been, woman. I was damned well starving for you. But I was dead set determined I wasn't going to take a taste."

Mischief twinkled in her eyes. "I've always heard there's nothing crabbier than a hungry man."

"Damned straight!"

"I'm hungry, too, Cade. So hungry to touch all of you."

She came undone, her hands on his shirt buttons, tugging at them, popping one loose in her haste. The button bounced on the hardwood floor, rolled under an antique armoire as romantic and otherworldly as Finn herself.

Vaguely Cade wondered how the hell she'd gotten it up here by herself. Or was that what the Captain had been up to the day he'd borrowed a dolly from the hangar?

"Oh, God!" Finn gasped peering after the vanished button. "I'm sorry."

She hesitated, suddenly shy. He curled his finger under her chin, rubbed his thumb over her full bottom lip. "Don't stop now, sugar, whatever you do."

"But your beautiful shirt…it looks expensive."

"Christmas gift from Jett and his wife last year." He fingered the torn place. "I can't remember this ever looking better. It makes me hot, Finn. Knowing you're in a hurry…"

He circled her wrists with his hands, pulled her fingers to the strip of naked chest visible between the open edges of his shirt. "I wish I could tell you how it feels. To have your hands on me after all this time. To know you're going to let me…"

He froze for a heartbeat, the words still hard to say. Necessary, after all the times he'd tried to downplay what this flare of passion meant between them.

"Let me make love to you, Finn."

"You'd better." Dark sweeps of brow lowered over her Irish meadow eyes.

"What?"

"Stop now and I'm going to have to kill you."

He threw back his head, laughter welling up inside him, pure and fresh and clean. Lord, would she ever stop surprising him? With her joy? Her honesty? Would he ever be able to believe what a lucky son of a bitch he was to have her in his arms?

He turned his back to her, needing to hide the flash of fear that sliced through him, the doubt that this thing they felt could be real, survive in a world that didn't believe in fairy tales. Didn't believe in women like Finn.

He stripped off the rest of his clothes, head ducked down, trying to hide how raw he felt, how suddenly, terribly scared.

Too good to be true…a voice mocked him. *Too good to be real… Only someone like Finn could believe…in* this. *In* us.

But Finn believed. With all her heart. Maybe enough for both of them.

He felt her fingers explore his bare back, down cuts of muscle defined in hours of lifting weights, to his waist, his left buttock. She teased the sensitive skin, let her fingers glide back up, leaving fire in her wake.

"You feel so good, all hot satin and steel," she whispered, pressing a kiss to his shoulder blade. Driving back his sense of dread, like that fairy princess in the story Emma loved, releasing her embattled beast from the wicked spell that kept him trapped inside walls.

Cade let the stone barriers inside him fall away. He turned to face her, his arms at his sides, his fingers gently curled, waiting to see response in her eyes. Desire flared, hot, dizzying, in the green depths, as if she'd trapped flame in her eyes. It licked him, deep, where even her touch couldn't reach him.

Or maybe, just maybe it could. With devastating delicacy she rested her fingertips on his collarbone, traced its path to his throat, then down, through the mat of dark hair on his chest, the edge of her little finger grazing his nipple, making his erection jerk in answer. Hell, if she didn't touch him there soon, he'd die.

But she took her time, her gaze following the trail she blazed, down his flat stomach, to where he ached for her.

She touched him, the velvety tip, down his length, then enclosed his shaft in her hand. A ragged groan tore from Cade's chest at her intimate caress.

He grabbed her wrist, held her still, afraid if she moved at all he'd lose control. And he wanted to take this slow for Finn's sake, take his time, make her writhe and gasp and scream while he imprinted his body on hers. So she'd never forget this night.

"Want to hear something crazy?" he said, taking her hand away from where he throbbed and burned.

"What?"

"Tonight, I'm damned glad I'm a man."

"Me, too."

Finn swept back the coverlet, revealing sheets so mellow smooth and soft she must've gotten them in some antique shop. Her eyes burned as she lay back on her bed, draping

her body across the creamy white cotton, edged with cro-
cheted lace. A bed that screamed woman, smelled of
heaven…of…Finn…. Cade sank into them both.

Finn shivered as his big body hovered over her, arms
braced on either side of her, long legs bracketing hers, his taut,
tanned skin sheened with a fine layer of sweat. Powerful
thighs pressed against her, broad shoulders gleaming, dark
hair softening the proud warrior angles of his face.

She traced the swell of his lips, marveling at their softness,
the burning sexuality so much a part of him, the unexpected
vulnerability that was Cade McDaniel's most guarded secret.

Threading her fingers back through strands silky dark as
night, she urged him downward. Cade lowered his big body
on top of hers with heartbreaking care, loving her with his
mouth, his tongue tracing her lips, slipping between them to
tease her inside.

His deft, calloused fingers stroked her, stoking the flames
curling beneath her skin, hand to breast, fingers to nipple,
softly rubbing the too-tender crest until she thought she'd
scream if he didn't soothe it with his tongue.

She gasped, twisted against the sheets as he kissed his way
to her breast, suckling her as if he were starving and she
could give him sweetness, peace. And she wondered, in a
flash of awe and delight what it would be like to nuzzle
Cade's baby to her breast, to feel its tiny mouth fasten, stubborn, insistent at the place where his father's had been.

But Cade drove the sweet image out of her mind with
erotic mastery, kissing his way downward, across the trembling swell of her stomach, until his breath stirred the down
at the apex of her thigh.

He drew away, touched her there, where every atom of
her being was centered, aching, throbbing, damp with need.
How could hands that were so big, so strong touch her so

delicately? A man so physical, so turned on be so maddeningly slow?

He was tormenting her, teasing her, a low growl of satisfaction and need rumbling through him as he spread her legs, dipped his finger inside her.

Finn stiffened at his gentle probing, as he kissed her waist, her hip, dragged his lips to her center. He kissed her, then lifted his head, the dark silk of his hair brushing her stomach.

"Let me?" It was a question, a plea. His gaze pierced hers.

Finn couldn't squeeze a sound out of her throat. She nodded, barely able to breathe. He smiled, hot satisfaction in his eyes. His head dipped down.

She cried out, head tossing, hands clutching first the sheet, then the dark waves of his hair.

He was so good at this, she thought, sobbing with pleasure as he tempted her closer to the edge. She'd known he'd be good at this... But she'd never...never imagined...

She whimpered in protest as he pulled away, rose above her. She felt the tip of him, firm, velvety, press against her.

"Hell," he swore. "Protection...it's in my wallet...."

"No! You don't have to. I'm safe, Cade. I want to feel you...just you. All of you inside me."

Cade groaned, low, his laser-fierce gaze locking with hers, piercing deeper than his shaft ever could. With a cry of triumph, he thrust his hips forward, burying himself to the hilt.

He kissed her, touched her, his hands as hungry as his mouth, his body crashing against her like waves against a shore. Finn wrapped her legs around his hips, arching her body up to meet him.

She couldn't get enough of the power in him, the passion. He filled her past bearing. Deeper than her womb, burying himself in the depths of her heart.

She wanted more. Wanted everything. Wanted to fly with him when he came.

Cade bracketing her hips with his big, hard hands, drawing her higher, tighter to meet his thrusts, the crisis building in them both.

The place his tongue had teased rocked against his body, his shaft so deep inside her, hurling her higher.

She cried out, shattered, her teeth closing on the naked curve of his shoulder with savage tenderness as her world flew apart.

Cade drove deep once more, twice. He cried out her name, his whole body going rigid against her as he came in a white-hot rush.

He collapsed atop her, and Finn held him with all her might, knowing how much it had cost him to let himself go so completely, not just his body, but emotions far more dangerous.

Face buried in her pillow, tremors still working through his sweat-glossed body, he lay there, terribly quiet.

Why didn't he say something? Finn wondered, alarm flickering inside her. Was he already regretting opening himself up to her? Leaving himself vulnerable?

She swallowed hard, shaken to her core by what had happened between them, knowing her world would never be the same.

"Cade?" she breathed, softly, stroking his hair. "What is it? Tell me."

He lifted his face from the pillow, looked down at her, wonder in his eyes. "So that's what it feels like," he breathed, touching her cheek with awe.

"Pretty nice, huh?"

"I couldn't even imagine…"

"Don't try that line on me, mister. Remember? You told me you've done this before."

"Not this, Finn. No. Never this. Here with you was my very first time."

"Your first…? I don't understand."

"I never knew this is how it would feel to—" His voice cracked, his gaze flicking away.

"To what?" Finn urged, her heart bursting, her spirit soaring as Cade whispered against her throat.

Make love.

"Oh, Cade!" she laughed, cried. "I love you so much!"

He rolled to one side, peered down at her so intensely she felt naked in a way no stripping away of clothes could ever have left her. "You sure about that? You love me?"

"I wouldn't have said it if I wasn't."

"Then…how about marrying me?"

Finn scrambled upright, sitting on the bed. "Wh-what did you say?"

Cade levered himself up beside her, the white sheets stark against his long, tanned legs. "Marry me, Finn. Not a pretend wedding. A real one where I can make you my wife."

Finn clutched at reality, tried to reconcile this man with the one who'd sat across from her at Ella Fitzgerald's, his face wracked with pain, doubt.

"Are you crazy?" she said. "You can't be serious. This is supposed to be our first date. Well, first official date, anyway."

"We've been together every day since that disaster with your ceiling. I feel like I've known you forever. And you know me…really know me better than anyone else ever has before."

"You told me you'd never wanted to get married after your family—"

"That's how I felt—until you. I know this might seem sudden, but I've been thinking about you all the damned time for weeks now."

"Are you sure?"

"Finn, I've never been more sure of anything in my life. Hell, can't you see? I'm crazy in love with you. If you won't marry me, what the hell am I gonna do?"

Panic fluttered beneath Finn's ribs. *Oh, God. Marry Cade?* It was one thing to dream that far, that deep. But the reality… It's what she wanted, wasn't it? A husband who loved her?

But what if he changes his mind? A voice tormented her. *Decides he doesn't want you? Your father did.*

Cade is nothing like Da. Wasn't that why she loved him so much?

"Well?" Cade said, a worried crease between his brows. "I seem to have the hardest time getting you to say yes."

Tears welled up in Finn's eyes. "Yes. I'll marry you. Yes, yes, yes!" She flung her arms around him, tears dampening his shoulder, laughter bubbling up through her tears.

"Are you sure you don't have any doubts?" he asked, earnest.

Only about me. Finn pushed them aside. "Oh, Lord. How am I ever going to survive the next few months."

"What do you mean, darlin'?" He crooked her a devilish grin. "Believe me, there's plenty more of me where tonight came from."

Her cheeks burned at his sexy promise. "But we can't spend the night together for real until, well, it's official."

"Can't we?"

"I was thinking about Emma…."

"Ouch. That puts me in my place. Here I thought you were all dazzled about me. Pretty hard on a man's ego when he's just given his woman all he's got. Don't get me wrong. I love Emma. But I wasn't expecting to be upstaged by a kid who's clear across town."

"She won't be across town after tonight. And she's going to need some time to get used to the idea of the two of us getting married. Therein lies the problem," she explained. "With a ten-year-old in the house… It just doesn't seem right to…"

"Be all over each other under the covers?" Cade wriggled his brows suggestively, his face so boyish, so relaxed Finn knew even when she was eighty she'd remember how he looked at this moment. "That would be a challenge all right. But I'm a damned impatient man when it comes to you, Finn. I mean, after all, I did propose to you on our first date." He grinned in satisfaction. "You've taken the edge off, sugar, but I can tell you right now, I'll never get enough of you."

"I'm counting on it," Finn said, praying he was right.

"Speaking of the little monster, what do you say we go tell her?" He climbed out of the bed, shameless in his nakedness, comfortable in his skin, as if she'd seen him standing there, all tanned and bare skinned a thousand times. Finn warmed at the knowledge she would.

"Now?" she exclaimed. "It's the middle of the night!"

"Emma will be so thrilled with our news she won't care."

"You can't be sure how she'll feel, Cade."

"Yeah, I can. The kid's almost as crazy about you as I am."

"What about your father? We can't wake him up!"

"Why the hell not? Serve the ornery old buzzard right. He's dragged me out of bed in the middle of the night plenty of times. Nothing like a call from the police station to buzz you out of bed like a blasted air raid siren."

"The police? The Captain's been arrested?"

"Far as the local cops are concerned there's nothing illegal about breaking up gang fights and chasing down drunk drivers and such. Though sometimes I wish I could put him in a cell somewhere and keep him out of trouble. Come on, Finn, what do you say? We'll go get Emma, tell her she can have her damned wedding, but it won't be pretend. Hell, I don't even care if you wear those crazy dresses Emma loves, and have the ceremony in the gazebo with Emma's paper lanterns in all the trees as long as I get to put my ring on your finger."

"Oh, Cade." Finn slid out of bed, went to him, wrapping her arms around him, sinking into the warmth, the promise of him, skin to skin. "Do you really think it would make Emma happy? I want her to be happy."

"What about you?" He tipped her chin up, looked deep into her eyes.

"You even have to ask?" Finn didn't want him to see any shadows, any doubts.

"You're both gonna be happy from now on," Cade vowed, the resolute edge to his voice reminding Finn of a soldier going into battle. "I'm going to give you the home you want. And Emma—she won't ever have to worry about her mother again."

Dread slipped like a sliver into Finn's heart. She wanted to caution Cade, warn him. Life wasn't that simple. And little girls' hearts were far trickier than he could ever know. But the thought of shadowing his joy kept her silent. There would be time later, to talk. To try to make him understand…

"Emma won't even care that Deirdre's off God knows where," Cade insisted. "You'll be there. And maybe someday if I completely lose my mind she'll even have cousins, little boys who want to fly and girls with your eyes."

Finn's heart leaped, hardly able to believe what he was saying.

"I'm not promising anything. You'll have to, well, give me time to get used to the idea."

"While you're getting used to it, think about this. The girls might want to fly. You never know."

"They can walk on the goddamn moon if they want to." He scooped her up, whirled her around, until they were both breathless, laughing.

When he set her on her feet, he sobered. "I'm going to give Emma and our kids what we never had. You watch. I'm holding on tight to this chance, Finn. I won't let anything take it away from Emma. From you. From me."

Finn kissed him, tried to brush foreboding away. He'd

known so little love, this proud, strong man, she thought, clean love, free love, without hooks and tangles and traps. But in time, she'd show him, find a way to help him understand one of love's greatest mysteries.

You had to hold love like butterfly's wings, lightly, carefully, willing to let it fly. Because the tighter you tried to clutch love, the more likely you were to crush it in your hand.

"*YOU* WANT TO MARRY *HIM?*" Emma blinked like a baby owl. Roused from sleep a few moments earlier, the child perched next to her grandfather in the Captain's living room, and stared up at Finn with a disbelief that made Cade laugh out loud.

"Thanks a lot, you little monster!" he said, acting wounded. Then he grinned. "Hard to believe, isn't it? But then, I told you she was crazy when she bought that old house. Guess this proves I was right."

"Well, you smell nice, Uncle Cade. And you're real good at fixing things like leaky pipes and stuff. But you do get awful growly sometimes. Like when I wanted to cut up the uniform and make you all handsome."

"Give it up on the uniform bit, kid. I'm still wearing a suit to the wedding. But you and Finn can dress up in clown suits for all I care."

"What about after the wedding?"

"Then I go right back to jeans and flannel shirts—whichever ones you haven't bothered to cut up yet."

"I don't mean what're you going to wear. I mean where you gonna live?" Emma asked. "You've got two houses."

Cade frowned. "I don't know."

"We haven't really talked about that yet," Finn said. Cade knew by the flicker in her eyes they should have. The cabin was finished, in prime shape. They wouldn't have to touch it for ten years if they didn't want to. While March Winds…

they'd gotten a start on the place, but it would be a hell of a long time before it could be restored good as new.

"It's got to be March Winds, doesn't it, Finn?" Emma insisted. "You love it and it's home and—the cabin's real nice, too, Uncle Cade, but you don't care about it like we do."

He hadn't thought he did, until now. Funny, he suddenly remembered, picking out every log, making sure every nail was set, perfectly. He'd claimed he didn't want roots. But he'd built the cabin's walls solid—to keep the wolves out. Or the memories. Even so, Emma was right. He wanted Finn happy. That meant moving into a house he would've claimed was ready for a wrecking ball years ago.

"Now that I think about it, we could sell the cabin, use the money to expand Flyboy's," Cade said. "Jett's been wanting me to do it, but I kept stalling. Wouldn't feel right, not putting up half the money."

Finn touched his arm. "Cade, you don't have to do this. There's time to think this over."

"Emma's right. There's no contest. When you think of home you think of March Winds." In spite of the fact that the place was going to make the house in the *Money Pit* look like a teensy little no big deal quick fix-up job. He and Finn would be working on the Civil War–era house for years.

"And there's something else that's bothering me," Emma said. "Where's her ring?"

"Uh, this whole proposal thing came up kind of sudden," Cade said. In bed. After the best sex of his life. "We'll have to go to the jewelry store and buy one."

"Jewelry store?" Emma scoffed. "Finn wouldn't like one from a jewelry store, all new and shiny and boring, like everyone else's. She needs the one in grandma's jewelry box, Captain. That real old one with the green rock in it."

"Emma," Finn protested, "I don't think—"

The Captain looked at her, old pain in his craggy features fading. "I think you're right, Emma."

"Captain, you don't have to this," Cade said, uneasy. "That emerald is supposed to be Deirdre's ring. She's the girl."

"It's supposed to go to whoever I decide it goes to," the Captain asserted stubbornly.

"Mom wouldn't like it, anyway," Emma insisted. "Nobody could see when she's on stage."

"But what about Emma?" Finn said, turning from the Captain to the little girl standing there, so hopeful. "You love old things, don't you sweetheart? Your grandpa should save it for you."

"No! I want you to have it. It's not real that you're getting married until you got a ring," Emma said, concern furrowing her brow. "She's just gotta have it, doesn't she, Captain?"

"Go get it, Lieutenant," the Captain said, flashing his granddaughter a crisp salute. Emma's small hand swept up in a perfect imitation. Cade remembered when he and Deirdre had done the same thing, mimicking their invincible giant of a father to make him laugh. Emma bolted out of the room.

The Captain turned to Finn. "The ring was my Irish grandmother's. A hell of a fighter, she was. Got mixed up in the Easter Uprising and had to run for her life. Came to America at sixteen years old, didn't know a soul. Eloped with the son of the family whose floors she scrubbed. The whole world was so damned sure the marriage would be a disaster. Should have been, different as they were. But I never knew anyone else so much in love. That's why I thought it didn't matter Emmaline and I were so— Maybe I should have known when she didn't want the ring when I tried to give it to her."

The Captain stopped, looked away. "I was wrong where your mother and I were concerned. But you, Cade. You're different. So much smarter than we ever were. I think you've got a hell of a good chance at finding the kind of happiness my grandfather did with his Irish bride."

Cade's throat tightened. He'd always know how badly his mother had hurt at the disaster of her marriage. He'd just thought it made the Captain mad as hell. The old man wasn't used to failing at anything he turned his hand to. But the pain, the regret in Martin McDaniel's face was real.

"I wasn't very good at being a husband, little girl," the Captain said, taking Finn's hand. "My son will be a better one. I was starting to think his mother and I botched things up so badly he'd never take the chance to try. He's a good man, my boy is. Take care of him."

Finn's eyes welled up as she stood on tiptoe to kiss the Captain's cheek. "I will."

Emma dashed in, triumphant, her fingers clutched tight in a fist. She came to Cade thrust it in his hand. "You gotta put it on her now. Go down on one knee, like they do in the movies."

"I already did that part—the asking part, I mean." Cade objected, resisting the prospect of making an idiot of himself in front of the Captain and Emma. "Remember? She said yes!"

Emma pouted, her dark eyes pleading, like she was afraid it was too good to be true. Wanted proof, to see for herself. Cade couldn't blame her. He could hardly believe it himself. "You have to, Uncle Cade. And the Captain and I'll make sure you do it right."

"Terrific," Cade grumbled. But hell, what could he do? With Emma giving him the Big Eyes, and Finn's face, tear-washed and glowing and the Captain looking as if he were about to bark out a command at any moment.

On your knees, soldier!

Cade looked down at the ring Emma pressed in his hand. Thought of all the disappointments the child had faced, how many times she'd been let down. And his father—the grief Cade had glimpsed on the old man's face.

Cade had never known his mother had rejected the antique ring. What had it done to the Captain, when his own wife had turned the ring down, as if it weren't good enough. And later, rejected the Captain as if *he* weren't good enough. Not cruelly. Subtly, in a hundred little ways.

After everything fate had given Cade tonight, Finn's love, a future, what was a little embarrassment if it would make Emma and the old man happy?

Cade turned to Finn and sank down on one knee, his cheeks burning. He could feel eyes boring into his back, Emma's, the Captain's.

"Finnoula O'Grady, will you marry me?" he asked gruffly.

"He's growling again," Emma whispered to her grandfather. "See what I mean?"

Cade shot the kid a glare. "You gonna let me handle this or not?"

Emma made a quick hand motion, like she was zipping up her lips. Cade tried hard not to smile.

"So," the Captain asked, impatient as always. "You going to say yes or not, missy?"

"Yes." Finn laughed. "Again."

Cade slid the ring on her finger, the square cut emerald framed by tiny winking diamonds that his great-grandfather had chosen for the woman he loved. A woman with courage, and the fairy lights of Ireland in her face. He wondered if that rebel colleen had been half as much a miracle as Finn.

He surprised himself, catching hold of Finn's fingers, drawing them to his lips. He kissed the hand now adorned with his ring. Emma was right. It did make it real.

Choked up, he fought to school his features back in a scowl as he looked over at his niece. "That pass with your approval, you little monster?"

Emma nudged her grandfather's leg with one bare foot. The Captain's gaze flashed to hers. On cue, they snapped to attention and saluted.

Cade laughed, gathering Finn in his arms, loving them.

His family. The McDaniel clan—crazy and difficult, quick-tempered and stubborn. And so damned wonderful it hurt. Everyone he loved. All together on the biggest night of his life.

Not all of them. A voice whispered in his head. *Not Deirdre.*

Guilt flickered through him, and he wondered if she would mind about the ring. Not that it should matter. Emma was right. Deirdre wouldn't want it. If it didn't dazzle people when she was up on stage, she didn't want to be bothered.

Like she hadn't wanted to be bothered with her daughter.

Cade tried not to mind that Deirdre was off God knew where. He just hoped to hell she'd stay there. He didn't give a damn if he ever saw his sister again after what she'd done to Emma, to him.

But if she hadn't left Emma with him, he never would've gotten to know what an amazing kid his niece was, would never had the chance to fall in love with Finn, have his future filled with love, with laughter.

But that doesn't change what Deirdre did. Abandoned Emma. Hell, dumped the Captain and me. All three of us, like we didn't matter at all.

Bitterness welled up inside him when he thought of his sister's face—pale from staying up all night, eyes a little wild lost in dark circles, like an animal, trapped. But she'd been the one who'd trapped him, sneaking out of the cabin in the middle of the night without a word.

Hell, sometimes the past months he thought he hated her. Except that he'd done his share to screw her up, leaving her to watch their mother die, the Captain diving into a bottle.

Leaving her to take the brunt of it when the whole world fell apart.

Maybe he had kept the secret their mother had saddled him with at sixteen, but if Deirdre ever found out the truth—hell, she'd be the one hating him.

"Uncle Cade, what's the matter?" Emma probed, sounding worried.

"Nothing. Just thinking. Wondering if I got this whole proposal thing right."

"Yeah." Emma sidled up, grabbed his hand. "If you got any more questions about stuff like that, just ask me."

"Count on it," he said.

He closed his eyes, trying to concentrate on Finn, on everything he had to be grateful for. He didn't expect another face to drift into his memory. Not the life-hardened planes of the lead singer of an on-the-verge-of-stardom rock band. Not the defiant, reckless sister who'd told the Captain to go to hell. No, the other Deirdre, who still haunted him.

His baby sister, trailing after him as if he were cooler than a superhero, her chin tipped up, eyes locked straight ahead, so damned serious she looked ready to go to war. Deirdre at six years old, saluting, before a hundred bad choices made her so lost she could never find her way back.

DEIRDRE MCDANIEL stood by the window, staring at rivers of headlights pouring away from the city in the dark. She'd always loved night—even as a kid. Daylight was far too glaring, showing every crack, every flaw.

Night was the music's time. When clubs would start to fill, cigarette smoke swirling in a cloud above an audience's heads, like wisps from a sorcerer's wand in one of Emma's storybooks. And they waited, a roomful of strangers, for Deirdre to pull out the magic. She'd blast her voice into every dark corner, every crevice in people's souls, until the music pounded down the walls inside them. She'd play and sing until her ears throbbed and her throat felt sandpaper rough and somehow, in all that mad whirl of sound, she'd find her own quiet center.

It was only later, after her buzz from the applause wore off and she was finally alone that the world got too loud and she wanted to reach for Emma.

Emma. Her baby girl. Smelling like baby shampoo after her midnight bath—somehow Deirdre hadn't been able to stand the smell of smoke on her hair, had wanted to wash it off of her the moment they got home, wherever home was.

Emma hadn't griped at all about being thrust into the tub when the rest of the kids her age were asleep. She'd loved that time, with Deirdre sitting on the cold tile floor, listening as Emma jabbered herself into oblivion. God, she would love to hear her baby's voice now. But Emma was back in Illinois with Cade. She'd be tucked in bed, sound asleep, a contraband book and a flashlight abandoned under the covers. Emma safe and warm in the kind of home she deserved. The home Deirdre couldn't give her.

Deirdre's heart squeezed, loneliness washing over her in crushing waves. Emma could always make the world seem brighter. Better. And not just her mom's.

What had their last landlady said after baby-sitting one night? *She's such a funny little thing. The things that come out of that child's mouth, you'd think she's lived a hundred years. Why, makes you forget all your troubles, and start wondering about the people in the stories she tells. I swear, there's not a thing in the world I wouldn't do for that little girl.*

Like letting Deirdre break her lease and head off to a better gig in Atlanta when her band put the pressure on. She'd hated feeling like she was taking advantage, but her bass guitarist, and aspiring lover, Travis Langdon, had been in a hurry to blow town, dismissing her scruples with a wave of his hand.

You should always find old grannies to live with from now on. The grannies get their rent, and as long as the rest of the band doesn't bunk in with you, nobody trashes the place. And when it's time to blow this Popsicle stand for a better gig in some other city, Emma can charm your landladies so much they won't hold you to the lease. It's the perfect setup.

It *had* been better for Emma—some of the women had actually liked baby-sitting her. It had done Deirdre good to come home and find fresh-baked cookies sometimes, Emma in bed. Maybe it had done Deirdre too much good, seeing her little girl sink into a home. Until she had to be yanked out by the roots again.

She'd been so stoic, most of the time. Her little gypsy, until...

Deirdre winced, remembering her little girl's last goodbye. How she'd clutched the bag of cookies. Shaken the gnarled hand that had been so kind to her.

Like Emma's grandmother would have been if she'd been alive....

Deirdre fought back a stab of pain. Her mother would have been crazy about Emma. The kind of little girl she'd always wanted. Instead of a hotheaded, rebellious, music crazy daughter who was better at stirring up trouble than cookie dough.

But her mother was dead. Probably a good thing she couldn't see what a mess Deirdre had made out of her life. And the Captain— She could imagine what he had to say when Cade told him what she'd done. He was probably still yelling about what a failure she was for leaving Emma behind.

Deirdre closed her eyes, burning from smoke and exhaustion. She'd done the right thing for her daughter. Done the best she could. Not that her best had ever been good enough where her parents were concerned. No, she was always the devil child, in counterpoint to Saint Cade who always did the right thing. Like he'd do what was right for Emma.

"I wonder if she misses me?" Deirdre murmured, flattening her hand against the windowpane, wondering why she hadn't known—how much it would hurt, how long it would burn, how slow time would crawl without Emma to make her smile.

She'd made her decision. The right one. She'd been so sure. The music—that's who she was—the only thing she'd ever been good at.

She sure stunk at being a mother—she'd seen it in Cade's eyes, heard it in his voice the night she'd tried to tell him…she was drowning. Scared. Couldn't handle it all alone. Failing Emma…

But then, hadn't the Captain told her she would? She closed her eyes, remembering the scene when she'd broken the news.

I'm pregnant.

What the hell are you thinking, having a baby? You can't even take care of yourself!

She was taking care of Emma now, wasn't she? Leaving Emma with Cade? She was strong enough to let her little girl go. But if she could just see Emma, be sure she was happy. If she could just gather Emma onto her lap for a little while, drink in the smell of her, feel the warmth of those small arms wrapping around her in a hug.

You'd just have to walk away again. It would be cruel. Hurt her again.

But it wouldn't hurt just to *see* Emma, would it? Look at her from someplace the child would never see her? Make sure she'd been right—that Emma was growing, thriving…happy the way Deirdre wanted her to be.

She had a two-week break between gigs. What harm could it do to slip into Whitewater long enough to get a glimpse of her daughter? No one would have to see her. Not Emma. And sure as heck not Cade. What her big brother would have to say to her was something Deirdre didn't want to hear.

"Hey, gorgeous?" Travis leaned in the nightclub doorway, his blond mane glossy against the black of his expensive new leather jacket. The newest addition to his wardrobe accenting his sexy guitar man body as he flashed that "come and get me" smile that made groupies scream.

Deirdre remembered when he'd been so sure he could make her love him—at least enough to get her in bed. "Yes?"

"Take a look at this. Steve-o got it in a package from his girlfriend." He handed her a newspaper clipping. "Isn't this the brother you left the kid with?"

"She's got a name," Deirdre snapped. "Emma."

"Okay. Okay. Emma. Man, are you on permanent PMS lately."

She stared at the engagement announcement, stunned. Finn O'Grady to Marry Cade McDaniel in Garden Ceremony.

Married? Deirdre thought, stunned. Cade was getting married? She'd been sure Mom and the Captain had cured him of ever trying the 'til death do us part thing.

She held the clipping up to the light, regarding the woman in the picture. Whoa. She didn't look like Cade's usual girlfriends. She looked smart, and had real soft-looking eyes, like she'd seen trouble in her life. Maybe she would understand…understand what? A voice mocked her. That you abandoned your daughter?

I was trying to do what was best for Emma. Because I love her. But it hurts. It hurts so much being without her.

"Hey, Dee?" Travis said. "Read the thing later. The audience is all revved up and waiting for you to dazzle them. Come on, honey, let's go do what we do best."

Deirdre stepped out to make the music that had always made her happy. But the lights weren't as bright, the songs weren't as powerful, the audience gray instead of splashed in rainbow hues.

She'd never missed the sunshine. But, God, how she missed the light in her baby girl's eyes.

CHAPTER EIGHTEEN

VERNA SOPHER slipped the last tray of goodies into Finn's refrigerator as deftly as a book on an overfull shelf, then shut the door, making the engagement announcements Emma had plastered on the front of the overstuffed appliance ripple like ruffling feathers.

Emma clasped her hands, pleasure softening the solemn lines in her small face.

"You got it all right, Miss Sopher! The baby cakes and the strawberries and cream will be perfect for the bridal tea tomorrow. And it'll be good practice for when you bake the wedding cake, all homemade like Addy's sister's was!"

"Got the recipes out of my mother's old cookbook, so they should be about right. Glad they pass inspection," Verna said, favoring Emma with a smile.

"White cake was my mom's very favorite." A haunted shadow fell in Emma's eyes. Finn winced at the child's use of the word "was," as if her mother had died. Was never coming back. But wasn't that what Cade wanted? Legal custody of Emma? Deirdre and what he saw as the chaos she'd brought to Emma's life banished like a bad dream? But there were good memories hiding in Emma's mind, too. And a loneliness Finn understood all too well. An emptiness even someone as wonderful and loving and responsible as Cade could never fill.

Gaps and holes where a mother should have been, painful

spaces Finn herself had felt in the weeks leading toward her wedding. A void Verna Sopher, in her capable kindness had tried to fill as best she could. Just thinking about the trouble the older woman had gone to for a virtual stranger made Finn's eyes burn.

"Everything you made is beautiful," Finn said. "But you shouldn't have gone to so much trouble."

"I thought we'd settled this at the library. You haven't a mother of your own to take charge of all this. Someone has to fuss over you."

"Yeah! Like me! I've been fussing a whole lot!" Emma said, seriously. "I made them put that announcement thing in the papers and do you know, if it wasn't for me she wouldn't even have got that ring? Men just don't know how to do this wedding stuff right these days." She shook her head with a sigh.

"I've been helping with the cabin, too. I practically got it sold all by myself—Uncle Cade won't even need that icky Realtor lady that used to get so crabby about the stupid For Sale sign on the tree. Those new girls were real nervous about moving to Whitewater, even if their mom and dad were just thinking about the cabin—until I showed 'em everything. Even my secret hiding place under the deck, and how to sneak out the bedroom window if you—"

"Not a good idea, Emma," Finn warned, tugging a silky black curl.

"But I want them to buy the cabin real bad. Jessica, the oldest girl, liked me. Maybe…maybe she'll be my friend." A spark of hope Finn had never seen before lit Emma's eyes. Hope Finn knew was all too fragile, excruciatingly painful if fate should ever snatch it away. "It would be real nice to have a friend who could talk back to you for real," Emma confided, "not just imagining like Addy."

"And just exactly what does this Jessica like to read?"

Verna asked, as if the answer to that question would tell her everything there was to know about the child in question.

"She had a real special copy of *Little Women* an' she won't let her little sisters touch it. But she said I could read it if I wanted. I told her about my mom leaving and Jessica said the mom in that book was the best mom ever. If I read about her, I bet I won't miss my mom at all anymore."

Finn's heart ached, and she wished it were that simple. How many hours had she spent reading the *Little House* books with Pa Ingalls, the fiddling Mad Dog playing, adoring father who had carried his little family across pioneer America? She'd followed the family's trek book by book, from the Big Woods in Wisconsin, across Indian Territory and Plum Creek to the Dakotas as Pa searched for the perfect home. Always thinking the crops were better, the land richer, the game more plentiful somewhere beyond the horizon.

Laura Ingalls's fictional father had been like Finn's own da in his wandering. Except that Pa Ingalls had kept his daughters with him every step of the way. And yet, hadn't the books just made Finn feel sadder in the end? Left her wondering what it was about her that made her da able to leave her behind?

"*Little Women* is a wonderful story," she said, praying the most beloved mother in children's literature wouldn't make the loss of Emma's real mother all the harder to bear.

"Finn," Emma said, "Jessica was talking about a mailbox between Jo and Laurie's houses, so they could pass notes and stuff. Do you think we could nail one to the picket fence?"

"*If* Jessica's family buys the cabin, and that's still a big *if*, I'm sure your Uncle Cade would be happy to put a box up for you. It'll be a nice change from working on that gazebo."

She glanced out the window, to see Cade and his father stroking the last coat of white paint onto the restored posts. Cade had done stroking of another kind when he'd shown the gazebo to her late last night, creeping out while Emma lay sleeping.

The posts were plenty sturdy, Finn thought with a secret smile. Cade had shown her by pinning her up against one and making love to her until they'd both been gasping. Her whole body tingled, remembering the desperation in him, the hunger as she'd tried to pull away.

What about Emma? We need to go back...

To the house where they'd limited themselves to surreptitious touches, stolen kisses when Emma wasn't looking.

"I want you now," Cade had said so fiercely, her blood caught fire.

She'd thrown herself into passion, even hungrier for their joining than he was. As if, when she blinked her eyes he might slip away.

Like her father had. Even after all the promises he'd made.

No, Finn told herself, firmly stifling the strange flutter of panic under her ribs. Cade kept his promises. Stalwart, steady, dependable. He was everything Patrick O'Grady was not.

Cade would never even have done the *Little House* bit, and dragged his girls halfway across the country, through Indian uprisings and railroad camps and winter blizzards that nearly froze and starved his family to death. No. He'd stay right where he was, dug in with that stubbornness that had kept him in Whitewater with his father, kept him fighting for his sister until Deirdre had done the unforgivable and left Emma on his doorstep.

Finn remembered how it felt to be pinned between the gazebo post and Cade's hard body. Trapped for a heartbeat between the future and a man as rooted as the cabin he'd built, solid, painstakingly hewn by life's sharp edges, pieces put back together, not someplace else, but exactly where he stood, when it would have been far easier to slip away, make a fresh start.

Like Finn had, so many times before? The insight taunted her. But that had been different, not at all like her father, Finn told herself. She'd been looking for something tangible. Now that she had March Winds she'd settle into one place, never be tempted to wander again.

Not with Cade burning her up inside with desire and Emma, looking to her for the love her mother couldn't seem to give. Dread feathered through Finn, a subtle sense of danger. It was crazy to love anyone this much. Life had taught Finn that lesson ever so clearly—love meant risking the pain of losing.

You're being ridiculous, Finn told herself sternly. *Cade is marrying you next Saturday. He's going to promise to love you forever.*

Forever, filled with days of his loving, nights of his wild, primal need for her body and soul so deep it thrilled her, terrified her. The relentless passion he'd shared with her in the night-dark gazebo with his hands all over her body, reaching so deep he brushed the secret raw places in her soul.

"Did you see what Uncle Cade and Finn did in that gazebo, Miss Sopher?"

Finn started, her cheeks afire as Emma piped up. Oh, Lord, she thought, dismayed. Emma couldn't have been playing Peeping Tom last night. "Emma, tell me you weren't sneaking around last night?"

"What do you mean, last night?" Emma looked so bewildered Finn let out a sigh of relief.

"Nothing," Finn said, painfully aware that she and Cade had been so lost in each other they wouldn't have noticed if an earthquake had shaken the newly shored up roof of the structure down on their heads.

Emma turned to Verna with a long-suffering air. "Weddings make people's brains leak. Uncle Cade even waked me up in the middle of the night last night to make sure I was sleeping."

So Cade *had* checked on Emma after he'd left the gazebo, probably dreading the same thing. Thank God she'd been sound asleep!

"That gazebo is just *gorgeous,* Miss Sopher!" Emma said. "And do you know Uncle Cade hasn't even growled once the whole time he's been fixing it!"

"Amazing," Verna laughed. "I seem to remember some very questionable language last time your uncle was working on Louise."

"Louise?" Emma asked, curious.

"My car. No one but your uncle has ever so much as peeked under her hood. That's why baking a few sweets for this wedding is the least I can do."

"Did you see our dresses? Mine and Finn's?" Emma asked. "They look like lace waterfalls, all white and foamy. They're hanging in the bedroom until the wedding. I got a blue sash and little blue slippers. Slippers are hard to find these days, you know, 'cause everybody wears tennis shoes."

"We settled on ballet slippers and had them dyed," Finn explained. "They were the closest as we could come to Addy's satin dancing slippers."

"But I had to promise I wouldn't wear 'em to school." Emma grew wistful. "I'd just adore to wear them to school. My mom let me wear any shoes I wanted. I even wore a red tennis shoe and a blue tennis shoe once, like a joke. She said it's good to have your very own style. Be an individual, instead of a cookie-cutter kid. If *she* was here—"

Emma paused, caught her bottom lip between her teeth, a wave of sadness settling across her face. She seemed to gather herself up after a moment, square her small shoulders. "But Finn says I can't wear 'em because I could slip and get hurt. And I got to listen because you're going to be my mom now, aren't you, Finn?"

Finn shrank away inwardly from taking on that label. She

might love Emma. Nurture this sensitive little spirit. But Emma had a mother. And Finn wasn't it. "I'm going to take care of you," Finn said.

"Yeah. I'm going to belong to you and Uncle Cade," Emma said, seemingly satisfied with Finn's response. "My mom left me," Emma told Verna, her chin bumping up with a defiance belied by the pain that still lurked in her wandering angel eyes. "I don't care if she never comes back!"

Finn touched Emma's hair gently, wishing it were that simple. But she'd said the same thing herself when her father went away. Trouble was, it was a lie. She did care, and so did Emma, with all of her broken little heart.

"Why don't you show Miss Sopher the dresses," Finn said, trying to distract the child. "Ask her what color flowers she thinks we should wear in our hair."

Emma brightened. "There's a jillion colors in the garden. Finn said I can pick every single flower if I want, but Uncle Cade says the bumblebees'll carry me away if I stick too many in my hair."

"Bumblebees?" Verna tried to tease. Finn could see the older woman was trying to hide the sympathy she felt after hearing the little girl's confidences. "I wouldn't advise putting any of those in my hair."

"I wouldn't put the bumblebees in my hair. They'd get in it all by themselves," Emma told Verna, her mind on spring roses and violets instead of the mother who'd thrown her away.

The phone rang, and Emma dodged over to get it. "McDaniel residence, Emma speaking. Well, not McDaniel residence yet. Not 'til the wedding next week. May I help you?"

Finn imagined the bewildered party on the other end of the phone. Who on earth could it be? The Captain was helping Cade out back. Verna was here. It's not like there was anyone else in particular to call her.

Emma frowned, her little face furrowed with confusion. "Some man with a really bad cold wants to talk to you alone. His voice sounds all funny."

"Weird," Finn said, suddenly uneasy. "Why don't you and Verna take that lemonade we made earlier outside to the menfolk. It'll cool them off and make room in the refrigerator. We don't want your Uncle Cade fainting from dehydration."

"Okay, but you'd better drink some lemonade, too. Especially before the wedding next week. It's always the lady who's swooning in books when they're all crunched up in those corset things."

Emma turned her attention to holding the back door, helping Verna carry out the tray, but as Emma shut the screen, the little girl cast back one last, worried glance at Finn. As if Emma knew Finn was almost waiting for something to happen....

Knew Finn's doubts, her edginess, her fears, that unexpected sliver of panic that jabbed under her skin whenever she thought of the wedding. The strange urge Finn had to gather up her belongings, ready to bolt just in case things went wrong.

Because things did go wrong. Finn had seen it before. So had Emma. The little girl was looking for trouble. Finn had done the same thing plenty of times herself after her father had left her.

But Finn wasn't going to let anything spoil this—not for her, or for Emma, or Cade.

Finn scooped up the phone. "Hello?"

"Ms. O'Grady?"

"Yes?" Emma was right. Whoever it was sounded terrible. She couldn't even tell if it was a man or a woman.

"You don't know me, but I need to talk to you about something important."

Finn's nape prickled with unease. She felt a moment's

panic, thinking of her father. She'd had to pull him out of trouble in the past. But Patrick O'Grady was dead. What trouble could there possibly be? "Who is this?" she demanded sternly.

"Someone who needs to talk to you. Meet me at Fuller's Mill in Fairbright. It's a little town forty-five minutes from where you are."

"Are you out of your mind?" Finn said, confused, off balance. "I'm going to have a garden full of people at a bridal tea here tomorrow. And even if I wasn't, there's no way I'm going to meet a complete stranger God knows where. Don't you watch the evening news? Goodbye."

"Wait!" A woman's voice stunned her. Suddenly clear. Strained. Desperate. "Don't hang up! Please."

Finn froze, a heartbeat from hanging up the phone.

"It's about Emma," the woman said. "I need to talk to you about Emma."

"Emma?" Suspicion tugged at Finn, setting her hand trembling. "Who is this?"

"I won't keep you long," the mysterious caller hedged. "I'm begging you. I need your help."

"Deirdre? Is that you?" Was this Cade's sister? Finn wondered. The little girl who'd followed him around? The kid who'd fallen off the wing of a plane and almost died? The rebel who'd felt rejected, without understanding why?

Was she talking to the Deirdre who'd turned her back on her family without knowing her own mother's terrible secret? Cade's sister who'd left behind a little girl who missed her mother, in spite of Emma's claims to the contrary?

Oh, God, Finn thought desperately. *Don't let her hang up. For Emma's sake, for Cade's, let me say the right thing!*

"Deirdre, Emma's going to be so glad to know you're all right. And Cade—he's been searching for you."

"I'll just bet he has," the woman said bitterly.

Finn started toward the back door, hope flooding through her. This was what she'd prayed for—a chance for Cade and Emma and Deirdre to heal—a wedding gift beyond price. If Cade wouldn't be too stubborn to forgive…. "Cade's right outside, Deirdre. Let me get him."

"No!"

Finn's ear rang as the woman all but shouted in alarm.

"Don't tell Cade! You're the one I want to talk to."

"You don't even know me," Finn reasoned, wanting desperately to hand the phone to Cade, pass the crushing responsibility of this call over to him. Cade, who'd had so much practice dealing with impossibly sensitive family situations while Finn… Finn had had none. "Your brother loves you," Finn soothed, wondering if Deirdre McDaniel had any idea how lucky she was. "He wants what's best for you and Emma."

What he *thought was best, anyway,* a voice inside Finn whispered. She tried not to remember the stony look in Cade's eyes, the hard anger, determination. *I'm going to sue for custody.*

The memory made Finn tense, Cade's determination set in counterpoint to his niece's desperate struggle, Emma torn between clinging to her love for her mother and letting that mother go.

"And Emma…" Finn said, hoping to find some way to touch the heart of this woman she'd never met. "Whenever Emma talks about you, she gets this look in her eye. I know you were a good mother to her, except for…"

"Except for dragging her all over the damned country following the band? And dumping her on my brother's doorstep? And God knows what other things I've done wrong? Yeah, I've done such a great job I should get Mother of the Year."

"You kept Emma with you for ten years. That alone proves you love her. As soon as Cade understands that, he'll move heaven and earth to help you."

Finn prayed it was true. But if it came down to the wire, what had Cade said? *Grown-ups can take care of themselves.* It was Emma who needed protection, he believed even from her own mother. "Your brother—"

"Don't try to tell me about my brother!" Deirdre snapped, agitated as a skittish animal ready to bolt. "I think I know Cade a little better than you do. Either you come and meet with me alone, or I swear, I'm outta here. This is a onetime chance."

Chance for what? Finn thought, suddenly cold. A onetime chance to set things right for Emma, reunite the hurting little girl with her mother? A onetime chance for Emma to heal. And yet, at what cost? Deceiving Cade the week before their wedding? Doing something Finn knew the man she loved would see as betrayal? Finn's stomach lurched as she peered out the back door window, saw Cade's dark head bent over Emma's, listening intently to the little girl's chatter.

Oh, God, if Finn botched this would he ever forgive her? Put aside the wound she'd cut in his spirit? She shivered, remembering the unrelenting tone in his voice, his determination to close even his own sister out when she'd done something beyond his stubborn code of honor.

If Finn lied to him would his reaction be the same? Why in God's name did Deirdre have to come back to Whitewater right now? And how in the world had she found out about Finn in the first place?

Finn shuddered, remembering the feeling she'd had sometimes, as if something was going to go wrong, the future Cade promised too good to be true. She tried to calm the panic inside her, the sense she was going to ruin things, the impulse to run before she did. Her hand clenched on the receiver as she tried to steady her nerves.

"Deirdre, are you all right?" Finn asked, wondering if illness or calamity had driven the woman to call.

"Come and see for yourself," Deirdre dared her, pushing in a way that knotted Finn up inside. "Just…just come. Please."

Foreboding chilled Finn, the clouds that had been hovering on the edge of her mood darkening.

Fear, cold dread that came from knowing the truth…the danger in loving anyone was that you might lose them.

Finn imagined Cade's face when he found out what she'd done, sneaked away to meet with a sister he now saw as his rival, the person who could take Emma away.

"Let me meet you next week, then," Finn said. "After the wedding." When she had Cade, safe.

"No. It—it has to be today. I won't be here next week."

Finn hesitated, feeling torn in two. Oh, Lord, what to do? Didn't she owe it to Emma to find out what this was about? But Cade…oh, God, Cade…if he found out—*when* he found out it would hurt him so badly. What would it do to him if Deirdre took Emma away?

Finn wavered, loving them both. But what had she sensed for weeks now? A hard, cold truth. That if she could fix things somehow for Emma everything would be all right. All Finn's own doubts would be swept away. The restlessness, the waiting and watching for happiness to slip away would disappear if only Finn could prove to herself there could be happy endings.

But not the ending Cade had wanted, she thought, aching. If she met Deirdre, she might lose Cade's trust. If she didn't meet Emma's mother…she might lose forever the chance to make Emma whole, heal the hideous tearing wound left in the sensitive child's soul when her mother had pulled away from her.

She vacillated afraid that no matter what she did, she would hurt one of the two people she loved most in the world.

Sucking in a deep breath, she took the biggest risk of her life. "All right. I'll be there as soon as I can get away."

"You won't be sorry," Deirdre said.

Finn's stinging gaze searched out Cade, his throat arched back as he took a long drink of lemonade, a few drops running down his corded throat, the frosty glass curled in hands that had made Finn feel excruciatingly alive, loved for the first time in so long. Emma solemnly showing Verna and the Captain the steps of the waltz Finn had taught her, as if the little girl was testing her precious slippers out for dancing. And the Captain, looking calmer and happier than she'd ever seen him, working side by side with his son to build Cade's new family dreams.

Finn wanted those dreams to be perfect for Cade, as well. Why hadn't Deirdre's call waited one more week? Until the wedding was over without facing all the pain and hard choices Deirdre's return would bring?

Finn shivered as the sun shifted under a cloud, throwing Cade in shadow.

What had Deirdre said on the telephone when Finn agreed to meet her?

You won't be sorry.

Too late.

She already was.

FULLER'S MILL crowded along the bend of the river, waiting for the evening crowd to pour in. A restaurant by day, club by night, a neon light-up board boasted an upcoming band, Muddy Waters, cover charge, three bucks.

Nervous as a wet cat, Finn entered the dim room, trying to let her eyes grow accustomed to the lack of light. A few couples were scattered across the room, the busiest part of the lunch crowd past.

A lone woman sat in one of the little tables closest to a ply-wood stage. She half rose when Finn walked in. Two cups and a carafe of coffee already sat on the table, but the woman beckoning to Finn already looked as if she'd had too much.

Finn's heart tripped as the glow from an overhead light illuminated the person's face enough so she could see—the beautiful woman who'd been in the photograph on Emma's bedside table.

"Deirdre?" Finn asked as she approached the woman.

She looked so much like Cade—her dark hair and piercing eyes, but Deirdre's fine-boned face was too thin, pale, her slender body in black pants and a flowing white poet's shirt agitated, as if every so often she brushed against a hot stove.

Her chin had that "take your best shot" angle to it, but she was so tiny it looked as if one tap would shatter her. Until you looked into those fiercely intelligent eyes.

"You must be the bride."

"Finnoula O'Grady."

"Whoa, that's a mouthful. Bet the teachers butchered that one on the first day of school."

Irritation sparked in Finn as she remembered a dozen or so incidents like the one Deirdre described, people making fun of her Irish name. She almost snapped a reply. But losing her temper with Deirdre in the first five minutes of this meeting wasn't going to help Emma.

Finn forced herself to remember Cade's surliness during their first encounter in the garden. Maybe McDaniels should come with some kind of warning label the first time a person met them. "Introduce yourself at your own risk."

She sat down at the table and rested her elbows on its edge. "Call me Finn."

"Finn. At least it's unique. I was always afraid Cade would marry somebody named Tiffany." Deirdre fiddled with the silverware, her fingers almost never still. "I ordered coffee and told the waitress to get lost. Figured we didn't want to be interrupted. If you want something to eat I can call her back."

"No. I'm not hungry." Lying to Cade killed her appetite.

Deirdre examined her with sharp curiosity. "I have to say you surprise me. You're not exactly my brother's type."

What is Cade's type? Finn almost asked, insecurity twisting inside her, but she had the feeling Deirdre had a gift beyond her music—ticking people off. If they were irritated, off balance, Deirdre had the advantage. A true McDaniel, Finn thought, but this one didn't fight with her fists.

Finn heard a rustle as someone sat down at a table near them, didn't even bother to look up. "Deirdre, I don't like deceiving Cade. I'm a rotten liar and when I'm stupid enough to try it, I always get caught. So let's just get straight to the reason you called."

Deirdre started at her bluntness. "I told you on the phone. I want to know how Emma is doing."

"Come see for yourself." Finn winced, imagining the reception she'd get, ushering Deirdre into March Winds' garden. She'd had to make some excuse to slip off alone, so she'd told the cluster of lemonade drinkers at the gazebo—*I'm working on a surprise for Cade.*

Oh, Cade would be surprised all right, if she pulled this off. So surprised Finn would be lucky if he didn't murder her.

"I...can't go see Emma." Deirdre balked, dropping the fork against a soup spoon with a clatter. "I just need you to tell me how she's doing. Is she all right?"

"No. She's not. How could she be without her mother?"

Deirdre flinched as if Finn had slapped her. Finn saw Cade's sister stifle the pain, exchange it for defiance. Deirdre's pugnacious chin thrust out even farther. "Emma's better off without me." Deirdre gave a brittle laugh. "Surely one of the times you two lovebirds came up for air my brother told you what he thinks about my mothering skills."

"It doesn't matter what Cade thinks. It matters what Emma thinks. Doesn't it?"

"She's a kid. What does she know?"

"She misses you terribly. She doesn't understand why you left her. She's all torn up inside wondering when you're coming back. *If* you're coming back at all."

Finn hated the cutting edge to her words, knew she had no choice but to use them. God knew how long Deirdre would sit here, listening to what must be painful.

Deirdre's face tightened, and Finn knew she'd cut to the quick. "I don't think my coming to see Emma is such a good idea. It would just confuse her." Deirdre sucked in a sharp breath, staring at Finn's finger, light from the table candle setting her emerald aglow with green fire. "That ring," Deirdre squeezed out painfully. "Where...where did you get that ring?"

Finn's cheeks burned. She covered the emerald swiftly with her opposite hand, guessing just how it must have hurt Deirdre to see it on someone else's finger. "I'm just borrowing it for a while," Finn faltered. "Until you or Emma want it back."

"Like hell you are!" Rage and pain flamed in Deirdre's eyes. "Saint Cade would hardly give his fiancée a revolving engagement ring. Besides, it wasn't his to give anyway. It was my father's." Bitterness welled up in her words, searing Finn. "I guess that shows just what kind of a welcome I'd get if I was ever stupid enough to follow your advice. Looks like the Captain's already picked himself out a new daughter. Good for him. I was rotten at family stuff anyway."

"Your family hasn't known where you were for six months. The Captain hasn't seen you for five years. He was worried. Angry. Angry people do things they wouldn't even think of any other time."

"Like give away my great-grandmother's ring? Oh, yeah, if I were pissed off at someone that's the first thing I'd think of. You're a real asshole, now where is that ring I buried in the back of a drawer twenty years ago?"

"Emma's the one who remembered the ring. She was all excited when we came to tell her we were getting married—"

"I'll bet. Why wouldn't she be? She gets a brand-new mom—a children's librarian, for God's sake. She was probably thrilled to take the ring away from me."

Finn might have bitten the woman's head off if she hadn't glimpsed the misery all but hidden in Deirdre's eyes. Self-doubt slicing even deeper than Cade's ever had. And Deirdre McDaniel didn't even know the most painful family secret of all—the stark betrayal in her birth.

Empathy welled up in Finn, and she focused on the tales Cade had told her of Deirdre as a girl, wild and brave and craving her big brother's attention. She gentled her voice. "Emma is understandably insecure right now. And yes, she craves having a woman in her life. She insisted the engagement wasn't official without a ring and she knows I love antique things while you...from what everyone says, you don't."

"Is that what everyone says?"

"Yes. The Captain probably figured you didn't want it."

"He sure as hell didn't bother finding out first, did he? But then, why should I get the ring? I ditched my family, didn't I? And you're going to play house with my big brother."

"Deirdre, I love your brother. And your little girl. But so do you. You made a mistake. You didn't do something unforgivable."

Deirdre ran her fingers back through her hair, a Cade-like gesture that tugged at Finn's heart. "You're wrong about that one, Finnoula. I—coming here was a mistake. I never should have called you."

"Don't say that! If you could only see Emma, hear her, you'd know how much she misses you. She talks about you letting her wear two different shoes to school, and letting her draw on the walls of your apartment. She gets this sad lost look on her face, and Cade tries to hold her—I do, too—but it's you she really wants."

Deirdre's hands knotted around her coffee cup. "I'm not cut out to be a mother. Cade can tell you."

"Well, you should've thought about that before you had Emma, because you're the only mother that little girl has got! If you leave her, you leave a big hole in her heart and nobody else can fill it. I know what that feels like. And I think Emma deserves better."

Deirdre reared back as if Finn had slapped her. "Don't you see? That's what I'm trying to give her by leaving her with Cade? I don't want to interfere in her life. I just want to make sure that she's well. Safe. Happy. She's not like other kids, already has a tough enough time getting along with them… being different…without having a crazy musician mother who drags her all over. I don't want to screw up her life anymore."

"You're doing a hell of a good job of it by staying away from her. I love Emma. And God knows I'd love to raise her. Teach her how to wear lipstick and pick out her prom dress and fluff her wedding veil. I'd love to hear her call me Mommy and hold her when she cries over her first broken heart. But even if I do my very best, it will never be good enough. She'll always wish that I was you."

Deirdre's bravado crumbled, her lips trembling. "You don't understand."

"Oh, I understand all right." Finn knew she was hitting below the belt, didn't care as long as it gave Emma the chance she never had. "My father abandoned me after my mother died. Dumped me in a foster home and went off to live his life. He was doing the only thing he could under the circumstances, trying to do what was best for me—I heard every excuse in the book. I wanted to hate him, but the truth is I'm a grown-up and part of me is *still* waiting for him to come get me."

Tears welled up in Deirdre's eyes. Finn sensed how rare they were. A sign of weakness. What had Cade said? McDaniels weren't allowed to cry? "I'm…sorry."

"Yeah, well, I'm sorry, too. My father's dead now. It's too late for us. It's *not* too late for you and Emma."

Deirdre lowered her head, fingertips against her eyes, hiding beneath the curtain of her hair, so vulnerable Finn ached. "But after what I did…how could Emma ever forgive me?" Deirdre whispered.

"Ask her. She'll surprise you. She's an amazing little girl. She didn't get that way all on her own. You had to help make her someone that special."

Deirdre's hand fell away, and she raised her tear-streaked face, an act of courage, trust that gave Finn hope. "Emma is special, isn't she?"

"Yes."

"What—what about Cade?" Deirdre asked, hot color staining her cheeks. "He must be mad as hell."

"Do you blame him?"

"No. But he'll blame me. I mean, he made it clear the night I came to the cabin he didn't want the responsibility of Emma, didn't have a clue how to deal with a kid. I left her anyway. He never was comfortable with the *Sesame Street* crowd. Especially after the accident…." Deirdre's gaze sought out Finn's. "Did he tell you about the accident?"

"He told me."

"He thought it was his fault. But it was mine. It… changed him."

If only you knew why…

"I never could forgive myself for that. He always took everything too hard, carried the whole world on his shoulders. The Captain, Mom, me. Cade felt responsible for all of us. I tried to lighten his load a little bit. Got so wild I figured he'd have let me take care of myself. I wasn't worth that—

that sad look in his eyes whenever he thought I wasn't watching."

So that explained it, Finn thought, throat tight. The wedge driven between two kids who had loved each other, banded together in their unhappy family. They had been so busy trying to protect each other, they'd broken each other's hearts.

Finn searched for some way to reach past the pain, offer comfort, soothe. "Deirdre, I'd be lying if I said Cade was thrilled when you first left Emma with him. He wasn't. He growled and roared and made all kinds of mistakes. He wanted to drag you back by the hair if he had to."

"That's the big brother I know and love."

"But Cade has the biggest heart I've ever seen in a man. In time, well, he got over his temper fits and got to know his niece, really know her, for the first time." Finn's voice broke, memories wafting through her, a hundred pictures of Emma and Cade together, flipping pancakes in the cabin's kitchen, sewing quilt blocks out of Cade's lucky shirt, going flying for the very first time, Emma fascinated as Cade told her the tale of Amelia Earhart.

"Cade adores that little girl," Finn said. "In fact…he loves her so much it's going to hurt him when she's gone. *I'm* going to hurt him, bringing you back into Emma's life." The thought of Cade's pain devastated Finn, to hurt this man who loved her, trusted her so much.

"Then why are you doing it?" Deirdre asked softly. "It's obvious you love my brother. I'm nothing to you. A stranger."

"Emma deserves this chance. To heal. To be whole. You're the only one who can give it to her. In time, Cade will see that, too."

Silence fell between them. And Finn could see Cade's sister weighing all she'd said. After what seemed forever, Emma's mother squared her thin shoulders. "All right," Deirdre said. "I'll do it. Go home."

"For how long?"

"I don't know. It's too soon. I—" Edgy again, she looked ready to run. "Emma needs me. You said so."

"I'm sure of it."

"But I don't know what to do. I missed her so much. But my music—it's the only thing I've ever been good at. If I don't have my music, who am I?"

"Maybe it's time to find out. You can stay at March Winds until you do." She winced, imagining Cade's face when he heard, his feeling of betrayal. How could she do this to the man she loved? Maybe she'd been right all these years after all, to keep moving. Maybe she didn't deserve the love of a man like Cade after all. If she could hurt him like this.

"You really do understand we McDaniels, don't you?" Deirdre broke into her thoughts. "Inviting me to stay with you and everything. You're trying to make sure Cade and the Captain and I don't kill each other in the meantime, living under the same roof."

"I'll do whatever I can to help you. I never really had a family. Just me and…Da. And he was always gone. I spent my whole life imagining what it would be like to belong." And she might just have blown her best chance of realizing that dream clean out of the water.

"Just because you have a family doesn't mean you belong there," Deirdre confided.

"At least you've got the chance to try. Take it, Deirdre."

Cade's sister squared her slim shoulders. "I will. Listen, if I'm going home, let's get it over with. Before I change my mind."

Finn gathered up her purse, pulled out a five, left it on the table to pay the bill. Deirdre touched her arm. Finn turned to Cade's sister.

"Finn…do you think Cade will ever be able to forgive me for what I've done?"

"I hope so," Finn said, raw with pain and doubt. "Because if he can forgive you then maybe, just maybe, he'll be able to forgive me, too."

CHAPTER NINETEEN

CADE STOWED the last of his gear into his toolbox, Emma's chatter making him grin. Sometimes he didn't even care what she was saying, just the sound of her happy was enough to warm him up inside. At the moment, she was trying to guess what Finn's surprise was going to be. Something wonderful, Emma was sure: anything from a white horse for him to ride up to the gazebo on his wedding day to a baby cousin for Emma to play with.

Cade closed his eyes for a moment, imagining his baby nursing at Finn's sweet breast. A picture terrifying and amazing at the very same time. *Don't rush things,* he told himself. *Take your time to enjoy every minute. It's not every day a man gets a miracle.*

Cade opened his eyes, that idiotic grin back on his face. Who ever would have believed life could be so damned good? He was getting married. Hell, just the thought of the *M* word had made his blood run cold for years. And now he felt the same wild, wonderful thrill he had the first time he'd taken the controls of a plane.

He'd been right in his suspicions—the sex *was* better than flying. But with Finn, the mind-blowing sex was just the beginning. It was all those little things, woman things, about her that took his breath away. Her honesty. Her generosity. Knowing he could trust her and never think twice.

His chest still felt tight whenever he thought of her, across the table from him in the smoky jazz club, listening to him spill his guts about the most painful time in his life, her green eyes misted with tears for him. Every line in her beautiful face seeming to promise she would never let anything hurt him like that again.

He was a hard-assed flyboy, plenty able to take care of himself, and yet, just seeing that protective light in her eyes had touched him in a way he could never explain. *He* was the one who took care of other people. The guy who fell on the grenade. It would take some getting used to—having someone looking out for him.

And Emma.

Emma's luck was about to turn. She was one lucky little girl to have Finn to mother her.

Cade shoved away the memory of Finn's worried face when he'd told her as much, her quiet warning. *Emma already has a mother.*

Deirdre was almost as good as gone. He'd called a lawyer, set up an appointment for after the wedding. The minute his ring was on Finn's finger, he was going to push the issue and sue for legal custody of the little girl they both loved. He needed the right to make decisions that would give Emma the security she needed, and the assurance that nobody, not even Emma's mother, could sweep in and screw things up for the kid again. Finn would see that he was right in time.

"Uncle Cade, Uncle Cade!" Emma cried. "Hear the car? Finn's back!"

Cade hoped she was right. "Sounds like more than one car," he said, the well-tuned hum of Finn's Volkswagen, already under his care, not quite masking the nasty rattle of an engine that sounded about ready to fall apart.

He straightened, reaching for Emma's hand. "Come on, we'll go see what this big secret of hers is all about."

Emma skipped over, slipping her fingers so trustingly into his, as if his little niece wanted to hold on to him forever.

They rounded the side of the house, as somebody killed the engines, two car doors slamming. Cade's eyes narrowed. What was that Alice In Wonderland quote Emma loved to use? *Curiouser and curiouser.* Finn must have brought somebody with her. What the blazes was the woman up to?

Whatever it was, he knew he'd love it. She knew him to his very bones, every crack, every flaw. And she loved him.

Would he ever get used to that? Take it for granted that she'd always be there when he needed her, reached for her? Cade's pulses throbbed in anticipation, and he could hardly believe how hungry he was to see her. Wondered if he always would be.

Cade pushed past a rhododendron that was taller than he was, and used the hand that wasn't holding Emma's to hold a low hanging branch back so the child could duck underneath. The Volkswagen was blocking his view of the other vehicle, but he could just see a flutter of white shirt, someone almost hiding behind Finn.

Finn had insisted on doing all of the wedding preparations herself, or with the help of people she loved. Could this be some friend of hers brought in for the occasion? Cade tried not to mind the idea of sharing Finn's time during this next, precious week.

"So, my beautiful almost-bride," Cade teased. "Where's this surprise of yours?" His smile died as he caught a good look at Finn's face. She looked like someone had set fire to that big old house of hers.

"Finn?" Cade said, dropping Emma's hand. "What's wrong."

Green eyes darkened, pleading. "Nothing's wrong. Things can be *right* now. Please, Cade, try to understand."

Emma edged forward and peeped around Finn, that half-scared look on the little girl's face. As if she was waiting for something to explode. Cade hated it.

"M-Mommy?"

"What the hell?" Cade's heart plunged to his work boots as Deirdre stepped into clear view.

"Hi, baby." Deirdre went down on one knee, as Emma flung herself into her mother's arms.

"Mommy, where—where did you go?" Emma cried, touching Deirdre's face, her hair. "I couldn't find you."

"I know." Deirdre stroked Emma's dark curls, with fierce, desperate joy, as if she wanted to gobble the kid up. "But I'm here now."

Blood roared in Cade's head, blind fury, stark betrayal. "Just like that? You just drop out of the goddamned sky? And say 'I'm here now' and everything's just supposed to be fine?"

"Cade, stop. Think for a moment…" Finn closed the space between them, laying a hand on his rigid arm. He shook it off, rounded on her, temper blazing.

"Goddamn it, Finn, is this your big surprise?" Bitterness spilled out, thick, black poison.

"Don't yell, Uncle Cade! Don't yell!" Emma wailed. "You'll scare my mommy away again!" Emma clung to her mother as if she were terrified Deirdre would disappear.

Why didn't the kid just plunge a knife in his chest? "Emma," he said in a strangled voice. "I never scared her away. She went out of pure selfish—"

"Enough, Cade!" Finn shoved him, hard enough to startle him, cut off words he could never take back, never erase from sensitive little Emma's mind. "Stop it! I know this is a shock, but— Emma, honey, we grown-ups need to talk, sort some things out for a few minutes. Why don't you go inside and get some lemonade ready for when we're done. Your mommy is probably thirsty."

"No!" Emma trembled, terrified. "She might go away again! She might—"

"I won't go away, baby," Deirdre choked out. "Not ever again. I promise. You go on now and do as Finn says. Emma, I love you."

The words fell like water onto Emma's parched little soul. Cade could see her drinking them in, feel the child he loved so much greening like flowers in Finn's precious garden. How could Emma do that? Forgive Deirdre after what she'd done? Look at Deirdre with those big eyes as if...as if Emma's heart had gone missing and Deirdre had brought it back to her again?

Emma drew back, her troubled gaze darting between the three grown-ups standing so rigid underneath the lightning-struck chestnut tree. Sensing disaster—but what could such little hands do to hold back the tide of anger, betrayal, lies?

Cade watched Emma until she slipped through the shiny green of Finn's freshly painted screen door. Why did it hurt so much? Seeing the love in Emma's eyes, the hope when she looked at her mother? Why did he have to face what he'd been fighting to deny for months? The fact that he hadn't been enough for the child he'd come to love as his very own?

"I have to be the worst present you've ever gotten."

He tore his gaze away from the door and faced his sister.

"Not that you shouldn't be used to it." Deirdre turned to Finn. "We had this crazy great-aunt when we were growing up who gave him bunny pajamas when he was eight. Guess I've even got that present beat."

"Damn it, Dee, this isn't a joke."

"You think I don't know that?" Deirdre glared at him, defiant, alive. Had he ever even admitted to himself that in his heart of hearts he'd feared that she was buried in a ditch somewhere and he would never find her?

"Not a word in months—hell, you could've been dead for

all I knew. And Emma—didn't you give a damn how she was doing?"

"I knew she was with you. You'd take care of her." Her voice softened in spite of the anger in her eyes. "Just like you always took care of me."

Cade stiffened. "And that's just what I'm going to do. Take care of Emma. She's staying here in Whitewater with me, Deirdre. That's final. She needs a stable home. A school where she can make friends when she's ready. She needs a mother who doesn't just take off whenever things get too hard."

Deirdre's chin bumped up a notch. "That's not what Finn says."

Cade slashed a pain-filled glance at the woman he loved, the woman he'd trusted. Trust she'd broken all to hell. Why did she look like she was the one whose heart had been drop-kicked across the floor?

"Yeah, I'll bet Finn had plenty to say. Of course, since I'm supposed to be her husband in six days she might have said it to my face instead of going behind my back."

"I'm sorry," Finn said. "I didn't—"

"I didn't give her any other choice," Deirdre cut in. "You know what a stubborn pain I can be, Cade. I scared her. Threatened her. Told her if she didn't meet me—alone—I'd take off again and never come back."

"Yeah, and that would've been a crying shame."

Deirdre flinched, the pain of his rejection darkening her eyes. Rejection she'd felt before, from other people who were supposed to love her.

Unconditionally, Finn would say. That's how a family is supposed to love each other. But what did she know? She'd never had to deal with the messes, the ugly spots, the raw, bleeding wounds those same people could rake across your heart. *Except for her bastard of a father.*

"You're right, you know," Deirdre said, some of the steel melting out of her spine. "It is a crying shame. What I did. I hurt my baby girl. And I hurt you. I was trying to do something right for a change, but what I did was…wrong."

Cade planted hands on hips, trying to take it in. Deirdre, admitting she was wrong? Hell, she'd spent her life dead stubborn, never willing to give an inch. Had he ever heard her say she was sorry?

Once…when she'd regained consciousness after her fall from the airplane wing. It had ripped him up inside as badly as she was, his baby sister crying, breathless from the broken ribs that lay beneath her hospital gown. "I'm s-sorry, Cade… I'm s-sorry. Did I break it?"

Did she break the goddamned plane? No. She'd stomped all over his heart.

Damn this irresponsible Deirdre for looking at him through his little sister's eyes. "Cade, I know I made a mess of things," Deirdre said. "But I want to do better. Do right by Emma."

"Then give her to me, Dee," Cade pleaded hoarsely. "I love her. I can give her a home. Finn and I… I thought… Emma could be so happy. Don't take her away like you did before. I don't think I could take it."

Tears welled up in Deirdre's eyes. She went to him, grabbed his hand. "I won't take her away. I'm going to stay at March Winds until I figure out what to do. Whatever it is, it'll be in Whitewater. And you and Finn…you'll have kids of your own someday."

"Will we?" Cade looked at Finn, her face so stricken, so pale, that haunted expression in her eyes. The one that scared the hell out of him since the day he'd known he loved her.

"Of course you will. You—you've got to marry her. She's the first one of your girlfriends I've ever liked. We're going to team up and make your life hell, big brother. So don't mess it up or you're going to have to deal with me." Deirdre kissed Cade softly on the cheek. "Now I'm going to go and see my daughter. Give you two a little time to talk. And Cade," she gave him a stern glare that wracked him up inside. *"Keep—your—temper."*

His temper? Hell. It was his life that was falling to pieces. With his back to Finn, Cade watched in silence as his sister walked away. Even after Deirdre disappeared, he couldn't bring himself to face the woman standing, so still, behind him.

"Do you want to—to go to the gazebo?" Finn asked. "It's…quieter there."

Cade's face contorted. Anywhere but that. The gazebo was too painful, the place where he'd made love to Finn, planned to make her his wife with no mistrust between them, no shadows, no deceit.

"Over here." He pointed to the bench he'd fixed underneath the chestnut, but that only reminded him of the first time he'd laid eyes on her. She'd been wearing that gauzy peach dress, her slim feet in delicate sandals, and she'd been trying to pry off the For Sale sign with an old claw hammer.

She'd been so full of light then, of hope, so sure everything she'd dreamed of was now within her reach. She looked like a shadow of that Finn now—uncertain, weary, sad. But damn it, she was the one who'd lied, who'd gone behind his back and done exactly what she knew he feared most. Brought Deirdre plunging back into Emma's life, leaving chaos in her wake.

Hell, Deirdre was even staying at March Winds at Finn's invitation. What did that mean? Would Emma scoop everything she owned into her little suitcase and go live there, too?

Cade's chest hurt as he thought of Emma's room empty. Swept clean, as if no little girl had ever slept there at all.

He arched his head back, trying to control the grief and

loss tearing through him, his gaze fastening in the chestnut's splintered, blackened branches. Yet, still somehow growing, green shoots pushing their way toward the sky. How could the love he and Finn shared be like that? Cade wondered. After the blow it had taken?

Finn sank down on the bench. "So," she said, picking at a ragged piece of bark. "Why don't you just say it?"

"Say what?" Cade bit out.

"I lied to you. I let you down. I ruined all your plans for Emma and…and us."

"Yeah. You did. And it hurts like hell."

Finn's throat constricted. He saw her turn her face away, sensed she was struggling not to cry. "Why doesn't anyone tell you that? How much it hurts to love somebody?" she said, forlorn as an angel banished from heaven. "When you make a disaster of—of something that could have been so perfect?"

"Perfect?" Cade snorted in derision. "Who ever said love was perfect? It's a goddamned mess."

"One you'd be better off out of, I'm sure."

"Exactly what the hell do you mean by that?"

"Tell me the truth, Cade. You can't possibly feel the same way about me after what I've done today."

His jaw clenched. "No. It's not the same."

"Everything was so beautiful before…like a fairy tale. I should have known it couldn't last."

Impatience blazed through Cade. He raked his hand through his hair. "Of course it couldn't stay that way forever. Life isn't a fairy tale, Finn. It isn't riding off into the sunset and happily ever after and the music swelling up to the fade-out shot of some damned romantic movie. Life is messy and hard and sometimes it hurts a lot. Love is the same way."

"It can't—can't be like that."

"Why not? Because you want the glass slipper? Who the

hell thought of that in the first place, huh? Some idiot starry-eyed woman?"

Finn looked as if he'd snatched one of the damn shoes right out of the fairy tale and smashed it in front of her eyes. It only made him madder—at who? He wasn't sure. At her, at himself. Deirdre's warning echoed in his mind, but the red tide of rage was too far out of control.

"A shoe made of glass?" he scoffed. "You damn well *know* that thing's going to break."

"At least we found out before it was too late."

Cold dread ran down Cade's spine, but he couldn't stop pushing. "Just exactly what did we find out?"

"Look at you. In your eyes. I can see how badly I've mangled everything. I'm not going to take the chance that—"

"That we'll be human? That we'll break each other's hearts sometimes?"

"You want to take that kind of chance after what your parents suffered? After the mess mine made out of their lives? Doesn't that scare you at all?"

"Hell, yes. It fucking terrifies me."

Finn stumbled to her feet. "We should have known this would never work. It was too good to be true."

Cade caught her arm, whipped her around to face him. She meant to leave him. He could see it in her eyes. Pain knifed through Cade. Was it only a half an hour ago he'd been picturing his baby in Finn's arms? That baby would never be. Cade would never build a cradle or hear Finn cry out when he loved her. "Damn it, Finn—"

"Don't you get it?" she cried. "I need to get away—"

"What are you going to do, Finn? Run when things get tough? You're just like your father."

Finn's stomach heaved. "Don't say that."

"It's the truth. You tell me you've spent your whole life desperate to sink down roots. How many times have you bounced around in the past ten years? From town to town? Job to job?"

"I—I couldn't afford this house…until Da left me the money."

"Bullshit. It didn't have to be March Winds or nothing. If you were serious about putting down roots any house would do, as long as it was yours, in any of the towns you worked in."

Finn wanted to deny it. Couldn't. Her eyes widened, sick with realization.

"Face it," Cade said. "You're no different than your old man. You've been running away your whole life."

"You're a real bastard, Cade."

"I never pretended to be anything different. You're the one who tried to make me into some damned Prince Charming."

"Then it's a good thing we found out, before—"

"Before what?"

There's something missing in me, she wanted to explain. *Something broken…*

"Before *what,* damn it?" he roared. She flinched at the rage contorting his face, but she couldn't squeeze words passed the lump in her throat.

"Before we had a little girl of our own, so you could leave her, too?" Cade snarled.

Finn fought to breathe, couldn't, images spilling through her, horrifyingly vivid. Cade shattered because she'd failed him, a child sobbing into her pillow, desperately needing things Finn could never give. She sank down onto the bench, cold inside, dead.

She caught a glint of green, the sunlight sparkling on the emerald Cade had slipped on her finger when forever seemed possible and he'd trusted her with his embattled heart. She remembered how beautiful he'd been the magical night he'd knelt down before her and slipped it on her finger. Following Emma's directions about the proper way to ask Finn to be his wife.

He'd been lit up inside, so happy, so young. He looked old now, haggard and tired.

"You're right," she said in a small voice. "About everything. About…me." She slid the ring from her finger, held it out to him, cupped in her palm.

His eyes locked on the ring, his jaw clenched. "What the hell?"

"Take it, Cade."

"No."

"You have to. Please."

McDaniel rage hotter than she'd ever seen blazed in his eyes. "Throw the damn thing in the river if you don't want it."

"You don't mean that. It was your grandmother's."

Finn set it gently on the rough concrete bench. "I should never have taken it in the first place," Finn said.

He glared down at the ring for what seemed like forever, unyielding as granite.

"Remember how Emma's eyes shone the night she insisted I wear it?" Finn asked softly.

God, yes, he remembered. She could see it in his eyes. He remembered going down on his knees, asking her to be his wife. He remembered laying his heart open, making himself completely vulnerable. Cade's face hardened.

"Don't you think Emma deserves to have the ring someday?" Finn urged.

"That's the way you want it?" Cade said. "Fine." He scraped the ring up, the concrete raking his knuckles. "To hell with love, lady, and to hell with you." He jammed the ring in his jeans pocket and stalked away.

Finn fled into the home she'd thought she'd wanted forever, slammed the door shut on her dreams.

"You're just like your father…just like your father…running away…"

Cade's accusations seared her inside, all the more agonizing because it was true.

But now she understood why her father had run. Because it hurt too much to love. It hurt and she was afraid.

She glimpsed Deirdre's worried face as she ran past the parlor, saw Emma, cuddled on her lap. Knew, with terrible certainty, she'd never hold a baby of her own in her arms. She was too much of a coward. Just like Cade said.

Thank God we don't have a little girl...

"Finn?" Deirdre called after her.

Alone. She had to be alone. Cut off from all this confusion, the weight of Cade's disillusionment, pain. Safe.

She locked the bedroom door behind her, flung herself on the bed where Cade had made love to her until her bones melted and her spirit soared. Until she'd believed in the fairy tales Cade scorned. She had thought she held forever in her hand. She cried as if her heart would break.

Deirdre knocked softly on the door, rattled the knob in an effort to open it.

"Leave me alone!" Finn cried.

She closed her eyes against the agony, the memory of Cade's stark, beloved face. It wasn't fair. His faith in what they had together had been shaken, too. She'd seen it—his fury, his doubt, his fearsome sense of betrayal. He'd had as many doubts as she had.

And he'd hurt her on purpose, leveled the most brutal accusation he could at her, striking where she was most vulnerable, raw, shattered.

You're just like your father, Cade had snarled.

Wasn't that what she'd always been afraid of?

She was just like her father.

She was.

She was.

CHAPTER TWENTY

FINN STOOD in March Winds' garden, the sky overhead sprinkled with a hundred stars. Had it only been five weeks ago Cade had guided his Porsche down the river road and shown her the North Star that navigators had used forever to guide weary travelers home?

Tonight there was only one light Finn longed to see. The glow of Cade's cabin windows against the night. It would have made it easier, somehow, just to know he was nearby. But not once in the past three days had she seen so much as a flicker to show he was still just a garden away. Not that it mattered. He was as far beyond her reach now as his boundless sky.

She touched her naked ring finger, wondering how long it would take before she'd get used to the terrible void where Cade's antique emerald had rested for such a short, such a precious time.

Before she'd gambled with Cade's trust. Before she'd faced the gaping flaw in her own character, felt the panicked need to run.

Finn stiffened, the soft crunch of footfalls on the garden path making her heart leap. In what? Hope that she'd turn around to see Cade? It wouldn't change anything. She couldn't let it.

But a much slighter form stepped from the shadows. Deirdre, her face even paler and more drawn than it had been when Finn had met her at Fuller's Mill. Finn sucked in a shuddery breath, trying to banish an insane sense of disappointment. Seeing Cade would only make it harder do what was best for both of them.

"How's Emma?" Finn asked, seeking what comfort she could in the reassurance that she'd done at least one thing right, giving the little girl she loved a chance to heal.

"She's asleep. All curled up tight…you know, like she does. Every time I tried to let go of her hand she'd wake up, beg me not to go."

"She loves you so much."

"Yeah. Even after I ran away. God, Finn. How could I do that to my baby?"

"You'll have to answer that question. And then, somehow, forgive yourself."

"I'll never be able to do that. Or forget…what you did for me. You didn't even know me. But you risked everything."

"You and Emma be happy. Love each other."

"We will." Deirdre's voice quavered. "All these years I thought music was my life. Without it, I was nothing. But I was wrong. I was Emma's mom. She didn't even care if I wasn't perfect. She could have had you—earth mother incarnate. But she wanted me. She told me. She always wanted me. It's so damned scary, Finn. How can I be sure I won't screw up again?"

"You will, but it won't matter. Not as long as you love Emma. That's all any child wants. And you won't be all alone anymore, in some strange town with no one to help you when you're exhausted and overwhelmed. Cade…" Just saying his name tore at Finn's heart like shards of glass. "You and Emma will have Cade to depend on."

"We'll have you, too."

"Deirdre, I told you it's over between Cade and I."

"*Over* my Aunt Fannie's ass! He just has one giant-size

McDaniel style mad on. And after I warned him to keep his temper!"

"It's not that simple. Things never would have worked between us. I…"

"Betrayed him?" Deirdre supplied. "Lied to him? Let him down?"

"Yes."

"Oh, I know just what my big brother is feeling right now. He's hurt, Finn. By both of us. And Emma…God, when he brought her things to the door, it was like I was ripping his heart out." Dee's voice broke. "I've only seen him that way one other time. When I woke up in the hospital after I fell off his plane. It was hideous, all that pain."

Memory seared through Finn, the scene her imagination had painted at Ella Fitzgerald's, the sensitive boy Cade had been, keeping vigil at his sister's bedside, blaming himself as his world blew apart. Shouldering the terrible burden of secrets alone.

For a brief, precious time, she'd hoped she could shift some of the weight of the world off of his broad shoulders. She'd wanted to give him a safe place to put all the love he'd held inside, cry if he needed to, the McDaniel ban against crying be damned. And laugh…she wanted him to laugh with that same reckless freedom she'd seen as he'd barrel rolled the plane he loved in a vast, cloudless sky. But in the end she wasn't strong enough. Wasn't brave enough.

"The Captain just phoned. He's been acting like some kind of sadistic cross between General Patton and a Jewish mother since the big blowup, giving Cade no peace. Said Cade's on his way to Jett Davis's ranch for a few weeks."

"I'm glad." Finn tried hard to mean it. "It hurt too much thinking of him alone in that great big cabin. At least he'll be with friends."

"Not my big brother. He's bypassing the big house and

heading straight up to some little shack in the mountains where there isn't even any electricity. Typical. Going off like a grizzly bear to lick his wounds when he knows damned well he's blown things. I don't feel sorry for him one bit. I hope he suffers the way he deserves to."

"Deirdre!"

"How else is he supposed to figure out he's making the worst mistake of his life? My brother loves you, Finn. And no matter what went on between the two of you the day I came back to Whitewater, I know you love him, too."

"Not enough, Dee."

"Cade doesn't know how to do anything by halves. When the guy loves someone, he hangs on. Look at me. I couldn't drive him away with a stick, and God knows I tried."

"You're his sister. It's different."

"That whole blood is thicker than water bit." Dee made a face, looking suddenly younger, softer. "I know Cade. Love doesn't come easy for him. But when he takes the jump, he doesn't let go. He won't let go of you."

"I'm the one who's letting go. He'll be better off without me."

"Oh, *puh-leeze*." Deirdre rolled her eyes. "That's exactly what I told myself the night I left Emma."

"You don't understand."

"Everyone *wants* to run when they get in over their head. I don't see you doing it. The way I look at it, you should be neck-deep in plans to get the hell out of Dodge if that's what you intended to do. But you're still dug in right here."

"Deirdre—"

"Just give Cade a little time to cool off and he'll be begging you to take his sorry ass back. And when he does you'd damn well better have the good sense to do it."

"And ruin the rest of his life? There's something wrong with me. Something...missing," Finn said. "I can't explain it."

"You don't have to. I know how scary it is to think you're going to fail the person you love most in the whole world. I believed I was completely hopeless as a mother. If you'd told me a month ago that I was going to be back in Whitewater, trying to build a life for my little girl, I would have said it was impossible. But I was wrong. You are, too."

The tiniest ember of hope flickered to life inside Finn. Terrifying, but real. She tried to deny it. "I can't afford to take that kind of a chance."

"You can't afford not to. Have a little faith, won't you, Finn?" Deirdre said. "You're Irish, for God's sake. You people are supposed to believe the impossible—in rainbows and pots of gold and that happily ever after kind of stuff. Aren't you the luckiest people on earth, or something?"

"Or something," Finn echoed, reaching for her old cynicism.

She tried to look hard reality in the face. There wasn't any hope. Cade had said the unforgivable, comparing her to her father. And what was worse, he'd been right.

As for the rotten luck of the Irish, she'd had it her whole life. But what if this one time Deirdre was right? What if there really could be a chance? For what? For Cade to forgive her? For Finn to find the courage to stay?

Could she dare to dream that it was possible? Her luck might be about to change?

IT WAS ALMOST TEN when Finn crawled out of bed, feeling like she'd been run over by a truck. The refrigerator was blessedly emptied of all those little tea sandwiches Verna had worked so hard on. The engagement announcements were off of the refrigerator, the house swept clean of any sign of the wedding plans that had gobbled up Finn's attention for the past week.

But Miranda March's wedding dress still hung in her bedroom, with Emma's blue satin ballet slippers tucked stubbornly beneath its folds, the child unwilling to surrender her conviction that two people she loved so dearly were going to make her fantasy wedding come true.

Finn tried not to hope too much herself. She still felt panicky, still felt the desperate urge to run. And yet, she felt an even deeper fear when she imagined the rest of her life without Cade's hands on her body, his mouth on hers.

Maybe she *was* crazy, but a part of her listened for him every moment, holding her breath, hoping…hoping he'd stride through March Winds' door just like Deirdre had promised he would, that he'd kiss her and make her fears melt away. Show her that she wasn't like her father after all, that she was meant to have a family, to have the man who loved her in his arms forever. If she ever did get Cade back, she would never let him go.

A knock on the front door made Finn's heart jump. She strained to listen for the deep rumble of Cade's voice. Surely he'd have to come back to Whitewater soon. Deirdre answered the door.

"It's important that I see Ms. O'Grady." A completely unfamiliar masculine voice insisted.

"Ms. O'Grady has had a hell of a few weeks," Deirdre snapped back. "If you told me you were the prize patrol ready to give her a million dollars I wouldn't let you in. Come back some other time."

"What would you say if I told you I'm a private investigator? I have news about Ms. O'Grady's father."

A frisson of dread ran down Finn's spine, just the mention of her father setting her nerves on edge. Why on earth would a private investigator have any information about her da?

"I'd *still* tell you to get lost before I sic the dog on you."

The P.I. chuckled. "You don't have a dog."

"Deirdre?" Finn called, entering the hall.

"This guy's just leaving," Deirdre said, trying to close the door. The tall, dangerous-looking man slipped his size twelve boot into the crack so she couldn't. He touched the brim of his black cowboy hat, and met Finn's gaze easily over Deirdre's head.

"Ms. O'Grady? My name is Jake Stone. I'm a private investigator. I've been working on a case involving your father, Patrick O'Grady."

Finn's hand shook as she brushed a wisp of hair off of her cheek. "My father is dead."

"Please, Ms. O'Grady. I won't take much of your time."

"Time is the one thing I've got plenty of now." Finn gave a pain-filled laugh, her shoulders sagging.

"Are you sure you want to deal with this jerk right now?" Deirdre demanded. "I mean, your dad's six feet under. Obviously this can wait."

"It's okay. I'd just as soon get this over with." Finn led Stone to a chair in the freshly scrubbed kitchen.

Deirdre, hands on hips, stood a few feet away, like a crabby guardian angel. "Put the woman out of her misery and spit out what this is all about," Deirdre insisted.

Stone removed his hat and set it on the table, then folded his long body into the chair, his eyes so hard, watchful, Finn shifted uneasily as she took a seat across from him.

"Four months ago I was hired by the nephew of a Mrs. Bessie Aronson, a onetime friend of your father's. Have you ever heard of her?"

"No. My father and I weren't close."

"She's a real nice lady, Mrs. Aronson. No kids of her own. Cozy little house. Got a big insurance settlement when her husband was killed in a shop accident. She never could bring herself to touch the money. Said it had her Henry's blood on it."

"I don't understand what this has to do with me or my da."

"She loaned the money to your father to sink into some kind of investment he conned her into trying. He disappeared."

"What do you mean, he disappeared?" Deirdre demanded.

"He took the money and ran," Stone said.

Finn's stomach pitched. Cool gray eyes locked on her face, giving her no quarter. "Mrs. Aronson's nephew contacted me when he found out what had happened. The lady is elderly, alone. Maybe not quite as sharp as she once was. An easy mark."

Finn could just see a vague, gentle little old woman, pitted against her father's charm. Mrs. Aronson wouldn't have stood a chance.

"How…how much money did he take?" Finn asked in a small voice.

"Over half a million dollars. Five hundred fifty-eight thousand and some odd cents."

"Holy shit!" Deirdre gasped.

Finn pressed her hand to her mouth. She was going to throw up. Oh, God, she'd thought things couldn't get any worse!

"Ms. O'Grady, did your father give you that money?"

"He died. A few days later I got this…this box. Everything he owned in the world. He'd had somebody at the hospital mail it."

"You mind telling me what was in that box?"

"His keychain—this lucky charm he always kept with him—a four leaf clover preserved in a plastic oval. His tin whistle. A few books—just a jumble of things anyone else would have called junk."

"Except?"

"Except for a cashier's check." She raised her anguished gaze to the gray eyed P.I.

"That's it," Deirdre broke in. "Hold it right there, mister. Finn, I don't think you should talk to this jerk anymore without a lawyer. I'll find some way to get in touch with Cade wherever the hell he is in the mountains. He'll know what to do. Jett will be able to find him in an emergency." Dee headed for the door.

"No!" Finn exclaimed. "I…I don't want a lawyer. And Cade… No." She couldn't tell Deirdre she didn't want him. She'd never wanted Cade's solid strength more in her life. "I can handle this on my own."

"Da wrote that he'd saved the money his whole life," Finn explained weakly. "That I was supposed to buy this house— the one I always wanted."

Stone quirked a thick black brow. "You didn't find all that a bit strange?"

"Everything my father did was strange! He was never like other fathers. It made crazy sense that he'd be living in suits from the Goodwill and have this kind of—of stash hidden away. Maybe the reason it made sense is because I wanted it to. But even I would never have believed…believed he could do something so awful."

Finn wrung her hands, trembling. "If my father stole this woman's money, why aren't the police here instead of you?"

"Your father charmed Mrs. Aronson so much she wouldn't press charges. Her nephew just wants to get the poor woman's money back."

"But—but I don't have it," Finn said, stricken. "I put most of it in the house."

"I figured as much. A house like this—it would be hard to afford on a librarian's salary."

He knew she was a librarian. Of course he knew. He must have been poking around in her life for weeks now. The thought of someone watching her made Finn's skin crawl. Did this man know about Cade? About the wedding? About all the dreams she'd hoped for, and almost…just almost captured in her hand?

"March Winds is a spectacular place," Stone said.

"It would have been. Someday." A sudden realization turned Finn's blood to ice. "Oh, my God," she choked out. "How much money did you say my father took?"

"Five hundred fifty-eight thousand and—"

"But a hundred thousand is missing! He didn't—didn't send it all."

"He made a stop at the casino on the way—probably thinking he could make some quick cash—then he could return the seed money to Mrs. Aronson and send what he'd won to you. That shouldn't surprise you, Ms. O'Grady. From what I've learned, your father was a gambler all his life."

Finn nodded, mute with agony. That was Patrick O'Grady all right, moving from town to town, throwing the dice, no matter how much it hurt the people he loved. Patrick O'Grady, the man with the luck of the Irish.

"Ms. O'Grady, it's obvious from your reaction that you didn't know where the money came from. And I've leveled with you, and told you no charges are going to be filed. But that still leaves the question of Bessie Aronson's money. She's had a hard life, losing her husband the way she did. The matter is in your hands. What are you going to do?"

"Finn, this isn't your fault," Deirdre burst out, curving one hand over Finn's shoulder. "It's too bad about Mrs. Aronson. I feel terrible for the lady. But what are you supposed to do about it?"

Finn gripped the edge of the table, trying to catch her balance in a world gone mad. Oh, God why this? Why now? March Winds…the lifelong dream that was supposed to be her home, a loving gift from her father. It had been one more con job, bought with money her father had stolen from someone who trusted him.

And now—Deirdre was right. What *could* Finn do about it? She'd spent almost every penny on the house she had wanted so badly.

"There's only one thing I can do," she said hoarsely. "Sell March Winds."

"No, Finn!" Deirdre erupted, grabbing her hand. "You can't. You love this place. Haven't you given up enough? You and Cade…you'll find a way to fix this. Cade can fix anything!"

"No," Finn said so sharply she stunned Deirdre to silence. Finn wished she could have married Cade, had this woman she'd come to love as her family. But even if, by some miracle, Cade *had* forgiven Finn and Finn had managed to scratch up the courage to marry him, any union between them was impossible now, with half a million dollars of debt hanging over her head.

"It's not fair!" Deirdre cried, outraged, glaring at the P.I. as if he were the one who'd created this mess.

"It's the only possible solution," Finn said. "But there's still the question of the missing money. A hundred thousand dollars? How am I ever going to raise enough to pay that back? But I…I'll find a way. No matter how long it takes."

"I have to confess, you surprise me, Ms. O'Grady," Stone said. "The whole time I worked on this case, I figured like father, like daughter."

Finn's shoulders slumped in surrender. "I guess I'm more like my father than I knew. It's time to move on."

"Finn, no!" Deirdre pleaded.

Finn groped instinctively for her left hand, fingered the place where Cade's ring used to be. "It's okay, Deirdre. Maybe things will be better someplace else."

But if she left this time, everything would be different, Finn realized, her heart heavy. She had always looked ahead, beyond the horizon, into the future for all the dreams she had wanted. Now she would look behind her.

Back to Cade in his rugged log cabin. To the white picket fence she'd almost had, and the love that had slipped through her fingers. Even the tiniest chance their love had was gone now. A hundred thousand dollars…it was a fortune. She wouldn't let someone innocent suffer the consequences for the wrong her father had done, no matter how much that someone claimed to love her.

Maybe she wasn't like Patrick O'Grady after all.

Tell yourself that if you want to, Finnoula, her father whispered in her heart. *But you should have known better than to love anyone, anything. Didn't you learn the truth when you were a little girl? If you love someone too much, God snatches them away.*

Deirdre glared at the P.I. "I think it's time for you to go, Mr. Stone."

"I suppose so."

"Yeah, what else can you do to her? You're a real jerk, sticking your nose in other people's business. Wrecking their lives."

His hard gaze caught hers, held it as he retrieved his cowboy hat. "I didn't steal the money. Patrick O'Grady did."

"Yeah. And now Finn's going to pay for it."

Finn heard the door slam, Deirdre's footsteps coming back.

"There has to be something we can do," Deirdre insisted. "I know you and my brother are fighting right now. But nobody's better at getting people out of trouble than Cade. He's had plenty of practice with me and the Captain. He'll fire up like a blasted grizzly bear the minute he finds out—"

"No, Deirdre," Finn said flatly. "I forbid you to tell him anything about this. I mean it. After what I did for you and Emma you owe me that much."

Deirdre squirmed. "I owe you everything. Getting my daughter back. My head on straight. Getting the chance to make things right. Don't ask me to walk away and let you bleed."

"It's over. Don't you see? Finished."

"Cade won't be an idiot forever. The man loves you. Just give him a chance to get over being hurt."

"And saddle him with an astronomical debt? How can I even be sure this is the last of it? God knows what else my da might have done. You want Cade saddled with a lifetime, waiting to deal with the next of my father's messes?"

"The guy's dead! How much more trouble can he be?"

"I don't know. But I'm not willing to risk Cade's future to find out." Finn sucked in a steadying breath. "This whole disaster—it's like a sign from God. Even if I had been stupid enough to hope that, well, that maybe… It doesn't matter now. It's over. I've always been terrified I'd turn out to be like my father."

"You're nothing like that jerk! You don't have to be alone anymore. Cade wants you, Finn. So does Emma. So do I. I'm going to need a sister like you to help me get this mother thing right."

Finn gave her a wan smile. "You'll do just fine. Funny, after all these years I can finally see that my father had a gift after all."

"Yeah, for screwing up people's lives even when he's dead. That's a terrific gift. Just swell."

"Maybe not." Finn squeezed Deirdre's hand, loving her, wishing she'd be around to see who Deirdre McDaniel would be when she grew up. "But his other gift, well, I guess I'll have to settle for taking that one to heart. My father knew when it was time to go."

The LAST THING in the world Cade expected to see as he pulled into March Winds driveway was the For Sale sign nailed to the chestnut tree. He jammed his truck into Park and tried to keep his heart in his chest. Amazing how it could just keep slamming away against his ribs, no matter how much it hurt. Not that he hadn't gotten exactly what he deserved after the things he'd said. But in spite of all that he couldn't believe his eyes.

Finn was leaving.

How could Finn do this? Sure, he'd been gone for a month—it had taken that long to cool off, sort things out, realize he hadn't really wanted to call off the wedding at all. Hell, yes he had, if he was blazingly honest with himself. At least for those few fiery minutes he'd been in a killing rage. He'd lashed out, hadn't held anything back. So how could he blame Finn for believing he'd meant the ugly things he'd said?

But Finn should have known me better, a tiny, unreasonable voice argued in his head.

She should have known that once he cooled off he would come to realize why she'd brought Deirdre back to March Winds. For Emma's sake. And, to save Cade's relationship with his sister, as well. He'd wanted to sue for legal custody of his niece, so damned sure Deirdre didn't deserve the little girl she'd deserted. But even the wild beauty of Montana had done nothing to erase the image that drove every other thought out of Cade's mind: Emma's face all aglow as the kid flung herself into her mother's arms.

Cade's gut knotted. Grueling as sorting things out in the mountains had been, that was the easy part. Going to Finn, telling her he'd been wrong…hell, he'd rather run the length of a football field under machine gunfire. In fact, the only thing he could think of that would be worse was the chance he'd have to live the rest of his life without her.

And now he had to face the fact that Finn was already taking steps to move on with her life when he'd expected…what? For the woman to be wearing some of that gorgeous lingerie of hers, waiting for him with open arms?

What the hell was he supposed to do now? Beg?

He winced at the thought, his McDaniel pride kicking in. Finn wouldn't make him do that. Maybe she'd jumped the gun and put the house up for sale. But hell, they could pull that sign down inside five minutes. After all, she still had the biggest heart he'd ever seen.

In the month they'd both slept alone she had to be as edgy as he was, remembering how good it had been between them before he'd blown it out of the water.

She'd forgive him, Cade assured himself.

She had to.

He froze, catching a sudden glimpse of Finn, hauling a big box onto the porch. She looked beautiful. Sad. So sad. The way Emma had looked before Finn had come into their lives. Cade turned off the engine and climbed out of the truck cab. Heart in his throat, he jogged over to help her.

"Cade!" Finn gasped, face paling at the sight of him. He grabbed hold of her burden, took it out of her hands. "You don't have to do that."

"I know."

She pointed to a corner, where other things were stacked— the wicker chairs she'd bought for the veranda, the little mosaic table made of broken bits of china. He had meant to grow old with her, taking morning coffee there, watching laugh lines about her eyes deepen and her hair soften to gray. Just the sight of that table made it real as nothing else could have. She was serious about selling March Winds. Leaving him for good. The thought hurt.

"How was your trip to Montana?"

"Quiet. I had a lot of time to think."

"I have, too," she said. "I decided it's time to make some changes in my life."

He couldn't disguise how much that hurt. "I can see that."

She drew back a few steps, making a show out of adjusting a pile of flowerpots. "Isn't it funny? You think you know exactly what you want, and then suddenly everything changes."

"Everything?" Cade hated the rough edge to his voice.

"I don't want my life all—all cluttered with stuff," she said, waving her hand toward the stacks of boxes and furniture. "I'm just getting some things ready for an antique shop to pick up. Should be able to raise a little mad money for my trip. And I won't be able to take everything with me."

"I wouldn't have believed this if I hadn't seen it with my own eyes," he said more stiffly than he'd intended. "You're really going."

"To Santa Fe," she said with forced brightness. "I hear it's beautiful there." Then why did she look like she'd rather go to hell. Or that she'd already been there?

Cade searched her face, looking for something, anything, to hang hope on. "Are you sure that's what you want? You were so…in love with this old house. Do you remember? And you loved me."

She flinched away from him, and he felt cold all over. "Things work out the way they're supposed to, Cade. Signs from God and all that stuff. If I had any doubts about leaving, well— I don't anymore. Emma was right about me and March Winds. I don't belong here."

She angled her face away, and he almost thought he saw tears. She swiped one hand across her eyes. "Dust," she explained. "It's everywhere in an old house. I think I'll try an apartment this time. As new as I can get. You know, just for a change."

He tried to picture her in a place pristine, sterile, without the whisperings of the past. She'd told him once that old things carried imprints of the souls who had loved them in the past. He remembered the way she'd cradled that old wooden bread bowl against her heart, as if she were feeling the pulse of the women who had used it before her, nourishing those they loved.

It scared the hell out of him, glimpsing that same bowl on top of one of the piles. How could she change her mind so completely? Selling away things that had painted that soft glow of pleasure on her face? Or had she come to hate him so much after the hard things he'd said to her that she just wanted to get away?

Where are you, Finn? Cade wanted to ask. *Why are you going where I can't follow?*

"Have you heard Deirdre and Emma got a new house?" Finn asked.

"No. I...hadn't heard. As soon as I landed in Whitewater, I came straight here." To see you. To tell you how much I love you. To ask you to forgive...

"It's a darling little place, but it needs a lot of work."

Cade grimaced. "If I know my family, Dee and the Captain will probably kill each other before it's done."

A wistful smile toyed with the corners of Finn's mouth. It seemed like forever since he'd seen her grin, that heart-stopping glorious life-is-wonderful grin that had stolen his heart. "I know a man who has magic hands," she said. "Word around town is that he can fix anything."

"That's why I'm here, Finn." He folded her fingers in his own. "To see if I can fix the only thing that matters."

"Cade, please don't." Green eyes, always so straight forward, shifted away. Cade's heart skipped a beat, cold dread seeping through him.

"Don't what? Tell you I'd do anything if I could take back what I said? I'll never lose my temper with you again. I swear it."

"Cade—"

"Okay, we both know I'll lose my temper. But I'll love you, even when I'm losing it."

Pain flashed into her eyes, grief and hopelessness and loss. Shouldn't her face be lighting up now? Glowing with that soft, sweet forgiveness so much a part of her. Shouldn't she be in his arms right now? Telling him how much she missed him?

Instead, she pulled from his grasp, wrapping her arms tight against her middle. Green eyes leveled on his. "It's too late."

Cade felt like he'd been sucker punched. Panic flooded through him. He fought to keep his voice calm, even. "You don't mean that. The past few weeks have been hell. Maybe I don't deserve you. But God dropped you right in my backyard so I'm not giving you back. I'll give you everything you've ever dreamed of, Finn. A home. A dozen babies if you want them. Think about that, Finn. Our kids running wild all over March Winds. Waking us up at the crack of dawn to get their stockings on Christmas morning."

"Cade, don't! There's nothing you can say to change my mind," she said. "The truth is, you were right."

"Right?"

"I kept telling myself I wanted to put down roots somewhere. But if that was true, why didn't I do it? All this time I've been on my own I've bounced from place to place just like Da did. Once the novelty of Whitewater and this old wreck of a house wore off, I would've gotten restless."

"What the hell?"

"These weeks you've been away have been good for me, Cade. It's given me a chance to think things through."

He was losing her. For good. Panic wrenched through Cade. "Finn, the woman I know could never leave everything she loves behind."

"Then maybe you didn't really know me at all. I'm my father's daughter."

"You're not like him," Cade said fiercely. "You saved me.

Just like that beast in Emma's fairy tale. You can't just walk away. That's not how the story ends."

Bleakness turned her green eyes to winter, some new sadness haunting her, something he couldn't name.

His fist clenched with the effort it took not to grab her in his arms, kiss her, beg her…to what? Love him? He didn't understand—couldn't grasp that this was real. She wasn't going to forgive him, let him make this up to her. She wasn't going to give their love a chance.

"Please." Pride all but made him choke on the word. "God, Finn, don't leave me."

"Be happy, Cade," she said. "I'll always think of you in that—that beautiful old plane of yours. High above the clouds. Barrel rolling and looping and…flying, so free."

"That being free—it doesn't feel so great anymore. It's just another word for alone."

Finn turned, started to flee toward the house.

"Finn!" he cried, so sharply she paused, angled her face to look back at him.

"One last thing before you go. If you need anything, you come to me. If you're ever sick, you tell me. If you ever change your mind, promise you'll remember where to find me."

"How could I ever forget you?" Finn said. "My beast. My…growly white knight swooping in to slay dragons—even the ones that disguised themselves as leaky pipes?" She forced a wobbly smile. "Goodbye, Cade," she said, and left him alone.

CADE SAT in Emma's old bedroom, the silence closing in on him until he couldn't breathe. He'd finished the bottle of Glenmorangie he and Finn had started the night of the storm, trying not to remember how she'd tasted the first time he'd kissed her.

He'd get used to it. Not kissing her. But damned if he could get used to the quiet.

The cabin felt like someone had died. Maybe someone had. The father he'd meant to be to Emma. The man Finn's love had made him, before she'd decided to move away. She'd promised to stay forever. All lies.

Lies like his mother had told the Captain. Lies like he'd told Deirdre. Not *told* exactly. He'd just poisoned the truth with his silence. Hell, he should be good at swallowing pain by now, gritting his teeth and charging into life even when his heart was smashed into pieces so little not even God could put them all back together again. But nothing in his life had ever hurt this bad. She was leaving him behind.

His eyes burned and he ground his thumb and forefinger against the lids, trying to rub away the images that gave him no peace. Finn, so quietly determined. So sure things would be better someplace else. He'd told her she was like her father—hell, he hadn't expected that she'd believe him.

He buried his face in a T-shirt Finn had forgotten at the house one day when they'd gone swimming and got caught in a downpour. The soft cotton still smelled like her.

"Cade?"

He started at the sound of Deirdre's voice, tossed Finn's shirt aside, in an effort to salvage some shred of pride. But it was too late. His baby sister's big eyes glistened with tears.

"I was beginning to wonder if you were ever coming home," she said quietly.

Home. This wasn't a home without Finn. Without Emma. Now it never would be, Cade thought. "You know, Dee, you're one of the last people on earth I want to see at the moment."

"I'll bet. If I was still off God knows where, singing, you'd be married to Finn right now. And Emma…"

"Emma would be pretending my love was enough for her,"

Cade said. "Acting like she didn't miss her mother. Yeah, that would be terrific."

"You look like hell."

"Yeah, well, no one asked you to look. How the hell did you get in here anyway? I know I locked it when I came in."

"I told you that you needed stronger locks."

Cade glared at her. "That's right. My little sister the expert lock picker. Did you know Emma can do it, too? Great skill for a ten-year-old." He couldn't stand the way Deirdre winced. He swallowed hard. "I'm being a bastard. I'm sorry. I just—just saw the For Sale sign, talked to Finn. I need to be alone."

"That's the last thing you need." She planted herself right in front of him, arms crossed over her chest. "I'm not going anywhere until you and I get a few things straight."

Cade raked a hand through his hair. "Dee, I really don't need any bullshit right now. No more big emotional scenes or temper fits."

"Finally something we agree on. The infamous McDaniel temper has done quite enough damage already, thank you very much. Not that I've got any room to get on your case. Look at the crazy things I did because I was just plain mad. I stayed away from you and the Captain for five years. Kept Emma away from the only family she had. How could I do that?"

She knelt down like she used to when she was a little girl, reached out, took his hand. "Cade, I'm so sorry. For everything," she said, heartbreakingly earnest. "I wouldn't blame you if you hated me forever."

"I don't hate you," Cade said hoarsely.

"Maybe not now, but if looks could kill there would've been a chalk outline of my corpse on March Winds' driveway the day I showed up."

"It wasn't about you…so much as…as what Finn did. She should have been honest with me."

"Yeah, and I shouldn't have been a damned coward. I'm the one who stuck her in the middle of this. I should have had the guts to face you, Cade. But I was so scared. I don't give a damn about what anyone else in the world thinks of me. Truth is, I'm like the Captain. I love ticking people off. But when it comes to you…you're different. You matter. You've always mattered to me so much it scares me. My perfect big brother. The golden boy. I let you down."

"I'm far from perfect. When I went into the Air Force I just left you, knowing what a mess the whole family was. But you acted like you never cared if you saw me again. God, it hurt, feeling like you were glad to be rid of me."

"I wanted you to escape, Cade. For both of us. That's why I acted like such a jerk, so that you'd get fed up and leave. I was trying to do something good for you. But you just got sucked right back to Whitewater because of me. I hated that."

"You're my sister. I was supposed to take care of you."

"We're supposed to take care of each other. That's what families do. But…sometimes things get so complicated they just don't sort out the way you want them to. If I look back on my life there's plenty I'm not proud of. I could give you a list of excuses, but they don't matter anymore. Maybe they never did. I never felt like I was worth much as a daughter, a sister, a mother."

"Deirdre, you're—"

"A first-class screwup. But not anymore." She squeezed his hand so tight it hurt. "You just watch me pull my life together, brother. Make a home for my baby girl. We're going to be a family again. Emma and me and you."

"And the Captain?"

A smile twitched the corner of Deirdre's mouth. "He's going to do everything in his power to make my ass tired, but I'm gonna have to put up with him. What else can I do, Cade? I love him."

"According to Finn there's a lot you could do. Sell everything you own and just walk away. I stuffed my pride and went to March Winds, ready to tell her what an idiot I was. Ask her to forgive me. I was so damned sure she loved me. Really loved me. That she'd give our love another chance. But…God, Dee, if I live a hundred years I'll never forget the look in her eyes. My temper—my goddamned McDaniel temper! I said she was like her father."

"People say things when they're angry—things they don't mean."

"She trusted me with secrets no one else knew. And the minute I got really pissed off I yanked them out and stabbed her right in the chest. Maybe it is best that she's leaving. What the hell do I know about loving anyone?"

"Cade, you have such a big heart that—"

"Yeah, I was Mr. Understanding the night you showed up on my doorstep with Emma. Emma said my yelling scared you into running away. Maybe that was my fault, too. Maybe I deserve exactly what I'm getting. Finn's lucky to get out while she can."

"That's not how it is!"

"Isn't it? She doesn't love me enough to stay." Putting that truth into words was the most painful thing Cade had ever had to say.

"She's leaving *because* she loves you!" Deirdre insisted. "So much, she's willing to…to…give up everything she ever wanted."

"Dee, what are you trying to say?"

"That I'm an idiot. Completely hopeless. And Finn's going to want to string me up from that tree of hers somebody should have cut down. I know I promised to keep her damned secret. And I owe the woman big time. But if Finn's learned one thing about we McDaniels since she hit Whitewater, she should've known this."

"What?" Cade's heart leaped with hope. He grabbed his sister, glaring down into her eyes. "What should she have known?"

"Damned if we can keep our mouths shut."

CHAPTER TWENTY-ONE

FINN STARED UP at the tidy white house on Elm Street and wished she were anyplace else on earth. Bright blue shutters and a lipstick-red door seemed to smile at the world, giving the modest house the aspect of a cheerful, welcoming face.

But she doubted the woman who lived beyond that door would have any welcome to give. Not that she hadn't warned Bessie Aronson she was coming. She figured she owed the woman time to compose herself. Part of Finn had wished she could just say her piece over the phone. But Mrs. Aronson deserved the chance to yell at Patrick O'Grady's daughter face-to-face. And Finn needed to do her best to put the woman's mind at rest, let Mrs. Aronson see that Finn was an O'Grady who meant what she said.

Finn squared her shoulders, trying to muster the strength to knock on the door. But before she could do it, the red door flew open, revealing an apple-cheeked grandmother with wise brown eyes.

Ash-blond hair was caught up in a soft bun at the nape of the woman's neck. A housedress printed with forget-me-nots flowed around her plump figure. She was round and soft in all the right places, Finn realized. With a perfect grandma kind of lap and blue eyes meant to smile warmly over story-books.

Finn felt a twinge of loss and longing she'd all but forgotten. She'd never known her grandparents. Had envied other kids, not only their parents, but those eye-twinkling, completely indulging scions of unconditional love that had whisked into the lives of so many of the other kids in the homes where she'd stayed.

They'd often come bearing presents and candy for their real grandkids. What had touched Finn most were the ones so kind that they didn't forget her. Somehow she knew that Bessie Aronson would have been that type.

"So, you must be Patrick's daughter, Finnoula," she said. "Come in and sit down. Can I get you something to drink? I just made a fresh pot of tea."

Something about the woman's kindness in the face of what Finn's father had done made Finn even more desperate to get this ordeal over with, get out of this house with its cabbage rose sofa and its innocent-eyed owner as quickly as possible. "Please don't go to any bother. I don't want to take up your time."

"As if I have anything but time now Patrick is gone," Bessie sighed. "No company except old Byron, here." She scooped up an ancient tabby. "Much as I love him, he's not much of a conversationalist." The cat hissed fiercely at the insult, revealing toothless pink gums. "Your father surely could talk."

Yes, Finn thought. And he talked you right out of your life savings. So why was Bessie's voice tinged with unmistakable affection? Maybe her nephew was right, and the poor woman's mind was slipping.

"My mother used to say that if he'd been paid by the word like Charles Dickens he'd be a millionaire," Finn said.

Bessie chuckled. "He could eat, too. Ate as if the simplest meal was a feast fit for a king. Did my heart good to watch him. He thought apple pie could cure any of life's ills. So, with all we have to talk about, I baked one fresh this morning."

The thought of eating anything at all made Finn's stomach heave. Oh, God, she thought, this was even more horrible than she had feared it would be.

Trying to hide her reaction, Finn crossed to a white painted fireplace. A serious mistake. She winced, as she was forced to look at the row of framed photographs on the mantel. A fresh-faced young man decked out in Navy dress whites grinned jauntily back at the camera, the same man years later, smiling with his arm around a far younger Bessie, a cake before them with a silver "25" on top.

"That was our last anniversary," Bessie explained, touching the picture as if she'd followed Finn's gaze. "Henry was killed three months later. It's been thirty years since that day, and I still miss him."

"You were very lucky to love someone like that." Finn's throat felt tight. Would she and Cade have glowed that way on their silver anniversary? Still so much in love? He'd begged her to come back to him, said he loved her. But the choice was out of her hands now. Her father had made certain of that.

Finn cleared her throat. "I wanted to tell you in person that I'm sorry for what my father did. I got a call from the Realtor today. My house is sold. Well, we'll sign the contracts next week. You'll get most of your money back as soon as it's in my hands. I won't have it all. My father—well, a hundred thousand is gone. I'm sure the private investigator told you that."

A pained look crossed Bessie's face. "Yes. Mr. Stone made it clear that you had nothing to do with the missing money."

"You'll get the full amount back. It will take time, but I'll pay it off. To the last cent."

"But how can you do that dear?" Bessie's brow crumpled with worry. "I know you have a nice job. But I can't imagine librarians make a great deal of money."

"I make enough."

Bessie's face softened. "Listen to you. So independent. Your father said you were. He was very proud of you, you know, for working your way through college and all. A librarian, he'd say. Proud and amazed as if you were to be the first woman on the moon. Patrick said there wasn't a career in the world your mother would have liked better for you. But are you sure, dear, about paying such a large amount back? It's not as if I need it."

"You can't know that. You might have medical bills, or…anything can happen. The money is yours. You'll get it back. You have my word on it." Finn looked away, shame burning into her cheeks. "Not that you have any reason to trust me, after what my father did."

Bessie stepped into Finn's line of vision, and looked her straight in the eye. "I trust you just fine. You're a good person, Finnoula. Honest. I suppose that's rare these days. Plenty of people would say I got what I asked for with Patrick—a fool of an old woman, taken in by all that Irish charm your father had. But it touched me, a man who loved his little girl so much."

Finn cringed, appalled that her father had used her as a weapon to soften this poor woman up before he robbed her blind. "My father stole from you, just like he lied to me. I'm afraid he didn't love anyone but himself."

"Is that what you think?" Bessie cocked her head to one side, like a curious bird. "It's strange. People keep telling me what a bad man Patrick was. But I don't believe them. I think he just ran out of time. Mr. Stone said he lost the hundred thousand at the casino. I'm sure Patrick believed he would win. He always believed he was on the brink of something wonderful about to happen."

Finn bit the inside of her lip. This woman didn't need to see her cry. But Bessie had seen enough of the world to know grief, even the most silent. She patted Finn's cheek with a gnarled, blue veined hand.

"The one thing I do know for certain is that Patrick loved you. Whether the world approves of the way he showed it or not."

Finn tried to fight the spark of hope struggling for life inside her, knew how painful it would be if she let it flare. She should know by now, her father would only carelessly stomp it out. He'd robbed her of her childhood, and now he'd taken away the chance she had at finding love, home, all she'd ever wanted. But Bessie looked so certain, as if she held some secret key to unlock people's hearts.

"How do you know that he loved me?" Finn couldn't keep herself from asking. "I've spent my whole life wondering."

Bessie laughed. "Oh, my sweet, sweet girl. It's so obvious. There's nobody in all the world more Catholic than the Irish. And Patrick was as Irish as they come. Why the man spoke of hills and glens as if his very blood ran green."

"But how does that mean he loved me?"

"We spent hours and hours just talking," Bessie said. "My nephew and that detective of his might think I'm a flighty fool who'd just usher a strange man into my house and hand him my bank book. But they're wrong. Patrick was…my friend. He understood how I felt, losing Henry. Still feeling like a piece of me was torn out even after all these years. Patrick felt that way about his own wife, too."

Then why didn't he take better care of her? Why wasn't he there to make her go to the doctor? Why didn't he see she was so sick?

Because he was always afraid to see anything but rainbows…

"Patrick always said you were so much like his Mariel. Sometimes, so much so it broke his heart."

Finn tried to remember her mother's face, but years had

blurred the edges of memory. What would it be like? Seeing
the wife he lost in the face of their daughter? Knowing you
could have prevented your wife's death? If he had loved
Finn's mother that much, the guilt would have been devastating. How could a man like her father have the strength to
look, day after day, at a mirror image of his wife's face?

"But this doesn't prove anything except that it hurt him to
look at me."

"Ah, but there you're wrong. Patrick told me he'd been
waiting his whole life to get to heaven to see your mother
again."

"But you don't know. You don't understand. He let her
down, too."

Sorrow misted Bessie's face. "He told me that. It didn't
mean he didn't love her with all his heart. Just that he was
human. Maybe more human than most."

"Maybe."

"The way I see it, the man was in an all-fired hurry to get
to heaven, Finn. But when he took that money from me, he
was willing to take his chances with hell. Maybe you're not
proud of the way your father lived his life. And maybe you're
ashamed of what he did before he died."

Finn nodded, her throat to tight to speak.

"You don't think your father loved you, child? Why that
man risked his own eternity to keep his promise to you. What
more proof do you need?"

Tears welled up in Finn's eyes. "I never—never thought
of it like that."

"That's the reason why I wouldn't agree to press charges
once I knew the money was gone. He betrayed me. He stole
from me. But I kept remembering how Patrick had looked
when he talked about his little girl. Now that I meet you, I
can see why."

An hour later, Finn wandered out into the sunshine, her

eyes blurry from weeping, her heart sore. Her father *had* loved her. That was something to hold on to.

And Cade…?

No. She couldn't drag him into this mess for the very reason that she did love him. He'd try to fix it, feel responsible. She'd be one more chain to drag him down, because his heart was too big, his spirit too generous to turn away, even if he wanted to.

But maybe someday if I can pay that money back…

And then what? What if something else happened? Another one of her father's crazy, reckless schemes came crashing down on her head?

No. Cade had spent so many years waiting for his life to explode, with his parents, his sister. She wouldn't put him in that position again. She loved him enough to give him what he'd never had, what he deserved. A chance, just a chance for peace.

And what did she deserve? The question whispered in her mind. She'd always been so sure of that. A home. Roots. The rambling old house of her lonely childhood dreams. But now, she was right back where she'd started from. Wandering. Alone.

Strange, she didn't care so much about losing that dream, the house she'd thought was her heart's desire. It was that other home, her home that almost was whose loss was breaking her heart.

A home without walls that she'd found in Cade McDaniel's eyes.

FINN SMOOTHED the flowing folds of her black skirt, feeling as if she were going to a funeral. She'd dressed accordingly because in a way she was—the final internment of her dreams.

But it would all be over soon. She could move on to whatever the future held. Even so, she doubted she'd ever touch again the joyous wonder she had found in Cade McDaniel's boundless blue sky.

She headed for her Volkswagen, parked beneath the chestnut's branches and wondered if the new owner would chop the broken tree down. She'd always hoped it would keep on growing, heal the black scorching wounds that scarred its beauty. But there were times when a quick, clean ax blade might be more merciful. To dreams, as well as struggling tree branches.

Finn heard a noise, caught a glimpse of someone standing atop the stone bench, folds of a soft yellow sundress riffling in the breeze. Emma. Finn's heart squeezed. The child's small hands clutched a pry bar obviously snitched from Cade's tool box, as she renewed her old battle to wrench the For Sale sign off the trunk of the tree.

"At it again, huh?" Finn said, startling the little girl. She expected that "uh-oh, I'm busted" look Emma did so well. But the child peered back at her, utterly shameless.

"Somebody has to yank this stupid thing off," Emma said. "And it looks like you grown-ups are too stupid to try. You can't leave here. Addy will miss you, and so will I."

"Oh, sweetheart."

"You remember those people who looked at Uncle Cade's cabin? Well, since he's not selling it anymore, they had to find someplace else. And guess what? They bought the house right down the street from Mommy and me."

"That's wonderful, Emma."

"Yeah. I promised I'd show Jessica your attic. Remember that book? *Little Women?* Well, Jo wrote all her stories in the attic. I bet it was just like the one at March Winds. If I want Jessica to keep being my friend, I got to keep my promises, don't I?"

"I'm so glad you and Jessica are getting along so well."

One less thing for Finn to worry about when she was gone. She was so tired and so sad, she wasn't sure how she felt about two ten-year-olds bursting in on her, but if there was anything Finn could do to help cement Emma's friendship with a real live girl instead of a ghost, she had to try. "We've still got a few days left. Why don't you girls come over tomorrow."

Emma's chin thrust out, that stubborn angle that reminded Finn poignantly of Cade. "No. Later. Maybe weeks and weeks from now. See, there's got to be rain on the roof when I show her. It sounds so pretty up there, all that pattering sound. Who knows when it's going to rain? It might take a long, long time."

Emma was stalling, trying to hold Finn at the house as long as she could. Touched, Finn stroked Emma's hair.

"I'm sorry, but it has to be tomorrow, kiddo. Maybe we'll get lucky and a storm will blow in for you."

Emma peered up at her, solemn, suddenly far too much like the lost little girl Finn had met under this tree a lifetime ago. "You're going away just like Mommy did. You said you'd always stay."

"You don't need me anymore. You have your mom back."

"I guess. But Uncle Cade doesn't have anybody at all."

Emma's words slipped like a knife blade under Finn's skin.

"He's all alone in that big house," Emma said. "There's nobody to hear him at all. It's no use being growly when there's no one else to hear you. But he wasn't growly when you were going to get married. Remember? He was happy all the time. He doesn't laugh anymore."

Oh, God, Cade, Finn thought, her heart aching. *I'm so sorry...*

"He'll get better, Emma. In time." *When I'm far away and he doesn't have to see me on the other side of the fence...* Finn had to believe that was true.

"Yeah, well. Maybe you'll have to stay here forever. Maybe nobody will buy this place at all. Uncle Cade always said a person would have to be crazy to buy it. Maybe you're the only crazy person around." Emma eyed the sign with an intent gaze. "You go ahead, now. I've got stuff to do."

Finn slid her hands down the child's arms, trying to keep from breaking into tears. "Emma, you can take down the sign if you want to."

Emma brightened, her smile so precious Finn knew she would remember it forever. "You mean you've changed your mind?"

"No, honey. The sign doesn't matter anymore. You see, that's where I'm going right now—to the lawyer's to sign the papers. March Winds is already sold."

FINN WALKED TOWARD the redbrick building that housed Whitewater's only law firm, her heart all the heavier, burdened now by the desolation she'd put in Emma's eyes. Her one comfort knowing that it would not take much longer now, this tearing herself out of the fabric of the McDaniel family's lives. Boxes crowded March Winds' entryway, loaded and waiting for the moving van. The sooner she could leave Whitewater, the better. Seeing everything she'd dreamed of packed in dull brown cardboard, out of her reach, was more than her heart could bear.

One sweep of a pen and it would be over, she told herself as she wound her way toward Alec Shoeve's office. Then again, maybe it never would be. Emma's warnings had come true. March Winds carried ghosts of its own.

Finn knew the world she'd built on Jubilee Point would haunt her forever. The future she'd almost had. She pushed open a glass door and entered a tidy waiting room, decorated with wildlife pictures, tabletops littered with old copies of *People* magazine. Not that Finn felt like reading gossip about other people's lives today. She had enough to deal with in her own.

A pert young receptionist flashed her a harried smile. "Ms. O'Grady, isn't it? I'm afraid we're hopelessly behind schedule today. Your buyer was supposed to have finished up his part of the contract process and been out of here an hour ago, but Mr. Shoeve is still in court. A nasty case of property rights. The neighbor built a shed that spilled over the Hendricks' property line. My dad always said if you want good neighbors build a really strong fence to keep them on the other side."

Finn smiled wanly. "Seems to be a widely accepted bit of Whitewater philosophy. Maybe I should come back later."

"No, no!" The girl protested. "That will only tangle the schedule up even worse—and frankly, I need to get out of here on time. Hot date. You know?"

Finn did know all about hot dates for the first time in her life. Her body yearned for Cade, an addiction she couldn't seem to shake. At night, she'd wake up, sure she felt the sensual power of his hands tempting her to love him. How could it be possible that she'd never feel him touch her again?

"Mr. Shoeve should be back soon," the secretary assured her. "You might as well wait in the office. That way you and the buyer can both sign off on the property at once."

Not knowing what else to do, Finn walked past the reception desk and entered the office beyond it, a large, sunny room that boasted a vast mahogany desk. Two imposing wing chairs faced it, their red leather backs to the door.

Someone had already claimed the nearest chair, a curve of arm in a crisp blue dress shirt just visible, braced on the supple leather.

Finn almost ducked back out of the office. The scene with Emma had been difficult enough. She hardly wanted to have to make chitchat with some stranger who was buying her dreams.

But she had promised herself she was going to face down whatever she had to this next week, instead of avoiding pain the way her father had. She tried to paste a smile on her face and walked toward the occupied chair. "Hi, let me introduce myself," she began. "I'm...*Cade?*"

She choked out his name, staring into the agonizingly familiar planes of his face.

"Hello, Finn." He stiffened, a dark flush spreading across his cheekbones.

"But wh-what are you doing here?"

Blue eyes regarded her, stoic, steady. "I'm buying March Winds."

"You're what? That's—that's ridiculous. You thought I was crazy when I bought it! Why on God's earth would you do such a thing?"

"I think you know the answer to that." Emotion flickered in his face. "Deirdre spilled the whole rotten story."

"But she promised she wouldn't!" Finn's heart sank. "She shouldn't have told you."

"Oh, yes she damned well should have. Why didn't you?" He shoved himself up from his seat, towering over Finn, so close, so far beyond her reach. "What your father did was a goddamned shame. But you've waited your whole life for a home. I'm not going to let you lose it."

Finn refused to back down. "Why didn't you just come to the house? We could have discussed this rationally."

"So you'd have a chance to feed me more of that bullshit you handed me the day I came back to town? No thanks. It sure wasn't easy, but I figured I could keep my mouth shut long enough to get my signature on the contract. Once the closing was over, there'd be nothing you could do to stop me. If Shoeve hadn't gotten hung up in court my plan would've gone through without a hitch."

"Cade, I'm not your responsibility."

"No. You're the woman I love."

Finn caught her breath. Who would ever have believed that words that had given her such joy weeks before could hurt now, so deeply. "Don't be absurd, Cade," she attempted to reason. "The money to buy March Winds—it's a fortune. And that won't even wipe the slate clean. If you count what's missing—"

"Dee told me about what your father gambled away. A hundred thousand dollars." His gaze hardened. "Don't worry. I'm good for it."

"Oh, God, Cade! This is insane! Where could you possibly get your hands on that kind of money?"

His jaw knotted, eyes blue fire. "I sold the Avenger."

Finn sagged against the desk in horror. "Your beautiful antique plane?" She cried, tears streaming down her face. "No! You loved that plane."

She saw the flicker of loss in his eyes, saw him shutter it away with stubborn tenderness. "There will always be other planes, Finn. Even ones as rare as my Avenger. But there's only one you."

Finn shook her head in disbelief. "But I told you I wouldn't marry you. I told you I was going away."

"I know. I was there." Pain lanced across Cade's face and it devastated Finn to know just how much she'd hurt him. His jaw tightened. "That doesn't change the fact that I love you. Nothing ever will. No matter what you decide now—whether you agree to marry me or not, it's my choice to do this. There's nothing you can say that will change my mind."

"But this is crazy! This could only be the beginning! Who knows what else my father might have done? Any day now someone else might come knocking at my door searching for money he took or—or God knows what kind of a disaster he left behind? I won't let you be dragged into this. Sorting out other people's messes. That's been the curse of your life. It's not fair, Cade. I refuse to allow you take that kind of risk, make that kind of sacrifice."

"Do you really think you can stop me?" A raw sound rose in Cade's throat. "Woman, don't you know I'd give up everything I own for just one more night with you?" He cupped her face in his palms, his strong, work-toughened hands trembling. "For God's sake, Finn, if you won't—won't forgive me, at least let me give you the one thing I can. The house you love so much."

He was breaking her heart, shattering it a piece at a time. So vulnerable, so tender, her Cade, trying to shelter her from the storm her father had unleashed. Willing to sacrifice the plane he loved, not expecting anything in return.

But he was hoping. She could see it, stubborn in his blue McDaniel eyes, no matter how hard she'd tried to extinguish it.

It was too much. Too hard. Too painful. This treasure of a man seeming so alone.

"But I don't even want March Winds anymore!" Finn protested.

Cade's jaw knotted, stubborn. "I don't believe you."

"It's true! I thought March Winds was what I wanted. But I was wrong. All those years I thought I wanted that house," she said. "But I wanted a home, Cade. Not four walls and plaster and leaky plumbing. A shelter for my heart. That's what I found in your arms."

"Did you?" Stark, vulnerable, he searched her face, every scar from his childhood laid bare, every hurt she'd dealt him stripped naked. How could anyone possibly save a man like him from taking on the burdens of people he loved? Even, God help her, Finn's own?

She wrapped her arms around him, holding this man, this miracle, everything she'd ever dreamed.

"I want to live in your cabin," she said, "the home you

made with your own hands, every nail, every log, filled with the essence of the man you are. I want to sleep with you every night and put our babies in your arms. I want to make love with you and fight with you and feel like I did when you barrel rolled that plane of yours every time I kiss you," she vowed with all her heart. "I love you, Cade McDaniel. I don't ever want to leave the home I found in your eyes."

Cade reached for her, offering his love, his life. "Come home, Finn," he murmured.

She stepped into his arms.

NOT FOR ONE HUNDRED and fifty years had March Winds seen a wedding—at least, for all any of the guests gathered in the gardens could tell. They might have stepped back through time into an age before florists and wedding planners and caterers with ice sculptures of brides and grooms. Not that anyone in Whitewater thought Finn O'Grady was practical—she'd bought that rambling old house, after all, folks whispered. But Cade McDaniel, the town's favorite son, should have had a sight more sense.

Little did they know, this wedding had been taken over by a ten-year-old dreamer with a stubborn McDaniel chin. And when Emma dreamed—Finn thought, love squeezing her heart—Emma dreamed big.

Impractical as it was, setting up Bride Central in what had quickly become an otherwise empty house had been a stroke of brilliance. And even when she'd been married for fifty years, she knew she'd still be glad Emma had insisted she be married out of March Winds. A precious thread, connecting Finn's old dreams with the new.

Finn laughed, remembering the furor the child had caused just yesterday. Commanding her crotchety grandfather and doting uncle to drag mirrors and chairs and a white draped dressing table up two flights of stairs to "the prettiest room of all." The tower where Finn and Cade had first made love, the stained glass peacock reigning over March Winds, resplendent in its window.

Maybe, Finn thought, on that long ago Fourth of July day when her da had boosted her onto the veranda roof, and she'd crept across its slippery surface to peer into the house of her dreams, her father had taught her the only lesson she had ever needed. That no matter how scared you were of falling, you had to reach for your dreams. Cade had shown her that the risk was worth what awaited you on the other side.

He had used the money from his plane to pay Mrs. Aronson back. Finn vowed she'd return every penny to Cade as soon as March Winds sold. But they both knew that could take a very long time. It still astonished Finn every time she thought of what Cade had sacrificed for her. Gladly. Generously. Lovingly. And today Cade McDaniel would make her his wife.

Finn stared into the full-length mirror, trying to believe that the woman reflected back at her was real. Bright-eyed, brimming with hope, even the shadows of worry about her father swept away.

Miranda March's wedding dress fell in creamy waves about Finn's body, the exquisite antique garment holding a special glow of its own as if it rejoiced at being resurrected from the shadows of time to play a part in yet another happy ending.

Finn wondered if Miranda and Angus, wherever they were now, minded that she'd added a new line of her own to the history written in the woven threads of this dress. Somehow, she was sure that they would understand.

A clatter on the tower stairs announced the arrival of the busiest member of the wedding party. Emma swept in, an angel in Addy's gown, an adorable solemn aura to her face, as if she were excruciatingly conscious of the important part she was about to play. Unfortunately, the fact that she'd tucked half the flowers from the garden in her dark hair made Finn want to scoop her up in a most undignified hug. "Aunt Finn, the Captain says it's time."

A tingle of pleasure ran down Finn's spine, and she wondered if a human heart was strong enough to hold so much joy.

But the real miracle was that Cade had promised to love her, not only in times like these, but when the glass slipper broke and the castle fell to pieces, when men like her father would run. Cade had proven time and again that he was as good as his word.

"Emma." Finn swept her into an embrace, unable to resist the little girl another moment. "I hope you're this happy at your own wedding someday." She caught a glimpse of Deirdre in the doorway. Her heart squeezed with affection for Cade's rebellious sister. "You, too, Deirdre."

Deirdre made a face. "I'm pure trouble. Just ask my brother. All this love stuff is for sweet angels of women like you. A man would have to be crazy to want someone like me."

"Mommy, Finn was crazy, too, when she bought March Winds," Emma said earnestly. "Uncle Cade said so. Maybe there's someone crazy out there just waiting for you."

Deirdre laughed, tugging one of her daughter's curls. "I've got you back again. What else could I possibly want?"

Finn wondered. Remembering the woman who'd wished for crowded concert halls and bright lit stages, applause for the music that poured from her very soul. Where would it all go? That passion for the life Deirdre would never have? Finn prayed Cade's brave, reckless sister wouldn't ever feel regret. But that was inevitable, she supposed. Deirdre's heart was torn in two. She'd done the best she could with it—given all she had to her daughter.

With a smile so determined, it was as if she had read Finn's mind, Deirdre handed over the bouquet Emma had gathered just that morning. The riot of pink and blue blossoms tumbled over a bow of shimmering blue satin ribbon that matched the sash bound about Emma's slender waist.

"I'd get moving if I were you," Deirdre teased. "You don't want to keep that brother of mine waiting. You know, we McDaniels have absolutely no patience. He might come charging in here like some hero in a romance novel and carry you down in his arms."

Finn treasured the image, knowing Deirdre was right. "That would make this day a wedding to remember."

"Oh, it's already got lots of remembering to do," Emma piped up. "Just wait 'til you see the surpr—ow!"

Deirdre clapped her hand over her astonished daughter's mouth. "Emma, hush!"

"Don't tell me." Finn cast Deirdre a nervous gaze. "Another wedding surprise?"

"Emma, you're scaring her. Remember what happened the last time the poor woman got a surprise before her wedding?"

Finn hated the regret in the other woman's face, wondered if a lifetime would be enough time to wash it away. She squeezed Deirdre's hand. "I'll be grateful every day of my life that you came back," Finn told her. "Into Emma's life and Cade's life and mine. Our world would be so much emptier without you."

"Yeah, well, there are times I think the Captain would like to ship me back off to boot camp. But Cade says it's because we're too much alike. Like father, like daughter."

Deirdre winced, and Finn knew she feared stirring up old pain. "I'm sorry. I didn't mean to… God, why am I always putting my foot in my mouth?"

"Guess it runs in the family," Emma said with a comical resignation that made both women laugh.

"You are like the Captain, in so many ways," Finn said. "You're lucky. Your father is a good man, in spite of all the bluster." *Please, God, you'll never find out that his blood doesn't really run in your veins.* But surely fate wouldn't be that cruel, Finn prayed. All the McDaniels had suffered enough.

Finn swept down the stairs, through empty rooms with gleaming hardwood floors. Emma whisked the door open and they stepped into the garden. Sunlight warmed Finn's face as she walked toward the gazebo, the elegant white structure gleaming against the riot of early summer flowers.

But though the modest number of guests they'd invited were sitting in the linen draped folding chairs Cade and Jett Davis had set up that morning, the supposedly impatient bridegroom was nowhere in sight.

Come to think of it, Jett's bubbly wife wasn't where she belonged, either, Finn realized. Robin Davis should have been in her place of honor in the front row, but she stood, baby daughter in arms, silhouetted against the overgrown hedge beyond the white picket fence. A cat in the cream smile wreathed her face.

Attired in his dress uniform from the army years ago, the Captain swept up to Finn, offering her his arm. Finn smiled up at him, knowing there was no one on earth she would rather have give her away.

"My son is a lucky man," Martin McDaniel said gruffly.

"I hope so," Finn said, pressing her thumb against the emerald ring Deirdre herself had insisted she put back on.

"Be happy, girl," Martin said. "Happiness is…very rare."

Finn stretched up on tiptoe and kissed his weathered cheek. Music welled up, liquid and lovely, the string quartet Verna Sopher had commandeered from her Chamber Music club filling the garden with silvery strains.

Finn's eyes stung as she gave thanks for all the people she

had found to love. Emma, basket of flowers in her hand, walked up the white-carpeted aisle with the dignity of a princess, dropping rosebuds she'd been up gathering at dawn. Finn's throat tightened as she glimpsed the bright purple Harry Potter bandage on her hand, covering the little cut a thorn had bitten into Emma's skin.

Finn had told her not to risk picking anymore, she didn't want her getting scratched. But Emma had shaken her head, so small but so wise as Finn and Deirdre had put on antiseptic and bandaged up the tiny wound. "You got to have thorns," Emma had said earnestly. "Without thorns, there wouldn't be any roses."

Finn knew that she was right.

She tried to smile at the guests as she approached the gazebo where the minister waited to perform the ceremony. But she couldn't stop searching for the one face in the world she longed to see. Yet even when she reached the makeshift altar, Cade didn't appear. Wasn't it the groom who was supposed to have to stand there in front of everyone, waiting for the bride to show up?

"Where is he?" she whispered to the Captain, a little uneasy.

The captain smiled, mischief in eyes incredibly young in his old man's face. Emma strained up on tiptoe, staring expectantly back at the white picket fence. The fence…. Finn's heart squeezed. Thank God, Emma hadn't followed her uncle's orders and stayed on her own side.

Finn swallowed hard, thinking how far they'd all come since that very first day. Her eyes blurred with tears. She blinked, hard, the green of rhododendron bushes and azaleas pink with blooms shifting, somehow, moving, transforming into something white.

Finn swept her hand over her eyes, heedless of the makeup she'd applied so carefully hours before. Surely, it couldn't be…

She gasped as her vision cleared, snapping into crystal clear focus. Her jaw fell open.

Cade.

It was Cade, his dark hair gleaming beneath a dashing plumed hat, swirls of shining gold braid decorating the rich navy blue of a cavalry officer's frock coat from the time of the Civil War. Glossy black boots encased his legs to the knee, a gold fringed sash wrapped around his narrow waist while a sword and scabbard hung at his side.

But most unbelievable of all, he was on a white horse—riding straight toward her as if he'd ridden out of the pages of one of Emma's books.

"Surprise!" Emma said, with a skip of pure delight. "Isn't he handsome? I told you he'd be handsome! Jett and Robin did it, but not gray like Angus's. Robin said gray isn't Uncle Cade's color. And a man had to look good for his wedding. Don't you just *love* it Aunt Finn?"

"Oh, yes, Emma. Oh, yes." She watched, heart overflowing, as the man she'd dreamed of forever swung down from the saddle, looking so vulnerable, so sheepish, a dark flush on his cheeks. Had any other man ever been so handsome?

"Uh, the strangest thing happened," Cade murmured. "The cleaners lost my suit."

Finn threw back her head, laughing. Cade took her hand in his, the soft leather of his cavalry gauntlets sweeping up to his elbows. Tucking her fingers possessively in the crook of his arm, he led her up to the gazebo, making promises Finn knew he would keep.

Cade's hand shook as he slipped his ring on her finger, as he vowed to love, honor and cherish, as long as they both lived....

But Finn wasn't finished, even after she placed the smooth gold band on Cade's hand. She had a surprise of her own. Deftly, she slid something from beneath the blue ribbon tie of her bouquet and pressed it into the palm of Cade's glove.

He peered down at the white embroidered thistle she'd snipped from the sleeve of her gown.

"So you'll always have a piece of me with you," she said, astonished as Cade's burning blue eyes gleamed, over bright.

Maybe McDaniels did cry after all. For joy.

He gathered her tight in his arms, kissed her with all the love and all the strength and all the tenderness in his generous heart. He banished pain, doubt—this honorable, decent, deliciously sexy man who had sacrificed so much for her, fought so hard to give them both this chance.

Finn vowed she wouldn't waste it. She might have stayed in Cade's arms forever if Emma hadn't tugged on Finn's skirt, and looked up at them, beaming. "Aunt Finn?" Emma whispered. "Isn't this just exactly like you and me dreamed it up in the attic that day?"

"No," Finn said, her voice ragged with emotion. "It's so much better."

Time whirled away in a storm of hugs and congratulations, laughter and delicious treats made by Verna Sopher's loving hands.

They danced until long after sunset, laughing and loving, sharing so much joy, while Emma's paper lanterns glowed in the branches above them, splashing the everyday world with vibrant blues and oranges, pinks and greens.

It was almost midnight when Cade stole Finn out of Jett Davis's arms in the middle of a waltz. "It's time to go, Mrs. McDaniel," Cade murmured against her ear, sending shivers of desire rippling through her. "I want you. Now."

Finn pressed herself against him, an answering thrill washing over her. It had been so very long since she'd had him in her bed. But they'd agreed not to make love in the weeks leading up to the wedding, wanting to make this night even more special.

Finn lost count of the times Cade had grumbled in frustrated desire: *What in the hell were we thinking?*

"The gazebo's a little crowded at the moment," Finn said, feeling his arousal stirring against her.

"Don't worry. I'll find us someplace else. And quick. Say goodbye to everybody. Your chariot awaits."

"My chariot?" Finn drew back in disbelief. "Cade, you didn't—"

He gave her a comical look. "Good lord, woman! Wasn't that damned horse of Jett's enough? I mean, I even wore this blasted uniform. It's wool, you know. It itches."

Finn laughed. "Then we'll have to see about getting it off you as soon as we can."

"Damn straight." Cade growled, tipping her head back so he could nuzzle her neck. "I may spend the next week naked."

"You can't do that!" Emma's voice all but made Cade jump out of his skin, leaving him flustered.

"Damn it, Emma! Tell me you didn't hear that!"

"Yeah, yeah, yeah. You're doing all that kissy face stuff. I'm not a baby, you know. Now you just listen here. You can't go yet. We've still got to let the wishes go."

"The wishes?" Cade groaned. "What the heck is that supposed to mean?"

"Addy wrote about it in her journal. Setting candles afloat on the river to make your wishes come true."

"Fine," Cade grumbled, resigned. "Anybody ever tell you you'd make a great dictator, kid?"

"Not a dictator. A general. The Captain says."

Emma grabbed her uncle's hand, dragging him toward the river, Finn following a few steps behind.

"Come on, everybody!" Emma called. "Get your candle boats."

The guests followed Emma's lead, taking the cupcake papers she'd pierced with birthday candles in the days before the wedding. Emma brandished a big candle to help light them, so excited she was in danger of setting Jett's little boy on fire instead of the paper wish he held.

"Whoa, there, partner," Jett said, whisking his boy out of danger. "How about if I help you out here."

He was a wonderful father, Cade's best friend, Finn thought warmly. Cade would be, too.

Cade came to her, two of Emma's little paper boats cupped in his strong hands, the candle wicks glimmering.

"Make a wish, Finn," he said, looking deep into her eyes.

"I can't," she said, cradling one of the little boats in her hand. "I have nothing left to wish for, at least not for myself."

Her gaze caught a movement by the riverbank, Deirdre helping Emma set the first paper wish afloat.

"But maybe for someone else," Finn said. "I wish Deirdre could find a happy ending just like we did."

She watched as Emma's flickering candle drifted out in the current, such a fragile vessel to carry the wishes of a little girl whose imagination was so very rich. Deirdre bent close to her daughter, as Emma straightened, and gathered her little girl in her arms.

Their journey was just beginning, Finn thought. There was still so much for them to heal. At least they'd made a start of it.

Finn set her own little candle gently into the lapping water, Cade hunkering down to do the same. Other wishes were being launched into the night, set afloat by people they loved. The tiny flames glinted like stars as they drifted down the river, stars fallen down from Cade's sky.

Finn linked her fingers with her husband's, leaning against him as the bright glow of wishes drifted off into the night, dreams she knew would come true.

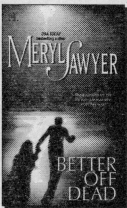

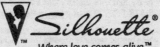